ANOTHER ENDING,
ANOTHER NEW BEGINNING

Albert Speer entered and stood uneasily.

Hitler knew he was supposed to be annoyed with him for refusing to be optimistic about the war. He sighed. This hardly mattered now.

"My Führer?"

"Sit . . . Sit down, my friend," Hitler said in a soft, hoarse rumble.

There was no chair so Speer sat on the edge of the bed. The lights flickered, the painting rattled.

The Führer coughed and cleared his throat several times. "If only," he finally said, "if only I could have turned aside from my destiny . . ." Speer crossed his legs. He noticed the pistol on the pillow for the first time, compact, shiny. A tic gripped the left side of Hitler's face briefly, violently knotted the cheek.

"The Russians are a few streets away," Speer said. His leader didn't appear to notice.

". . . before *it* chose me . . ."

"*It*?" Speer asked. "Do you mean destiny, my Führer?"

"No," came the reply. "I do not."

UNTO T

UNTO
THE
BEAST

Richard Monaco

BANTAM BOOKS
TORONTO • NEW YORK • LONDON • SYDNEY • AUCKLAND

UNTO THE BEAST

A Bantam Spectra Book / April 1987

ISBN 0-553-26144-4

Published simultaneously in the United States and Canada

PRINTED IN THE UNITED STATES OF AMERICA

O   0 9 8 7 6 5 4 3 2 1

"I never read novels. That kind of thing annoys me."

Adolf Hitler

PROLOGUE
(APRIL 1945)
In the Ardennes Near Germany

PFC Frank Astuti was running through the misty, grayed twilight shadows, the dim earth speeding and rocking past, machine-gun bullets whipcracking the air and spanging into the torn earth around him. He was running, lungs aflame, ducking, weaving across the open field that had been farmland before the war smashed across it. Sundown was burning red at his back, the red tinting only the tops of the wall of trees a few hundred yards still ahead. Tracers pumped and skidded from both sides and seemed to seek him, personally.

His thoughts fugued:

A little more just a little more and I'll be okay just a little . . . yes . . . oh, shit shit shit . . .

The guns blasted blindly as if (he wildly thought at one point) the sunset were at war with the smoking woods. His objective was a low ridge that cut across the fields. He intended to dig in there, if he could, and wait for his own people to catch up. If they did.

Suddenly a pool of darkness opened under his feet and he tripped, staggered, and went down flat on his face, rifle in front, pack slamming his broad shoulders into soft, powder-reeking dirt. A shell hole.

He lay there sucking wind and cursing steadily and inaudibly. After a while, the firing seemed comfortably far away by sudden contrast; he rolled onto his back and thought about smoking. Then he saw the blotted outline of the man sitting there in the last, thinning wash of twilight, rimless glasses faintly gleaming. His hand flew to his bayonet handle even as he realized the other could have killed him a dozen times in the past minutes.

1

"What the fuck are you doing here?" he said. He noticed that he was a civilian. Even in the shadows he could see the baggy, dark suit, collar, and tie.

Doctor Rudolph Renga had been watching the lurid sunset and deciding whether to crawl on to the next hole and try to reach the ridge that way. He kept losing time. Then he'd turned and studied the German lines, or at least the broken, smoking forest to the east that was spewing bullets. He was holding up, he'd decided, pretty well for his fifty-odd years. And he'd never expected to be caught out in the center of a battlefield. He'd assumed he could slip through the lines and hadn't been prepared for the fluid speed of this war. For days he'd been literally chasing the front and today the Germans had counterattacked and the front had caught up with him. And then this American soldier dove out of the fire-spitting sky. He'd been tempted to wrench his rifle from him while he lay on his face, winded, but knew if the rest of them were coming it would be a hopeless, probably disastrous gesture. Even if they sent him back, he could try again somewhere else. Never mind that, this fellow seemed to be isolated . . .

"You hear me?" the soldier wanted to know, crouching to his haunches, rifle across his knees.

"Staying alive," Renga said over the rattling of the guns.

The soldier nodded.

"Not a bad fucking idea," he agreed, "except here ain't the best place for it. How'd you get out in the middle of this?" He gestured around with his free hand and ducked a little as a stray line of machine-gun bullets chewed earth a few feet away. A light dirt spray clittered over them. "Huh?"

Renga was thoughtful, studied the fellow as best he could in the diminishing light. The hole seemed a bath of shadows they were both up to their necks in. The soldier was short, stocky, dark, curly-haired with a pencil mustache. He thought, idly, how the mustaches today were pathetic beside those masterpieces of the First World War. *Lord Kitchener. The Kaiser. My friend General von Moltke.*

"I'm going into Germany," he finally answered.

"Uh-huh. Okay. So you're nuts." The GI clamped an unlit cigar in the corner of his jaw. "I got relatives at home who're nuts. I'm used to it. My cousin Frankie's nuts, for instance."

The battlesounds had lessened somewhat in the last few moments. Renga peered over the top.

"You going somewhere, Professor?"

"Yes . . . How do you know I'm a professor?"

The American was amused.

"I know people, you know what I mean? There's three things I know. I know broads, food, and human nature. What I don't fucking know is horses." He grinned. "That's beyond my powers."

"And you say I'm nuts?"

"You're a German, right?" The GI wanted confirmation.

"Originally."

"But you sound a little British."

"I went to school there . . ." He peered around. The firing had slackened. Down the line a flare went up. It threw wild red shadows and a few guns sputtered. "It looks clear now so—"

"*Managgia*, don't you get it, Professor? There's umpteen Krauts out there who'll blow your ass off and wear it in the fucking Easter Parade." The stocky soldier leaned on his rifle and peered up into Renga's long, rawboned face and jet-black eyes that seemed to focus far away and rarely blink. His gaze made the GI uneasy. "Unless maybe you're a Nazi spy . . ." he pursued without real conviction.

"That's absurd. What would I be spying on out here?"

"How do I know?" The other shrugged. Crouched down and carefully lit his cigar stub within his cupped palms. "This war is for shit, you know what I mean?" Took a deep drag. "I liberated these. . . . This here's a good hole so we just sit tight for a while, you got that? What the fuck do you want to go over there for, anyway?"

"Come along and see," Renga said, sarcastic.

"That's fucking amusing." He squatted down and rested his back against the soft earth that still retained a moist, burned-powder smell. Down the line small-arms fire continued to crackle. This sector was quieter. The woods were a grayish blot of twilight going to black about a hundred yards ahead. High up, wisps of clouds glowed faintly pink. A star trembled into view.

"You're lost," Renga suggested mildly, "aren't you?"

"That may be, bud," was the measured reply, "but at least I ain't fucking nuts." Puffed the cigar carefully behind his hands. *"Capisch?"*

"What?"

"That's Italian. I talk a little Italian. My old lady was born near Naples." The smoke, invisible now, floated around them, dry and tangy. "In fact, I found some fucking cousins when we went through there last year. It's a fucking hard life over here, you know what I mean?"

Renga nodded, somber, remote. A flight of planes went over very high up, heading back west. The droning echoed in the hills and valleys.

In a little while, he thought, *I'll go on.*

He hoped the American would be all right. For some reason he had no fear for himself. Perhaps, he considered, he'd seen too much death already to presume to worry. He certainly didn't wish to die. Smiled, rueful. He'd been certain he was done with wars long ago. *Just like the whole world,* he thought.

No one had listened so he'd come here alone. He'd known it might come to this. Fate was fate. Any soldier learned that fast. And then the odds. Smiled again. No sense getting into the odds. They didn't bear thinking about. But he was going to try because he didn't see a choice.

Like any man on a lulled battlefield, he realized, he was thinking about the past.

"My wife was Italian," he murmured.

Ah, he thought, *Eunice . . .*

"Oh yeah?" his chance companion responded. "I ain't married. But what the fuck, worse things could happen, you know what I mean? I ain't worried." He'd let the cigar go out and now chewed the unlit stub. "When I get out of this fucking miserable, lousy country of scumbags and this cocksucking, *stunato* army, then who the fuck knows, right?" Paused. Shook his head. "So she's dead, huh?" he said quietly.

"Yes."

Now it was dark. There was no sense waiting. Reason said she was dead, at least.

"That's rough," the soldier said. "I can't believe you come this far in one piece."

"Good fortune."

"I don't know how *I* got this fucking far, to tell the truth . . ." He shifted the cigar stub. Spat. "My name's Frank Astuti, by the way."

"It's dark now," Renga told him. "I have to be going."

Astuti bounced over on one knee and gripped him by the sleeve as he was easing himself over the lip of the hole.

"Come on," he shout-whispered, "—you got to be kidding. You can't go fucking around out there, for crissake. Use your head. This ain't a joke. Sit tight right here and you'll be okay. You hear me? Huh?"

Renga carefully disengaged himself.

"Excuse me," he murmured, "young man. Good luck to you." His glasses faintly showed out of the dimness of his shape. The soldier was unconsciously scratching under his arm. The scattered firing went on. A shift of breeze brought a fresh sting of smoke. He continued scratching and staring as the older man got to his feet and moved off into the darkness. He watched for a while, then lost him altogether. Frowned. Punched his fist nervously into the earth. Spat again. Stared into the black blankness under the stars . . .

"Forget it," he whispered to himself.

A hissing red flare arced overhead suddenly, harshly laying the area bare, catching Renga out there in his dark suit in a mad shifting and shaking of shadow and flame-light.

"Holy shit!" Astuti muttered—because he knew what was coming, and a moment later it came: the thin, penetrating screams arching down one after another after another . . . mortars hitting everywhere, ground buckling, leaping, shrapnel humming and ripping the air and earth, splintering in among the trees, each bright burst blinding, twisting the landscape into a smoky, blazing, dissolving hell. "Holy shit . . ." he repeated, flattening himself against the concave wall of stony dirt, pressing his face close, helmet digging awkwardly into his neck as the world opened up into shriek and pound and blast and then the German lines answered, 88s screaming overhead, the famous flat, barking blasts: *Bap! Bap! Bap!* . . .

Holy shit, he thought.

PART I

I
(APRIL 1945)

The pain shot down from his hip to his foot when he shifted his weight. His left arm trembled in uneven spasms as he limped heavily across the gray, windowless room. The carpet muffled his footsteps. His back ached. He kept trying to tilt his head up straight but it was stiff and hurt.

He briefly gripped the chairback by his bed to steady himself, then struggled on into the adjoining bathroom and fumbled among the bottles around the basin. He dropped several pills before he was able to press a few into his mouth with the palm of his hand. There was no glass so he bent his head to the faucet and sucked at the feeble, sour, rusty stream in order to swallow.

"This is what we've come to," he muttered under his breath.

He stayed bent over the sink, waiting to see if he was going to vomit. Breathed the stuffy air, heavily. His gray uniform now had a water stain on the lapel.

A generator whined steadily several rooms away, and there was a continous vibration like distant thunder. Every few moments the room trembled and the little bottles clinked.

Finally, painfully, he straightened somewhat and was met by the mirror reflecting the gray walls and the blotchy, yellowish-gray face, sweaty with pain and effort, almost-lightless eyes, faded blue, behind steel-rimmed spectacles. The nose was thick and putty-like, flesh bagged and sagging. His hand automatically brushed his cowlick from his eyes and rubbed the famous smear of mustache.

My God, he thought.

Because this was the first he'd really looked in a long time. Even when shaving he'd left the reality blurry. He stood there, breathing and sweating and waiting for the drugs to bring the sweet, familiar, soothing softness.

His hair was gray too and he stared, blinking at the ruin of a face.

My God.

He blinked slowly. Left his eyes unfocused so his image was a pale ghost to him. His lips moved but no sound came out.

Betrayed . . . you betrayed me . . . you brought me to this . . . you . . .

The lights flickered as the room shook hard enough to stagger him back a step. The shadows closed in for a moment, hollowed his face. He looked around, lips pressed together, eyes flashing brief anger.

"Scum," he muttered. "Dirty, filthy pigscum!"

The rage translated into a sudden burst of energy and he limped quickly back into the dreary bedroom.

The day will come . . . he began thinking, then broke off because the day was never coming. It had passed. His stomach sank again. He felt like a child waiting for his father to come home and punish him. Except this time, father was half a dozen nations and ten million men. . . . The pain was diminishing but the thrill of anxiety remained.

He sat down heavily in the hard-backed chair, locked his trembling foot around a rung, and stared at the featureless green-gray wall near the steel door.

This is like a tomb, he idly thought, *this bunker.* But at least he was spared seeing the rubble and flame and horror of the surface world. Yes, that was some slight compensation.

He had felt despair and terror like this a thousand times in his life. And always fate had turned aside for him. Because he'd been chosen . . . Yes . . . He remembered.

A thousand times, he thought.

. . . when those boys from the other school had trapped him by the fence before he quite reached the gate to his house.

Over forty years ago, he recalled. The room vibrated. The bombings had stopped because the Russians were too close. These were shells. Pounding without respite, day and night. Pounding the capital into rubble.

His mind took up the memory; a cool evening, the boys closing in on him . . .

That was the first evidence of the power, he thought, nodding. *Yes . . . the first . . . destiny secured me . . .*

He had been backed up against the man-tall fence that masked him from the house. Tough peasant boys. He remembered the leader was short and thick-shouldered with big ears. He never forgot those ears. His hands were big and callused.

"We got you now, you little flowerboy," he jeered.

Adolf stood there in his baggy leather shorts. The boys were on three sides, their backs to the sunset that burned like hot coals beyond the hills. A few city buildings were visible downslope in the middle distance. Twilight shadows and silence lay on the autumn earth. He heard a girl singing a few houses away; a distant dog barking in the valley. He backed against the hard wood thinking if he were only on the other side he'd be safe, only an inch of material locked him out from safety. Felt hopeless fear as they closed in, a tall, skinny, long-armed youth and another, a total blur in his memory.

He didn't want to fight but there was no choice. He thought about pleading, kneeling down . . . thought about blindly running. All he needed was a step. Could he climb the fence? He was sweating with fear. These three had broken a farmer's arm in a recent brawl. One of them had been in jail more than once. They hated him, he didn't know why. He had avoided them before, but they'd waited on his street—though it may have been chance, he didn't think so.

"Please—" he heard himself rasp, "what's the trouble?"

Laughter. The skinny one hooted.

"No trouble, faggot," he explained, "we're going to kick the shit out of you, that's all."

Laughter.

"Unless he blows Reini," said the blurry third.

"That's right," the apelike one agreed. "Should I take it out, faggot?"

"That's a lie!" Adolf cried. "Shut your mouths!"

But his body leaped in panic as the tall one reached a bony hand for his arm (he suddenly remembered the boy's flared nostrils and a boil on his cheek) and then the

fenceboards were blurring by . . . shouts . . . panting
. . . curses . . . the sky and dark street reeling, spinning
as he struggled to run, shadowy hands reaching from dim
outlines to clutch and strike at him and then he was
running and then a sharp blow struck the back of his head
and he fell and rolled in the dust and had an abstract idea
that they'd thrown water somehow because his head and
neck were wet—the stone that hit him was just rebounding
in the road. Laughter, jeers, and then someone standing
over him in a great sweep of satiny billows that glowed (to
his stunned senses) mysteriously in the fading light, part of
the garment covering him, the long broom in her raised
hands a terrible weapon in the shadowy dusk, her fair hair
and fierce eyes shining (he distantly thought as the dull
pain began to pulse in his bloodied head), driving the three
attackers back by sheer inner force and fury. He stared
from partly under the smooth, lavender-scented robe. One
hand unconsciously gripped a bare foot underneath. Now,
as the last light died, they were featureless outlines against
the palely streaked horizon, seeming to shrink as she took
another step toward them, brandishing the broom and
raging, robe billowing just as he was rolling over onto his
back and glimpsed (where it parted) a sweep of long white
legs and then his father's voice yelling from the house (he
could see him from where he now lay), leaning bare-
chested from the bedroom window. *He's still drunk,* Adolf
thought, struggling to his knees, wobbling.

"Klara! . . . What's going on? . . . Come back inside! . . . What's going on?"

The attackers moving off, leaving without even a jeer
as his mother stood there, lowering the broom, as he
watched and pushed away his father's voice deeper into the
background.

I was protected, he thought, forty-odd years later as the
light dimmed again and the concussions echoed and shook
the earth.

His left arm began to tremble violently and he gripped
it, held it down with this right hand. Stared around at the
blank walls.

"You deserted me," he whispered. "You promised
. . . you betrayed . . ."

He felt empty now, unable even to work up any real

resentment. Rocked slightly on the chair, blinking, staring, oblivious to the knocking until the door acutally opened and an orderly thrust his head in. His uniform collar was open. The bony head was blond and pale; the sleepless eyes, haunted.

"My Führer," he said, "Speer is here."

He didn't break his stare. The thunder of shell impacts vibrated the portrait on the far wall. The glass kept rattling faintly. He said nothing. At this point protocol was loose.

Albert Speer entered and stood uneasily.

Hitler knew he was supposed to be annoyed with him for refusing to be optimistic about the war.

He sighed. This hardly mattered now. It was reflex to keep Speer standing there uncomfortably while he held a frown and was silent.

"My Führer," Speer finally said. "I stand totally behind you."

Hitler's hand was under control now. He glanced up, glasses flashing the dull electric light. The drug was soothing; invisible, gentle hands running along his burnt-out nerves. His stiffness eased. Speer was still saying something. He'd missed the first part.

". . . therefore, my Führer, this is what I must express to you."

The tone of conciliation was adequate, the words didn't matter. He felt the deeper tension soften a little now. It was, he reflected, so easy to get along with him: just be reasonable, just don't force him to have to struggle. Resistance was so needless, peace so sweet.

The English could have had peace, he thought, shaking his head, *but no. Naturally not. They had to provoke me. Just agree . . . just agree with the truth, it's so easy. If the Jews had been sensible we would not be fighting today.* He wondered if Speer realized this. *This idiotic war! If they hadn't insisted on their age-old selfish plans, if they hadn't had to undermine the great nations and pervert all beauty and values.*

Shook his head, sighing now. What was the use? No one ever really understood. Well, a very few, special men.

"My Führer?"

"Sit . . . sit down, my artist friend," he said, in a soft, hoarse rumble.

There was no chair so Speer sat on the edge of the bed that had clearly, he noted, not been slept in. Across from him was the door to Eva Braun's quarters. The lights flickered, the painting rattled again. Speer looked tense and resigned.

The Führer coughed and cleared his throat several times. The pockets under his eyes quivered.

"If only—" he finally said, rasping, "if only I could have turned aside from my destiny . . ." Shook his head. Speer crossed his legs. He noticed the pistol on the pillow for the first time, compact, shiny. "It was not to be . . . to have really just been an artist, to live in the mountains at peace with nature, what happiness that would have been . . ." A tic gripped the left side of his face briefly, violently knotted the cheek.

"The Russians are a few streets away," Speer said, for some reason, perhaps lingering resentment. His leader didn't appear to notice.

". . . before *it* chose me . . ."

"*It?*" He faced the hollow, somber eyes and saw them flash a strange fear and longing that disturbed him. "Do you mean destiny, my Führer?"

The heavy, aging head shook slightly.

"No. I do not," was the reply.

There were footsteps and shouts out in the corridor. Someone seemed to be threatening someone else who was singing. Then a sound of shattered glass, scuffling, curses, all blended into the incessant, rumbling explosions far above.

The Führer swayed in his seat, left leg vibrating again. But his voice was distant and almost peaceful.

"All I ever realy wanted to be," he said, staring, "was an artist . . ." He was weeping now. Tears trickled into the bumps and creases of his face. "I will be dead very soon . . ." Nodded. "The poison, they tell me, works very well . . . a bullet is certain only it it cracks into the skull squarely . . ." A pause. "Often it merely glances off the side of the head leaving the victim alive but helpless . . ." Pause. He removed his glasses. "I face the fact that there's no hope," he murmured.

The architect didn't know whether to agree or not. He just sat there depressed. The cramped quarters, the dankness, the glaring artificial light, the relentless pounding, kept him terribly tense. He hated the bunker and yet outside was a hell almost beyond imagination. It was too late

for anything now. There was nothing left to say. Yet, Hitler
went on and on, in spite of anything he claimed to accept.
What compelled him? What did he dream of, even now?
After all these years he still really didn't understand what
had driven the man to this point; what demon. And even at
this moment, at bay, at the end, still words, words, against
the irresistible storm.

He looked at the aging man, broken face, gleaming
tears, the lost loneliness and misery. What had driven him
to wade in so much blood? Not for what he told them, not
for land or monuments. No. Nor for Germany either.
Germany was a tool and if it broke he'd cast it aside without
compunction. Always without compunction—that was one
of his terrible advantages over other men, as if he'd been to
the devil's mountain and received the ten commandments
of hell. Where had the strength and madness come from?
Speer had already faced the madness because he'd been
part of it, even, he thought, bowed down to it.

*The whole country is going to be destroyed. Millions have
died, my God, it's too much for the mind to bear. This man who once
painted pictures wearing rags sits here and burns the world down
around himself as if he held Lucifer's torch to it with his own hands.*

"My Führer," he said, afraid as always to resist him, "is
it, do you think, at all possible . . ." Held his breath and
tried not to look directly at his ruler's eyes.

"Hmmm?" Hitler was restlessly rubbing his knee with
his hand.

"It is, perhaps, possible, if as you have just said, there is
no hope, for the war to end soon and spare our country
total destruction—"

He was already stopping even before the ravaged man
snapped upright suddenly, bright-eyed, clenching his good
fist and thundering with amazing violence through his
rasping throat:

"Germany has failed! Don't you see that? They were
not fit . . . not fit for the immense task it demanded!"

'It' again, Speer thought.

"They must be destroyed," the Führer thundered on,
all his old energy back for a moment, power pouring
through the shattered frame, and Speer felt his nerves leap
and sing an echo, almost against his will. "They failed in
labor to bear the superman and it was for this alone I
sacrificed my own life!" And then his rage was suddenly

gone and tears flowed again. "My God, old friend, I gave up everything for this . . ." Choked on a sob while the architect was horrified by this terrible transformation. "Gave up everything . . . everything . . ." Shut his eyes and shook silently with palsy and self-pity. "God, I am weary," he whispered. "I can't express it, old friend . . ."

For an instant, with his eyes closed, there were flashes of green and red fire that he blinked away, like afterglow, but not before he'd glimpsed something . . . an impression . . . darkstone structures . . . lurid glimmering in what had to be windows . . . billows of smoke or mist.

No, he told himself, *go away . . . I won't look anymore . . . not at that place . . . not anymore . . .*

Superman, Speer thought. *He still talks this nonsense.*

The older man in the baggy gray uniform reached out.

"Give me your hand," he said, biting his trembling lip. "Give me your hand. Remember when I went back to Linz? I swore I'd never go home until I made something of myself, just as my father had sworn." The lights went out totally as a tremendous blast shook the bunker walls; dust fell and the picture clattered wildly. It seemed to Speer, as the lights brightened again, that his ruler rose, pale and amorphous, from shadowy depths to take transient form there in the hardback chair where he shook and twitched as if currents of aberrant and terrible energy grounded through him like dark, unseen lightning. The blast that had nearly killed him last year (another one of his frighteningly miraculous escapes) had surely wrecked his body, he thought. "Well," the Führer went on, smiling now, reminiscing, almost as if senile, "I certainly came home and showed them a few things. That was a memorable and historically significant day . . . Old Alois's son came home!" He chuckled and shook his head. "What clean joy we all felt in those days, Speer! What joy . . . The world was there like stone to carve into a new and magnificent work of art for the first time, led by the spirit without confusion . . . Well, there will be a way out of these present difficulties too, old friend, you'll soon see that!" Nodded jerkily. "There always is a way. What time those drummers kept in that parade! I went straight to my mother's grave and wished that wonderful woman could have seen our triumph!" Smiled and nodded.

II
(1907–08)

The yard was partly overgrown with dense brambles and
berry bushes. The humid air lay unstirring under the
midsummer brilliance of sun. He stood in the weedy grass
under the open bedroom window. His shadow lay across a
bed of drooped white flowers.

He could hear his mother's breath, slow and sighing.
The window was just higher than his head, so he couldn't
see her lying inside.

The sweat beaded around his neck. His hands were
thrust deeply into the pockets of his leather knee-length
shorts. He just stood listening, and after a time he heard
her praying and he knew she would be fingering the gilt
rosary that she kept wrapped in her long, hard, pale
fingers. Somewhere in the village a dog began listlessly
barking. A man shouted, unintelligibly, and then the heavy
silence closed in again.

He pictured the lacy coverlet, the oversized pillow
dented by her head in its wreath of matted hair; her set,
pinched face, flushed, the eyes restless, wild, too bright. He
knew the light was slanting into the dim cottage room
through the parted, leaded glass, crossing the bed and then
the wall as the sun sank and seemed to measure away her
life. His bright, pale blue, somehow almost hollow eyes
burned with unshed tears and his lips trembled.

His sister, Paula, was now standing on the narrow
porch. She had come out noiselessly. Behind the house a
green tilt of mountain showed above the near pine trees.

"Come in now, Brother," she said, watching him from a
round, set face that showed nothing.

He shook his head, chin lowered, belligerent,
stubborn.

"Mama is asking for you again," she told him. Her

long, neutral-colored dress revealed nothing about the shape of her body. Only her hands moved, twisting a shawl-end where it crossed her bosom.

"No."

"But Ade—"

"No. I won't watch her die."

He could hear her praying now and he drew his hands from his pockets and clenched them at his sides.

"Why does she pray?" he muttered. "It means nothing!"

"You know this?" his sister responded. "Nineteen years old and you know this?"

"God will not help her!" The unshed tears burned but didn't leak a drop. "There is no help." Shook his head in a single, violent jerk. "Nothing."

"Come in, Adolf," she repeated. "Your mother asks you to come in to her."

"I refuse!" he almost shouted; and heard his mother's voice cease.

Oh, Mama . . . Mama . . . he thought. He felt as if he stood at the edge of a bottomless pit, everything empty before him . . . everything. *Should I lie again? Is that best? Could I stand there and tell her I failed again?* He suddenly tensed his jaw and frowned, lowered his chin. *I didn't fail I wasn't given a chance by those pigs—those academic pigs who know nothing anyway.* But it didn't matter why and he knew that too. The fact was, he had no diploma, no trade, and the art professors had turned him away. He clenched his fists in his pockets and the unshed tears burned and burned. He shook slightly with self-pity and grief. *Those damned pigs! God, I'd like to break their necks! God! Can I say to my mother, look, I have nothing? Can I say such a thing?*

A memory flashed from five years ago: the same backyard, a hot, bright summer morning, sitting on the lush grass with a sketchpad, trying to draw his mother while she bent and straightened, clothespinning sheets and blouses to the washline that stretched from the house to a tree. He had just given up and started to sketch the porch when a shadow from behind darkened the bright, white paper and as he twisted around (already afraid, heart leaping) he saw his mother had turned, still holding a dripping, empty shirt up to the line. Struggling to his feet and still turning (glimpsed the other shadow merging with his own on the lawn) as the hard, harsh hands clawed into the back of his neck and then he was struggling, raging, smelling the sweat, sweetish warm alcoholic breath and the sweat and must of the stained uniform as the voice bellowed over his own;

"Picture painter! I'll show you who's a picture painter!"

"Let me go!"

". . . I'll teach you picture painting, you stubborn swine!"

They spun together, the house going past, then his mother (a step closer to them, the shirt suspended, falling behind her) then trees, a neighbor's chimney. He strained to pull away, arms flailing madly. The house, his mother, long dress and apron fluttering, running now, the shirt on the ground, shouting into the gasping, cursing, and the pounding of his blood. He struggled around to face the stocky old man—nearly seventy, hale, unsmiling, granite-eyed—who hit him a terrific punch and the boy reeled and went over into the flowerbed by the porch, seeing the sky and earth rock and sway, Mother almost there now, shouting:

"Stop this! My God, stop . . . stop . . . stop!"

As his father's big hands had the sketchpad, ripping, the halves and quarters of paper flying into the air and then his mother (he saw through his blurred and darkened sight) shaking the much older husband, plucking at his clothes without moving the stolidly planted figure who kept staring at his son. The thirteen-year-old struggled to get his rubbery legs under himself; his body had crushed his shape into the white and yellow flowers, cheek just starting to pulse and sting (he could feel but not yet taste the blood in his mouth), watching now as his mother was flung aside in a ballooning of frilly garments, long hair loose and shaking, as the bearded, barrel-chested former policeman with harsh and scornful lips loomed over him again. Then the golden-bright and green day blotted out as the hard hands (he heard his father's racked panting) gripped his face and the sagging, softly massive torso covered him and he gagged and screamed, felt suffocated, twisting his head against the stiff cloth in a panic for breath, smelling the stale beer smell he'd always loathed, clawing, muffled and desperate . . . Father raging, spittle flying:

"You little bum! I'll teach you . . . you little bum!"

And his mother, from far away:

"Alois, stop this! Leave him alone, Alois!"

Adolf bellowed, tears streaming, punching, punching, kicking at the stifling, mountainous hulk pressing him down, sinking his teeth into the harsh cloth, then into a thick finger, bone grinding—his father's howls of pain—rolling apart, the hand still clenched in his jaw, the suffering man's free fist pounding his son's stubborn head. Adolf tasted the salt-sweet blood now, his own and his sire's. The day reeled and darkened. Voices became a single, mounting, formless roar. Alois jerked free, leaving the battered boy on his knees among the blossoms, blood welling and flowing from between his bared teeth and down his chin as he swayed, seeing and hearing only in his mind now, aware of a vast, black storm of somber fire sweeping over the earth filled with a monstrous, burning, dripping shape of heads and horns and blazing bestial eyes. Another blow and he seemed to hear the wailing of numberless beings in a sea of smoke and torment and hissing blood, rising, flooding over him, as if he'd slipped and stumbled and fell in a breaking surf, and he tried to cry out, and then nothing . . .

His aunt had come out now and was standing beside his sister on the porch. She was a big woman with folded arms and red, frowning cheeks. She stared at him.

"Why doesn't he come in?" she asked Paula. She was stocky and stood there with the solidity of his father.

"He's upset," Paula said.

"You don't understand," he said.

"I understand," the aunt said. "I understand you very well, Master Hitler. You deserted her and went away to live like I-don't-know-what. You took money and sent none back."

Paula touched her aunt's arm.

"Don't say these things," she murmured, glancing back at the house.

"It needs to be said," the aunt insisted sternly.

"You're a fool," Adolf muttered. He really wasn't looking at her or paying close attention. He stood alone with his chill of guilt and fear.

"He'll end up like young Alois," the aunt went on.

Young Alois was his half-brother. "He'll see the inside of a jail in due course."

"Leave me alone," Adolf said quietly, without energy. He turned his back and walked toward the fence. The air was rich and heavy; the sweat itched on his face and neck. They were both talking now but he didn't hear it. He rested one hand idly on the clothesline and stared at the tall boards. Gray and peeling.

Now what do I do?

He remembered it now, bleakly, without even rage:

The following took the test with insufficient results, or were not admitted to the test: . . . Adolf Hitler, Braunau a. Inn, April 20, 1889, German, Catholic. Father civil servant . . . Test drawing unsatisfactory.

"I don't give up," he whispered. The aunt was still saying something from the porch into the stagnant, hot afternoon. Then, after a few moments, the door opened and shut. He stared at the blank boards as if to read something in them. "Never," he whispered. Gave a deep, sighing hum and suddenly smashed his fist into the fence, felt the pain leap from his hand up his arm, and he almost smiled with pleasure and satisfaction. Leaned forward and rested his forehead on the humid boards. Shut his eyes. Remembered it again . . . and again, as if enjoying that too, like the mere physical pain that meant nothing, the numbing arm limp at his side. Remembered as if to engrave it forever, as if to be sure the wound could never heal: . . . *unsatisfactory . . . unsatisfactory . . .*

And then, muffled from within the house, a sobbing groan that chilled the back of his neck and made him sick with helpless fear. Another, and he spoke to drown it out, muttering into the fence, over and over:

"I don't give up . . . I don't give up . . . I don't give up . . ."

III
(APRIL 1945)

I am almost there, Renga thought. Down the line there was distant firing and a shout that might have been a scream. The sheltering ridge was very close now. He stumbled down through another shell hole, kicking something soft. He crouched and discovered a boot, then someone's leg; recoiled in horror because that was all there was—no someone—and refusing to think about it he went on, scrambled out of there, shuffling, careful. *I am mad, naturally,* he thought. *I will never confront Hitler . . . I will die hopelessly . . . but I owe her that death . . . and the rest of them, I owe them too . . .*

He twisted his head around to watch the softly sputtering parachute flare, swaying and sinking almost directly overhead, a brilliant red that he gaped at, for a moment, as if he were a child at a fireworks show. And then his body seemed to hear first (because it spasmed into action while his mind was still engrossed), the incoming, mounting scream of the first shell; the mind rambled and wondered even as the rest of him sprang for life.

(1907–08)

Rain, Winter chill. Raw earth smell.

Always the rain, he was thinking. *Always cold* rain . . .

He stood apart from the others, away from the umbrellas. The water spattered over his head and face. His bad lung throbbed a little. No one could tell if he was weeping into the streaming downpour.

Paula stood beside his aunt across the grave where the mounded, fresh earth ran to mud and slowly dissolved.

The priest was under an umbrella held up by an altar boy. His voice seemed to wash away with the cold storm.

Adolf was staring past the little church, across the fields into the billowing mists that poured over the hills. His sister was looking at him. What was going to become of him now? she wondered.

Paula was sure her brother was going to leave. The men of the family, her mother always said, gave themselves no peace. Were never, for a moment, content. Stubborn, proud, angry men.

"Poor woman," the aunt had just said over the spatter and rush of rain on their umbrellas. "God grant her rest."

"We have to help him," Paula said, weeping now, staring across the grave at her pale, awkward, thin brother, his hair plastered along forehead and cheeks. "He's very unhappy."

The aunt crossed herself with the priest who was finishing up. Gusts of wind cut the rain sideways now, billowed it over the onlookers.

The priest was finished and moved quickly away, skipping and long-stepping in his robes over the muddy pools. He headed for the church.

Adolf watched him go, feeling at this moment a strange rush of almost exultant energy. The priest seemed a feeble, black scarecrow, a meaningless shadow dissolving into chill grayness. The priest was powerless, like the rest of them. He saw this with sudden clarity. God . . . ah, God . . . God was this uncanny strength pouring through death and life, streaming into him . . . each being was endlessly wiped away with their misty hopes and plans and dreams, wiped away like smoke to nothingness. He clenched his hands to check their trembling. The chill rain washed over him. His clothes were sodden. The cold force poured on and on . . .

He smiled. An elderly cousin, turning to leave, huddled under her parasol, glanced at him and was startled by the haunted look on that avid, pale face. Adolf shut his eyes. Swayed there for what seemed a long time . . . then rain and time came flooding back. He blinked through the blur. The damp air seemed to burn in his bad lung. His aunt and sister were standing close to him, the water beating down like a wall between them.

For a moment he thought they'd come to him for comfort and he wondered if he would be capable of expressing this truth, this movement, that had possessed him. Did he have the power to make them feel it too? For a moment he felt mighty words, words from the storm and forever, beginning to fill his throat and then his aunt was saying something brusque and Paula something quiet over the drumming, steady, gusting, grayly darkening downpour.

"Come home, Ade," his sister said.

He brushed the water from his hungry, staring eyes. He looked vague, almost stunned, she thought. And he felt suddenly vacant, weary, chilled, dull as mud.

"I . . ." he hesitantly began.

"Please," she said. "It's the best thing. Aunt says you can . . ."

"We have to comfort one another," said his aunt, "in this hour of sorrow."

He blinked at her, frowning. Said nothing.

"You can work for Uncle Karl," Paula said. "Come out of the rain now."

"In the sausage shop?" he asked, needlessly.

His aunt nodded, once.

He'd worked there one summer. He remembered stuffing the meat, organs, gristle, and sometimes bone into the grinder, working the crank, pressing the mass through, getting sprayed with blood and fleshy muck that caked on his clothes and stank. Karl, stolid, silent as stone all day, chopping meat and stuffing scraps into his mouth so that he always seemed to be chewing blood that stained lips and chin.

"No," he murmured.

"What is he saying?" the aunt demanded.

"Please, Ade," Paula said.

"I'm going to be an artist," Adolf said. He stepped back, murmuring, "I'm not part of all this." He gestured vaguely.

"He's a fool," the aunt humpfed. "What did I tell you?"

His voice suddenly filled with stunning power, as if the energy he'd sensed flowing through death moments before had poured strength into him.

"Never!" he boomed, gesturing stiffly with one hand. People already at the cemetery gate turned to look back through the drenched air.

"Ingrate!" said his aunt. "Think jobs drop from the sky, do you?"

"Be quiet," he said firmly, glowering at her.

"Go sleep in the ditches, you bum!" she raged, shaking the open umbrella in her fury. "Your father was a *man* and you're a bum! He made something of him—"

"The time will come, fat woman—" Adolf roared in a thunderclap of concentrated fury that riveted the mourners paused at the gate. Their pale faces gaped across the muddy, misty, boiling graveyard. "The time will come when you'll see what I *am!*" She was already storming away, half dragging Paula through the mud, turning only once to fling back a last shout:

"Get a job, you tramp!"

And his thundering voice, breaking with tears, finally:

"You'll see, you old fool! You'll see! You'll all see!"

Then on his knees, chilled, miserable, he flung himself on the muddy grave earth, sobbing in his throat, clawing wrist-deep in the icy mire that yielded back nothing, murmuring, choking on his mother's name . . .

He seemed to be dreaming for a while, as in a fever. Some time later he raised himself to hands and knees, smeared with muck. Stood up, the rain thickly washing it away. His eyes still dreamt a huge, open-air theater where a gigantic Wotan raised a long spear over his horned helmet and shouted in a ringing, singing voice, something more than words, that brought all truth and time into a single, magical moment.

He blinked. The upturned, pale faces of his ecstatic audience was now melting into the dull wet gravestones all around him as the fantasy washed away too.

He reeled slightly. All sound suddenly blended into a roar as of unnumbered, shouting voices and then the earth suddenly rolled up . . . up and over the sky and he never felt the saturated ground, as if it had gaped like a mouth and swallowed him into blackness.

IV
(1908)

It was a clean, cool autumn morning. The air seemed washed pure. The still-green fields and trees, streaked with gold and dull reddening, seemed to sparkle as if polished by the refreshing breezes.

Adolf went on steadily, not even breaking a sweat yet, descending the long hill, following the stream that he knew eventually crossed the main valley road heading toward Vienna.

He climbed a steep bank in the pebbled shadow of the old stone bridge. The stream rushed quietly past, spattered with light and shadow. He felt warm and confident. Exhilarated by the air, the day, the immense prospect of his life opening before him. He did as few quick peasant dance steps, a little jig, raising from the rutted road a fine dust that floated like pale smoke across the violet glow of heather.

Then he froze, heart leaping with a kind of fear and shame, as a pale, blond teenage girl was just crossing the near bend in the road. She passed through the shadow of an overhanging tree and the sunlight seemed to burst in her golden hair. *Gretlin,* he thought. Had she seen him jumping like a fool? Almost ran the other way. Controlled himself.

She hadn't seen him. Went on into the trees . . . was gone. He relaxed. Blinked rapidly. Tried not to think about that night on her family's farm. *She saw nothing,* he repeated to himself. *Nothing . . .*

Because he'd seen her in church and had thought about her and watched her and dreamed and sketched poems about it. He'd said no more than a shy hello twice and then, on impulse one evening, because he believed, suddenly, that she'd been watching him and cared in

26

agonized secret as he did himself, he'd walked out of Linz to the farm country where she lived—not far from where he now stood. He had no real idea of what he'd do when he got there. Just wanted to be near where she was . . . he had vague ideas about getting her to walk with him, telling her he loved . . . perhaps a kiss . . . and then he was crossing the open land in full moonlight, slowing as he neared the far end of the potato field. Saw the house lights glowing dim yellow on the rich earth. Climbed the rear fence, oblivious to both the flurry of geese in the barn and her parents' voices inside the house.

He stopped near her window: he could see the lantern on the dresser, closed door, parted drapes. Ideas flew through his mind, quotes: ". . . . only through love of Thee can my soul live, O princess! . . ." He'd knock on the glass. ". . . . Thou art my hope and prayer and redemption! . . ." He drifted closer and closer. Could have touched the sash from where he now stood. A steady draught kept the drapes parted.

As his eyes adjusted from the moon dimness he had an impression she was wearing a skimpy, dark garment until he realized her naked body was crossed by shadows. She was standing beyond the lamp, twisted around as if to study the backs of her legs, and he took it in, stunned breathless in the warm, summer-drenched night, dizzied by the exquisite bright hair, the golden shimmer flow of limbs to the graceful, arched feet that bore her so sweetly he imagined kissing them. Dizzied with longing, heat, and a kind of terror, he discovered his hand had slipped inside his leather shorts. *I love thee*, he kept thinking. *I love thee*. Part of his consciousness tried to rip the fingers away from that shock of dark sweetness, her pale, golden form floating in a web of trembling reddish light, darkness dissolving the world around them and leaving her only an image, his flesh melting as his hand flew on, straining, scraping and pressing desperately under the tough leather, unable, and no longer wanting, to release himself from his own grip even for an instant, left hand fumbling at the fly buttons, right wrist aching, spasming on . . . all sounds and movements vague and infinitely distant until the other window had already banged open, the dog crashed raucous in the kitchen and her father's breathy voice called: "What is this? Who's out there!" And Adolf went to his knees in panic as Gretlin, covering herself, raced to the window with the wavering lamp as he was already scrambling away (feeling the futile, feelingless pumping in his shorts, muffled and almost painful), climbing and tumbling over the fence, fleeing in shame and frustration across the uneven fields, dog, lights, slamming, outcries, fading behind.

He stared at where the blond hair had last glinted in the blue-green shadows. He vowed he'd put all the past behind. He would remain pure and set his feelings into irresistible poetry. Paint beautiful images that would haunt all mankind with the bittersweet, tragic illusions of dreaming youth . . . and she would someday suffer to know what kind of heart had broken for her.

"I'll not fail," he whispered. "I'll not fail . . ."

V
(APRIL 1945)

Sultry late afternoon. Oberführer Kurt Fragtkopft yanked the comb through his lank salt-and-pepper hair, wincing with pain as he ripped out the knots. He peered into the greasy mirror: a thin crack divided his soft-fleshed face and part of the cramped office behind him. The mirror, for some reason, had been tacked to a beam in the dimmest corner.

He straightened, clattering the comb onto the littered desktop, and struggled to close his jacket collar over the undeniable jowls he refused to accept. He wouldn't order a larger coat.

"Dammit," he gasped, fingers thickly struggling, face red, pale eyes bulging.

Why must he come out here today? he asked himself. *Little Heini. Full of great ideas every five minutes. Why kid ourselves? It's about over.* He locked his teeth together for a moment. Slit his eyes. *Still, we've got a few tricks left.*

Sighed with relief as he finally got the collar closed.

Looked for his cap. Outside was a pale sunny day. With the windows shut and sealed with tape the office was very stuffy.

He moved in front of the window as he buckled on gun and holster, staring down into a little, neatly tended garden where a row of fig trees was newly green. He sighed to think how it would be autumn before they were really ripe. Shook his head.

What will be left by autumn? Those assholes really made a mess of things. The pressure is on. He was petulant. *We've got to clean up the mess now. The assholes.*

Beyond the garden were rolling, green empty fields and spurs of rich woodland. A peasant's house on a distant slope showed white and toylike. At the horizon dark masses of smoke piled higher and higher where the city burned and the armies clashed. They were that close now, he took note. Shook his head.

Assholes . . . hopeless, ignorant assholes, undid all our efforts and sacrifices . . .

His stomach felt hollow with anxiety but he shrugged and set his black SS cap over his damp hair, thinking how that would leave a ringlike indentation when it dried.

Paused at the door, glanced out the window on the opposite side from the garden and the sweeping vistas. This had a view of a flat yard of pale yellowish dust, green-gray barracks and high double lines of barbed wire set with sentry towers. The yard was clear. He squinted: saw no sign of the Reichsführer's car at the main gate yet. Decided he'd take a walk.

Wrinkled his nose as he opened the door and immediately shut it again. He'd forgotten the wind was from the east today blowing back over the camp. Acrid smoke-stink lingered in the room.

He found the little jar of French perfume on the window ledge and dabbed it under and around his nostrils. Then went outside, down the wooden steps, crossing the shadow of the smokestack that towered over the blackened, factorylike building. The sweetish stench immediately penetrated the scent he'd put on. He never had become used to it.

The smoke, sucked down by random eddies, stung his eyes as he crossed the inner yard past the squat, dark, windowless prison barracks. He locked his hands behind his back and strolled toward the gate. His stout body cast a

long shadow across the barren ground. Each bootstep
raised a fine dust that drifted and was lost in the general,
acrid haze.

His shadow flicked over the splintery chink between
the boards where she stared dully, crouched bony and
barefoot on the rough floor in her sacklike prison rags.
One hand feebly picked a sore on her frighteningly thin
calf. Her face was shadowed by purplish stains of starvation
and utter, wasting exhaustion that underscored the bony,
ravaged face, stringy grayed-out hair, and sunken cheeks.
All the women crammed into this narrow space seemed of
one old age though some had clearly been children not
long before. She had realized, at some point, that even if
some survived, the true horror would forever remain
indescribable.

She sat there facing the bare wall. Behind her the
voices were constant but muted by weakness and despair
into sobs, mutterings, prayings, lingering moans.

The shadow had caught her faded, starey eyes and she
focused on the commandant's soft profile a few feet away,
as he passed. She'd never seen him so close. But then, she'd
only been transferred to this camp recently, just ahead of
(though she had no way of knowing it) the Russian
advance. She knew dimly there was fighting but it seemed
there had always been fighting . . . or did she really
remember some long-lost world where soft, white clouds
gathered over a green hill and rustic cottage where
immense roses grew sweetly on the trellis? It was as vague
as an old dream. She had no idea anymore how long she'd
been in the camps, though there had been a time when she
kept careful, outraged, then finally anguished and hopeless, count.

She pressed her face as close as possible to the space
between the planks and blinked at the portly black-
uniformed man clumping by with a certain middle-aged
weariness in his tread. He sniffed and wrinkled his nose at
the fecal-rot stench seeping from the barracks that she was
long past noticing: stench of sickness, death, and burning
flesh.

He winked out of her sight a moment later, but the
sight of his face had stirred something deep in the lost, dim
channel of her remembrance. That face . . . that face.

Heard a voice, a conversation, a bright, brief flash of image that seemed from that other past world and time . . . where? . . . when? Knitted her blotchy brown brows straining to get it. Sighed and rocked back and forth, staring at the bare slit view of dusty earth where a single, skeletal spray of weed vibrated slightly in the light, smoky, warm breezes.

What did they expect? Commandant Fragtkopft was now asking himself. They want a miracle. Did they have any idea of how many of his men had gone insane, not to mention killed themselves, in the past three years? He wondered. *We don't do miracles here.*

A roar echoed in the sky and he looked up. Waves of bombers, American, he realized, going over, contrails traced long and pure white behind them. Not a fighter left in Germany, he reflected, to challenge them. Not much left of Germany either, as a matter of fact.

He paced on. Almost at the gate he frowned.

What's this?

As the sentry saluted, Fragtkopft pointed to the naked, emaciated man caught in the barbed wire half a dozen yards down the line, head drooping, limbs bent and shattered, looking like, he thought, a broken stick figure. Very little blood had oozed from the fat, purplish bullet holes. He lay tangled in wire and shadows as the sun lowered, now a vivid, swollen red touching the top layers of the mass of rising smoke and dust to the west.

"How long has this one been here?" he snapped.

"Not long, sir," the sentry answered.

Well, I was probably in the shower and so heard nothing.

"Is anyone interested in getting him out of there?" he wondered sarcastically. "Or do we leave him for the Americans?"

"Are they so close, Commandant?"

"They'll be using your toilet and giving your wife chocolate bars before you can blink, Corporal."

"Yes, sir," the pale young man said. "Herms went to get a burial party, sir."

Fragtkopft went on through the gate, thoughtfully.

Burial party, he thought. *Some joke. The bastard must have been part rabbit to get as far as he did. Must have taken off when he realized what was happening. Some of them do.*

He was amazed that any of them retained either

strength or instinct for life at this point. How could you
expect them to really face the fact of what they were? You
couldn't. It was as easy to spook a mass of them as it was a
rafter of turkeys, he thought. *Now we've made a cleaner world
for the Bolsheviks and Yankees to enjoy. What irony.* They
refused to face the fact that what they were caused their
doom. He recalled a book he'd read many years ago: *Jew,
See What Thou Art!* it was called. Very clearly written, he
seemed to remember.

Turned around just outside the double gate and
looked back, facing the crematorium belching thick, greasy
smoke. He heard the car coming now across the long,
straight stretch that reached to the gate. Himmler's car.
Driving in daylight too. *How brave,* he thought. Didn't turn
around. Rocked on his heels, lost in this thoughts.

You try to go on, he reflected, *you try to be decent.*
Frustrated. Bitter. His stomach felt hollow again. *I'm caught
like that pathetic bastard in the wire. Who's better off? Those
stinking assholes.* He spat in the dust. *You can't kill everybody.
Some of the swine are bound to escape.*

There was a ping in the purr of the motor as it came
closer.

In for a penny, the English say, in for a pound.

His shadow stretched alongside the wire in the lurid,
red sunlight that dimmed rapidly. His mouth was suddenly
dry when he tried to spit again.

You take a step . . . then another . . . another . . .

He lit a cigarette and sucked deeply at the smoke.
Between that and his perfumed nostrils he barely noticed
the burning flesh.

He heard the brakes squeak at his back.

*And you go on and on like a drunken man who can't stop and
can't fall either . . .*

Back in the barracks, the woman stood up, wobbling,
weak, leaning on the wall, streaks of feeble light coming
through ventilation slits high up, submerging in twilight
(almost as in a church) the bony, wraithlike shapes in their
rags and tatters, swollen, seeming to be all eyes, eyes that
glowed and stared out of the shadowy vaguenesses of
themselves. She stood up, gasping, lips pressed together,
expression fierce and wild, shocked too because she remembered, she remembered him. She remembered.

(1909–1913)

The fat woman was just tugging down her garters and rolling her dark stockings off one after the other, standing there, tipping, losing her balance slightly, hopping for an instant as she freed her heel, massive breasts swaying in the smoky, bluish light. Now she was completely and (Kurt Fragtkopft thought) obscenely nude. He was making sure the single set of French windows opening onto the terrace were locked. He glanced out briefly, as he readjusted the drapes, at the lights of Munich, a glimpse of muted, restless reflections in the river seen through the reversed image of the room in the glass panel. The bald, gleaming head of Drecklicht, the chairman, chewing his cigar; Schatz, stooped, bearded, hooknosed (worse than a Jew, his colleagues said) and the half a dozen others floated, superimposed, dim, hollow, over the city. In the blurred and hazy illumination he imagined they all looked like a stag party of petty businessmen. A passing notion. He smiled and went back to the circle around the woman who now lay down on the rug and opened her legs wide. Began taking deep, uneven breaths. Her sagging face was too soft, in the shadowed light, for the little eyes to be visible.

I hope she's cleaned herself, Kurt thought.

Someone lit the incense and the thick, acrid perfume burned in his nose.

Minna hates the smell, he thought. *Probably it was stupid of me to let them meet here. What could I do? Burning that stuff is unnecessary superstition but everyone likes cheap hallowed effects. There's a scientific basis for all this, naturally.* He shifted restlessly in his seat. He was the youngest member and it had taken a lot of convincing to win him over. He was known to be very critical and logical. *And this nude cow, my God! She looks about to give birth to a child or a fart.*

He joined his hands matter-of-factly with the men on either side of him. Schatz, on his right, gripped with chilly, bony fingers. The fellow on his left (he'd forgotten his name) always reminded him of a book salesman, elfin and quick. His hands were always moist.

Drecklicht was watching the clock on the wall. He sat

directly across the circle from Kurt. The woman's head was between his feet.

"It is now . . ." Drecklicht began, holding the syllables, ". . . now . . . time!"

Because, Kurt was thinking, *the moon has just entered the mansion of power.* He was wry. *What would Minna say to that?* He began chanting, murmuring with the rest. *She'd say I am mad.* He imagined trying to explain to her the necessity for the sound.

Drecklicht was intoning, above the chanting, as the woman sighed; mountainously heaved and quivered.

"We ask you, dread lords of the past," he was saying, "to come to us tonight, to speak with us under the stars of power and truth, to speak from beyond the illusion of time. We call you without fear. We bid you open the doors of death. We *command* you! We *command* you!" The chanting rolled on, gathering volume and intensity. Kurt wondered if she could hear it downstairs. He hated having to do this but his voice seemed pulled out of him by the others and he wondered (for a flash) if he could stop if he wanted to. "We *command! Command!* Now speak."

And the woman grunted and gurgled in her throat. Belched so hard her vast breasts and planetary belly shook, then she began to talk in a blurred, stiff, male voice, harsh and fragmentary.

". . . fuck you fuck you fuck youshitcockfuck cunt . . ." She spat and drooled.

A low entity has her, Kurt thought, still in the steady chanting. Drecklicht would have to drive it out or they'd get nothing.

". . . cunt cunt cuntshit fuck cock I piss you piss he shit . . ." Dry, crackling, robotic laughter. "The devil sucks your asses you virgins! You—"

"We *command* the power," the leader shouted, "of a great lord of the past! We demand, without fear, the clear truth!"

"I am a lord you toe-licking shit-suckers, you cocks, you—"

"*Go!! Out!!*" Drecklicht bellowed.

Now a dim, quivering, amorphous, bluish-glowing shape began flowing like a blind worm or headless snake from between the fat, wobbling legs.

Kurt was startled. This was new, and disturbing.

Ectoplasm, he remembered. It was supposed to be common with trance mediums, though this one, apparently, had never gone beyond speaking before.

Meanwhile the voice had changed: the sound was well-modulated now. A trifle hollow.

"Ask," it said, from the drooling, flaccid mouth. The strange, mistlike, fluid stuff kept oozing out, swelling into a lumpy balloon now. Or was it a light effect?

"Who are you?" demanded Drecklicht.

"The past," was the answer.

"Were you a member of the great race?"

"Believe what pleases you."

Drecklicht grew stern, concentrating, words powerful and steady.

"Will the great race be reborn soon?"

The hollow, flaccid woman babbled and moaned for a moment. Kurt saw her fingers clench and dig deeply into her fat palms.

"In part," the voice pronounced. "It has never died."

A sigh went around the room. The chanting hesitated briefly.

So, Kurt thought, *is it possible? These prophecies would seem to have been remarkably accurate.*

He partly shut his eyes and pictured the days of the great race to himself. He often did this before going to sleep, trying, so to speak, to recall it from the memory of nature. Sometimes while walking in the street or during a class at the university. He edited and altered the images as he read or heard or conceived of new elements: the stupendous towers dark against the evening sky, the great fernlike trees, the lush fields in the violet wash of glimmering twilight. The bent, dwarfish slave people working silently; the giant masters, eyes radiant, penetrating, cool, moving gracefully in their black and silver robes, performing magic to swell the growth of plants, directing beams of golden force into the sky to form and unform the clouds. Sailing through the heavens in chariots of rainbow fire. Masters of all creation, raising immense, jewel-like cities. Commanding all things to their will. Trees a thousand feet high lit by the rising moon so close to the earth it covered a quarter of the sky. Thousands of the giant masters moving in their matchless, lordly beauty, holding talismans of superscience, floating out from the mile-high towers to pray and delight in the endlessly mild weather.

He narrowed his eyes to better visualize:

One of the long-limbed, magnificent women had stripped off her robe and stood proudly as a naked, golden-bodied male demigod crossed the velvety, softly luminescent grass and embraced her. They soon were caressing one another's sleek, inexpressibly vital bodies and kissing deeply.

He was startled back to the moment by a deep, long, bestial roar from the now twisting, twitching medium:

"Yaaaaaaaaaargg!" she screamed. "Relti! . . . Relti is here! . . ."

The luminescent cloud that he seemed to see flowing from her flesh seemed to briefly shimmer and form an uncertain, shadowy outline: a human head, fierce face and bony forehead, going blurred, foggy, crumbling as she sat upright, sweat streaming down her skin, panting, eyes rolling, a trickle of bile and foamy vomit creasing her chin and spattering the obese torso.

The chanting had stopped and Drecklicht was standing up, stretching his cramped limbs as were others now. Kurt gratefully released the two hands he'd been holding and thoughtfully sat back. The conversations began, muted and fragmentary, around the room.

Someone had put on the gaslight and the medium was now squatting on the rug. For a while no one paid any attention to her. They were all too engrossed with buzzing about the oracular news.

Schatz was rapidly nodding his narrow, dried-up head and grinning liplessly at Kurt.

"Ah," he was saying, tapping his long fingers on the younger man's knee which made him want to pull the leg away violently, "what do you think of this, Kurt? Eh? The—" He lowered his voice. "'The Osiris of Bremenhaven' was right again." Eyes twinkled as he used Drecklicht's nickname. "It would seem the times are ripening for us, eh?"

Kurt Fragtkopft was getting nervous about the nude medium on the rug. He was afraid Minna might come upstairs before he called her. He didn't want to show any middle-class inhibitions, however, so he squirmed inwardly and waited.

"Well, I hope so," he began, "but I'd still like more evidence that—" He looked up.

"What's this?" Drecklicht was standing over the woman

who had just urinated on the pale rug. Kurt instantly saw the stains. His stomach sank. There were a few titters here and there as the discussions hesitated then poured on over this minor obstruction.

Kurt was on his feet.

"Get her dressed!" he shouted.

"Better put her to bed," Drecklicht suggested. "For a bit."

"The pig," Kurt muttered.

"Well, well, Fragtkopft," Drecklicht said soothingly, "she can't control herself effectively after a session like this. You know that. Did you see the manifestation?"

"The ectoplasm? I never believed in such things. I assumed they were tricks."

"Well, you saw it." The older man was short and carried his bald head hunched forward on his stocky body. "Eventually we may see the actual form of one of the lords."

Kurt and a uniformed officer, a captain in the Austrian guards, were assisting the groggy medium to her feet and working her way toward the adjoining bedroom. She was sweaty, heavy, and (Kurt thought) sickeningly soft. One of her pendulous breasts slapped against him as they released her over a bed that sagged and popped internally as it took her weight.

I saw it, yes, he was thinking, *but that proves little. Who knows what actually causes such a thing.*

"Some mess, eh?" the captain remarked, tossing a dark, red-and-white patterned robe over the heavily breathing hulk.

"I hope to God she doesn't soil herself again," Kurt muttered.

"Isn't it worth the inconvenience?" the captain wondered in a vital tone that made Kurt feel he was part of something very manly. "She's a good contact. One of the best. Take it from me."

Kurt had never met this man: vigorous, tall, in his late thirties. Striking figure, he thought, with his braid and monocle. Perfect officer class, he stood out among the grayer, frailer types.

"Yes," Kurt murmured, standing there a moment, catching his breath as the captain lit up a thin, black cigar. His monocle flashed the matchflame.

"You're a new face," he said, exhaling through his nose.

"Yes. I recently was . . . became a member."

"They must trust you or you wouldn't have been here."

"Well, it's my home, you see."

"Ah," said the officer as if that fact totally confirmed him. He puffed almost constantly on the cheroot. Kurt was fascinated. He'd never seen anyone smoke like that. He thought of a fire-breathing dragon or a defective stove. "We are pretty much on the *inside* of things here. This group has connections that would surprise you." He winked, the smoke jetting out with his words and streaming around his fluffy mustaches. "Above us here there's just the inner order."

Kurt had heard this himself. And the inner-circle members were said to be often drawn directly from this group; Drecklicht was supposed to be one of the chiefs. Well, he certainly didn't mind being one of the elite. It was his university reputation that had done the trick. A brilliant paper on how the historical process was the "anvil on which the dominant nations are formed." His subsequent study on "Myths and the Root Races" was no sooner published than he received an invitation to meet certain members of the Thule Group. They'd praised his occult research and Drecklicht had insisted that what for him had been theoretical and mystical was, in fact, a present and practical (if he could be allowed the word) reality. They'd promised that if he got through the initiation process, he would experience, for himself, the reality of the great race and their supernormal powers. He thought it nonsense, but something in himself wanted to be persuaded. Well, wanted excitement, perhaps, entertainment. Why not? And you never really knew, did you, unless you took a chance. . . .

So here he was. Except explaining all this to his wife, Minna, was another story. He saw her now, past the smoking captain's shoulder, kneeling, wiping furiously at the rug while Drecklicht worked at being charming.

God, he thought, with a husband's resignation, *she had to come up now. Why didn't they leave the door shut?* Sighed and closed his eyes for a moment. He remembered trying to discuss all this with her the other night.

"I don't like that man," she said.

They were under the quilt in the darkened bedroom. Nippy autumn air stirred the fluffy curtains. Street light poked vaguely along walls and ceiling, barely penetrating the deep shadows.

"Well," he returned, "he's a brilliant fellow. Drecklicht has his points, Minna."

They lay there not touching. He stared at the ceiling, idly following the abstract patterns of darkness defined by the dim threads of glow. He respected her opinion. Always had. Not many women had spent even two years in the university. He was proud of that fact.

"I have disliked brilliant men before," she said. "Napoléon was a genius, according to some; still, I doubt we would have been friends."

"Come now, Minna. Let's—"

"And all of a sudden you believe in . . . I don't know what kind of nonsense."

"How do we know it's nonsense?" He frowned and whistled softly between his teeth. "We have to have open minds."

"Some of us have holes in our heads."

He grunted and went on whistling unconsciously.

"Stop that, will you?" she whispered, fiercely.

"What?"

"You know I hate when you do that."

"I don't think it *is* nonsense. Not at all. There are more things in heaven and earth—"

"It's crazy. And all those men are crazy. And if what they can do can be done then it's all the worse."

He sat up violently.

"That's ridiculous!" he hissed. "I won't hear it! That's materialist, middle-class littleness. You sound like your father."

"Don't involve my family, if you don't mind."

"There are powers," he said, staring into the depths of the room. "Powers that stand behind the kings and presidents and international bankers. Powers beyond death, I think . . . I have seen—"

"Tricks, Kurt," she insisted, sitting up and taking him by the shoulders. "Tricks! Those cultists are taking you in. They want your academic credibility. Those fools . . . those . . . those fanatics!"

"Oh, everyone's a fanatic or a fool now. Me, too, I imagine." He brushed her arm away and flung himself from the bed to stand uncertainly on the cold floorboards, feeling the draft around his ankles and chest.

"*Kurt.*"

"The world is coming to crisis. Have you read Chamberlain? Everything's going up in flames and Germany will—"

"Oh, stop it! I hate this talk. Please, let me go to sleep in peace . . . please . . ." She flung herself down and partly covered her head with the pillow.

"Minna," he murmured. Shook his head. Folded his arms against the chill. "Minna . . . listen to me."

"No," she said, muffled by the pillow.

"Listen . . . I don't want to be a little university nothingness." He shivered a little. Rubbed his hands slowly up and down his arms. "I mean what I say. I want to have an effect. Germany will be great and I want to be part of that greatness."

She twisted around to look at him, a pale, vaporous, shadowy figure in the dim room.

"Those crazy astrologers or whatever they are," she said, "are going to make Germany great. That's a good one. Let the Kaiser worry about the country. You should teach and have children and live your life, in the name of God . . ." She stared, trying to focus on his face, seeing only the pale outline. "Kurt? . . ."

"I can't explain it to you," he finally said.

"Come to bed, Kurt. Please come to bed."

"I can't explain so you'll understand. I'm sorry this is so . . ."

"Kurt . . ."

"Certain men will be on the inner circle of power."

"Come to bed . . . for God's sake . . ."

She came to the doorway where he was standing with the captain. The mountainous medium on the bed groaned softly under her covering sheet. Minna was holding a damp cloth that smelled of roses and disinfectant. She glared at her husband, silently, furiously.

The officer clicked his heels and stiffly bowed.

"Madame," he said.

She ignored him, totally, watching Kurt who stood in the folds of fuming smoke from the reeking cigar. He was consciously keeping up a firm appearance.

"An unfortunate accident, my dear," he said uncomfortably.

"I don't know what you and your *friends* were doing in here," she said coldly. "And kindly don't ever tell me."

As she turned and went almost fiercely through the gathering and out the door, Drecklicht watched her with a faintly raised eyebrow. The captain snorted and smoked. Kurt felt a little dizzy and went to the nearest window just as the dull-eyed medium rose vastly up in her sheet and began heaving around for her clothes, grunting, face blank.

VI
(APRIL 1945)

The cement room shook, dully echoing the booming impacts up above. The few guests already seated at the laid table stood up as the bride and groom entered. Martin Bormann hummed a strain of Wagner's wedding march. Dr. Haase perversely wanted to counter with Mendelssohn's to spite him. He never found out if he had the nerve because at that moment a tremendous blast knocked chunks of plaster dust loose, killed the lights for a few seconds, and clattered the china on the table. As the greenish-gray-walled chamber brightened again Herr and Frau Hitler sat down. Haase noted he seemed quiet, more relaxed than ususal, perhaps resigned finally.

Haase was tall, thin, silver-haired, almost ghostly-looking. Tuberculosis had consumed one lung already and the other strained for air in the heavy, foul bunker atmosphere. He had replaced Dr. Haase recently, at Hitler's request. Haase was dying.

Goebbels, showing his teeth, stood up for a toast.

"To the Führer and his bride," he cried with nervous enthusiasm.

The Führer nodded, picked up his knife by the dull blade, and tapped it steadily on the tablecloth. Stared straight ahead while Eva Braun Hitler chatted with Frau Goebbels.

"But when we were in Berghof," she was saying, "we used to dance all evening on the terrace. That was really so wonderful. My figure, I've been told, was surely at its best in those days . . ." She sighed, glanced at her new husband. "If only we could go back, but I suppose that's no longer possible. The air was so good. I haven't had a real appetite since . . . and see how *he* looks . . ." Indicated Hitler. "He hasn't been himself either." She shrugged, coquettish, and touched his hand that was tapping the silverware. He didn't seem to notice. Stared. "But it's all duty, of course."

"Yes," agreed Magda Goebbels.

"No man has ever given more to his people than this man," Dr. Goebbels added, refilling his champagne glass.

"My husband," Eva went on brightly, as Hitler this time patted her rather plump, smooth-skinned fingers and didn't look at her as he said, absently:

"Yes, *Tschapperl.*"

"Ah," said Goebbels as the orderly set down the wedding cake, "bravo, bravo!"

"Very nice indeed," someone else commented.

Bormann was now on his feet. He swayed slightly, speech blurred. He'd been drinking since the night before.

"Führer," he said hoarsely, "you will be preserved."

A charming choice of words, thought the physician, Dr. Haase, and nearly said out loud: *But he insists his body must be destroyed.* Shut his eyes as if to divorce himself from all of it.

"Heil Hitler!" Bormann suddenly cried jarringly. Even Goebbels winced before he sprung up and saluted, a desperate edge in his voice as he breathed:

"*Sieg* Heil!"

The Führer barely seemed to notice. Then glanced up, tensed lips twitching slightly. Everyone now waited, expectant. Haase stared at his plate where the orderly had just plopped the sugary cake. As he watched, the icing crumbled and fell away like a broken wall. The lights went off and on again; plates and silver rattled from the concussion. Another brief taste, Haase thought, of the terror of total underground darkness. They all seemed to resurface from bottomless depths. His own body had instinctively jerked in fear. Hitler was now speaking.

"Vienna was still my greatest struggle," he said, "because, you see, then I did not have my purpose fixed

unalterably. This came later. I had not yet been consecrated." He was strained but still resonant and rumbled on.
"So, it was, therefore, not easy for me . . ." He stared, not
at anything, as far as Haase could tell. ". . . for me to resist
despair and surrender . . . or, worse yet, the temptation
to a middle-class existence!" He nodded, somber, eyes
engrossed beyond their heads. "Yes, I resisted . . ."

"Thank God for that," interjected Goebbels.

"Naturally, for someone like me, there were ample
opportunities for commercial success . . ." He smiled.
"Imagine, I might have owned a small business!" Laughter
all around the table.

My God, Haase thought, *but why didn't you? What force
was it moved you on your path that you call 'providence'? My God,
what was it?*

". . . naturally, as history testifies, I went in another
direction."

(1909–1914)

Reinhold Hanisch was staring at the greasy windowpane. The reflected room was low, long, narrow, with dark
board walls warped and stained and peeling. A row of beds
glowed in the gritty glass. Men lay stretched out or were
glumly sitting, isolated, staring. One, about seventy, muttered continuously, frail hands trembling on the filthy
covers; another, younger, wrapped in rags, barefoot with
swollen red ankles and blue toes, was catching lice in the
bedclothes and cracking them with his nails. Down the end
of the line someone groaned in his sleep over and over.

Hanisch sat on a tilted stool, big feet in battered boots
braced on the floor. He scratched his itchy beard and
focused his eyes on the dim street below. The gaslights
gleamed on the wet cobblestones. Feathery ice was forming
on the glass.

"Where is that pig?" he muttered.

He turned away. Covertly unwrapped a hide sack from
within his patched, tattered clothing. Peeled off a few
greasy bills, shook a scattering of coins into his palm and
pondered them with depression and disgust. His lips
moved silently.

He nervously looked up as a shadow fell over him. A
thin, scraggly bearded young man with a cowlick and wild,

penetrating eyes stood there in a ragged, baggy floor-length coat.

"So," Hanisch said, nagging, "you decided to finally show your—"

"Great news," Adolf said. Smiling, shaking a wad of newspapers in his friend's face.

"Unless you've become rich, it's not great news."

"Reinhold, listen to me—"

"No speeches. I want to hear that you've done the pictures you promised. Müller, the stove merchant, is waiting. He paid fifty kroner in advance, Ade."

"Fifty. It should have been a hundred and fifty."

"What's the difference? You never do the work."

"That's a lie, Hanisch. But you don't bother me. I'm too pleased tonight." He tilted his head stiffly back and smiled. "I brush off your insults. Listen to this—" He unfolded the paper, eyes greedy, intent. "Here it is . . . so . . . Ah, 'liberal committee ousted!' What do you think of that? There's a defeat for the damned Slavs! Germany and Austria must join hands. This is historical inevitability. All resistance will be brushed aside. 'The will of Germans to mix their blood in a common pool cannot be resisted for much longer.' That's what this writer says. And I agree!" His eyes widened with triumph.

"I don't know why you give a damn," Hanisch said. "What do I care? Look how I live, and I'm supposed to worry about whether Germany and Austria wave the same flag? Don't make me laugh."

"It isn't funny," Adolf said, firm and intense. "This is a great issue. Everything is affected."

One of the inmates of the Home for Men was in the process of spitting up phlegm when he could stand no more and broke in. His voice was wheezy and harsh.

"Shut up," he interjected, bloodshot, watery eyes squinting as his turkey neck rocked under the weight of his long head. Spat a wad on the floor. "You damned Germans . . ."

Hanisch slumped back on his stool in disgust.

"You changed the subject," he muttered to Hitler. "Let's talk about the drawings." But his reluctant client was already embroiled with the tramp on the bed. Hanisch sighed and shook his head.

No more, he thought, *no more. He's never done a thing on time, not once. I have to scramble around and make a fool of myself. No more. I'll draw them myself. I thought I had something with this Hitler but he's as big as a bum as the rest of them.*

". . . all you Germans," turkey neck was saying, wheezing, "are homosexuals! You don't fool anybody."

Hitler was bouncing up and down on his toes, brandishing the newspapers, the uneven gaslight at his back flailing abstract shadows over the dingy walls and sagging ceiling as a few other inmates sat up and took notice, starting to enjoy the scene.

Hitler seemed bursting with zest for life as his voice rose in thundering intensity to override the gesticulating scarecrow before him who now was kneeling on the lumpy coat and clawing the air with vacant frenzy.

And worst of all, Hanisch went on morosely, *he thinks they're great works of genius! What an ego! And wastes his breath on every idiot he meets. Senseless. Someone wants a picture for the sausage shop, very well, paint it and we eat! That's simple enough. My God.*

Shook his head and refolded his money in the scrap of leather purse as Hitler was shouting, red-faced, floor-length coat flapping as he shook his fist in the skinny, jeering face while the audience cheered and mocked. One fat man rose on all fours and aimed his bared buttocks at the pair of them.

". . . and," Hitler was going on, "Germany's destiny is clear! As Chamberlain said: 'The German spirit will restore civilization at the abyss of decadence'!"

"At the *what* of *what?*" someone asked, amidst laughter.

Those were the wrong words for these people, Hitler discovered.

Someone else threw a shoe which clattered between the beds. The man on all fours farted ringingly in the moment's silence following Adolf's last bellow. The broken wind brought down the house. Even Hanisch glanced up from his dour ruminations, smiling.

"Germans are all pigs!" the skinny man chanted. "Germans are homosexuals! Long live Franz Josef! Long live—"

These men in rags, Hanisch thought bleakly, incredulous, *are actually fighting over emperors! God help me!*

As the man opened his mouth to yell again, the opponent leaped forward and with a sudden stab thrust a rolled wad of newspaper into the gaping, gap-toothed mouth and rammed it home with the heel of his hand and stepped back triumphantly as the man gagged, coughed, and chewed, fingers clawing between his lips.

The audience went wild with approval. Adolf gave a bouncy little bow, grinning.

"Good work, kid," a man said.

"That's how to shut them up," the farter said, sitting back down on his bed.

Another:

"Did you see that, eh?"

Way in back:

"That German's no fag, no sir."

A round, filthy little bald man with a drooping mustache suddenly leaped up, beating his palms together and screaming and howling like a tormented wolf. He flung himself on the floor in front of Adolf who was startled and embarrassed.

"God bless this man!" he shrieked. "He's an angel from heaven!" Shriek-howl. ". . . I see his light! . . ." Howl. "Yes, I believe . . . Ai . . . Aiiiiiiii! . . . Ai . . . Ai . . . Ai . . . The moon is burning my brain! . . . Ai! . . . The moon . . ."

Began writhing and kicking between the beds, rolling.

"Shut him up, somebody."

"Kick him in the head."

The skinny man was spitting the last of the paper out. He aimed a vicious kick at the madman who rolled away, whining now like a cur.

Hanisch jumped up and slammed his stool into the wall.

The howling, barefoot, dribbling, panting man suddenly started crawling up and down the aisle between the beds on all fours, rapid, thumping.

"The moon burns," he cried. "It burns . . . Ai! . . ."

"Where are you going?" Adolf asked his companion.

Hanisch stormed past in disgust.

"Out of this sinkhole!" was the raging reply, and he kicked the scampering lunatic in the ribs, without much effect, as he went out.

Adolf caught up with him across the street in the Schwartzer Schwanz beer parlor. He came in from the cold night in a fluttering billow of oversized coat and sat down beside Hanisch on the hard bench. He dropped a sheaf of drawings and pale watercolors on the warped, gouged tabletop. It had started to snow and the flakes turned to droplets on his coat and hair.

Hanisch nursed his beer in silence. Didn't look at his partner who'd remained in a sprightly mood.

"Come on," Adolf placated, "have a look at these anyway." Poked the pictures with a stiffened forefinger.

His companion didn't look up.

"I'm through with you," he said. "You act like impressing those . . . those gutterscum in there means something. You're off your—"

"But it does," Adolf insisted seriously. "I dominated the situation."

"Is that what you think?" Hanisch squinted sidelong at him.

"I do." Adolf sat up, very straight. "If I can do it here I can do it there."

"And where is *there*?

Adolf Hitler shrugged.

"Anywhere I choose," he said.

"Don't make me laugh. My empty stomach would bounce on my bones." He thumped his fist on the pictures. "Müller is still waiting for his—"

Adolf frowned.

"A bourgeois pig," he retorted. "Listen, Hanisch, my friend, all men are the same. Except for circumstance those bums upstairs would be bankers." He grinned.

"Oh." The stooped, shrewd-looking man shook his head wearily, raising an eyebrow. "Tonight all men are the same. The other day some were great and the rest fools. Make up your mind, young Adolf. Make up your mind."

"Only a few *are* great, that's true," he admitted, "but not by right of title or money. No. They only may be great who let the sacred spirit fill their souls!"

Hanisch pushed himself back from his beer, still shaking his head. He wasn't quite amused.

A fat drunken woman in tatters was clinging to the tavernkeeper, a bald, beefy, mustached man who was sliding her with tilts and staggers toward the door. They seemed to be performing a strange dance over the slick tile.

"The sacred spirit of my asshole," Hanisch muttered.

Adolf Hitler was slapping his palm repeatedly on the wood, nodding to himself.

"But all who are not great," he said deliberately, "are all the same." He compressed his lips firmly.

The woman cursed and fell down on the yellowed tile floor near the door; the man struggled to raise her and push her out. Adolf could see their reflections in the shadowy glass of the door where they seemed amorphous shapes wrestling in darkness. "All who are not great are the same, regardless. Because they live blindly and follow like sheep." Nodded, excited, trying to express perfectly what he saw in his mind. "Because," he said, hitting his left palm with his fist, "they are without the inspiration of the spirit. Without the spirit, life is a dull and meaningless sham, Hanisch!"

Adolf was staring at the dully gleaming bartaps. The fat woman was out the door now and the burly landlord was clearing tables.

Adolf's eyes unfocused and the reflections blurred into cold, flamelike shimmers.

His pale hands gripped one another restlessly. His white, gaunt, sleepless face tensed with inner strain. He was thinking about Wagner again. Tracing his career from defeat to ultimate triumph was deeper than a consolation: it was proof of grace. The great man, he thought, asked no one's permission to be great. He sighed and momentarily debated whether to buy a sweet cake. Hanisch was talking but he really didn't hear him.

"Aaah," the older man sighed, "we may as well go over to the soup kitchen before they shut down for the night." He pushed himself up from the bench, weary, resigned. Noted his friend sat staring straight ahead, hands trembling slightly. He wondered if he was going to have one of his outbursts.

Adolf had never felt such hopeless emptiness. Not even at his mother's cold, gray grave. Licked his lips. Tried to pull his mind away but it kept slipping down . . . He felt trapped in a colorless dream. His great architectural designs, a year's work, useless! His plans for rebuilding the city—who would ever glance at them? Men were walking shadows on the treadmill of the world. Blinked. His head ached. Was afraid the feeling wouldn't stop. What would he do then?

Just keep pushing, he thought hollowly, *the door finally opens.* Let others work at meaningless jobs for pale survival. Anyway, he'd tried that a week ago after a bitter snowstorm, staggering, thin, bareheaded, shoveling the walk in a meat-cannery yard, hands freezing, bad lung burning, struggling in the ragged gang under the eye of the manufacturer himself who stood, all the while, in the latticed window, bulky glasses gleaming blank flashes of sun and snow, long curved pipe fixed between his immense mustaches. Adolf had raged to himself as he wobbled and listlessly chopped his outsized, awkward shovel at the icy layers that the sun had crusted harder. He shivered.

See what I've come to, he'd thought, *—just to eat! While that fat bastard watches over me.* After a time the exhausting monotony had floated his thoughts through memory into fantasy: remembering his father overseeing his work in the yard, always critical, always taking over—*Well, the old man tried, I suppose but he really laid bare for me the pettiness of the middle-class mind*—imagining himself (as he did when a child) leading a charge (in the costume of 1870 based on drawings he'd seen) into the massed French ranks, breaking through at bayonet point in the wild, exploding chaos of shells and buzzing bullets and yells and screams. Squinted into the dazzling cold, scratched at the ice and pictured the battlefield and the desperate charge almost as vivid and absorbing as an actual dream.

Kubizek was a childhood friend, now a musician in the capital. He was back in Linz to see his family and had stopped to visit Hitler's sister, Paula. She served him tea in the kitchen, at twilight. The air glowed cool and shadowless and still. Where the hill sloped up slightly were rows of abandoned beehives (once old Alois's apiary), dim, Kubizek thought, tomblike shapes in the sourceless dying light.

"Tell me the truth," she insisted, "how is he?"

She sat across the narrow table, large eyes glowing, features swallowed in the misty dimness.

"I suppose he's well enough, Paula," he replied uncomfortably. "Doesn't he write you?"

"Not often," she said with a shrug. "He wrote Elli at Christmas. But I'm really worried . . . What is he doing? How does he live? Tell me, August, please."

The tall young man touched his pale forehead and stared out the window at where the fence cut a dark slice from the grayish-glowing sky.

"He does drawings," he finally answered. "Does this and that . . . He has great confidence in himself." Sighed. Fluttered his tapered fingers down to the tabletop. "He was always very idealistic, you know."

"He thinks he's living the life of Richard Wagner," she sighed. "Doesn't he?"

He inclined his head.

"That's a way to express it," he admitted.

"In all honesty, August—as his friend—is this possibly justified?"

He raised both hands in a pale flutter.

"How can I answer? How can I judge?"

She stared directly at him. He avoided her intense eyes.

"You already have," she told him. "What is he really doing in Vienna? He's not going to make a living painting pictures."

The trees and sky had melted together into a blotted night. The last gleaming showed on the grass, the paled sky, the teacups on the obscure table, and her eyes . . .

"I don't know," he finally replied. Toyed with his cup, the delicate porcelain, fragile as a breath. "He tells me he's waiting . . ."

"Waiting? For what?"

He was lame and uncomfortable. Long fingers wisped around the cup, vaguely.

"He once said something about an invention," he finally told her.

"What kind of invention?"

"I wasn't paying attention, really. We were at the opera, standing room for *Trist*—"

"Invention!" she cut in, eyes outraged. "Invention!"

The dusk had blotted them both out. Everything but the sky over the hill of trees was dark. He noticed something moving, floating across the yard like a swirl of mist . . . and then his stare resolved it into an infant, wobbling slowly and wide-legged over the grass, light hair almost a substanceless glow.

"Whose child is that?" he wondered.

"Geli," Paula said. "Angela's daughter."

"Your niece. I didn't think she was even this big."

"They grow so fast," Paula said. "And then, God knows what happens."

The little girl wandered up the slope, fading as he strained to follow her steps. She blurred . . . was lost . . . Her mother's voice called from around the house.

(APRIL 1945)

Frank Astuti kept his head pressed down as the world reeled and bounced and rattled. The sky ripped at him; dirt flew and shrapnel whined. The top of his helmet was just below the lip of the hole.

He didn't bother to think anymore. Just waited. Felt naked, felt each scream and hiss was aimed just at him, was surprised at each miss. Each fraction of life was a surprise. The world had closed down to the delicate business of taking breaths from the burned, shocked, acrid air. The wonderful delicacy of heartbeat and blood and bone.

Felt something watching him, weighing the fast-falling, precious inches of his living . . . The professor out there, Renga, the Germans, his own people, the whole rest of everything in the universe that surrounded this little space had ceased to exist; all other things were fainter and further off than morning's last dream at midday. There was only now, breath and pulsing, only each begrudged instant leased by each fallen shell, by each successive miracle.

(1909–1914)

Adolf sat on the bench in a semitrance as Hanisch looked quizzically at him.

"Hey," he said, touching his shoulder, "are you coming?"

Hitler didn't respond. Stared. The first night had been the worst: he'd run out of money and had to sleep on a park bench, waking, shivering, from a dream where dark forms rushed past and fell in silent, bloody heaps all around him, and then a giant knight in glittering, icy greenish armor had struck down at him with a great mace and he'd struggled and screamed and pleaded for pity and life . . . and opened his eyes to see the tight, dark uniform brass buttons bright in the chill dawn, writhing away as the club fell again on his shins, ringingly. "No tramps here!" the officer had said, the jacket tight around his plump little belly. "No tramps," he repeated. Adolf's scraggly beard had shaken as he spoke: "Excuse me, sir," he'd said, wincing with pain, scrambling away. No sense, he'd thought, in provocation. Why make it worse than it was?

The memory now brought rage and bitter disgust. That stupid, unjust bastard! That mindless nonentity, slave of a decaying state! tool of whatever nameless forces dominated the blind herd, the mass beast that knew nothing but its endless appetites.

He was a little amazed at the clarity of his rush of venom. He realized he'd summed up much of his recent reading and thinking in a few words. He wished he'd spoken them aloud where they might do some good, stir the consciences of conscious men and sting the exploiters. The blind tyranny of a uniform! At least at home in Linz the constable had been friendly. The streets were clean and the inhabitants, however dull, fussy, narrow-minded, and pretentious, were at least well-fed and civil. The memory of the town seemed very bright and warm now. The people in this place were degenerate, that was clear. A spiritually decaying metropolis, sick with vice! Here he was in relentless misery, alone . . . alone . . . How could he dare think in sweeping terms? And then he came back to himself in the grimy present in the foul beer cellar beside Hanisch who was still staring with remote contempt at nothing. Adolf felt vaguely feverish, pale, and his recent reveries seemed more like sleep than daydreaming.

Hanisch glanced at him.

"Are you all right, Hitler?"

"Hmm?"

"Listen, I'm hungry. I'm off."

"To beg food for your supper?" Adolf was disgusted by everyone, suddenly. They were all apathetic, futile.

Hanisch sneered.

"But you're a fine gentleman," he mocked. "I forgot." Snorted. "You, who tried to beg pennies from a drunk. Don't make me laugh!" He snorted again, and lurched. "You're such a great genius, I forgot that too. Above the rest of us swine."

"Be still, Hanisch." Adolf was back into his fitful, burning inner images. They showed in his eyes. He wanted to sit in silence and let them unfold.

"What about your big plans with that Jew," his companion went on, blinking heavily. "What's his name? The old clothes dealer . . . your pal!" He'd had enough of this provincial egomaniac. "Why didn't you go to Germany with him? Eh? You're probably half kike yourself. Your big ideas to make an easy million!" He laughed. "Excuse my lack of faith." Took a step away, looking back. Adolf just sat on the bench and Hanisch realized he was barely aware of him. "At least—" he raged, heading for the door, "at least I have common sense." Stopped. "Talk to me about begging!"

"All right, Hanisch," Adolf rumbled. "All right."

"You're the biggest bum here!" he yelled, and slammed out through the greasy frosted-glass panels. The clientele had barely taken notice and Hitler went back to his thoughts. The answer to something, he was sure, lay under his nose . . .

Two weeks ago he'd gone out to beg. *Others do it,* he'd reasoned. *If approached scientifically I might make a decent amount.* That made sense. On a crowded street, he had calculated, he might approach at least one person every ten seconds. . . .

Yes, this has possibilities. He paced thoughtfully along the pavement toward the main thoroughfare, holding his caftan shut with one hand where the buttons were off. The wind sliced into him. His eyes watered and nose ran a little. The winter sun was wan. He went up the steps to the library, paused, and stared over the carriage traffic in the square where an occasional motorcar huffed and banged over the uneven cobbles. Swarms of people were going to work, face after face, pale in the chilly light.

He decided it would be futile to approach anyone at this hour. They were all in a hurry, their time accounted for. He pictured the thousands, millions all across Europe, struggling out of bed, grinding themselves through another bleak day. He'd been up all night and that alone gave him a certain detachment from all this . . . this endless streaming of bundled coats and featureless faces, feet clumping, he felt, like machines. For a moment he had a confused impression he might be sucked up and drawn away and utterly lost in it, and he unconsciously backed a step or two higher from this gray, menacing mass.

He kept telling himself he wasn't part of it, that it had no power over him! He stood there, coat open and askew, hard breaths frosting, cold hands clenched into fists. Sensed some strange will shaping, directing the mass that was not the will of any individual. A dark, tidal energy. The idea was frightening and exciting. He could almost see the immense flow of history.

Took a nervous step higher. Remembered he had to beg money. Sagged slightly and tugged his baggy garment closed. Money . . . His lips trembled as he clenched his teeth. Money . . . Yes, the gold of Wagner's *Ring*: the materialism that had darkened the waters of the spirit!

He stared at the brightening sky above the massive gray buildings. He felt a strange, feverish wonder, comprehension, and a rage that knotted into fists. The dark will that powered the dead mass and set it crunching to blot out every shred of human light, fed on gold! The dulled, gray minds bowed to that power without even knowing it! But he would fight back! Too many artists stayed passive and were sucked down in the end. He would fight! Yes . . . For an instant, feverish, he was almost ecstatic; swayed, wanted to pray or swear an eternal oath but didn't know how yet, or to what.

His life was beginning to make sense. Every time he weakened he found new strength. He'd always known he was chosen for some monumental task; even lying on the hard cot in the dim roomful of stinking, snoring, hacking, sometimes raving men, he knew it. How many times had he almost given up and gone to work, headed home to take the factory job . . . or be a bank clerk . . . He snorted. Shoe salesman.

He turned and headed into the library. Anyway, he could always get a cup of coffee from the guard. A nice fellow. Sometimes even a sandwich was possible.

After a day's reading in the steamy quiet and impersonal luxury of the library he came down the steps thinking how philosophy was abstract nonsense unless you grasped it from within yourself. He'd been reading Darwin today and mulled it over as he huddled along the chill, twilight streets. The superior forms survived by destroying the others. This was the divine movement toward perfection.

The darkening blur of the crowd flowed around him where he aimlessly walked, gaze on the dimming sky above the dark roofs. People avoided the shabby figure who seemed to be talking to himself with intense excitement. His long coat trailed on the bleak sidewalk.

A woman glanced at him and half-skipped to pass at a distance. A man unconsciously checked his wallet in his pocket.

The world has been committing racial suicide!

Recently, he'd screamed at Hanisch, sitting up on his lumpy cot beside him in the greasy, brownish flophouse air:

"Nietzsche said it best: 'Rise above the noxious humane illusions spun by the unfit and crippled spirits to ensure their own'"—"Bah!" cried the other, pulling up his ragged blanket and lumping his back to Hitler—"their own worthless survival . . . purge the blood of its poisons, to shrink from no terrible deed, then—"

"Then my arse," Hanisch had retorted. "You quote like a gramophone. Who cares what anybody said?"

"These ideas are alive and will shape history!" Hitler beat his fist into his bed, and dust flew. "You'll see! 'Shrink from no terrible deed and then the evolution of the new, vital man will follow'!"

"That's what we need around here," Hanisch muttered into his hard pillow, yawning.

"The earth can still be saved, I'm telling you, from the stupid, cowardly, talentless, gray mediocre—"

"Hitler, for God's sake, let me sleep!" He'd pulled the blanket over his head. "Just because you never do doesn't mean—"

"The new leader must be a ruthlessly inspired artist who will be king, creator, and—"

"Good night, Hitler!" Muffled, raging.

He leaned against a lamppost for a moment. The crowd blurred by. As the last glow faded above the buildings the gasflame hollowed his wild, drawn face. Occasionally someone would stare at him and pass on.

"I must be patient," he whispered, "and trust in the spirit . . ."

He wandered on, then stopped by a line of brightly lit shops. First realized he'd walked the wrong way. Blew on his hands, then thrust them under his coat.

He smelled hot food from some kitchen and his stomach seized up with a violent cramp of hunger. He looked around. People were already going out to early dinners. He pressed his lips together. It wasn't fair.

The icy wind seemed to have driven contemplation

from his brain. He looked around with nervous contempt.
Hesitated, trying to get up energy to act.

You're in the gutter, he told himself, *that's that.*

He went up to a portly woman in black silks and
shawls. Cleared his throat and she brushed past. He turned
to a mild-faced young man in a dented top hat who smiled
before Hitler could speak and shook his head.

He was embarrassed but there was a grim satisfaction
in it too. Utter failure was better than any mediocre gain.
Cheat him out of his fair chances and he'd sleep in the
gutter to spite heaven!

He followed a couple, a bearded, solid-looking man
and stocky wife. After a few steps they turned and stared at
him, sternly, and he pretended to study a shop window.
Looked in bleak anger at a display of sweets and cakes. Pink
and green icings. The counterman glanced out at him once
or twice while he served customers. Hitler's breath frosted
on the glass. He saw the reflection of the long, greasy coat
Neumann, the old-clothes dealer, had given him.

I'm an artist, he thought, *I can look shabby if I like.*

Noticed a policeman across the street. Started walking.
Felt the official eyes on him. Almost ran when he turned
the nearest corner. Then snarled with terrible venom. Spat.

I'd like to take that club and split his fat head for him!

The begging wasn't going too well. Decided to post-
pone it.

He was passing a restaurant. A gleaming cab had just
halted. A flash of a tall blond woman, a rush of white silks
going up the carpeted steps to the waiting doorman as her
escort swayed, fumbling to pay the fare. The horse backed
and shifted in the traces. As the man turned, still holding a
sheaf of bills, he saw the scarecrow figure close to him, pale
hands clasped nervously, staring at the money.

"I . . ." Hitler began to say.

The man shook the bills, gestured.

"Want this, eh? You rogue!"

Hitler nodded vaguely. The doorman was just coming
down, silver braid gleaming, eyes narrowed. The formally
dressed patron wobbled and belched. Hitler smelled the
alcohol, sweet, warm, and slightly nauseating.

"I . . ."

"Trying to rob me, eh?" said the man.

Hitler was already backing, then walking away as the

man lifted his cane. He ducked into the gathering crowd
and heard the doorman's voice, conciliatory, irritated:

"Another tramp. That's three today."

Then something about the police as he turned the next
corner.

The memory dissolved into the next thoughts as he
eyed the dingy barroom. What had created this situation?
Why had the races fallen so low? How exactly did the Jews
fit in? Everyone made such a stir about them. They seemed
no more wretched than the other petty merchants or local
dregs he spent his time with. The Christian prejudice was,
of course, absurd. Why he even liked Neumann much
better than Hanisch, for instance. The French and the
Slavs seemed a much worse menace. He frowned. He
would have to dig deeper into this famous question.

Decay was everywhere. Look at that one: long-nosed,
yellow-eyed, bluish-pale flesh. A human germ, evidence of
disease. Hitler's hand strayed under his greasy shirt and
scratched a flea bite.

I used to think poverty alone produced these effects, he
ruminated. *A mistake . . .*

Peered at another man, puffy, crouching near the low
fire in the grate, ankles bare and swollen, swallowed into
iron-hard, shapeless shoes. Hitler blinked; he felt light-
headed but clear, terribly clear and objective. The fellow's
eyes were tilted like a Mongol's!

Hanisch had left his beer barely sipped. Hitler nervously began draining deep swallows, still staring. He
rarely drank even beer. But he felt it might cool the heat in
his brain. His eyes flashed around the smoky, low-ceilinged
den.

The man by the fire was poking a stubby finger into his
mouth, rubbing what Hitler assumed was a sore.

*Eyes like a Mongol . . . not German, not even Austrian
. . . what? . . .*

Poverty did not make this man, this man created
poverty! Not the world but his own tainted blood brought
him to this. He seemed to see the blood when he shut his
eyes for a moment and felt them burn. Like a dream-
image, the pure fluid stained with bubbles of darkness.

Took another long pull of beer. Wiped his mouth with

his tattered sleeve. Then the room spun slowly as he looked avidly around.

I'm hungry, he thought, *I haven't eaten since . . .* Tugged his scraggly beard. The long-nosed man looked up, noticed Hitler's bright, restless, violently bright stare. Hardly noted the jerking little nods and muttering which seemed normal enough there.

Each nation is like a single individual. Genius depends on racial purity. It was all so incredibly clear!

He stood up. The floor tilted, the faces around seemed to gape and grimace as in delirium. A morose Jew, long face in his hands, wearing a crushed hat, peered up at him with large, lost eyes. Against the wall two human wrecks, bloated and discolored by filth and drink, quarreled raucously with empty vehemence like skeletons in baggy rags. The man by the fire was picking his nose now and contemplating the results. A fat woman, who'd been tossed out earlier by the massive, turklike bartender, burst back in the front door, covered with blood from her nose, ragged coat flopping wild shadows around the walls, yelling, furious, defiant.

Hitler staggered a step or two on the slick tile.

"Men become shapeless lumps," he muttered. "Peoples become shapeless lumps . . ."

He bent forward, suddenly sick and scared. Was he dying? Going mad? He staggered for the door where the raving woman was wrestling with the big tavernkeeper.

He reached the opening at the same moment the wrestlerlike man flung and kicked the woman into the doorframe so that they both stuck there together. He was pinned, face pressed into her soft, sour massiveness while she shouted and belched and he kicked and clawed, gagging, suffocating.

Help me! his mind cried.

The tavernkeeper kicking and shoving them both now (Adolf felt white flashes of pain) until they burst free like corks from a bottle and he went spinning across the sidewalk and down into the icy gutter, looking up as a vast bulk that seemed the world itself fell on him, flabby and distended and stinking, and he tried to raise one arm against the darkness of it, the horror and weight, the gapped teeth, bloody face, inflamed eyes, the bleating, bellowing, voracious, drooling mouth looming to swallow

him, and he believed he screamed before blackness blotted
him out and he fell into a flash of green and red glow about
the brightness of embers . . . was looking down and over
a fortress that seemed to have been carved out of a
mountain . . . rivers of fire, masses of fog and smoke
billowing slowly everywhere, and a man, a king of some
kind on an iron throne set on a gigantic tower platform,
watching half a dozen young men and girls strapped to a
kind of rack . . . moments later (he tried to scream)
armored men were stripping the flesh from their living
bodies with red-hot blades while a slim, dark-haired, nearly
naked woman hung with silver hoops and bracelets and
wearing a silver and black crown too, danced, slow, stately,
formal, while strange instruments softly brayed and
clashed . . . and he screamed as the king seemed to turn
to look at him, screamed the night back down to cover
himself, and there was only blackness this time . . .

(APRIL 1945)

Rudolph Renga had almost reached the ridge that was
a long, low, wall-like shape of deeper darkness against the
stars when the blackness was torn to flailing shadowshreds
by the dense barrage. Even as his infantryman's reflexes
(wearing twenty-five years' rust) sent him diving for the
ground an immense concussion (so close it was a puff of
ringing silence) suspended him somewhere without direction—sky, earth, time, all whooshed away by the blast into a
stun of brightness and he fell or rose or vanished . . .

Frank Astuti eased his helmet, then his squinting eyes
over the lip of the hole. Most of the shells were hitting up in
the woods now, lighting them fantastically from within,
blazing limbs and shadows flying insanely. He was sure
about half an hour had passed. He was amazed nothing
had hit him.

That old fucker's bought it, he thought. *He ranked high
among the nuts of our time . . .*

Spat sour juice and tobacco fragments. He'd chomped
the cigar in half during the action.

In the flickering that now resembled summer lightning
he could see big chunks had been bitten out of the ridge.
The gunners probably assumed there were troops behind

it, he concluded. He tried to locate the crazy civilian and saw only the dancing, jumbled darkness and countless craters.

He was thick as a stone, that guy, he thought. *Fuck it. Lucky I didn't piss in my pants back there.* Spat. Picked at his teeth and gums. *Fongule. That old fuck's bought it out there. He was among the great assholes.*

He turned and looked in the general direction of his own lost lines. Sighed.

Astuti, you ain't such hot shit yourself, he thought, with disgust. He had no idea where he was. He remembered he used to get lost in Bronx Park. *Who knows where they are? If I go back, then what? I could get stranded miles in the fucking rear, that's what.* Because he knew there was no continuous front here. The action was too mobile for that. Patton's Third Army rarely formed connected lines. Rarely stopped moving. *What a mess!* Shook his head. He was fumbling through his clothes for a cigar. *At least if I go forward I'm okay. Nobody ever got boiled in piss for advancing.*

But he knew that wasn't the whole reason. Suppressed the fact, spat again, found nothing to smoke, adjusted his pack, and crawled up out of the hole, pushing a piece of gum into his mouth and chomping it steadily. Stood up in a loose crouch and moved cautiously ahead, dropping flat at any too-bright flash from the forest ahead.

He headed for where he'd last seen the man. When he got there he poked around for longer than necessary because he already knew there was going to be nothing unless you counted his torn and muddy clothes. He didn't want to think about the fact that he was actually following the guy: no reason made sense.

He had balls, though, you got to say that much. But he didn't pretend that was enough. He hated to admit he even cared enough to be curious about why a middle-aged German with a British accent and a teacher's manner wanted to risk his neck getting in someplace everybody else wanted to get *out* of. He shook his head, spat, and chewed.

Astuti went on toward where he assumed the Germans more or less were. He felt the strange anticipation of combat, moving steadily and calm while his body tingled, expecting a terrible blow at any moment.

If he's alive he had to follow this ridgeline unless he's stupid as well as cracked. Shook his head. *I'm breaking every fucking rule.*

Rules for staying alive that had worked for three years.

If I didn't talk to the fucking guy it would be a different thing. He was working his way closer to the smashed, stripped, and smoking trees. *One way's as good as anything else at this point in the glorious pages of this miserable, bitch-sweating war.*

Strained his sight into the hinting, incomplete darkness. Hands moved restlessly on his rifle.

Where the fuck is that clown?

Renga was among the ruined trees, wobbling and stumbling over the uneven ground, hand stretched out like a blind man, coughing from the smoke, following the vague and random beacons that were small, patchy fires or flowing heaps of coals. Rudolph Renga was naked: the shellburst had stripped him down to his shoes and socks, and his glasses were gone. His hair was a little singed but otherwise he was sound. His ears, however, hurt and kept popping and rumbling. And he kept thinking he'd lost his horse and armor and that his castle was burning and it was too late to save his wife and children. He kept weeping about that and vowing revenge over and over. He would destroy his enemy with his own hands, he would drink in his death like wine.

VII
(1912)

Helmut von Moltke was seated, leaning over a spread-out map on the polished, darkwood table as Rudolph Renga was admitted to his study. The single, bright oil lamp on the clean surface was the room's only light and spread slightly shaking shadows over the austere, bare whitewashed walls.

The general looked up, the gold braid and medals flashing. Renga was surprised by the place. He'd anticipated a more massive, ostentatious style. This was, well, he thought, rather more monastic than anything else.

As the grave orderly withdrew, after neatly saying, "Dr. Renga, my general," Moltke rose and held out his large hand which his visitor took firmly.

"Good to see you," the massive man said quietly.

Rudolph bowed slightly.

"Yes, General," he responded. He was tall, lean, sharp-faced, with deeply intent eyes that remained perfectly still without actually staring. He studied his host for a few moments. He was thick-necked, jowly with a Prussian haircut and a tusklike mustache. He looked precisely like what the doctor hated: the crude, brutal, unimaginative warlord. Except, he noted, the eyes weren't right—too distant, contemplative, inward.

Moltke tugged at his mustache with thick fingers before speaking again.

"My wife," he said, "will join us presently. Would you like a drink of some kind?"

Rudolph shook his head. Glanced at the map and saw it was Europe. Well, war was coming. You didn't need spiritual sight to see that. The armies, he thought with contempt, were chafing at the bit. The map was drawn over with what he assumed were military indications.

He looked away, waiting for the famous commander to explain himself: why should the chief of the general staff and his wife spend a private evening with an obscure mystic lecturer?

"Perhaps, Dr. Renga, this will interest you," the general said, indicating the map and reseating himself before it.

"I'm not very military-minded, I'm afraid, General."

"Ah. I wish I could say the same . . . openly," was the curious reply.

"Hmn?"

"I often feel trapped in this life." Moltke smiled wanly.

"Trapped?"

"By fate." He stared inwardly for a moment. "But let me show you something, Doctor."

His finger and its shadow traced along the map.

"These are not designs of war. I leave those for the day. At night I dream a little. Or do I? This is why I asked you to come. You mentioned the Grail in one of your talks."

"You have been to my—"

"No. One of my officers."

For a general he seems rather mild . . . sort of the reverse of

Father . . . He hadn't thought of his father in a while. Made a note to send a letter, soon. Hadn't seen him in the year since he'd taken his appointment and moved to Munich. His mother was dead. He had misty memories of her talking to him about how you could hear God if you kept still enough . . . how you could listen to the grass growing . . . he must have been six or seven . . . His father seemed soft, pale and stooped, but his eyes, he thought, glinted more like a warrior's than a postal clerk's.

"Yes?" Renga probed politely.

"On this map are marked places, possible locations where the Holy Grail was hidden in the past." He revealed a hobbyist's special, muted pride as he explained: "I have researched this for many years. Someday I mean to search for it, as the Christian knights did of old."

Renga wondered how to react. Was he serious? He seemed to be. Renga hadn't imagined his lectures at the university would have done more than baffle the few students who attended and amuse certain members of the faculty. He felt his position there hung by a thread, at best. If he lost the job he might have to go home. An uncomfortable thought. Well, the dean, at least, liked him despite his "peculiar" spiritual views, and Professor Fragtkopft defended him, for some reason. There was someone his father would admire: just Renga's age or less and already fully established. Renga believed the young professor supported him just because the others didn't. *He's not fond of his peers,* Renga thought. He seemed to want to be friends . . . well, that was one thing he surely needed!

"You find me eccentric?" Moltke squinted up at him, breaking into his brief reverie.

"Good evening, my dear," a woman's voice said behind them. Madame had just come in the double doors in a long, lacy white gown. She seemed vigorous for her years. Her gaze was remote, like her husband's. "Good evening, Dr. Renga. What do you think of our map?"

Our map? he thought. He was already looking forward to going back to his apartment. He loved to study through the night, alone in the hushed hours, probing, soaring without effort to comprehend centuries of history and human struggle to rend the inner veil, to discover truth naked, tracing golden clues, sifting the dreamers, the reasoners, the fearful, the certain, ripping open the vain fabrications of lost and hopeless materialists, doubting the avid seers . . . sifting all gospels and thrilling, finally, to find that every sacred work of every nation hinted or insisted the same as if there had been one author, a single mind with ten thousand temporary languages, faces, times. By midday Renga would doubt everything and then take up the search again after midnight; recently, in the warm mornings, pacing before dawn in the deserted park in the city's almost-stillness, hearing the first tentative birds as the gray and blotting dark gradually formed trees and grass and distant buildings, recently—he swore—he'd almost felt it, thinned the wall of his senses and almost seen it as the sun shocked the skyline with actual, streaming, shattering glory . . . for all his fear (because beyond that wall there was edgeless vastness) he was drawn back, again and again . . . for all his doubts too.

"Good evening, madame," he said.

"Yes," she said, waiting.

He sat in a tall, stiff medieval chair as if poised to leap up. She had an impression that his body was quite light and supple. There was an ascetic, pinched look in his face, she decided.

"I believe the Grail exists," her husband was insisting. "A cup of light hidden away in the darkness of this world. A beacon. A hope. The only hope, perhaps . . ." He leaned his massive body forward, the mustaches down-pointing like soft tusks. "You say this is not so?"

The shadows on the wall caught his attention. One of them suggested an armored man. His sleep had been fitful lately and he kept waking up dreaming about knights in outfits not quite like any he'd recalled seeing depicted: dark metal fine as fabric, form-fitting, skirtlike, with helmets that almost seemed modern or Japanese . . . images of great armies sweeping through a semitropical countryside full of hot, clinging mists, bubbling mud, steaming rivers, and active volcanoes . . . the faces of the warriors seemed too long, sharp-featured with stony, dark, pitiless eyes . . . in the dream's distances he kept glimpsing terrible moments of violence that would drive him, shuddering, toward consciousness. Scenes where women, children, or captured men were being stabbed, raped, sliced to pieces or suspended from supple-looking, fernlike trees over billows of hot smoke pouring from pits in the unstable earth . . . he sensed an unspeakably cruel war that had gone on for many lifetimes . . . he sensed he was somehow a part of it . . .

He looked away from the shadows.

Something's going to happen to me, he thought. As if the light and shadow was an omen shaped on the face of time. *Something I have no control over.*

"Well?" the general wondered.

Renga realized he was staring too long at the humped, black silhouette of his host and his own slender outline seeming prisoned by the chair's crossbars, locked in a two-dimensional cage of shadow.

"Yes," he murmured, trying to look straight into the general's moist, contemplative eyes, but the shadows dwarfed him distractingly. He shut his eyes and saw an image of his family garden in early springtime, as when he was a child, alive with white and yellow vibrance, the lawn, soft willow-green all around . . . Blinked. He was already saying, over his thoughts, "The Grail, I believe, describes stages of initiation. It may be no more than a . . . a symbolic object. The pure knights, in the tales, pass through stages of inward transformation."

Moltke tilted his massive head, thoughtful. He looked older than his fifty-odd years, strained, sleepless, puffy.

"Can you be certain of such things?" he asked.

"No. Not certain."

The general sighed deeply. One big hand began drumming on the desktop. He seemed to be coming to a decision.

"My wife," he said, at length, "receives *impressions.*"

"Of what sort, General?" He looked at her.

"We thought," she said brightly, settling back in her chair, "you might be interested."

"Someone like yourself, Doctor," Moltke put in awkwardly, "understands, I imagine, the invisible worlds."

"Ah."

"We trust your discretion," she said.

He was uneasy again. Crossed his legs. Tapped his foot. Kept trying not to look at the shadows. Felt he was being sucked into something, deeper . . . deeper . . .

"I'm listening," he murmured.

"Let me show you," she said, then to her husband: "It is better so, Helmut."

He nodded. She settled back with a slight sigh.

Moltke stood beside her, holding her hand as she continued to respirate deeply, eyes shut. It reminded Renga of a patient going under ether.

"A trance?" he needlessly inquired.

"Wait," rumbled the general, nodding. The medals gleamed on the rich blue of his Prussian uniform like golden stars.

Her face became peaceful and in a moment she was speaking, but not in her own voice. A sweet, almost flutelike tone.

"Have you questions?" the voice asked.

"Yes," said the general, looking at Renga. "Can the coming war be avoided?"

What is this? Renga wondered. *Does he mean to justify being a general?* The trance upset him. If there were discarnate forces and intelligences (and he no longer seriously doubted this), then a trance invited them into your mind.

"No," the voice replied.

Renga nervously moved his leg. His shadow flick flicked on the spotless wall. He pushed away an image of something all shadows, teeth and hooked claws lunging at him from the darkness beyond the wan flamelight, as Moltke was asking:

"Will the outcome of the war bring stability to Europe?"

"No," came the sweet reply, and Renga was startled by the compassion and grief in the voice that was not like the lady's. "It will not. It will open the gate to hell and loose the beast."

Renga was on his feet, unconscious of having moved. His heart pounded. He stood over the frail medium. His shadow dimmed her. Her breath twisted unevenly from her and she moaned.

Renga was familiar with the various doom prophecies for the twentieth century. But . . .

"What beast?" he heard himself asking. "What beast do you mean?"

"Quis similis besteia? Et quis poterit pugnare cum ea?" the voice quoted.

"For who is like unto the beast?" translated Moltke in a rumble. "And who can make war against him?"

But all Renga heard now was the doubled and re-doubled pounding of his heart filling body and brain as he moved and his shadow flashed over the wall; he lost himself and seemed to leap up above the suddenly shrinking world and sky. He sensed he was fainting for the first time in his life and out of flaming darkness a vast form swirled and gripped at him with cloudy talons like a nightmare trying to force its boiling horrors into waking's bright substance. The pounding of his blood became a voice like shook tin and smashing iron echoing the sweet and terrible tones repeating: *It will open the gate, it will come inside . . . inside.* As his consciousness tried to hide under the mounting shadow that screamed and rent at heaven and earth he saw the world ripped and wounded, saw the crack widened with each shattered soul that was sucked into the abyss by the indrawn breath of the great shadow. Saw one paw closing down over the golden light squeezing it dim . . . dimmer . . .

He yelled and was normally conscious by the time he actually struck the floor and stared up calmly at the shaken general, unaware that his voice still howled on while Madame Moltke shook and bounced and rocked her head, eyes rolling as she added her own rasping shrieks to Renga's . . .

The general was over him, shaking him, great mustaches flopping. And then he was still and shut his eyes.

VIII
(APRIL 1945)

The harsh overhead light caught the Führer's head where he bent over the map table. He'd clasped his hands below his waist to control the trembling left arm. As it was, the table vibrated slightly. The shelling was steady.

He was dimly aware of the officers clustered around him, just back at the edge of the light. Their medals, braid, and brass gleamed and winked as the light swayed slightly. Except for that, they blended in with the shadows in the concrete room. He stared at the map. He had always loved maps. His eyes followed the traceries, roads, rivers, railroads. A gloved hand reached into the light and gestured at something. The voice spoke deferentially, apologetically. He was aware of the tone but the actual words made no impression. He stared. What use were ideas and strokes and counterstrokes if no one was capable of the execution? Just see there, where they were dangerously overextended on the left of the river. A bold attack might crack their army in half! But what was the use? They were all defeatist or hopelessly stupid. The cleverer ones had been disloyal. It was so simple to be disloyal now . . . well, they'd see. What would they see? His mind passed over and on. Oh, God, if he only had one, single magical bomb that would crack the rotten world in half! Shut and reopened his eyes. Tracked, almost hypnotically, the textures of the map . . . Where was his physician? He needed another injection.

I was promised the magic, he bitterly thought. The gloved hand was back, the voice speaking again—or was it a new voice? No matter. He stared and glimpsed images of his new weapons, the black rockets . . . the images moved, volitionless as in a dream, and he saw thousands upon thousands burning the night skies, raining down, shattering and melting his enemies away.

Please don't let it all fall to dust and nothingness, he thought, blinking back to the grim moment. *Please.*

Put a hand on the table to steady himself. Someone said something from the shadowy group across from him. The gold gleams moved and winked. He felt a sudden chill.

I can frighten these men but I can't make them understand, he thought. *That's sad* . . . Saw the flaming weapons again blasting the dark earth to pieces.

Then looked up, eyes bright in the cold, white light. Spoke to the gathered shadows.

"Everywhere, there were to be paved roads and everywhere monuments to the heroes because, you know, the best are all already dead." He frowned and nodded with a jerk. "Now they'll have only rubble. This city was to become a monument itself! That's right!" His voice suddenly regained that ringing power that set men's nerves tingling. "I planned an immense golden dome over a thousand feet high. There would have been nothing like it in history. Towering cities of great stones that would last a thousand years! Only the noblest and purest would live there. I came to bring a sacred thing, to raise men from the ugly horror of history! To make you pure and god-like . . ." He raised a trembling fist before his face. "I have *seen* the god-men. I have seen them."

He suddenly was silent and stared back at the map. His head hurt again. He more or less forgot what he'd just said. Blinked rapidly. Where was that swine Haase, didn't he realize he needed an injection? And he called himself a doctor. He felt nauseated. Cold. Shivered.

(1912)

When Adolf Hitler opened his eyes he felt he existed only as sight, blurred and tentative. He seemed to be staring down a palely glowing slope of landscape, jagged and frozen where craters, ridges, and rills were marked by trembling shadows. Beyond floated a sea of darkness and vast, looming, dimly hinted shapes. Icy wind blew ghosts of snow over these wastes and stung his vision; and next he felt his numbed flesh, needle bites on his face, and heard the slow, shallow rasping of his breath.

He tried to grasp where he might be, to locate this arctic wasteland. There was a light in the air, wavering in the gusty snowfall, round, bilious, yellowish, moonlike. He felt a deep, hopeless fear, fear that he was lost forever from time, dead and doomed to this bitter, freezing eternity.

Lord God and sweet Mary, he thought, *return me to life. To sweet warm life. Let me love and live*.

He tried to move now and, surprised, found his arms painfully lifted him. Burning prickles coursed through his body.

I'm still living, he thought, grateful. *I'm still living!*

He'd felt dead. He'd been certain of it.

Lifting his face from the snowbanks, perspective returned and he realized he'd been staring from inches away at the deserted street. The strange moon was the nearest gaslight under the dark, shabby buildings across the way, masked by the heavy snow.

Got to his knees, remembering everything: the fat

woman was gone, the tavern was shut for the night. He
looked around. How long had those bastards let him lie
there? To freeze. What did they care? *Bastards!*

Swaying to his feet he was dizzy and sick to his
stomach. Chilled to the bone. Shaking violently. Eyes
burning. *Bastards!* He knew he had a fever. Huddled in his
coat and shivered. His bad lung twinged with each rough
breath.

The streets were empty as far as he could see. The
mounting storm billowed past. He forced his aching body
to move. Headed into the gusting sheets of cutting snow.

Just across the street, he kept telling himself. *Cross the
street and upstairs to rest. It's warm upstairs.*

He kept one arm flung up before his face but he could
barely squint into the vicious, ripping, freezing air. His
head pulsed. Felt the fever raging through him. Leaned on
the wind—and actually was so weak he slipped sidewise
along the tearing, shifting push—and decided he'd head at
right angles until he reached the building wall and then
work his way up to the lodging-house steps where he could
hold onto something besides wild, biting air. He knew he
was close to falling and was sure he'd die there if he fell.

He slipped and struggled on, holding his stiff coat
closed with numbed fingers, other arm groping in dark,
windy, freezing space.

Too long; he should have reached the sidewalk by now.
Tried to see, to shield his eyes . . . Hopeless. Could he
really be in the middle of a familiar street? Once again his
whirling mind felt an ominous supernatural something
here. Where was he? This was unearthly! If only he weren't
so weak. Saw only faint, glowing shapes that billowed,
ballooned, danced endlessly past. Clawed at him,
shoved . . .

He sensed he was circling now and didn't even have
the strength to panic. Staggering, tripping, sliding, groping
in wide, hopeless arcs, now seeing flashes of vision or
memory: long grass and full trees in soft, warm, ripened
sunlight; days that seemed rich as honey, a perfect seamless
blue sky; soft, swaying flowers, restless birds, the lawn, the
white fence. His burning lips kept moving, soundlessly
repeating: *Mother . . . Mother . . . Mother . . . help me
. . . help me.*

On and on, aware, distantly, that he must have gone

down the street with the wind and missed the far corner. So now he had to be (all this in a rational flash) out in the nearby square. Or was he lost in a world of dark and ghostly white, his body a dream and his soul being drawn away to nightmare?

He saw a blurred, remote glow in the violent night and had a rambling idea it was a gateway home—the light that used to burn on the front door of their house. He aimed for it.

And then felt hands as if she'd stepped to his side from the warm, sweet, syrupy land of eternal brightness.

Mother.

He couldn't voice a sound.

Warm, sweet hands, blur of face (the vision of childhood's other world the only thing clear) and he reached and touched living flesh. Tried to see with eyes sealed almost shut.

Mommy. Little Mommy.

Arms were holding him, helping him stumble forward, over the curb, then down a set of steps into a dark, musty place. The warmth was a shock to his shuddering body and he heard a voice (he didn't know was his own) moaning faintly and from far away heard her speaking in what seemed a liquid flow of wordless sound. Then a softness swallowed up his flesh, heaps of covers coming down, mounding over him where he lay in a blur of mismatched senses.

"Poor boy," he didn't hear her saying. He was already falling into a cozy doze, watching the landscape drift by: green and yellow earth, blue and white sky, soaring over flashes of water . . . lush fields where peasants seemed to be toiling and singing . . . clouds fluffing themselves up over the soft, hushed countryside . . .

He had only flashes of waking between mad sleep and bright images as the fever lulled and mounted again and again. Flashes of the narrow room: dim gaslight, overstuffed, elaborate furniture that seemed (to his burning, ravaged perception) to be menacing him with some strange truth, hinting with shadowy bulks, massed draperies, obscured bric-a-brac glinting in dark corners . . .

* * *

At some point he opened his aching eyes and the woman was sitting on the edge of the bed, her cool hand on his forehead. She held a steaming cup to his lips and he gulped and swallowed. She wore a billowy red robe. Smelled of roses. Then it went dark again . . .

Then she was back—or had she never moved? and this time he tried to sit up and speak, discovered, as the sheet slipped down, that he was nude. Felt weak and shaky.

He squeezed his lids open and shut, trying to focus. She was big. Tall and wide. Hair a copper-stained blond. Neutral eyes, more gray than blue. Like still pond water, he thought vaguely. Blurry features. Soft, anyway: a tiny, red-tipped nose. Fleshy chin. A vast bosom showing where the drapelike robe parted.

Her hand was round and soft stroking over his gaunt white face as if molding the flesh. She stroked straight to his chest and torso, lightly massaging the bony ribs.

"There's nothing to you," she told him, with playful scorn. "You need some meat and potatoes."

He lolled his head on the crinkly pillow. Breathing sighed.

"I . . ." he began but she was already tilting a mug of rich broth to his lips. It scalded but was rich and potent. He gulped carefully, the warmth seeping and exploding within him.

"There's herbs and weeds in this," she said off-handedly, "that'd make a dead man stir." She found this remark worth a soft chuckle.

She restrained the cup for a moment, then fed him more.

"Easy, young man," she almost crooned. "Easy, you want to grow up strong and tear into the ladies, don't you?" Chuckled again. Her bosom swelled liquidly.

He finished the broth and took better notice of things. He realized the sickness was still there, but the rest and this concoction had pushed it away for a time.

"You've got basic strength," she said, looking into his face. Then grasped his hand and tilted it into a stray strand of light. Poked at the palm with her small, surprisingly strong fingers. Squeezed and probed. Rocked her head slightly, nodding, as he distantly spoke and shocked him

with her comments. It took time before he understood that
she was actually reading his hand.

"Your father died before your mother when you were
young," she was saying. "He left you weak in the chest."

He shook his head. Blinked and frowned. His sight still
swam and her form seemed to shift its outlines as he stared.

"Do you—" he said, surprised by the softness of his
voice, "do you know me?" He kept trying to blink himself
clearer.

"The ladies like you," she remarked, squeezing under
his thumb. "So what's the trouble? Eh?"

He felt a little spasm of strength coming back.

"Women should be respected," he semi-whispered.

"But a woman likes a little affection from a fellow," she
said, smiling at him. "No?"

"It's too easy to take . . . to take advantage of their
weakness." He nodded, slightly. Tried to retrieve his hand
without success.

"Oh-ho," she said, raising both eyebrows. "Is that the
story? A true gentleman at last."

Turned his hand another way.

"There's nothing to be afraid of," she told him.

"It's not a question of that," he said weakly. Tried again
to free his hand. She was tilting it in a faint strand of light.
Was silent for a time.

"Are you a gypsy?" he finally asked.

She didn't react. Released his hand, staring not quite at
his face for a long moment.

"Well, then," he said, trying to joke, "what about my
future?" Smiled. "Do I die of lung fever by tomorrow?"

"No," she said, quite seriously. "You don't die."

He waited. Then, a little curious and not really
amused, asked:

"Well? . . . Nothing more to tell me?" Shut his eyes to
rest them. "Do I ever marry? Will I be rich and great?"

"Yes," she said, without expression.

He opened his eyes. Snorted.

"Well," he said, "that's nice to hear." Snorted another
laugh. But he was secretly pleased. Closed his eyes again.
Many of his historical heroes had consulted readers,
diviners, mediums. Part of the shadowy history of the
world (as gleaned from his astonishing library forays)
involved kings and conquerors with their private wizards.

At first he had assumed this was characteristic of cruder ages. But then many of these were first-rate minds. Anyway, he'd concluded, anything condemned by churches and hidebound professors was probably worthy of serious reconsideration.

He squinted at her: her form blurred into the dim glintings of the room, then came back as he feebly rubbed his eyes.

"If you don't show your feelings," she said seriously, "you will be very lonely in life."

"Feelings?" he distantly wondered. "Anyway, how did I get here? And where is this place?" He was suddenly surprised he hadn't dealt with that question immediately. It was as though, he thought, the fever had drugged or enchanted him . . .

"I found you," she murmured, touching his bare shoulder gently. "There's no need to be so lonely in life. To hold yourself apart." Her hand was neither hot nor cold, he noticed. But not unpleasant.

"You read these things?" he asked softly, hoarsely. "In my flesh?"

He tried to sit up but knew it was hopeless. He felt gently weighted down evenly all over his body. His energy seemed to drain away with the slightest motion. If he just lay still it was not too bad. He blinked and squinted but the room's outlines stayed fuzzy.

"How did you know my father was dead?" he asked her. Her hand still rested on his shoulder. "Did I say things in my sleep?"

"You said nothing." She wiped his brow with a cool towel. "You will be so lonely, sweet boy." She smiled. "Bad boy." She sighed. "Such a romantic dreamer."

"My father died when I was twelve," he was whispering. "And I didn't shed a tear . . ." He moved his head restlessly on the pillow. "I'm an artist . . . I believe I have . . . I have a great destiny . . ." His eyes flamed in their pale and somber bluish grays, found the pale glow of her shadowy face. "But I loved her . . . she was kind to me . . . and beautiful . . ." He shut his eyes. "In school I . . . I hated school . . ." He hardly was aware of actually speaking now. He seemed to sink down into a spreading, darkening pool. He groped instinctively for her hand. Found it and held on, weakly.

"Rest yourself for a while, young man," he thought he heard her saying. His sight darkened. The hinted room dissolved into a formless void.

"I hated it . . . useless . . . teachers were fools . . . weaklings . . . you have to be strong for life . . . strong . . . not lonely . . . the old bastard knew that, the old bastard . . ." He didn't know he was weeping. ". . . not lonely if you're . . . strong . . . I used to walk . . . by myself . . . watch her . . . hair so golden . . . I loved her . . . can't make me a fool . . . no . . . I'll kill whoever laughed . . . whoever . . ." The blackness came down firmly and he felt nothing at all. Only void. Didn't hear voice or thoughts or feel her neutral hand soothing him. ". . . loved . . . said nothing . . . nothing . . ."

It was like being underwater: sometime later he was aware of the dimness, the vague shapes that might have been walls and furniture, shimmering, wavering, as if the very fabric of reality were about to be totally rent and he felt fear and suffocation . . . suffocation! He struggled weakly to free his nose and mouth from a wet, stinging musk, sweet salt sourness, taste, smell, and roughness rubbing, pressing like a brush scraping over his face, rhythmically . . . his hands reflexed up to touch the great, bare, palely swinging softness above him, straining to gasp air, his head (he now realized) caught in a tight hot vise of soft, massive flesh . . . he pushed uselessly, hands denting in and slipping off . . . the weight kept rubbing and rubbing over his face, smearing him with thick musk; one plump hand locked in his hair, the other reached back somehow now and flung the covers away (he felt the cool air shock on his naked body) and then the hand gripped him, worked at him, and he heard her voice from high above, gasping, fierce, tyrannic:

"Come on . . . come on, bad boy . . . come on . . . lick it, you little fairy . . . you dirty little fairy . . . lick it . . . come on . . . come on . . ."

And he moaned in shock and fear as he hardened violently—spasmodic, sudden, helpless, electric . . . it was sinking, dying sweet . . . yes . . . yes . . . and terrifying . . . terrifying . . .

"Come on, lick!" she commanded. "Lick! Lick!" Grinding his face into her groin, and as if the two were one, pleasure and pain, and sweetness shame and fear too; his tongue working voraciously, almost frantic, all his strength involuntarily gathered, exploding as he sobbed and cried out, sucking air desperately, chest and throat on fire:

"*Uuuuuuuuuunnnnnnnn! . . . Uuuuuuuuuunnnnnnnn!*"

And she hissed and twisted in her ecstasies.

Daylight, pale and harsh, seeped around the curtains and sliced in wherever they parted. He opened his eyes. They hurt, whichever way he moved them.

He remembered, or thought he did. It might all have been delirium, after all. He was naked and sweaty under the tangled covers. The fever seemed to have broken. Looked around the room: dim tables and chairs, the stain of rug. No sign of the woman. He licked his gummy lips. Felt somewhat stronger and sat up gradually.

The pressure of her seemed to push him (not just physically) out of himself into a dreamish scene lit by dull, uncertain blurs of luminous green that resolved into two hanging globes of dull light swaying in a floor-to-ceiling window on thin chains, gusts of foggy wind shaking them, billowing heavy, dark parted curtains that seemed woven out of metallic cloth. Outside massive, gleaming buildings with green-glowing windows seemed like mountains in the rolls of mist and, dim in the distance, dull red fires that he somehow knew were volcanic . . .

He knew that world, somehow, and twisted in fear to escape it . . . failed . . . because the weight was on him and his body (smaller, thinner, more graceful) lay under a slim, muscular woman who was riding his hips, her face (in the tossed, greenish hinting) imperious, intense, cruel, eyes and hair jet-black, almost snarling in her ecstasy, crying out what had to be his name (except he couldn't make actual sound of it), head twisted around to look through a window where naked bodies sat on long iron stakes, chained, twisting in muffled, unimaginable agony as their weight gradually drove the honed points through the torso, fraction by fraction, and they (he realized) were struggling to speed the process and shorten the pain, desperate, mad, mouths stuffed shut with wads of wax. Three or four victims were visible from the bed where the king and queen copulated . . .

What had really happened? He felt nothing. It could

as well have happened to a stranger, he supposed. Heard a deep, rasping gurgle from nearby. Dragged himself to the side of the bed and made out the rounded, long shadow-spill of her on the rug, limbs gleaming wetly in the blunt but scattered light.

She went on snoring as he sat up, groggy and frail, and set his feet on the floor. Groped around the area for his clothes. He had a strange, unclear fear that if she woke up she would hold him prisoner here.

She must have washed him, he realized as he was bent over working his feet into his hard, battered shoes. He didn't smell and that was unusual enough for him to notice.

He stood up, wobbling, buttoning his seam-split shirt. His hunger was raw and fierce. Holding his coat he fumbled into the kitchen. The window there was dark and he could see a trashcan and realized the apartment was below street level. Found some stale bread and hard cheese. He clawed at it, stuffed it into his mouth, chewed and swallowed in a kind of spasm of appetite.

When he glanced up she was filling the kitchen doorway with her tremendous blond nudity. He looked at her with fear and sullen defiance. He doubted if he could overcome her physically in his present state.

He set his teeth and lips grimly and stared at her.

"So you're leaving?" she asked neutrally.

"Stand aside," he rumbled.

She moved closer, into the narrow space.

"We're all strong again now, it that it?" She wondered. "Want me to read the rest of your future?"

"No!" he said, too loud even in his own ears. He was betraying his fear, he thought. And yet the force of his voice was remarkable in itself. It seemed for a moment as if another person with total health and terrific energy had spoken through him. "I'm leaving."

"Can't tempt you a little?" She smiled. Moved even closer, thighs slapping together, breasts liquidly bumping. As he moved to try and pass her she leaned her body into his and one soft hand gripped into his crotch. He pushed at her, banging into some hanging pots and pans along the wall, smelled her flesh, hair, and stale but perfumy breath. Felt a moment of strange excitement and simultaneous revulsion as the last night came back vividly.

Then he slipped and twisted past her as she laughed

and pinched his backside. He was ashamed that he wanted to wait, to feel her mouth there again—almost reeled across the living room toward the gray-lit hallway beyond.

"A cup of coffee?" she called after, still amused.

Followed him to the hall as he wrenched the door open and went up the few steps to the street. A lacework of snow gusted chill and wet into the vestibule.

"Come back anytime, young man," she called up to him. "What was your name, anyway?"

Outside, in the bright grayness, snow falling steadily, he twisted his face back to her. Smiled and then frowned. Rubbed his lips nervously.

"Adolf," he told her.

Thought about her mouth, stared at the soft, bluish-veined flesh visible through the parted doorway as if she'd floated up from the inner dimness. Twisted himself away without another word.

It was all so ordinary, he was telling himself. The body reacted, spasmed, and forgot. Left no mark. Meant almost nothing without love.

The chill air seemed to cleanse his mind. He sucked in deep, biting breaths. He suddenly thought about going to confession. He hadn't gone inside a church since his mother died.

What a hold they get on your mind, he thought.

He struggled on through the gray-white shrouded lanes down toward the river. Very few people were out at this hour. Some shoveled walks, others ploughed along on early business, wrapped to the nose in woolens.

He passed a toiling postman. Next noticed a clergyman sweeping the surface snow from the church steps. His outline seemed without depth in the misty illumination. His breath steamed like smoke.

He glared, light-headed and fuzzy, at the dim man. On one level Hitler realized he wished he could go into the church and unburden himself in the contemplative dimness. The very desire infuriated him. Even the design of the building, the peace and timelessness within, was a clever device to entrap free souls!

They want us to be weak so they can rule us!

"You!" he yelled across the yard, the sound flat and muffled. "You invented sin!"

"What?" The clergyman cupped his ear with a mit-
tened hand.

Hitler spat in his general direction, invisibly at the
distance, and moved on, grayed away, as the puzzled man
stared after him, to a ghostly form, then vanished into the
quiet hissing pitter of snowy morning.

IX
(APRIL 1945)

Frank Astuti, rifle at the ready, picked his way through the
smoldering woods. Glanced at a German officer crumpled
beside a shattered tree trunk. His uniform and hair were
on fire. He winced at the broiling meat smell. The enemy
seemed to have pulled back. Which suited him. He'd seen
no sign of the crazy professor. Wasn't surprised. If he was
alive he wished him luck. Waded on through the fire-
shadows, alert, eyes restless.

While Renga was just wandering past two Germans in
a sandbagged outpost, he suddenly stepped out of the
smoke near a burning tree, sooty and naked except for the
shoes, his eyes and teeth bright white. He was picturing the
dark lair where the wizard worked his magic and hatched
his plans. He'd make his way there and strangle the filth
with his own hands. No weapons but those would serve. He
needed only a horse. Stopped near the two soldiers. He'd
ask these cowering warriors a few questions.

"Where is thy master?" he wanted to know, in old
German.

The one with the pale, round face and tiny eyes tilted
his helmet back with his gunbarrel.

"We thought you were a black man," he remarked.

"Where are your clothes?" the second, a dour, long-
jawed, practical corporal inquired.

"I seek thy master's castle, sirrahs," Dr. Renga explained. "And I will deal justly with him, I promise thee." There had obviously been a great battle here recently, he noted, stooping to pick what he believed was a great, spiked mace. "Tell me the way there or perish," he declared, brandishing the broken tree limb at them with energy. *These cowards here are afraid to even rise and face me like men. They crouch in their hole like beasts . . . like moles*, he thought. "Speak!" he commanded.

The round-faced private was almost merry.

"Aren't they cold?" he wondered, indicating Renga's genitals.

"How did you get out here?" long-jaw wanted to know.

"For sooth," guffawed round-face, "he knows not, I wager."

"Insolent dogs!" cried Renga, raising the stick. "Speak, I say, or by Saint Michael thou shall regret thy ways!"

"I'd say he's a *gauleiter*, from his manners," quipped round-face with some bitterness. "Listen, brave knight, why don't you go take it up with the Führer? He's the one you want." Pointed with his burp gun. "Just keep going that way, my lord, and you'll come to his castle." Guffawed.

"Maybe we should take him back with us?" the other wondered. "He could be escaped from somewhere."

"Well, then, good luck to him. What do you care, Gustave? We'll all be prisoners soon enough or dead."

"Never mind that talk," Gustave said. "Last night I dreamt—"

"Thou did well to direct me thus," Renga told them. "I swear to have his worthless life!"

He could see the face of the slayer of his family: the empty, pale eyes, the drooping, thin mustaches setting off the pale, hard lips. Remembered him sitting with his armored cronies at the Holy Emperor's palace, preparing his secret plots and betrayals.

"What's this?" the corporal said.

"Let me be," said the other. "If he can beat the Russians to Berlin, so be it." Chuckled and shook his head.

"Still," the other said humorlessly, "it's treason."

But Renga was already disappearing into the fitful flame and smoke and darkness, naked, blackened, mace over his shoulder.

"So be it," the soldier repeated.

* * *

Frank Astuti had happened on the same dirt road Renga was wandering down, and so it wasn't long before he passed the same point except that by then the two Germans had fallen back and the sandbagged dugout was empty. He went on through the flickering, smoke-choked forest figuring he'd take a nap toward morning.

Renga kept seeing his wife and children's slashed and burned bodies tied to posts in the castle yard. He'd seen the herbs and dried flowers and colored powders and wax drippings staining the earth around the cold fire. *Witchcraft,* he kept thinking, *those degenerates . . . God give me power! Oh, those degenerates!*

And seeing too, always, the hated face, the hollow eyes lit by inner bleakness. Renga went on.

(WINTER 1913
NEAR CHRISTMAS)

Rudolph Renga ws having coffee in a cafe. He was sitting at a tiny table facing the bright glare of frosty window. Outside the sun was blinding, chilly brightness on the snow and in the shimmering, stainless sky above the city and reflected in the icy Danube that showed over the low roofs where the hill sloped away. It was about midday.

No one understood why he'd come to Vienna this time of year. He'd gone on sabbatical. Because of his conversations with the Moltkes he'd decided to further research the Holy Grail. His friend, Professor Fragtkopft, had tried to argue him out of it. Insisted it was an irrelevant direction to take. Seemed almost angry as if the idea offended him, somehow. Which had puzzled Renga. He was starting to think that the young professor was consciously trying to guide him in some unclear direction. He wondered what and why. There was something a little secretive, he thought, about Kurt. He suspected there was a problem between him and his wife. Renga liked Minna very much. Found her very sensitive and open. At times, he thought, she acted as though Kurt made her uncomfortable.

He sipped his coffee. Wondered if his good suit was pressed. He'd have to check when he got back to the hotel. Moltke was in Vienna himself and had invited Renga to an embassy reception for the German Kaiser. The idea amused him a little: the politicians, rulers, soldiers, seemed like gray shadows in a dream world. His only regret at the moment, he decided, amused at himself, was that the libraries weren't open all night.

He realized he felt safe behind his senses again. For the first time in over a year. The feeling that at any moment, any time, all illusory walls would dissolve and leave him naked in an unknown world had abated. Was amused again because now that he was hidden he wanted to be found. Because the mind's hush was there beyond the ear's deafening acuteness, sight's blunt blinding, the sweet lies of taste, clumsy confusion of touch and baffling smell, beyond that screen of hopeless measurement was the hush (he only sensed) without limit, the light without stain.

Sipped the coffee, basking in the steamy heat and streamers of sunlight. Drummed his fingers on the clean marble where the white cup gleamed.

Easier to believe in engineering, he thought. Millions were trying. He imagined them huddling around the ebbing coals of the intellect's fire while the shadows and wildness pressed closer, seeping deeper into the last, wavering glow, as they tried to believe there was really nothing out there.

You think you're safe, he'd recently told a class, while you build your machines and count profits and say all you know is what you know but the vastness is there, all around, the mystery, immeasurable, uncountable, and only a mist of reasoning and hope between you and the eternal forces of utter violence and bliss.

He looked up as a strange man paused, then sat down in the opposite chair.

Oh, God, he thought wearily. It was either a tramp or a madman. Was he drunk? The nearest waiter had already paused, balancing a silver tray of cakes, watchful. Renga took in the dead-white face pinched around hollow blue eyes and bristly mustache under a wild shock of lank hair. The greasy coat was buttoned to the neck. For an instant Renga bizarrely felt the man had stepped from the roiling darkness of nightmare into the glittering, lucid afternoon. Then he realized he was losing initiative, should simply insist: I have no wish for company, at the moment, my dear fellow. That was the best line to take in these cases. Sighed. Felt strangely immobile and vaguely depressed . . . shook it off with an effort.

The man placed a folder of drawings on the table. "I'm an artist," he announced, in a throaty rumble.

Slightly defensive, Renga noted. Well, obnoxious perhaps, but at least he didn't seem mad. A Bohemian. With quite a commanding manner. Intense, but probably harmless. He'd see what this was about.

"Yes?" he responded carefully.

"You look intelligent," his uninvited companion said, leaning forward as if to mesmerize him. The eyes brooded.

"I try my best," Renga parried, leaning back, gaze steady and dark, meeting the other's haunted hollows. "What can I do for you, Herr . . . ?"

"Hitler. I got rid of my agent," he said confidentially. "Hanisch the crook. I took him to court. I've learned a few tricks." Frowned. "I found out lawyers are bigger crooks than anybody." Almost smiled, stare never breaking. "I'm selling my work myself now."

"You'd like me to look at some pictures?" Renga was perplexed as the fellow made no move to open the water-stained folder. He tried not to sound patronizing. Smiled at the secret pun. "Would you like, oh, a coffee, Herr Hitler?"

"No," came the deadpan response. He turned to the waiter who was hovering (without the tray now) indecisively nearby. "A cream puff!" he demanded with a jerk of his head.

So nervous, commented Renga to himself.

Hitler opened his coat and settled in. His tieless shirt was yellowish and patched. A shaving cut on his neck. Behind his head was the chill brilliant day, the river of ice.

"Have you had many exhibitions?" Renga asked, to fill the strange silence. The artist shook his head, once. With muted violence.

The waiter set down the pastry on a frail saucer and Hitler instantly took a large bite, staining his mustache with what seemed curds of snow. His tongue shortly found them out. Renga sipped his cooling coffee and decided to wait. The cream puff was vanishing like magic, he thought, amused. *He eats like a child.*

"Have you tried to arrange any?" he asked now, by way of conversation. For some reason he didn't want to give his name.

"Tried what?"

"To arrange an exhibition of your artwork?"

The chewing, grim fellow snorted. Began to speak in his steady, thundering voice, with shocking, sudden volume and fierceness.

"The classical values in art have degenerated to nothing!" he informed his questioner. Incompletely masticated fragments showed among uneven teeth. Renga lowered his eyes. He half-expected a fleck to fly out and hit him. "Do you imagine I'd be allowed a fair chance?"

"By whom?"

"The critics, the academics, the Jews, the bourgeois—"

Renga frowned. What was this?

"Just a minute—" he cut in, "have you already all these enemies? You'd think you were famous as Rembrandt."

"The same forces that left Rembrandt to die poor because of his greatness still exist and exact a worse toll today than—"

Renga was genuinely puzzled.

"The Jews?" he wondered. "Why not say Methodists, into the bargain? Roman Catholics too? Why not? The bourgeoisie, I might grant you. The academics—" he shrugged—"who cares?"

"The Jews may be a bigger factor than most people think," the stern, humorless-seeming firebrand asserted, thoughtfully.

Renga cocked his head and squinted one eye.

Amazing nonsense, he thought.

"Sure," he said, chuckling, "all across Europe they gather in their synagogues and pray to keep you from getting ahead in life." Hitler was forced to smile for an instant. Moved his hand as if to dismiss this line of thinking.

"Well, there may be more to it than you think," Hitler insisted. "I used to take it too lightly myself. There are Jews, and there are Jews, if you see what I mean."

"Perfectly. You think the Rothschilds are after you."

Hitler smiled again.

"They're a bad influence on art in general," he said rather lamely, brushing the specifics aside. "This is a decadent period. I'm talking about the sources of the decay." He seemed more comfortable now that (Renga noted) he could be more abstract and rhetorical. "There'll have to be a revolution before the art world gets cleaned up here. Believe me. Art is a totally certain index of the state of a people as a whole." He gestured stiffly, fist clenched. His

listener found himself fascinated by the cold, stiff anger. It
was as though a well, ever brimming with seethings, had
been tapped. "Europe is inert, dull, decaying. They deco-
rate this sterile way of life with their bits of *modern* trash. I'd
like to sweep it all away with an iron broom!" The stare
seemed to penetrate unguessed distances. "Modern life is
empty, hopeless. It has lost all spiritual foundation."

What's this? Renga wondered. *He sounds a little like
Fragtkopft.* The idea didn't quite amuse him.

"Yes?" he pressed.

The stare remained focused into unseen gulfs.

"It will be destroyed," Hitler rumbled, quietly, raptly.

"Does it have to be? Cannot we work to improve—"

"Too late," he interrupted. "Too late for half-
measures."

Renga noted that the conversation almost had a
dreamlike quality, as if he were actually petitioning this wild
young man to swerve the fate of the world. As if what they
said at this gleaming little table in the harsh winter sun in
the stuffy comfort of a Viennese coffeehouse would give a
spin to destiny. He normally would have smiled at himself.
Why wasn't he smiling? This man had a compelling effect
that was hard to shake off.

"I don't think," he finally said, "that it's ever too late for
people to discover their souls."

The stubborn head jerked in rebuttal.

"It's not for everyone," Hitler declared as if he had
authority to say so.

"How can you just say that? Any human being can
open his eyes to the spirit."

The artist leaned forward, swallowing the remnants of
his pastry, obviously delighting in both the discussion and
the lingering sweetness.

"A common error," he said. "I've studied the question
intensely." Rapped his knuckles on the tabletop. "Only the
highest types can hope for any enlightenment. Genius is
the least requirement."

"Or," Renga shot back, "isn't genius the result of
opening up to the spirit?"

Hitler was amused. He leaned back, smiling, shaking
his large head.

"You might as well," he said, chuckling, "claim an ape

could encompass a Strauss waltz as say the mass of mankind
could hope to—"

"I don't say it's impossible, my friend," Renga broke in
with a grin. "Maybe not Beethoven. But really, only the
humble, only the simple of heart and open—"

The other's face was suddenly stormy. Grim. Eyes
flamed.

"Christian claptrap!" he thundered. The waiter looked
over again. Renga jumped a little in his chair. "Was Wagner
humble? Was—"

"Was Wagner enlightened? He was a miserable man!
Unhappy and—"

"Genius is its own end! It—"

"Quiet down over there!" the waiter called over. "Is
this the public square?"

Hitler shot him a furious but nervous look.

"The swine," he muttered under his breath.

"Look," Renga was saying, "this is very interesting. But
I've looked into these things myself. Recall, for instance,
how Lancelot was too arrogant and worldly to find the
Grail while *Parzival*—"

Hitler's eyes misted over and he leaned back in his seat
again.

"What a work," he said, almost gently. "The music
lifted me from myself. I think Nietzsche was in error when
he attacked—"

"But I wasn't referring to the opera."

"I'd like to be Kaiser," the other remarked, "so I might
never be interrupted."

"Forgive me. But I was referring to the legendary tale
itself, not—"

"I know all about it," Hitler cut in.

He would be hard to really like, Renga thought.

"I wouldn't mind being Kaiser myself, from time to
time," he murmured.

"The knights of the Grail," his companion was now
informing him enthusiastically, "were chosen members of
the highest, most evolved racial types of the time."

"Weren't we discussing a legend?" Renga tested.

A curt head shake.

He and Kurt ought to get together, Renga thought.

"No," Hitler stated. "They were real people."

"You know this?"

The fanatical-looking artist rubbed his bristly mustache, looking suddenly, strangely, covert and careful. Glanced around the quiet room. The coffee machine hissed suddenly in back and someone was singing in the kitchen.

"Perhaps I knew then," he finally replied, seeming to joke.

"In another life, perhaps?" Renga smiled.

Hitler stood up, gathered his folder into his expressive hands. Seemed suspicious.

"Will I get to see your work?" Renga asked.

Hitler paused, then slipped a dog-eared drawing out and laid it on the tabletop. The edge bent over the coffee cup.

Renga cocked his head one way . . . then the other. Asked himself if he was missing something. Felt let down: he'd expected something stark, violent, a breaking storm, a titanic battle of gods . . . Was he selling someone else's work? Stared at the fussy, detailed, gloomy view of some massive state building across a semideserted square where little, shadowy human figures seemed lost and dwarfed by the exaggerated heap of dead stone . . . Well, was that the message? Was there a message?

"Ah," he murmured neutrally. The picture had an oppressive effect on him. He looked into a colorless, empty world where every dreary line and angle was rigorously straight; where perspective was frozen, exact. Where nature's luxurious ease was utterly absent. Trees wavered, pallid and sticklike as the people they could bring no comfort to. No living forms could possibly breathe and grow, he was certain, under the dark, immense architecture of that brain's design.

He sensed that if he reacted badly the touchy artist would vanish for good. While that would probably be just as well, he had to admit he was very curious about this enigamtic, clumsy, compelling, furious person.

"I'd like to see more," he told him, watching his face. "I need time to pick and choose. It's very interesting."

The set face showed nothing as Hitler shrugged and zipped the picture away.

"Why not?" he said. Smiled briefly.

Does he imagine that's warm and winning?

"It's up to you," the artist concluded brusquely and strode away with seeming purpose in his step, after saying (as if expecting to be believed); "I have an appointment," in place of good-bye.

Renga watched him cross the frosty glass into the icy glitter of the street, ragged clothes fluttering in the cold wind.

X
(APRIL 1945)

He doesn't like to come in the camps anymore, they say, Commandant Kurt Fragtkopft thought with faint contempt as he greeted the Reichsführer-SS who made no move to get out of the open Mercedes touring car after extending his hand and smiling bleakly. The sun was below the smoke clouds in the west and the fading red glow was caught in Himmler's round glasses so that, for a moment, against his black uniform and the twilight shadows the man's skull appeared hollowed out by smoldering flame. Then his head moved slightly and the effect was gone. He sat between two large officers unknown to Fragtkopft.

"Commandant," Himmler said, "I expect, after all, the best and most from you special men who have already given so much more than the others." Pause.

"Yes, sir?" Fragtkopft waited for the inevitable impossible order. He had never been disappointed. *Yes,* he thought, *we speical men who fill the ovens for you.*

"Are you keeping up with things here?" Himmler wondered.

Keeping up, thought the commandant.

"I am trying everything possible," he replied. "But there are technological limits to the operation, as I have many times informed the Reichsführer." He enjoyed these little moments. There was little else to enjoy.

"I am certain you are doing everything in your power," his leader assured him. "However, it appears that conventional methods have failed us." He stood up and got out of the car. He took Fragtkopft a few paces away from the others. His thin, prim lips added to the cool, remote expressionlessness of the wispy face. "I am trying a number of alternatives."

Yes, the other thought, *one of which already got Hitler to order your arrest.* He'd picked that up on the grapevine: Himmler was trying to negotiate with the Allies. "Ah."

"Even the most desperate measures," Himmler added.

"You mean these haven't been desperate yet?"

"We have to call on"—he dropped his voice—"the powers. You understand, I'm sure, Kurt."

Kurt stared at the single chimney where the foul, black smoke boiled and faded into the darkening sky, suggesting shapes (as when he was a child), landscapes, figures, mounting and dissolving. He suddenly felt unutterably tired.

"The stars have reached a critical alignment," the Reichsführer was saying. "The moment is here. We have the means. This is the largest camp still functioning. The moment the Führer dies, the forces of history will reach a climax. My researchers are certain of the moment, you understand?" Himmler's face showed nothing. "We are sending over as many more prisoners as possible beginning tonight. I, myself, will come back here at the eleventh hour to participate." He went on talking but Fragtkopft really didn't hear him.

"But," he said, "we can't possibly process more than we presently—"

"Naturally," Himmler cut his short, "but that doesn't matter anymore." His lips flicked what was almost a smile, his face a vague paleness, the glasses a glint. "It need no longer be entirely orderly." Schoolmasterish. "Only this once, you see." Nodded. "I hate confusion, myself, and sloppiness. But it will only be a temporary affair, I assure you."

How horrible, he thought, *it is going to be horrible.*

"Yes," he muttered, "I, nevertheless, am very much opposed to—"

"Yes. Naturally."

Himmler turned and headed back for the car.

". . . opposed," Kurt murmured.

"Everything's in order. Don't worry. Perhaps we'll surprise our enemies once again."

Fragtkopft was numb. He didn't really understand
because he didn't want to. He was aware only of a hollow,
sick fear within himself. His mouth was dry.

"I've done my duty here a certain way," he found
himself saying nervously, "and that's bad enough but I have
to keep the routine." His hands were shaking badly. "It's no
good otherwise . . ." Shook his head, too rapidly. "Don't
you see, it has to be carried out in an orderly fashion or
men go mad!"

Himmler was studying him. Patted his arm with his
gloved hand, twice.

"Steady yourself, Commandant," he said, mildly.

Fragtkopft bit his lips and sighed, deeply.

"But can't we just accept—"

"No," the Reichführer cut him off, "we cannot accept."

This is going to be terrible, Fragtkopft was thinking, *this is
going to be terrible* . . . stared at the smoke, the shapes,
something like a grimacing face, melting . . .

Inside the dim, reeking barrack the woman was still
struggling with the commandant's features and her thin
memory. He looked like him. Walked like him. She lay back
on the boards and didn't look around at the others, the
sighing, moaning, murmuring, dying shapes. Her memories suddenly flashed and stirred: she saw the old house,
the view from the kitchen window across the campus, the
rose garden and the white fence, the students walking. She
blinked. An emaciated little girl who looked fifty, hair
falling out in patches, tummy bloated, crouched, watching
her from a few feet away, stare wildly bright and glazy. Shut
her eyes to get the memory refocused: a man, a thinner
version of the commandant, was bent from the waist
smelling one of the roses. *God in heaven,* she thought, *God in
heaven.*

(1914)

Kurt Fragtkopft didn't look up from his desk as his
wife came into the study. A few pale streaks of daylight
leaked through the bulky drapes.

He was scribbling notes in a litter of opened and bent-
back books, papers, cards, pens, blotters, crumpled fools-
cap.

"It's time for you to go," she told him, voice a little tired. Her hand idly smoothed her dress.

He twisted his head around to look up at her. For an instant, she was almost afraid, shocked because he seemed a stranger, a surprise face.

We get used to seeing one another a certain way, she thought, *and imagine that's really what we look like.*

But he didn't, objectively (she believed), look himself: so pale, and glassy-eyed and strangely smug, as if he possessed some deep secret. You had to face changes in people, she told herself, but she liked the old Kurt better. Much better. The boyish one. A little cynical, to be sure, but boyish all the same.

Like those others, she thought, facing it squarely. *Those cranks, or whatever they are.*

He was smiling. Put down his pen and leaned back, looking more his (she thought) normal self. Enthusiastic, amused by life.

"Time, Minna?" he asked. She used to find him witty. *Is this what marriage does?* she wondered.

"The proctor's tea," she reminded him.

"So I'm to waste a day with those fools again?" Shook his head. "God, but they're a dull and hopeless lot."

She shrugged.

"It's your job," she said. "Anyway, you were grateful enough when you first got the position."

He smiled that secret smile again.

"That's true," he agreed. "But I'm sure Napoléon's gratitude for his early chances didn't hold him back later. You have to see things as they are."

"What does Napoléon have to do with anything?"

He shrugged and picked up a sheet he'd been working on.

"Just a figure of speech." he muttered.

"Why don't you open the drapes and let some light in here?" She went over and jerked back the curtains. Stood there staring across the snowy campus glittering under a cloudless, crackling sheen of blue sky. Looked at the soft gray stone buildings, the steeple on the hill, skaters on the river.

He blinked at the sudden brightness and shielded his eyes. Went on reading and humming under his breath.

"There's a new time coming," he said, at length, and

she couldn't tell if he was reading it, "which will put an end to mediocrity forever."

"The clock still says eleven today," she remarked. She kept staring into the dazzling landscape. "Are you bored with me, Kurt?"

He glanced up. Seemed to weight her mood. Laid the paper aside.

"What's this?" he asked her, carefully, she thought.

"Something's happening," she said.

"To what?"

"To us."

He frowned. Reached for a cigar. Then a match. A new habit, she thought. She smelled the brief sulfur reek, then the irritating sting of smoke. She didn't turn, eyes filled with bright reflections.

Something else he picked up from his new friends. He knows I hate it.

"I don't know what you mean," he said, quite automatically, they both realized.

That's right. That's the husband's next, inevitable remark, she was thinking. Sighed.

"Minna?"

She shook her head.

"I always hoped we would have a family," she said.

"Well," he responded, shifting the cigar from hand to hand and studying her, trying to gauge how serious this might become. "Well, why not? In time."

"Ah, Kurt," she murmured, "I never expected this . . ." She lightly touched the cold glass and watched her body heat leave the steamy shape of her hand briefly on the windowpane. Watched it fade . . . She heard him stand up.

Next, she knew, he'd take her by the shoulders and kiss her forehead, thinking all the while of whatever it was he always thought about that now and then distilled into remarks about Napoléon and so on.

He did. And said:

"I love you dearly, Minna."

She wrinkled her nose slightly at the tobacco.

"Do you, Kurt?"

He nodded.

"How can you doubt me?" he wondered.

"Then what is it?" She searched his face, his pale eyes. "What, Kurt? What?"

"Nothing," he protested. "I've been active. What do you expect from me? You're a good wife."

She looked down as she disengaged herself.

"I regret I ever married," she said softly, flatly. Turned back to the window, the sparkling winter day.

He chuckled.

"We could have lived in sin," he suggested. Kissed the side of her head.

"Maybe that would have been more exciting," she replied, "for you."

"You're exciting enough for me," he said. She heard him relighting the cigar and rattling papers. "But I'd better get going . . . I'll be back later . . ." Rattle, scrape, creak of the chair. ". . . later, for supper. I'll . . . I'll get loose from those fools as soon as possible . . ."

"Yes," she said inertly.

She heard him pause. Probably was studing her again, she decided. Making sure she wasn't about to get hysterical. Just be calm until he was out of hearing and what did he care? That was marriage.

"Are you all right now, darling?" he asked.

She nodded.

"Of course," she said, not looking at him. She didn't want to look. Everything was blank. He was blank. Marriage was blank.

"Good," he said. She heard him inhale deeply and head for the door.

Shut her eyes. Then reopened them. Heard his steps in the hall. The front door opening, muffled voice calling back into the house:

"I'll be back soon, my dearest."

And the door shut.

She couldn't even weep. She didn't even *not* love him. Just blankness, grayness, dullness. She could sense his relief to be outside.

XI
(APRIL 1945)

Damp, gray dawn. A dense fog rolled everywhere, yellowish, mixed with drifts of smoke from the smoldering forest.

The duke (Renga) still followed the dirt road, walking steadily, soot-black, singed, and nude to his silk socks and expensive, battered shoes, swinging the three-foot tree branch.

He had slept briefly just before dawn. He'd wakened suddenly, at first light. Stared nervously around at the blank, shifting mists. Remembered himself for a moment or two . . .

I must have blacked out. Where are my clothes?

Got quickly to his feet, the blood pounded in his head and his identity blurred . . . he swayed, and was back in the Dark Ages. He smiled grimly. *These fogs may be that wizard's work.* His deadly enemy might be hoping to screen himself from just revenge.

As he walked now he prayed, murmuring:

"Dear God Almighty, maker of heaven and earth, grant me strength and power to overcome this cruel monster who is possessed by the black beast of deepest hell, who is the very spawn of the anti-Christ. Dear God, bring his plans to confusion, his ends to blindness and uttermost defeat!" Crossed himself. "Amen."

Thunder, he thought, as muffled, echoing booms rattled hollowly through the hills. *Odd sounds, methinks.*

The flat, percussive bangings were totally unfamiliar. And then the crackling of small-arms fire not too far away. After listening a few moments he put it down to more magic and went on thinking how he still needed armor and a sound horse. Beyond that, he believed, God would guide him. After all, he was an adept of the Holy Grail. The wizard knew this well and hated him for it. He said they

were weaklings, the Grail knights, and that the Christ spirit
was a lie and would degenerate them into women.

He was hungry now, too. Not much hope of finding
anything when only a few glisteningly damp feet of ground
showed in any direction. Well, he'd keep on straight, and
the way would eventually open for him. These mists, after
all, hid him as well as they hid things from him.

Frank Astuti expected any moment that this road
would lead him to doom. The trouble was, he didn't dare
stop or go back since he had no idea where either side
might be at this point. To say he was lost, he reflected, was
like saying there was sin in a whorehouse.

He'd decided he deserved this. It would be a lesson to
him. You don't go walking off following a lunatic who was
probably already blown into so many pieces they'd have to
bury him with tweezers and a spoon.

He marched along and shook his head now and then.
Plus, it's foggy all the time. One thing about war, he
meditated, it made the Bronx seem good. Made him
homesick for a place where he was *bored to the fucking point
of insanity.*

He was sort of praying for cigarettes now.

*If He sent that manna in the fucking Bible why don't He send
me a fucking smoke?*

He strained his sight into the mists, fruitlessly. A
vague, sourceless glow everywhere. The sky was barely
brighter than the earth.

I'm probably going backward anyway . . .

The duke left the road and went a few steps into the
woods. The trees weren't burned here and he decided to
look for roots he could eat in the underbrush. Squatted
down and dug his fingers into the wet loam, probed and
sniffed.

(1914)

Rudolph Renga felt oppressed and tired. He stood by
the floor-to-ceiling window staring down into the snowy,
festively lit street. Christmas shoppers flowed along, three
stories below, some with bundles, some with small fir trees

over their shoulders, boys zipping snowballs at top-hatted men.

A mellow nostalgia came over him. He remembered childhood Christmases: the morning thrill, the excitement of racing downstairs to the tree, the stacked presents, the rich pine tang, the rooms filled with stove heat.

In the glass the bright, noisy royal reception behind him showed dim and remote. He saw the vague forms milling, drinking, snacking, under dull chandeliers in a hall rent with blots of darkness, hollowed by the outside world. There was the tall bulk of Moltke (who'd invited him) beside the gesticulating Kaiser himself, dwarfed by the towering ceiling and distant, fading walls. Massed dignitaries, he observed, in absurdly over-trimmed uniforms and regalia that made them seem like actors in a pageant.

He refocused on the clear, sparkling night outside and felt another moment of nostalgia: a dozen or so boys were having a battle. One group held a high snowbank and the others, ducking around carriages and horses and pedestrians, charged across the street, looping their snowballs on the run while the defenders poured a steady fire down on them. Covering their faces, ducking, staggering, they tried to mount the icy slope but the barrage was too intense. One, then another, attacker broke and fell back, a boy, hit squarely in the face and head by a massed volley, toppled and rolled to the bottom.

They're getting rough out there, he thought.

"Dr. Renga," someone was saying behind him. He half-turned, recognized Madame Moltke with a young woman by her side, an impression of honey-colored skin, dark hair, dark eyes, a slim poised figure. An impression too of seriousness with humor. The contradiction (or was there one?) took his attention.

"Madame," he was saying, glancing back at the window, caught between politeness and interest; the dazzle and conversational roar of the room and the silent view below where things had clearly gotten out of control: some of the boys were fighting hand-to-hand now, struggling, rolling, and punching in the spill of street and shoplight, their shadows wild and exaggerated, flashing over the snow and buildings.

Pulled his stare back to the two ladies.

"Is something wrong, Rudi?" Madame asked, concerned. "Outside?"

He shook his head.

"Not really," he murmured. "Just some boys playing."

He glanced back again: One seemed to by lying on his face, the others, in a loose circle, looking down at him. A few passersby were stopped, watching. He turned back to the glittering room. Blinked.

"May I present Dr. Renga," Madame was saying. "Contessa Eunice Malverde."

"Charmed," he said.

"By the window?" the contessa wondered.

"I warn you, Rudi," Madame said, watchfully amused, "Eunice prides being interesting above propriety."

"Being proper comes from owning property," the young Italian lady observed. "Eh? As a matter of fact, if you . . . ah, *ammucchiàre*, you know, *pile up* enough even your outrages become models of conduct." She smiled.

"I imagine she has read Karl Mark," the older woman commented.

"Marx" corrected the contessa.

"Exactly," agreed Madame. "You prove my point."

"A melancholy fellow," Renga added. "He thinks all history boils down to real estate dealings."

"Does it now?" the pretty contessa asked, watching him from under arched eyebrows.

Renga was amused. Glanced around at the pomp and flashing gold and mirrors, babble and banked lights of that immense room.

Madame von Moltke was fascinated by the two of them. Smiled warmly.

"This is a peculiar conversation," she announced. "But I think you two like each other."

"Are they both connected?" the contessa asked.

"Inevitably," the older woman said.

"I meant the conversation and the affection."

Renga chuckled.

"So did I, my dear," Madame replied. "Has it progressed so far as affection already?"

"According to you," said the girl with a shrug. Touched the tip of her sharp nose with the tip of her golden fan. Glanced covertly at Renga who had just glanced through the window again as they began to drift out into the room's hubbub. Squinting past the reflections (harder to do from this distance), he saw a crowd had collected though most of the boys seemed to be gone. One was still lying there, a dark, stretched-out stain on the snowbank, limbs flung wide as if to receive an embrace.

"We'll be at war soon, you realize," Madame was saying.

"Are you in the army?" the contessa asked, and after a moment Renga realized she meant him.

It was something he didn't think about. He blinked and frowned into the glitter.

"Yes," he murmured. "The reserves."

The contessa took his arm. Her scented hair sweetly stung his indrawn breath.

"This next conflict," some man was saying, "will be tremendous in scope."

XII

At about the same moment, across the city where all the lanes sloped toward the riverdocks, Paula Hitler and August Kubizek were plowing through the uncleared, dim alleyways where men clustered in baggy overcoats around bonfires or crouched in doorways, the iron cold closing down on them. Bundled-up street prostitutes paced, wrapped to the eyes so that they resembled (he idly thought) strange women of some desert tribe.

"My God, Gustl," Paula said as they read the sign: *Gumpendorfer Gasse.* "He lives here?"

Kubizek thrust his hands deeper into the coat pockets, tilted his head into the shifting wind. Shrugged.

"This is the address I had," he said. He turned and accosted a scarecrow of a man who was shuffling past, feet wrapped in rags, a bent stick (for a cane) slipping on the street surface. "Excuse me," he said. The man didn't react. "Excuse me . . . you there!"

Finally the fellow turned his long head. The eyes were

beaten blank but with a flicker of sullen, undying anger in them as if his existence had always been partly sustained and warmed by a slumbering rage. Kubizek barely took note. He was used to such things. You had to get used to them among the poor. The dormant furies of the broken and outcast.

"Excuse me," he repeated. "Where is the 'Home for Men' located?"

"Hah," the man said. He was the one Hitler had fought with in the lodging house. "You can follow in my steps and you can't fail to come there soon enough. Or, if you be impatient, run three doors ahead and climb the stairs." Then turned and went back into himself.

"But wouldn't he have written?" Paula asked Kubizek, who slogged along, shivering steadily. "I sent him a note insisting he come home for Christmas this year." She stared, rambling a little. "Angela wanted him to see Geli . . . his little niece . . . She's very fond of him . . ."

The scarecrow man went wobbling on, feet crunching, stick clacking and skidding.

"Let's get going," Kubizek said.

She was staring up at the door of the flophouse.

"But how could Adolf live in such a place?" she asked.

The hostile man was now laboring up the stairs, clutching the rail, rags billowing out in the gusts. When he opened the door, the wind groaned in the vestibule.

"Let's get to a cafe, at least," August said, tugging at her arm. "I'm rattling in my boots."

She searched his face, chapped hand gripping his lapel.

"Do you know something?" she demanded. "What are you holding back? Why didn't he answer my letter? Gustl? Please. Talk to me now?"

He tugged her along the snow-silent street now. Down an alley into a square, luminous, deserted.

"I know nothing," the musician told her.

"I have dreams . . . terrible dreams about him . . . That's why I had to come here."

"Dreams?"

"I wake up sweating and weeping . . . I feel sick . . ."

"What kind of dreams?"

"I see him held prisoner in terrible places . . . dark,

with green light and terrible shadows like . . . like wings beating."

"Maybe your bed is too soft," he suggested, hugging himself and bending into a sweep of wind.

"No, no," she insisted, "these are portents."

"Bavarians are all superstitious. It's in the blood. Your brother too."

"It means something," she insisted. "When did you see him last?"

"God, the air itself will soon freeze!" Teeth chattered. "I'll take you to your hotel." He turned his back to a violent cut of wind as they crossed out into an open square. Their coats flapped and fluttered. "I have a rehearsal tomorrow. My hand will be—"

"Gustl!" She squinted into the dark, freezing wind.

"A few weeks ago. We went out and drank beer. He even got drunk which he never does . . . We both did . . ." Teetered. "It's all ice underneath here . . ." She clung to his arm as the wind veerings pawed at them. "He ran in the street and kept flapping his arms and I told him he wasn't much of an eagle so he said he'd be a wolf instead . . . we were pretty far gone by then . . . He was in good spirits, I think, for him." They backed along now, faces starting to numb under the stinging. They huddled together out in the huge, empty, frozen space. She felt spasms of shivering under his bulky coat. One of the dreams was like this: she was trying to find her brother in a vast, deserted city and everywhere she went there were stiff corpses of men, women, infants; street after street and she had to climb over the dead in places where they clogged the way . . . "Then he shouted, you know how loud he can shout . . . he shouted that he had held the *spear* in his hands, whatever that is, and has seen the future . . ."

She pictured him, intense, insistent . . . *Always so dramatic . . . What is life doing to my brother? . . . He's so unhappy . . .*

"I told him he must have been feverish," Kubizek said, blowing on his hands.

"No," she said, trying not to lick her cracking lips. "Our family is like that. What they dream comes to pass."

He shook his head. Teeth clattered, shaking his voice that the wind seemed to suck away.

"Nonsense," he told her. "Listen, Paula, Adolf was—"

She slipped and leaned into him, clutching his coat. "*Ach*," she said.

"Listen," he said, shielding his eyes, staggering. "I think he was ill . . . he told me he talked to spirits—" he waved his free arm—"they *appeared* to him! He said he was promised the future . . . I told him, Paula, I said, Adolf, go home for a while, take a rest, it's been a strain and—"

She screamed and flung herself into him and they both skidded, dancing sideways, flails of snowdrift tearing at them, and then with a shock of terror he saw it was a few steps ahead, a nightmare demon glaring from a face of shadows, fangs glinting in the gaped, dark maw thrusting itself up from a mound of ice, snowghosts swirling and whooshing . . . a moment later he realized it was the head of a large wolflike dog, frozen, the faint light gleaming in the iced eyes.

"It's all right, Paula," he soothed, leading her past, shielding her with himself, teeth clicking. "Come . . . it's all right . . ."

XIII
(APRIL 1945)

The duke (Renga) was back on the road which had just ended at a blasted bridge. He could barely see the far shore, a gray sketch of rocky embankment. The fog rose like chill smoke from the steely river.

He paused, then waded in. Was amazed at how the bridge seemed to be torn to pieces as if a giant hand had smashed it. The water was cold but not unbearable. Out in the middle it was only waist deep. He sloshed along, club over his shoulder. He was sucking the meat from one of the roots he'd dug from the loamy ground.

He heard the strange sounds again: rattling bangs and pops, fog-muffled. Now and then he heard faint hummings overhead almost, he felt, like bees. He had no conception these were stray shots from a savage clash half a mile away.

He kept remembering his family chained to the charred poles, the burnt flesh and dark blood . . . Murdered by that foul king! He gritted his teeth in his blackened face. Snarled and smashed the tree limb onto the water with a sharp crash. "To thy grief!" he hissed.

His shoes squished as he went on around the next turning. The sun's disk showed now and then, fairly high up in the morning. The mists were brighter. The river had washed him pale white to about the navel. The rest remained sooty except for his hands and wrists.

By the side of the road he noticed a strange thing: two wheels with metal spokes joined together by mysterious gleaming tubing and disks and chains. Was it an instrument of torture? It stank of grease and God-knew-what. There was a man tangled in it all twisted and broken, which had given him the idea it was a new rack and wheel arrangement. He considered putting on the odd clothing except it was soaked stiff with dried blood. The man had certainly been shattered. He picked up his mushroom-shaped helmet and set it on his head.

This is, at least, a start toward proper gear, he told himself.

A little later, Frank Astuti, happy that the road seemed to be heading toward the sporadic firing he kept hearing (he wasn't sure if the fog was a blessing or curse), passed the same spot and noticed, with mild interest, the shattered German soldier tangled in his motorcycle. He went over and poked into the fellow's pockets looking for at least a cigarette. Found nothing. Cursed. And there was no liquor in his kit. Recursed. Went on.

Not too far ahead the duke stopped short, startled. A figure was floating in the mist ten feet higher than his head. For a moment the surprise brought him back to being Renga and he thought:

I keep blacking out . . . where am I now? . . . What's happening to me? . . .

And then moved forward again, club upraised, back in the past.

"A demon," he muttered and then saw it was a man in shorts hanging by the neck from what he took for a marvelously worked gibbet, smooth and round as a ship's mast with crosstrees near the top. Lines ran from it out into the mists and a little further on he passed another . . . then another. They seemed to be spaced evenly along the road and connected by the lines which made no sense. And each with a body, which, naturally, was no surprise.

Out of the shifting gray loomed a new shape; a low-roofed stone house. Looked like a peasant farmer's place. Perhaps he was getting near . . . He sensed he was in the right region. Could feel the dark pressure of the wizard's presence somewhere ahead. The strangeness of the landscape, he knew, was caused by the enemy's dreaming loosening and blurring ordinary reality.

He went up the rutted walk to ask directions. Stopped and stared at the picture pasted to the wall. Even though the fog had thinned he still had to get close and then his stomach seized up with fury and reflex fear when he recognized the portrait.

A wonderful likeness, in truth, he said to himself. *Though the subject lacks something . . .*

The wizard's face, though the mustache was oddly cropped. The unmistakable eyes glowed back at him, thin, grim lips set with chill, mystic ferocity.

He was bent close, staring at it, when the old woman peered around the doorframe. He was trying to read the script but the lettering was strange and, he mused, he was no monk.

"Go away from here," the woman said, startling him.

The scene swirled, changed.

I am Rudolph Renga, he thought.

"Where am I?" he asked her. He had a confused memory of where he had just been: through dim passageways, scuttling, hunched, with massive figures slinking around him at the outskirts of his vision in an undersea-colored scene; his armor clinkings echoed in the damp hollows and pits . . .

"Go away," she said, "murdering your own people! You miserable soldiers . . . Go!"

He staggered and lost himself again. His speech fell back into long-lost times.

"Old woman," he said.

"Disgraceful how you show yourself," she said. "Have you no shame? Go away, go away from here, murderer!"

"I am no murderer," he declared, "though a murdering fiend I seek."

She squinted at him and finally realized he must be mad. His half-black body, the stick and helmet, strained credulity.

"Poor soul," she said, "the SS will make short work of you, I think. You better hide someplace until the Americans come."

He blinked at her. A stern frown creased his lips. He pointed at the poster.

"Serveth thou him whose likeness is displayed on your hut?" he demanded.

"Never fear," she replied. "Down it comes once it's safe. You're not so mad as you seem."

"Which way from here to his foul lair?"

She shrugged, bending up her shoulders. She was quite stooped.

"Goebbels says he's in Berlin," she informed him. "If you can believe that." She narrowed one eye. "I say the Führer's in Switzerland. That's what I say."

No doubt she would have said more.

"Point out the way," he cut in.

"Take the train," she said, "when the war's over."

He raised his fist.

"Tell me, peasant!" he roared at her. "Stop mouthing mad nonsense!"

She drew back.

"Eastward," she said. "Eastward. God pity me but here I stand talking to a naked lunatic," she muttered.

"Toward the rise of the sun," he murmured.

She said no more but stared in disbelief as the madman suddenly urinated into his cupped hands and smeared the pungent brine over the portrait, chanting:

"May the dogs of hell lick thy foul blood. May the fat worms consume thy eyes. May nothing thou plantst take root. May thy offspring be monsters and rend thee to death!"

Then he advanced on her and kept her from shutting the door.

"Leave me," she croaked. "I—"

"Food," he said. "Give me food and drink, woman."

Then turned around as three men in black uniforms

and black helmets, blurred to shadows by the mist and his
bad eyes, seemed to have materialized behind him. The
woman slammed the door and darted inside. He stood
facing them.

(1914)

At the reception Renga was studying the odd man who
was standing between Moltke and the Kaiser. He seemed
drab and tentative in his civilian dress clothes, against the
gold, red and white, and blue military glitter. He had pale,
remote eyes and a snub nose. His German had a faintly
foreign, not accent, but style. Very subtle. Was he a Dane? A
Swede? A blanched fellow with a runny looking face. He
was talking and the circle of officers around him seemed
particularly attentive.

"That's Chamberlain," Madame von Moltke told him.

"An Englishman?"

"He wrote a famous book," she replied. "My husband
swears he's the German Rasputin."

"Your Kaiser seems impressed," the contessa put in.

My Kaiser? he thought, *What a strange idea.* Because in a
time of religious patriotism he felt no sense of being
anything but flesh and blood. He didn't feel the German of
his father or the Spanish-Russian of his mother. Nations
were ghostly lines on maps, habits of eating, kinds of
weather, various noises made with the mouth.

"What's so amusing, Doctor?" the contessa wondered.
"May it be shared?"

He shrugged.

"I was thinking that if you raised a German-born child
as a Russian he'd probably be willing to die for his Czar."

"That amuses you?" she asked.

"No," he said. "Not in the least."

He turned his head to try and focus on the conversation—or rather, monologue—going on a few steps away.
He watched the Kaiser listening, nodding his sharp face
repeatedly.

". . . therefore," the Englishman was saying, "because
of their greater ability they must accept a greater *responsibility.*" The Kaiser nodded agreement, lips grim. He kept
his withered arm close to his body, Renga noted. Spun his
monocle nervously with the other hand. It flashed the light

in a cold glitter. ". . . technological skills combined with poetic feeling plus tremendous vitality make Germay the true center of the Western world."

"What of Britain?" Moltke rumbled.

The Kaiser shook his head, eyes sharp and mocking. "That's because you're a great-grandfather, Helmut," he told him. "You remember the Englanders as they *were*."

Needlessly loud laughter greeted this sally of imperial wit, Renga observed. Wilhelm was noted for his power to offend everyone and anyone.

"The English," Chamberlain explained, nervously didactic and prophetic, "are a great people, but lack the method and mystical fervor of the Germans."

"Exactly!" cried Wilhelm, stamping one gleaming boot on the slick tile floor. "That's why we're not afraid of war. If war comes, we'll win it! And build a better Europe when we're done."

Of course, Renga thought, *others will have to die. A small matter.*

"You don't have to be so gloomy, Grandfather," Wilhelm said, clapping the older man on the shoulder. "Greatness, as this man says, is our duty."

"War, Your Highness," Moltke replied, "in the event, is not so jolly."

"God knows," His Highness affirmed, sincerely, as far as Renga could determine, "no one but a fool or a weaponmaker welcomes war. But, I repeat, if come it must—" he stamped his boot again—"we'll show the rest of them how it's done!"

Several of the women clapped their hands. A number of officers gave little cheers while most contented themselves with vigorous nods.

Moltke had moved a step nearer Renga and extended his hand to usher him forward.

"Dr. Renga," he said, "I present you to His Majesty."

Wilhelm nodded to Renga's bow.

"Do you know Chamberlain here?" he asked.

"No, Your Majesty." To Chamberlain. "How do you do, sir." He felt slightly absurd scraping through these senseless forms.

The contessa had joined the group, and the ruler and general acknowledged her as Chamberlain leaned his head forward and spoke to Renga.

His eyes were too bright, Renga thought, with flickers of fear in them. Strange. He remembered a few things he'd heard: the man was an English historian who'd become a German citizen out of fanatical conviction.

"Herr Renga," he said in a dry, somehow forced voice, "the general tells me you are a mystic of sorts?"

Renga shrugged.

"Of sorts," he replied, thinking: *This is one of those great men who ask questions to answer them . . .*

"What sort, Doctor?" the contessa put in. The Kaiser and general were listening now, too. "Do you believe in sprites and spirits, or merely God?"

The Kaiser laughed loudly at this. Nodded.

"God," he remarked, "is a very nice rabbit to pull out of your hat." Laughter. "But what do you answer, sir?" Kaiser Wilhelm loved acrimony.

"Can you see radio waves?" Renga asked. Paused, then: "Not everything is caught in the net of your senses, Contessa."

"You say God is radio waves?" She smiled, but not, he noted, maliciously. He sensed she was just testing his ideas. There were chuckles going around, except Chamberlain's face showed nothing but nervous, burning avidity.

"They should put receivers on the altars," Wilhelm troped, heavily.

Renga laughed and quipped, half-serious so she'd know that too:

"First tune in your heart, hm?"

"Bravo," said Madame von Moltke.

"Yes, yes," Chamberlain added nervously, seeming compelled to be speaking. "I know all about the invisible worlds." His hands clasped and unclasped. "I've witnessed it, after all. Face to face, soul to soul. It is a terrible confrontation!"

"Terrible?" Renga was curious.

"We are hemmed in by unseen terrors," the other explained. The haunting fear brightened like blown embers in his restless stare.

"But, sir," Renga insisted, "there's such wonder and beauty and—"

Chamberlain half-smiled. Nodded and shook his head at the same time as if opposites united in him, poured energy through his body. The Kaiser spun his monocle and raised an imperial eyebrow.

"It's a dark dream, I tell you," the Englishman said, stare flat, yet voracious.

Renga blinked and it seemed time was suspended between each eye-flutter. He somehow *saw,* as if the room had faded, thinned: and seeming to push through the melting substance was the flaming, cloudy bulk, a burning, bleeding storm glinting fanglike lightnings, rending forward, groping for him . . . and then his next blink seemed to disperse it and the noisy, bright reception rushed back into the brief vacuum of his senses.

"Are you all right, *Dottóre?*" the contessa asked, touching his arm.

"What?" he murmured. "Yes . . . Of course . . ."

"You went pale."

"I was just thinking . . ."

"Maybe thinking doesn't agree with you."

"Man," Chamberlain was saying, "has to master the terror. Harness the terror." He kept up his nodding and head-shaking. Renga thought, abstractly, that his skull might simply roll from his shoulders if he kept moving it like that. "Ride the terror! Man must rise in triumph over the dark, primal forces of time's nightmare!"

Renga blinked rapidly. Felt a little numbed. But the shadow and flame were fading from his mind.

"Yes!" the Kaiser was saying fervently, chin tilted up, lips set under the sharp mustaches. "Yes!"

"No," Renga heard himself say so softly that only the woman beside him could have heard.

"Salvation," Chamberlain was continuing, "will come from the German race, with sword and prayer!" He actually (to the shock of the entourage) took the Kaiser by the withered arm and gripped the floppy sleeve. Saliva gleamed at the corners of his mouth. "A leader of divine fire will ride in the forefront, all-highest." His snub nose was aimed into his ruler's face. ". . . all-highest, even if you are not the one, in the end, with the power, yet He will come. The German race will bear him forth from the womb of themselves!" He staggered. Renga could see the whitened fingers gripping into Wilhelm's sleeve as Chamberlain's eyes rolled his head jerked rapidly back and forth.

"*Dólce María,*" the contessa murmured, "but what is this?"

As Chamberlain staggered he dragged the Kaiser with him across the slick floor to a chorus of horrified gasps. They were so stunned that no one moved immediately. Servants gaped. Officers and ambassadors stared and frowned. Then a pair from the general staff, a red-faced older man with bristly gray hair and a skinny lieutenant, rushed and skidded forward to intervene followed by others several steps behind. Wilhelm struggled to keep his footing as Chamberlain whirled him around and around in a frenzied kind of waltz, giving out a high-pitched, continuous, inhuman little cry. For a blink-length Renga thought he glimpsed a cloudy, shapeless dimness around them shot through with the candle flames from the wall beyond. Chamberlain yanked his ruler in a violent circle, gripping him by the crippled arm which looked ludicrous stretched out to its slight length. The Kaiser struggled and raged in pain, cursing wildly. The first two officers arrived, caught on, and a moment later were spinning around too across the glassy surface in a glittering jingle of braid and medals as they tried to save the ruler from his spasming philosopher; others threw themselves into it and it became a mad maypole with Wilhelm in the center and then, with a terrible shriek like (Renga thought) a ravaged machine, Chamberlain whirled free, spun, and crashed flat, unbalancing the rest who went down like a scrimmage and, surprisingly, Renga didn't find it funny. He wasn't sure why not.

Moltke just stood there, brooding, massive, immobile, lower lip pushed out, arms folded, seeming to look on in great sorrow. Renga half-expected him to weep at any moment as the philosopher, lost in his racking fit, thrashed and foamed around the feet of the horrified nobility.

XIV
(APRIL 1945)

Nurse Feldbach went down the steep stairs into the heart of the bunker, holding the folder of reports with one hand and the banister with the other. She'd gotten through the shelling again, crossing over from the underground hospital, racing through the Reich Chancellery garden (a shattered moonscape of rubble) and finally descending past the SS guards into the musty, stale, and now (she noted for the first time) urine-smelling interior. The idea of being trapped and suffocating down there appalled her. This, she thought, was the government, living like trolls in a cave.

She passed a long table where Frau Hitler sat with two other young ladies and a few officers. They were drinking beer and eating cake. As she passed down the corridor she heard the Führer's wife saying:

"Berchtesgaden was really the most beautiful place in the world. The views were so breathtaking. Really, it's impossible to describe the . . ." her voice was muffled to nothing as Feldbach went down the musty corridor.

A stocky man she didn't recognize passed her.

Drunk, she thought with disgust. *God help us when the Russians get here.*

She frowned, wrinkling her pale, chubby cheeks. Even on the present Berlin diet, she'd remarked several times, she couldn't really lose weight. She thought she'd walked too far. There were no orderlies or guards down at this end, which seemed odd. Then she heard the chief surgeon's voice around the corner. The light bulbs dimmed and she winced at the touch of terrible darkness. The shells were letting up a little, though. The Red army was getting too close.

She turned the corner and stared with surprise into a narrow bathroom. The door stood open. Two men in black

110

uniforms were holding a lean, sleek, long-muzzled dog that didn't bark or growl but rather whined pitiously as Dr. Haase thrust a pair of pliers into its mouth and she had a vague idea that he was about to extract a tooth, which she knew was absurd and anyway, he wasn't even a dentist and this was, somehow, a greater shock than all the bloody bodies, the severed limbs that piled up like garbage from a meat factory in the operating room, because this animal was healthy and alive—its nails clicking and skidding on the white tile as it struggled and twisted its head—and had nothing to do with the human horror, slaughter, pain, and madness so she almsot screamed because she knew very well what they were really doing. She finally saw Adolf Hitler standing behind the three struggling men in his drab uniform with the single dull Iron Cross pinned to his chest, arm shaking, head jerking slightly, clasping his hands before him as he always did in public when not gesturing or posed.

The doctor withdrew the pliers and they all stepped back from the dog who frothed and briefly spasmed, vibrating rapidly, legs stiffened and kicking. Tossed its head and seemed to stare around once as if to take in the toilet seat, tile, sink, and the nervous-looking spectators. Then it flopped into stillness. Hitler just stared, expressionless. She knew this was his favorite dog, Blondi, and so she knew the meaning of what she had just seen.

Hitler's rumbling, strained voice rang hollowly in the little room.

"It seems very effective," he said. His left hand seemed to struggle to beat itself free from his right. "My God . . . I feel nothing anymore." The doctor was looking at him in silence. "I feel nothing."

The doctor was holding another one of the poison capsules in his fingers and for a moment she thought he was going to give it to the Führer. Then he slipped it into his pocket.

The two men stopped to take away the dog but Hitler spoke: "No! Everyone out! Do you hear?"

As she went back around the doorframe she glanced back and saw him standing there, staring down, and found herself thinking:

My God, if he weeps for that animal what would he do if he saw the city up there? Except she realized she meant *should*, not *would*.

The doctor looked at her and shrugged. The SS men leaned on the wall. No sound came from the bathroom. She wondered if he were cradling the dog, kissing it, or just staring. She wrinkled her nose. The foul air down here was stifling.

MUNICH
(1913–14)

Hitler looked around the lobby of the quiet, worn wood and rustically draped suburban inn. His hollow, blue-gray eyes concentrated the sparse lamplight and reflected the windy evening that filled the casement windows. Outside a few stars showed as the woods sank into dimness. As a March storm blew up, branches tossed and rocked against the cloud-streaked, chilly sunset. A few raindrops already spattered into the glass.

Two men, puffing their cigars furiously, were immersed in a confidential conversation across the rough-beamed room.

They look like they're on fire, he thought. He hated smoke. It always burned his bad lung. He shifted restlessly in his seat. Why had he bothered to come here? He should go back to the city. Catch a late train. Have some cold supper at that cafe near his new rooming house . . .

Wasting my time . . .

Stood up, brushing off his trousers, straightening his dark jacket. Shifted indecisively from foot to foot. Tapped one brightly polished shoe on the carpet.

He realized he was about to get depressed, sink into morbid realism. Ask himself how he dared dream so high, based on what? A few predictions, hallucinations? . . . Tried to force the mood aside.

Katerina Plutsky was crossing the lobby, smiling, looking him up and down.

"Quite the dandy," she said. Her hair, he noticed, had been rinsed reddish. She stood there, big and solid, in a black and red print dress. "Your fortunes seem to have already turned."

He made a deprecatory gesture and immediately affected quiet dignity the way he imagined a man of destiny would.

"Hardly a dandy," he said. "An aunt died." Chuckled through his long, vaguely beaked nose. "She'd forgotten to alter her will and so her money went to my dead mother and so to me. You should have heard their lawyer rage! It gives me a certain satisfaction to think that if the soul survives she may look down—"he smiled—"or rather *up* to see how I've been profited against her dearest wishes."

"Your gratitude would move her deeply," Katerina said. "It's unfortunate, what family feeling comes to, more often than not."

"The ironies of providence," he remarked, "never cease to surprise and impress me."

"I'm pleased you arrived. I—"

"But don't you remember?"

"Remember?"

"You predicted this. From the hand." He held his palm up to her and struck it with his forefinger. "The second time I saw you." He smiled and nodded. "This fact has had a decisive influence on my present thinking."

He'd gone back within two weeks of that first night when she'd found him wandering in the snow, shaking with fever. He'd been drawn back. At first, he'd told himself, it was curiosity: how did she know things about his past? Then the idea of foretelling the future . . . He never really admitted that sex might have been a factor. He simply believed that, contrary to his nature, he'd let himself have an extra drink of wine there and that would lead where it led . . . And at the climax he always found his mind became very vivid (with images as bright and portentous as when asleep), and in a spasm of physical bliss he would half-imagine things . . . amazing things . . . terrible things too . . .

"I don't recall," she said. "But I often forget much of what I say during a reading."

"All the same," he pronounced, "it has had an incalculable effect on my thinking."

He saw the occult as another threat to the materialistic conventionalists, the Bolsheviks, the Church who sought to conceal evidence of the mystical link between the shadowy, ephemeral individual and the eternal forces of time, of history. He stared at the cigar-smoking men for a moment thinking, peripherally, about the hopelessness of the dull, middle-class business mind. Considered how they lived (like his father) without ever looking into the shadows, unconscious of the terror and wonder of reality!

"Well," Katerina Plutsky said, easing into the stream of her purpose, "perhaps that's why I asked you here." He waited, watchful. "I sense something about you, Adolf Hitler. I did from the first. I want you to hear something."

"What?"

"A man. With a powerful and fascinating message."

"Here?"

"Tonight," she told him, nodding. "A talk. Downstairs."

"Ah. I hesitated," he said honestly, "because I was unsure of your motives, when I got your note."

She smiled, confidential, relaxed.

"Thought it was passion, hm?" Shook her head. "That was an old impulse. Anyway, I'm living with a poet now."

"I don't pretend to understand," he said, shrugging, "with any completeness, the fairer sex." He bowed slightly, from the neck only. "As I grow older, the mystery deepens." His slicked hair was cropped close and gleamed. He held his palm out to her. "But do you see if I die in battle?" he wanted to know.

She glanced at the hand and then away, without touching it. He clenched a fist.

"There's got to be war soon," he said fervently. His eyes shone. "It has to come." He nodded once. "It will clear the air."

"I don't believe you will die soon," she murmured.

As they spoke she walked him out of the lobby onto the deserted patio. They stood by a dry fountain, the centerpiece a snarling wolf at bay cast in cracked concrete, ghostly in the muted light. A scattering of last year's leaves, broken husks, lay in the basin.

He rested one foot on the rim. She folded her hands in

her fur wrap. A faint greenish and rose stain on the high
clouds still marked the sunset. The coming storm rattled
the woods and swirled the leaves in the fountain.

"Did you go and study the holy lance?" she asked
suddenly.

He pursed his lips. Reached and touched the wolf's
rough, brittle teeth. The tongue was split in half.

"Yes," he murmured. The wind gusted and spilled
through his hair, tugged at his clothes. Raindrop spattered.

He had stood there surrounded by the glitter of the
Habsburg treasures: stared at the crude spear with a space
in the head where a rough nail was bound by gold, silver,
and copper threads. She'd told him to go and see it; the
spear of Longinus, the holy spear, the spear of destiny. He
knew it was reputed to have been possessed by major rulers
and conquerors since the Roman centurion Longinus
supposedly struck Christ's mercy blow on the cross with it.
Standing there he'd felt a tremendous roar of energy
lifting him . . . and then it was as if he were wavering
between sleep and waking where dreaming washed over
him . . . images flowed, melted into one another, and he
reeled against the glass case where his dim, grayish
reflection floated featureless, hollow with the spearpoint in
his head . . . wavering, his brain insistent he was still ill,
hadn't been eating or sleeping . . . and then the reflection
was a dreamshape, tall, imperious-eyed, beautiful and
chilling . . . he'd wordlessly felt the message:

"Did anything happen?" she wanted to know.

He straightened up from the concrete fountain, not
looking at her. Chill rain rolled in on the gusts.

"Yes," he whispered, nodding, remote. "Something
happened."

He decided the famous man was a poor speaker. Far
too dry and precise. Yet, he grudgingly admitted, intense.
A tall, hawk-nosed, dark-eyed, cold-lipped fellow. He
found himself half-listening. Considered slipping out the
back in a minute or two.

A damned schoolteacher, he said to himself. *The great
Rudolph Steiner.*

Glanced around the low-ceilinged room. Perhaps two
dozen people on uncomfortable chairs, shifting, crossing

and uncrossing their legs, coughing, fidgeting, while the man under the hanging electric light sat very still, eyes never seeming to blink, voice certain and full of force.

Hitler noted Katerina wasn't present—unless she'd crouched down behind the back row of empty chairs. How did he get himself hooked into this? Look at these old fools! An aged man cupped his hand to his long, hairy ear to pick up (he thought) the ramblings of the lean man on the platform. Shook his head and smiled. What a crew! Hitler shook his head and smiled. A skinny woman, face like a stork, moved her lips as if repeating the mumblings she was hearing, to reinforce them for life.

Now the speaker's remote, far-focused stare seemed to be on him—no, just looking toward him, he realized.

He has eyes like an aviator, he thought. He remembered pilots he'd met in the war. *A gang of snobs . . .*

". . . for the Aryan," the man had just said. Hitler looked surprised and suddenly leaned forward a little.

What's this now? he wondered.

". . . but first, we have to investigate the origin of the term. It is not enough," the strong, almost soft voice said, "merely to say that the Aryan is the ideal but largely undiscoverable racial type related to the Indo-European. Nor to say he is a repository of certain cultural values. Nor merely related to Nordic-Germanic generalizable qualities . . ."

Hitler leaned all the way forward. The birdlike woman coughed thickly and he shushed her with a violent hiss. She glanced over with surprise.

"Is there truly a superior type of human being?—an evolutionary advance?—or, in spite of what common sense seems to suggest, are all beings equal?"

Of course, Hitler thought sourly, *the Hottentot beating his log drum is no doubt my equal.* He was amused. Perhaps this wasn't going to be such a wasted night after all.

The speaker shifted in his high-backed seat on the little platform. Cleared his throat. Tapped his notes with one long finger. The nail reflected the bright light with a glassy glint.

"So," he continued, "what does occult wisdom have to say about this question? What is the story of man's origin as read in the record of nature?"

Ah, thought Hitler, *the Akashic record of the Hindu.*

He knew about that. The composite consciousness of the earth said to enclose the globe like a magnetic field, recording everything, every event, word, thought, dream; the magnified soul of every living thing. *Fascinating* . . .

"Back before the rise of Atlantis," the speaker was saying with wonder and conviction, "before the Lemurian continent came to be . . ."

Possible, Hitler thought. *There's no way to definitely disprove it. Myth always has a factual basis.*

". . . the world was covered by a steaming sea where volcanoes raged and darkened the sky with cinder and smoke so that the earth was virtually formless and seething." He crossed his long legs the other way. "The highest intelligence was a fishlike, or eel-like, translucent creature, eyeless, earless, but with a single, crestlike psychic organ in its head which was otherwise just a mouth."

Fascinating, Hitler thought.

"With that organ it sensed others of its kind and remained in touch with the invisible worlds which were far more substantial to it than the physical." Cleared his throat. His almost fierce stare seemed aimed at Hitler again. "This creature was the primal form of sensitive intelligence." Set his legs straight beside one another. The single light bulb hanging above him sank his face into a mask of shadows whenever he tilted his head forward. "Beings from the higher planes of existence that later would be known as angels or celestial intelligences—the gods, in short—took substance, appearing to those creatures to teach them the upward evolutionary path, to inspire them to expand their strange consciousness, showing them auras of light that were beacons in the otherwise, unending, impenetrable, dreaming fog of that long-lost age. Some of those creatures fell back into slime, unable to endure the light . . . others moved forward on the road to humanity . . ."

Hitler was sitting rigidly upright. His hands trembled with excitement. The implications flooded into him: inspiring superbeings animated the most primal myths! It all fit! Some types decayed, some advanced, and some, like the Jew, were blind turnings on the path that clung to abnormal survival in defiance of nature.

He hardly was conscious of the lecturer.

". . . therefore, in the following age we find ourselves in the Lemurian period wherein—" He coughed and recrossed his legs, tilting his face into and out of the harsh electric light. Hitler now began to pick up the thread again. ". . . wherein man was not yet as we know him today. His body was supple, the bones elastic. The earth was shrouded in dense, tropical fogs. Volcanoes were everywhere. Wild jungles flourished; demonic, dragonlike creatures prowled. The man of this epoch lived with his psychic eye fully opened. The invisible world was still more real to him than the visible. He was only fully conscious in sleep. They still had more of a general race-consciousness, like bees or ants, in a sense . . ."

Hitler was concentrating now.

". . . than awareness as individuals." Coughed, dryly. Twice. A slight draft rocked the light fixture above him and his face went from stern fullness to dark hollow over and over . . . "This was a stagnant form and, in time, certain of these beings with more restlessness or personal energy ventured out of the sodden valleys into the rugged, volcanic highlands. There were the first who began the transformation to the true root race of the Aryan peoples. In the sun and open spaces their senses had to become keener . . ."

Hitler was rocking in his seat, hands locked together on his knees, gaze transported, seeming to keep hypnotic, unconscious time with the winking shadows on the speaker's face.

". . . they became the hard-muscled, sharp-eyed hunters. Runners. Fighters who progressively lost the psychic senses of their passive fog-bound brothers. Divine mysteries could no longer be perceived directly but were approached through ritual and totem"—cleared his throat —"therefore, from here on a new mankind emerged, more vital, tougher, and inventive . . ."

Yes yes yes, Hitler thought, exultant, *my God it's so clear . . . so clear! The eastern peoples are the direct result of the contemplative,* fellahin *fog-dwellers! Western man is born to be dynamic and fierce . . . to rule the rest.*

He shut and opened his eyes and realized there were tears in them. It fit. It fit. Everything.

". . . with the problem that he become too one-sided in his dependence and domination by the five senses. He tried to shape the whole world into that narrow, incomplete image so that, today, Western man suffers from a fanatical belief in mechanics, force, and a science that shrinks from the unknown, inner senses . . ."

Hitler was back with him at this point.

". . . a science that is not spiritual is no science at all. As religion became meaningless, nationalistic feelings and technology replaced belief in God. Once the inner eye is shut, the mind sinks into the mud of materialism . . ."

"Yes," Hitler muttered. The nearby woman with a storklike neck and nose glanced at him. "Yes . . ." He suddenly found himself on his feet, a kind of electricity crackling through him. He felt amplified, ten feet tall. "Sir," he cried, "what was the origin of the Jew? How did he come about?"

The lecturer stopped rocking and now sat with both feet firmly planted. Hitler now noticed Katerina across the room.

"You are ahead of me, young man," the speaker said.

"That's another trouble with Aryans, Professor," Hitler retorted, in fine spirits.

There were a few chuckles. He folded his arms. Waited a moment, then sat down again.

"The Aryan root-race," Steiner went on, "reached a peak with the Atlantean culture. The spiritual and earthly faculties were, for a time, in harmony. They possessed magical and scientific powers that made them seem like gods on earth." Cleared his throat. Coughed once, dry and rough. "Psychic and physical were fused in them."

Hitler saw images of towering buildings, pyramids of shadowed power, vast, sparkling flying ships, awesome-faced men and women . . .

"Amazing," he whispered.

"They held all secrets," the man on the platform said. They could visit other's worlds, foretell the future, read minds—yes, even control evolution, develop new forms of life. They hoped to improve on man, you see, crossed human and animal and ended producing monsters that peopled later myths and the dreams of generations: centaurs, hydras, gorgons, harpies . . . mutations that escaped control and survived for centuries in hidden places . . ." Clasped his hands over his knees. Hitler shut his eyes and swayed a little in his chair, seeing it, how it fit. ". . . some of this noble race mated with the hybrids, beast, and semibeast and further distorted the evolutionary plan—"

He was on his feet again, vacant, dreamy eyes flaming with fury, one hand cutting the air wildly.

"That's where the Jews came in!" he shouted.

The speaker sat up straight, watching Hitler as if with sudden recognition.

"What?" he responded.

"The Jews were obviously the offspring of degenerate matings! Don't you see?" He smiled. It was so clear he was awestruck by the insight. He could see the images: a golden, magnificent, godlike mother giving agonizing birth to a beast-engendered semihuman dwarf . . .

"The Jews," the lecturer said, shifting in his seat, "were the necessary bridge between Egyptian and Christian forms." His tone was dry and schoolmasterish which infuriated Hitler. "Just as today we are preparing for the passing of the Christian into the next Western cycle. In any case, anti-Semitism is meaningless because—"

The reason would never be known, as the young, harsh man let fly a thunderclap of words.

"Be still!" he yelled. Was everyone blind? "Look at the nature of the stagnation and decay all around us! Who are the leaders who suck the Aryan spirit down into the slime? Who profits? Turn over a stone and a Jew crawls out! The stockmarket, politics, the newspapers . . ." He swayed. In a moment these people would be on their feet, cheering the truth. He thrust out his chin and folded his arms. Waited in the stunned silence. Glanced around. Rudolph Steiner was standing up. He didn't look angry but rather (Hitler realized later) almost sad. Hitler felt uneasy.

"What's all this?" the old man with the hairy ears was asking a stout, expressionless woman with a tiny flowered bonnet set on her round head. His stork-faced neighbor was staring at Hitler.

"Why must you keep disturbing us?" she demanded.

He felt cold, then flushed. Fought an impulse to sit down meekly. Steiner was just looking at him as if he (somehow) knew him. He felt isolated. These people were obviously fools. For an instant he wanted to open his heart to them, explain how he'd suffered and learned his lessons in loneliness . . . Why was he always misunderstood? Hopeless; he was alone. Couldn't stay there and couldn't move. Sweated as the moments dragged in silence.

A man in the front row rose from the general blur and looked back at him. He wore some kind of uniform with gleaming brass buttons. He was big and bearded. "Are you finished?" he wanted to know.

Hitler suddenly jerked into motion as if rigged with invisible strings. That Steiner was clearly misguided. A victim of occult Jewish power. Yes. He locked his face into a scowl, not even voicing the *Damn you!* in his mind, whirling, jerky but fast, through the double doors, slamming through as the crowd began muttering among themselves.

The sounds were snuffed by the slammed doors as he almost ran, not letting himself feel, across the lobby and then into the stormy night. Not feeling as the wind and rain ripped at his face, stinging, cold . . . not feeling . . .

Katerina Plutsky had followed him to the entrance and saw the back of his dark suit vanish into the darkness beyond the streaky light from the inn windows. She stopped there, the wet wind tangling her hair as she stared into the blank night. The trees clashed and whooshed around her. She wanted to shout something after him—call him back, hold him, shake him—she felt pity, shock . . . and, she realized too, fear. She didn't know why but she felt very afraid . . .

XV
(APRIL 1945)

Commandant Fragtkopft was chilled, even in his woolen uniform, open at the neck. The morning was misty and gray.

You wouldn't know it was April, he thought, staring out over the rows of prisoners while a short noncom called the roll and checked off the names. The devil with anyone, he was still going to take the weak and aged and sick first. Things were going to be run decently here until the end. In a few minutes he would go down the line and make his selections. Whatever happened, after the war his records would speak for themselves and show he was no butcher or blind sadist like too many others, he thought, but a dedicated man trying to serve the larger interests of humanity. A radical surgeon in the most difficult operation in history. The hell with Himmler, when he came here he could take over himself! Nodded, his jowls quivering a little.

He began to pace along the line now, lost in his thoughts. The fog was so thick he could hardly see the rows of faded, wasted, wobbly men and women and children at the far end of the yard. Though he could smell the smoke, the charring meat, the towering stack itself was invisible.

He was near the end of the line, pointing with his gloved finger every few steps, the soldiers herding, helping, or ordering (according to age, sex, and condition) those selected into a separate line. At this point there was very little protest, just sighs and moans. If there could be an absolute limit to despair and suffering, one of his men had written in an intercepted letter, it would be found there.

He noticed an old woman trying to look spry. His eye was too practiced to be taken in. There was a time when this might have even bothered him; another when he would have been coldly amused; another time, perhaps with pity and fear; but today he just thought: *There's nothing for you to cling to* . . .

As he pointed one of them spoke directly to him. He blinked and frowned. What was this? Strictly forbidden. He searched the bony, wasted faces. Which one dared? The drifts of mist coiled among them like cold smoke. A woman stared. Her shaved hair was just growing back in a light fuzz, her eyes intent but not with the fear or hate he often saw or the more common hopelessness. No matter, no one could speak to him. This had to be kept very professional and impersonal. But as he strode on away he could have sworn she said:

"Kurt."

But he didn't pause to even find out. Afraid he'd hallucinated. His heart sped up. He took deep breaths. Sensed that if he once slipped he'd slide down and down into bottomless dark. Held himself, gritted his teeth, kept his gaze straight ahead as if the shift of an eyeball might dislodge him.

(1913–14)

Minna Fragtkopft couldn't believe she'd really gotten into this. She'd gone to her mother in the suburbs. Now they sat together in the dining room, sunset light streaky and rose-pale over the old woman's firm-lipped face and calm eyes that were the color of an autumn garden, Minna always thought, russet browns and faded greens.

"So what do I do, Mother? I'm perfectly miserable."

Her mother was munching a sweet cake, sitting plump and relaxed in the cushioned chair.

"The marriage comes first," she replied indirectly. "Doesn't it, Minna?"

Minna sighed.

"I would have thought so," she returned, distracted, staring out the window across the walled yard at the neighbor's bluish slate roof among the wintery trees. "But now I don't know anymore. Kurt is—"

"He's your husband," her mother said, setting down the remains of the torte on a gleaming porcelain saucer and licking the sugary stuff from the corners of her lips.

"Sometimes I think he's crazy."

"They're all crazy." Her mother shrugged with her hands over the polished table that shone like dark water. "Go along with his whims a little. What harm can it do? He'll come back to normal, never fear."

Minna was caught in a stare, watching the last light fade in the yard where she'd grown up. There was the massive tree overhanging the wall where she used to set her dolls up for tea. She sighed. She had known what her mother would say before she got on the train that morning. So she'd come just to hear it in person, to be able to say to herself, *I'll try my mother's advice.* Because she felt trapped and remembered she had always felt trapped. That's why she'd gone to college. That had been a fight. It was always easier to play with dolls and march in step.

"Kurt is quite intelligent," her mother said next. "No doubt you should give him your trust." Picked up the cake again, poised it near her ruddy lips. "Would you like more tea, child?"

She stared at the wall across the familiar walks and bushes that seemed softened by the twilight.

Was there ever such a life? . . . Remembered one summer when she was about thirteen, eating yellow-flavored ices under the soft-colored trees by the wall, sitting with dark-eyed, humorous Erika in a fine spray of morning sunlight. Erika poking her tickle-ribs and saying how she wished one of them were a boy so they could get married someday because who would want to live with a man who never knew what it was like to be a girl and then they laughed and mock embraced, kissed, totally relaxed . . . she remembered Erika's tart scent and the taste of the ices . . .

She smiled, remembering.

We had such easy joy, she thought. To walk in warm rain and not mind being wet and smell the turned earth in the gardens . . . to open your heart to your friend, without doubts. *After those years there was always a little dishonesty in everything* . . . In boys at formal dances and parties full of rustling gowns, unyielding-faced chaperones all moist, stifling lavender scent . . . even in intimacy after the boys mysteriously turned out to be men there was always the strain, the pattern of near-lies . . . She sighed, she imagined, for all the irreversible generations . . .

And two weeks later she was thinking: *All right, Mother, I'm trusting my husband, Mother. I'm being a good wife* . . .

They'd just left the street and headed down a steep, uneven flight of cement steps into the basement of a tremendous, block-sized apartment house. She followed her husband who followed the man in front who followed the several ahead of them.

The corridor was dim. Dusty bulbs spaced about fifteen paces apart lit the damp brick walls. The floor was cracked and slightly sunken in places. Dank and silent. She made out a faint, low moan that she decided was a generator because the floor hummed and vibrated slightly.

As they rounded a bend she smelled burning and thought how terrible it would be to be trapped down here. Streamers of bluish smoke drifted and whirled around the sparse lights. Then she recognized the tobacco tang.

Don't let this place affect your thinking, she told herself. *They're trying to create a mood. What's this now?*

They passed an open steel door that overlooked an immense chamber down below filled with huge, dim, hissing, and throbbing shapes lit by flickers of fitful flame and her heart jumped. A rush of hot air poured up and she realized it was a boiler room. Shook her head at herself.

Nerves. Next thing I'll be ready to believe all their supernatural nonsense!

They went on, down a cross corridor, followed a steep turn, then descended a long ramp. The tobacco smoke blew straight back into their faces.

"This is all too absurd," she said to Kurt.

"What's the matter now?" he wanted to know.

"What are we doing down here?"

"A meeting," he murmured, "I told you that."

"Of building porters?"

He glanced impatiently around at her.

"As a matter of fact," he stated, "one of our fellows is in charge of this place."

"In charge? Oh, fine, the superintendent."

"The manager."

"No doubt," she said sarcastically.

"Minna, please," he murmured. "You promised to be objective."

"I thought it was the other way around," she murmured.

She'd tried to keep her critical sense muffled during the preliminary meetings. With mixed results.

The group stopped in front of a blackened, buckled, rusty iron door. Now she saw the source of the smoke: the tall, rapier-mustached captain, long cigar atilt in his jaw, tugged the door open, a cloud of fumes gathered around his head.

The door stuck, scraped, then banged open with a squeak that sent a shudder and gooseflesh along her back. Like an animal cry, she thought.

They all went into the musty storeroom. Lanterns and candles were set on dusty tables and crates. She noticed, just within, a voracious, hawk-faced, dark woman sitting on an ancient spinet piano, as if about to sing while someone played the missing keys and snapped hammers.

"Looks like a big night, eh?" the captain remarked

confidentially to Kurt and Minna, tapping cigar ash into the floor's dark dust rolls. "Your wife has advanced rapidly. Congratulations. There's a chance that old Haushofer himself may turn up later on. The master himself." He crossed the big room to where Drecklicht sat in a massive armchair with one beveled leg missing so that it swayed slightly like, she thought, an eccentric rocker. Heaps of dusty, decayed furniture were roped and piled at his back and along the walls.

A plain white sheet was laid out in the center of the floor. Rickety chairs for the meeting were set in a loose circle around the room. They took seats and waited. Dry-faced Dr. Schatz sat beside her, grinning liplessly and nodding to himself from time to time as if it were a tic of agreement.

This is for my marriage, she told herself again.

"Why don't you have a child?" her mother asked as she stared out the window at the draining evening.

"I don't know," she replied listlessly.

"Is this an answer?" The older woman leaned across the table. "Don't you and Karl . . ."

"*Kurt,* Mama."

"Yes. Don't you—"

"No." Sighed. "I mean . . . sometimes . . ."

"Well, that's not good. That's not good."

"He'd rather go to meetings."

"Then you'd better go to meetings."

She thought she recognized other faces as the rest of the members drifted to their seats, except the candlelight was so streaked and blotted by shadows it was hard to be certain of features across the circle. She was internally bracing herself for another evening of interminable, obscure, and (she believed) utterly fanciful discussion and lecture about . . . well, what tonight? Astral travel? Demon raising? Ouija boards or weird forms of Darwinism? . . . the fourth dimension? . . .

Origin of Specious, she called it to herself. *Everybody loves evolution, it's a psychological need, but they never catch anything, much less themselves, in the act of evolving.*

She was squinting at a bald, dwarflike hunchback squatting up on a backless stool. He was talking from his perch to the man standing beside him, arms folded, whose face was mainly in darkness. His eyes flashed the candle-flame now and then and she was surprised by their almost catlike luminosity.

She felt a little shock of fear at what seemed an apparition floating through a doorway across the room. Seeming to drift down the aisle between the shadowy crates, broken tables, askew lamps, tilted chairlegs, shape-less tarpaulins. A massive, ghastly pale figure loomed up out of the darkness. Something, she felt, from half-dreams lost in childhood fevers.

Then the lumpy form passed through the ring of smoky light and squatted down with a grunt on the spread sheet. With a little start she recognized the gross medium from the meeting at her house, months past. The one who soiled her rug. The memory revolted her.

God, she thought, *and what are we in for tonight? How could he take me to . . . does he have no respect left? My God . . .*

Round, soft, bluntly nude, breasts rolling immense, curdlike, almost shapelessly to the sides of her chest and waist as she now lay back, opened her legs, and raised her knees.

My God . . .

The medium was taking deep, heaving breaths. Her flesh quivered.

"Kurt," Minna hissed, "I'll never forgive you."

"Quiet, Minna."

"Let's all join hands," Drecklicht commanded.

"This disgusting exhibition," Minna went on, looking fiercely at Kurt's set profile.

"This is part of the ritual," he whispered back, "it has religious significance. You—"

"Religious!" Her voice rose and heads turned.

"Be quiet, please," Drecklicht requested. "Please."

Religious, she thought vehemently, *a fat woman on a dirty sheet in a filthy basement. Religious. But where's the nearest asylum? That's the question.* Shut her eyes. *Just let me get through this tonight.*

She controlled an impulse to stand up and run. Wondered if the door was locked and if she could find her way out. Glanced around as the chanting began. Normally she would have been embarrassed by this. Even the staid

Lutheran services of her childhood left her uncomfortable. She heard Kurt's voice raised with the rest and somehow that repelled her measurelessly, as if this set a final abyss between them.

She noticed that the man who'd been standing beside the hunchback on the stool was now seated, hands gripped into the circle. A vague smear of wavering, reddish light showed his strong profile: large nose and jutting chin. He was leaning forward, strangely bright eyes seeming to stare greedily between the medium's massively outspread thighs.

Such degenerates! she thought.

Kurt held her left and Schatz her right hand in his dry, bony fingers. She shuddered. Glanced at his axlike face. He seemed to be grinning as he chanted. Head rocked.

Now the medium was vibrating rapidly, violently, legs flopping down, starfished, drooling and gasping. Drecklicht, at her head, was shouting (Minna thought) nonsense words continuously as the fat woman began to scream and twist as if she'd just been impaled by an invisible spear. As she rolled, Minna saw her lose control of bladder and bowels simultaneously and vaguely thought, because she was past even shock at this point, *Is that what the sheet is for? My God.*

Rolled and smeared herself in it as the chanting began gathering speed and force and she found herself getting caught up in the rhythm, lips moving, though soundlessly. She noticed the intense, powerful-looking man with the glowing eyes wasn't chanting either. His lips were grimly pressed together below his brusque mustache.

She wondered if she could possibly yank her hands free. Her body tensed. She decided to wait a little longer.

The medium suddenly roared like (she thought) a beast from a jungle of nightmares, howled, then fell limp, glistening, running sweat, stained with stinking excrement.

"Baaaaaaaa! Braaaaaaaaa! B'yaaaaaaaa!" The fat throat puffed up, cheeks swelled. Then the dead-white gleaming body lay still in the trembling flamelight and shadow.

"Look . . . look," her husband whispered, excited, "do you see it? It's here. Do you see it?"

She blinked and stared. Schatz, at her right, was

squeezing her hand so that the bones ground together. She struggled now and cried in pain.

"It's here!" Kurt shouted. "It's here!"

A sighing moan from the group. Minna saw the man next to the hunchback stand up, eyes like cold fire in the shadowed face, paleness set off by a cowlick and dark, uneven mustache. For some reason she was almost mesmerized and stared at him rather than the medium, thinking, distantly, that somehow Kurt had meant that man!

XVI
(APRIL 1945)

Renga, naked to his shoes, blackened to the waist below which the water had rinsed away the soot, stood facing the three SS soldiers. Two were cradling burp guns and were helmeted. The officer, in visored cap, flourished a riding whip. His colorless eyes seemed amused. He was long-bodied, the others stocky. The shortest had a too-large head and a somewhat-humped-up back.

"Well, well," the officer said, "here's something." Grinned faintly. "Probably a *Wehrmacht* officer, yes?" The last addressed to Renga. "Drunk and behaving obscenely in a war area."

"Be careful," the old woman murmured from behind the door. "They're security troops. They hang anybody they like."

The officer took a step closer.

"They're certainly taking them older and older," he remarked over his shoulder. The stooped soldier was peering around at the thinning mists that were now palely yellow as the still-unseen sun brightened. Renga was frowning, trying to make sense out of the strange accents and flow of nonsense.

"Out of uniform," the officer was going on, enjoying

himself. "Ready to desert to the Americans, eh?" Another step. "What's your name and rank, you miserable swine?"

The other two just stood there, guns leveled.

The black and white man holding the club squinted and frowned. For a moment the question threw him. He almost said "Renga" but that meant nothing. Frowned, then remembered.

"Charles, Duke of Thuringa," he said, "thou son of a whore. And equal to dispatching any such scum as thou. Even had ye armor of proof yet would I slay thee!"

The old woman shook her head where it lay alongside the door.

"No, no," she hissed, "hold your tongue, madman!"

"So," the officer said, widening his eyes with glee and malice, "an aristocrat, are you? Facetious as well. You degenerate cowardly deserter! All of you will be hanged before—"

But the duke could stand no more. He sprang forward with a speed and certainty that Rudolph Renga probably could never have matched and slammed his club on the officer's head, a blow that the futilely upraised arm did little to ease. The crack of shattered bone rang in the yard. The man staggered forward, desperately clutching at Duke Charles with his good arm, blood spilling from under his black cap and over his face, the real shock of the blow just beginning to pound into his wrecked brain, senses clutching, scattering . . . He was too close for his men to shoot. The bent-back one was shouting:

"Get clear! Get clear of him!"

The old woman had flung herself inside and slammed the door.

"Servant of evil," the duke snarled, shaking the officer who clung loosely now except for the madly clenched hand which was locked into his bare buttock, raising bloody welts. "Release me!" he yelled. Kicking and twisting. "Release me!"

Frank Astuti first thought he was witnessing a disgusting romance. He'd waded out of the mists, moving alongside a stone wall, and then heard the voices. Crouched down and moved on until he could see into the yard. Wondered what the Krauts were shouting about, saw a black-uniformed SS man on his knees embracing what he

took for a naked Negro (the pale legs were partly con-
cealed) in a helmet. On top of it two others seemed to be
enjoying the sight.

"Holy shit," he murmured.

A moment later he registered the violence.

They're trying to kill that there mooli, he thought, meaning
the black. He impulsively laid his rifle on the wall and
sighted and squeezed, mind saying:

Weirdest fucking thing I ever seen!

As the half-black and -white duke, the Nazi clinging to
his behind, charged what he didn't know were guns with
what he thought was a mace . . .

(SPRING 1914)

The air was mild. The new green was full on the
breeze that flowed across the river valley outside the city of
Metz.

Renga and the Contessa Malverde were facing one
another in an open carriage, liveried driver above them in
the box. They were stopped on a dirt road that slanted
down the crest of a long bluish-green slope that rolled to
the misty silver gleam of river. The sun was already below
the far hills so that the fields and woods floated in glowing
dimness. Tenuous rose-pale sunset faded into blue-black.

Her silky dress was like watershimmer when she
moved.

"What happens next?" she asked quietly.

"I really don't know."

He found himself getting lost in her eyes at times: their
color was elusive, deep dark, he decided, like the dusk with
a vague glow of some unspecific tint.

He was trying to picture himself going back to his life
at the university. He suddenly had realized there was no
desire to go back. Sometime during the last month here,
with Eunice and her friends . . . Oh, he still studied, or
pretended to . . . but . . . sighed within himself . . .
pretended.

One of the horses snorted and shifted in the traces,
rocking the carriage slightly.

"Yes?" She waited. "You really don't?"

He nodded, searching the dimness for her eyes again.

The coachman's back was just an outline against the mountains and sky where the stars were coming out.

She shifted her legs, the silk an obscure rustling paleness.

"I know," he finally murmured, "only what I *don't* want."

"Yes?"

"I'm one of those people," he told her, "who *almost* see the light."

"Oh? You seem quite . . . positive whenever the subject comes up."

"Which subject?"

"Seeing the light. You seem convinced there *is* a light, for one thing. You know . . . *come si dice* . . . holiness. That there is holiness in life." She was serious, he noted.

"Reflected light," he said, staring into the dusk, the vacant, melting landscape.

He felt her touch his knee.

"I'm very glad we met, Rudolph," she said. "I . . ."

"Yes?"

The touch went away.

"Are you going back to . . . Munich?"

"Have I a choice? It's my job there . . . I feel like I'm floating again. When I was younger—"

"How young?" She was warmly intimate.

"Nineteen, twenty . . . anyway, I floated. I fall into it. I have no particularly sensible ambitions, you see."

"Or any particular ambitions, either?"

"That too, Eunice."

"That may be one of your best features, *signóre*."

He stared at the faintly stained horizon, a violet-red edge. He saw himself, if he wasn't careful, drifting into a Bohemian life like . . . like that dreadful painter he'd met . . . what was his name? The one with the pale, brooding eyes. Remembered: Hutler or Hitler.

"I have to go back to Italy for a few days," she said, opening a cigarette case and handing him a metal box of matches. He took one out.

"I know that."

A long pause.

"Well, then?" she wanted to know. And a long pause again. "But do you object if I smoke?"

"What?" he murmured, coming back, striking the

match with a rasp that seemed very loud in the mountain stillness. Far down the valley, perhaps in France, a church bell tolled vespers. The breeze was like a sleeper's light breathing. "Would it matter?"

"Not much," she agreed as the flame flared and they both winced in the sudden, yellowish light. After blowing it out an afterimage of her face sprang across his sight. "But must I ask again?"

"I wish I could go with you," he said.

"Ah." She tilted the vague glow of her head and spoke to the driver. "All right, Albert." The carriage jerked forward softly. "That's what you really want, Rudolph? To drift on with me?"

"Yes. Drift."

"*Madònna* . . . you know, I was married. Had a child who died and a husband who went away to America."

"Yes?"

"And there are many other things about me . . ."

"I'm anxious to find them out, I think."

She was amused.

"Not all, *caro*."

"About the husband?" He smiled.

"*Che sorà* . . . never mind the husband."

"I don't."

"How old are you? Such a serious man. I think you're younger than I?"

"Perhaps. Does it matter? You act younger."

They rolled with slight creakings toward the dim outline of the castle. A light had just winked on in the tower.

"Well, then?" he pressed.

"It's not easy. But, you know, I only came here because I knew you were coming."

"Supposedly to work."

"Is it true you have a hopeless passion for Madame von Moltke?"

"What?" He chuckled. "It's certainly hopeless, Eunice."

Her hand touched him again and went away again.

"I feel good to be with you," she told him. "I wish I were . . . well . . . not so difficult a person."

"I haven't found you so."

"But I am. I take advantage of my money and so on.

That's the truth. I have to tell the truth. I don't like men to
get the high hand?"

"Upper hand."

"*Sí* . . . But you're too serious, my Rodolfo."

"Am I?"

"No question about it."

They were silent for about fifty yards. The castle walls
loomed over them now. The horse jogged on easily.

"Sometimes I'm frightened of the night," she said. Her
hands clasped one of his. "I feel . . . like it will open and
swallow me . . ." She sighed. "You want me to love you,
Rodolfo?"

A pause.

"Yes," he said. Almost surprised at his own voice. "Yes,
I do, Eunice." Raised her hand to his lips. The carriage
drifted into the huge, dimness of the gate, hooves clop-
clopped on warm, packed earth . . . "Don't be afraid," he
found himself saying.

The rain and mist were one substance as the rider
urged the supple, too-long-muzzled horse over the crest of
a hill where outsized ferns and long grasses were withered
and blackened by the volcanic heat and smoke from the
fuming, red-flashing mountains that were like a wall
behind him. He saw a stream of lava working its way into
the valley. Dead ahead through rents in the landscape that
seemed formed from the clouds pouring down from the
low, gray sky, he saw the fortress city of the tyrant carved
from a mountain, dark, miles high. He saw the besieging
armies gathered around it in fire and fury.

He knew a way inside. A secret. He smiled, grimly,
because he believed he was doomed. But he would get
inside and reach the king. One hand resting on the
pommel of his sword he rode on through the mist and
smoke. The tyrant would be more dangerous now than
ever before, he thought, because he was at bay and no one
could tell what dark weapons he might dredge up from the
depths of hell to smite with.

He had to reach him and try to stop him. He knew the
face so well: the thin lips, long, beaked nose, bony brows
with hollow, dark eyes that smoldered like ashy lava. The
warrior gritted his teeth, imagined his sword stabbing into
that throat, the rills of blood running and spilling from the

bright silvery blade. He felt rage and grief. Burned with it. Burned . . .

Blinked his eyes. A single tear broke from one corner. Stung. His hand went over his heart unconsciously, because there was a throbbing warmth there that wasn't quite pain . . . some kind of wound . . .

And next was jolted awake, twisting, sweating in his bed, awake in silence looking at calm moonlight frosting the long window that faced the deep, immobilizingly soft bed. So soft Renga felt drugged.

Then he heard Eunice breathing and remembered the night. Touched his wet forehead and tried to shake away what he nearly believed was just a dream.

"I do not sleep now," she murmured, shifting under the quilt. "*Amore mia.*" Her long, firm hands held his arm and chest. "Who can rest well in a new bed?" Outside the wind gurgled and sighed in the wall's chinks and edges.

"Would you like to go back to your room?" He worked his sticky lips. His mouth, he decided, tasted as if something had died under his tongue.

"Too cold in the hall." She sighed, snuggled. "How many women have you made love to?"

"Hm?" He was just drifting off a little. Smiled. "Not many." Which was more than true, he reflected.

"How old were you?"

"When? Yesterday?"

"Come on . . . the first time."

Tried to remember it, back in his undergraduate days . . . There had been no real feeling, unless you counted fear.

"It was nothing like tonight," he said, finally. When his body had seemed to melt into a common fire, intensities pouring up from shocked depths, dissolving him . . .

"But of course." She touched him intimately and sighed. "The present lover is always the best." He grunted and wavered toward unconsciousness again, wondering if the dream was waiting.

"Are you regretting anything?" she asked.

"No," he whispered. "No . . ." Her hairscent recalled warm springtimes. Relaxed him.

"Want to sleep?"

"Mmm," he agreed.

She waited, then whispered, close to his ear: "Bad luck to go back to sleep without making love."

"Mmm . . ." He responded. Snort-snored.

"Ah, my sweet young man . . . what's to become of us? You're something like a priest and something like . . . *che?* . . . *Madònna mia,* I wish you'd be awake." Sighed and stretched herself along his body. Stared at the ghostly light at the high window and let herself relax. It was always so limitless, she thought, in the beginning. So tenderly lush with promise.

He was just then sinking into a silver-black soundless sea . . . and then the fog and rain was billowing again and sheeting over the steps that led to a black iron door. He was there, resting his right hand on the door (which had no handle or keyhole) which somehow seemed to stick to the palm and open smoothly outward and the armored warrior (who was himself too) went into the dark corridor—the downpour roared behind him now—groped through a blurring of diffused light that resolved into an archway . . . passed into a tremendous chamber where misty rain-light leaked through slitted embrasures high up on the cold walls . . . and then the shadows stirred into form and he glimpsed what he took for glaring, empty eyes and a gaping, fanged mouth and he started to run (aware that it was the tyrant's protector seeking him because he was the sharpest fang ripping at the wizard-lord), the darkness sucking at him, slowing, softening his strides . . . he drew his sword but it seemed dulled by the cloudy, many-headed creature swelling around him, filling the huge hall, great, vacant paws lashing down . . . and then the throb in his wounded chest burned, became a sob, a sigh, a tender sadness, a pain that was a power too and a strange joy, and a golden-pale light suddenly shimmered around him and he felt the beast recoil; the light was blinding now . . . and next he woke, blinking into the sun that hung in the window opposite the bed, lying on his back with empty arms.

He shook off the dreaming and looked around the room. She was gone. He wondered how late it was. She was probably already at breakfast. He yawned. Kept shaking his head against the lingering, vivid, troubling images.

XVII
(APRIL 1945)

Astuti watched the taller SS man spin and flop down in a billow of mist as several slugs sprayed across his middle. At the same moment, the bent-backed one was already turning, bringing his gun level, strangely innocuous-seeming red flame flickering at the muzzle, and then the stone wall was being chewed up inches from his face as his own rifle swung with fantastic slowness (that he saw was going to be far too late) and hot stone chips ripped his cheek and he saw the duke (Renga), in the same nightmare struggle, free of the clinging officer, still charging, stick upraised, and he distantly understood that this was all a single moment and that somehow, whether he lived here or died, had been rehearsed for unnamed ages. A single sunbeam had just sliced through the leaden afternoon and flashed in his eyes so that all the slowed movements seemed to float in golden radiance and part of his vivid, shocked consciousness found itself absorbed by the pure, detached movement of tone and color as if there were no danger and no time . . .

(SUMMER 1914)

The evening was hot. The Mediterranean a lucent blue, deepening to violet as the sun sank behind the hills of Nice. Renga was astounded by the richness and color. He kept looking past the dinner table out across the water where a single sailboat, lightless, moved in phantasmal silence, pale and graceful.

A servant crossed the terrace with a silver tray of wine. The lanterns in the trees swayed with the sea breezes. The party was close to dessert.

Beside him, the contessa touched his foot with hers.

Smiled. The host was saying something at the far end of the long table. Madame von Moltke was listening, her fragile white-haired head tilted forward. Behind them there were greenish tints in the darkening sky.

Renga tapped his fingers restlessly on the pale linen. He was still trying to catch up with his life. So much was changing . . . And the contessa's surroundings made their affair so strainless, a perpetual vacation where the bed was always neat, the drink mixed, the food ready, the weather even, clear, and perfect . . .

The stocky, balding host, a weary-looking Rothschild partner, was shaking a stubby finger at a guest. His impeccable sleeve and gold cuff button gleamed the changing light. Two maids in white were serving melon in massive silver bowls.

Renga faced the fact that he was floating. Suddenly it was July. In two months he was due at the university. He'd have to make a decision. Kept deferring it . . . though, if he weren't careful, he'd defer his life away.

But these days have been like wine, he said to himself. And the rich, soft, languorous nights of silk and tenderness. *How long can I drift like one of those hangers-on?* . . . Living almost like a child, wandering on beaches or through orchards, planless and fascinated, discovering endless beauties without use.

Sipped from a goblet of fruit wine. Eunice turned and kissed him firmly on the lips and then headed, in a water-sleek rustle of silk dress, for the stone house that seemed dimensionless, insubstantial, in the twilight haze.

Madame von Moltke was looking at him. The servants were just lighting the pale Chinese lanterns in the dense dark under the trees.

"I'm leaving for home tomorrow," she said. "Helmut is nervous about the political situation."

Renga nodded.

"Yes," he said. "I can see why." Except it was so far away. Looked back at the sea which was all muted violet and seemed faintly lit from beneath. The sailboat was a vague misting he could hardly be certain he saw. "I can see why," he repeated. So many countries tied together, he thought, by strings of national fantasy, ready to shed blood for reasons no one could clearly explain . . .

"Any progress," she wondered, "with your research-es?"

He didn't look at her as he answered:

"Well . . . slowly . . . I've been . . ."

"Yes," she said. "In love. That's good."

"I hope so."

"Never doubt it. It's all we really have. What else can you keep?" She wasn't looking at him now. She leaned closer, scented with lavender and mint. The faint flames lit her creased face. "Memories die out as well."

"Yes."

"I never went back into trance, you know," she told him. "Last time it nearly had me. As it is, I hesitate to sleep deeply. But soon I'll sleep very deeply, eh?"

"Soon, Madame? You have many years left."

"But I'm too old to do much good."

Her eyes held wisps of glimmering.

"What good do I do?" Renga wondered. He remembered her trance and what had happened, the shapeless darkness that had clawed at him . . . but that all seemed far away and almost silly. What had he feared? Demons from the sleep worlds? Vague glimmers from the dead blocked out by flesh, bone, and the stony earth? Why did she want to go outside the wall, in any case? Into what? When the unseen filled her with hinting voices, and nightmares boiled up . . . There was a spark of light, a Grail, all through the dark of history but no book told him where it was . . . or her . . . or her husband . . . neither did the ephemeral voices, or any voice, for that matter. It was lost.

"If you love somebody you do good," the old woman told him, drawing back her quiet face. "Anyway, someday you'll have to face what I couldn't face."

"How do you know that?"

"If it's true, what does it matter?"

He smiled faintly. Glanced back at the bay: the boat was gone; stars gleamed in the glassy calm water. The guests were finishing their melon. The host was telling a joke. His round face bobbed, undefined.

He said nothing. Eunice came back and sat beside him. The sea seemed to breathe in the last wisps of day.

"Ah," she said, squeezing his hand, "what a moment this is!"

The musician had come through the gate and was standing under the massive chestnut tree, the warm flame-light glinting on the instrument.

"Such moments," she whispered, "die beautifully."

The music gathered itself to close, faster, deeper. There were almost tears in his eyes. He thought of so many old vanished things: loves . . . childhood . . . when life lay unstained before him in boundless, intimate promise . . .

The piece ended with a lightly plucked string. The table applauded. Contessa Eunice nudged Renga.

"*Bràvo signóre*," she enthused. "*Bràvo!*"

He was already playing again, a slightly harsh melody barely louder, at first, than the breeze in the long leaves.

Renga saw a young man in a dress suit come into the garden and cross over to Madame von Moltke. He spoke briefly, bent close to her. From her expression he first thought something had happened to her husband. So he got up (as the man was gone quickly) and went around the table to her. Heard her sigh, staring.

"It's come," she said quietly.

He didn't have to say *what* because he knew.

"Oh," he whispered, not feeling anything yet.

"I think," she suggested, "we should go back to Germany immediately."

"Yes," he said, not looking at anything, not even the dark sea where shiplights showed here and there like brightly mirrored stars. The violin was a ghostly whispering. Eunice had stood up. It was already going around the table.

"They shot someone or other," Madame was saying. "In the Balkans."

And I'm part of this, he thought, bitter and frustrated. *Why can't we simply say "no"?* He looked at the warm lights of the houses along the shore and thought how those people in there would actually leave their homes to go kill other men they had never seen.

Eunice was beside him suddenly, smelling fresh, light.

"I'll go back with you, *amore mio*," she said, tense. "I don't care."

(JULY–AUGUST 1916)

Helmut von Moltke, commander in chief, rose as the Kaiser and a civilian, Houston Stewart Chamberlain, entered the long, low room. The various members of the general staff came to surprised attention.

"Our Rasputin," one whispered, meaning Chamberlain.

Heels clicked. Lushly green trees and dark blue sky showed at the long windows. Late sun slanted through the branches.

"Good evening, gentlemen," the ruler said, moving directly to the map table where Moltke stood stolidly, pointer held like a rapier at his side. "Helmut," he greeted the commander, "all is well, I trust?"

"I hope so, Your Majesty." He saw that Kaiser was unusually nervous. War wasn't such a joke when you reached the reality. What did he need this civilian for? To whisper strange dreams in his ear? he wondered.

"Moltke," the Kaiser said, restless eyes flicking over the bright brass and silver uniforms where streaks of thinning sunlight caught them. "I have been in communication with the French. There is still hope of peace with them."

The plan, the timetable of attack, had been in development for decades and called for the defeat of France in six weeks before the vast Russian army could fully mobilize. Moltke thought about the sheer mass of what was already in motion, streaming to railway terminals, hundreds of thousands of troops pouring for the border . . .

"Yes, Your Majesty?" he asked, uneasy.

Kaiser Wilhelm kept his withered arm close to his body and gestured with the other.

"We can turn on Russia first," he said fervently. "A quick victory in the east while we hold the other front stable. The Russians will be totally disorganized. We can easily reach Moscow."

"As did Napoléon, Your Majesty," one of the staff officers respectfully put in.

Wilhelm glanced at Chamberlain as if for confirmation and support. The pug-faced philosopher licked his pale

lips, looking at everything and nothing as he spoke and
rocked his head.

"Germany's true enemies are the Slavic hordes," he
informed them. "We must destroy them in the east. They
threaten the purity of our blood." He seemed to nod and
shake his head in disturbing contradiction. Moltke wondered if he were due for another fit. "To lose territory is
nothing, but to lose our people is everything!"

"Where did this idea spring from?" the bulky commander wanted to know, ignoring the royal adviser.

"From yourself," said the slightly defensive king. "You
told me the German army could perform such maneuvers."

"Not now. Impossible, Your Majesty."

A pause. Everyone was waiting, watchful. The general
stared down at the map. Soon three-dimensional men
would track over that symbolic calligraphy, thousands,
millions of eyes, points of view, beating hearts . . . moments, dramas he would never know . . . Each millimeter
of map would express all that life is: hope, fear, courage,
futility, dream, compassion . . . rage, hate . . .

The Kaiser cleared his throat.

"Are we still talking about the German army?" he
asked, sarcastic.

For an instant Moltke thought the map shifted on the
table in a draught: suddenly there were hills and trees and
brilliant sky, dust and endless marching gray columns,
masses of men and guns, swarms, charges, heaps of fallen,
smoke and fire . . .

He thrust himself back from the table, then cried out
once, sharply, and then fell into the map which opened to
receive him like a dream. He was sprawled there, eyes
rolled back. They lifted him and set him in the chair. His
limbs lolled. A doctor was sent for in the camp.

"Well?" the Kaiser later demanded as the doctor
straightened up from the general.

"There's a faint heartbeat, Your Majesty." He looked
grave. "But I fear the worst."

"The worst?" The ruler kept glancing nervously at
Chamberlain as if he'd had something to do with it.

The doctor fluffed up his white mustache which all but
obscured his round, red nose.

"I believe he has fallen into a coma," he pronounced.

One staff member, stocky, stiff, monocle flashing the thinning, rose-tinted light, spoke up:

"Why?" he wondered.

"Too soon to tell," the doctor shrugged. "We can only pray the condition is not irreversible." He glanced down at the older man who seemed peacefully asleep in the armchair, face unfurrowed. "It may be some time before there's a change. He could simply die and never recover consciousness." Shrugged.

The officer looked faintly skeptical. The Kaiser paced near the window. His gold-inwrought spiked helmet gleamed dully.

"On the eve of war," he blurted. "Is this an omen?"

"Perhaps," said Chamberlain, moving his head, eyes tracking back and forth. "We will never be safe so long as Russia exists." His eyes seemed to be following some unseen, fluttering thing around the dimming room. Perhaps recalling the danger of a fit, the Kaiser kept part of the long table between them. "The spirits of the races have prepared their armies in the seen and unseen worlds. This begins the greatest battle of all time." He trembled slightly by the window. His back blocked the fading sunbeams. "They dream the world," he suddenly cried out, "and rise in dark omen!"

"Your Majesty," the doctor began to assure him, "to the scientific mind omens are—"

He was cut off as the general's eyes opened and he raised a hand to his temples.

"The hand of God," the Kaiser muttered.

"How do you feel, Excellency?" the stocky officer asked Moltke.

"Strain," the doctor was quickly explaining, "brought on by overwork. He must rest." He touched the general's pulse. "Simple collapse." He brimmed with confidence.

The commander pulled his arm free and heaved himself to his feet with great effort. Swayed by the map table. Though it was now dusk in the room no one had lit a light yet.

"The attack must go on," Moltke said, with finality. The Kaiser looked slightly sour but said nothing. "It is far too late to turn back." Locked his big hands behind him. "Far too late."

"You must rest, General," said the ruddy-nosed doctor.

"After the war," was the reply. "We must attack as planned. As planned!"

Because he'd fallen into the (he now believed) future. The map and the world had opened under him. He'd seen terrible sights and endless war, suffering, butchery without end, plague, hunger . . . saw a pale face, arms folded, high on a platform or cliff-face (he couldn't be sure), brooding over rivers of fire and blood, a shadowy, multi-headed, hydric thing seeming to sit on his shoulders—the god, he believed, of endless war—and so he knew they had to win at once and make peace at once or perish over slow ages and it would be his guilt if they failed because he knew what was coming . . . Knew . . .

(APRIL 1945)

Goebbels entered the bathroom, clubfoot boot clacking on the white and black honeycomb tile floor. For an instant he was startled and nearly fled because the Führer was sitting on the toilet seat in the stall, slumped back. But the little minister realized an instant later that the olive-drab pants were pulled up and belted closed. The dead dog had stiffened, the legs jutting out, jaw gaped with a mouthful of darkness.

"My Führer," he said, "excuse me. But the young heroes are assembled and waiting for you." He paused, quite calm, energetically erect, weight slightly off the twisted foot.

His leader stared and then stirred slightly. He wasn't trembling, for the moment. He worked his lips before he spoke, as if they were dry. There was a faint flicker, an almost smothered flame, in his pale eyes.

"So," he rumbled, "they fight on, do they?"

"Absolutely, my Führer. These are the last of the best."

Hitler nodded. Sat upright, one fist now clenched on his knee.

"They might have sired a race of gods," he muttered in bitter anguish. Changed the subject. "They want me to leave here, Joseph. To carry on from the south."

Goebbels gripped the edge of the gray partition. His teeth flashed as he spoke, earnest, concentrated.

"In that case," he said, "they have lost all faith."

Hitler looked interested. He'd once said of this minis-

ter: "The man burns like a flame!" Unwavering fanaticism
that many assumed was refined from cynicism.

"Are they wrong, then?" Hitler asked, not without a
faint hope, a clutching at (he thought) shadows. "What is
left? These are my last hours—no, don't deny it . . . you
who are my true spiritual heir, my loyalist companion in
struggle . . ." Nodded, clenched and unclenched his fist.
The crippled man waited to see if this were rhetoric or if a
question was coming. "*Is* there hope, Joseph?"

"My Führer, if there is to be a miracle it must come
here! In the capital. Remember, that disgusting Jew,
Roosevelt, died a few days ago. That was the first sign, as I
said at the time. Stalin or Churchill will be next!"

Hitler struggled to his feet, leaning on the partition.
Brushed at his grayed forelock with one hand. His expression mixed skepticism and hope.

"The Allies would fall to pieces," he murmured. He
quickly imagined the results, the lightning political moves
he could make. Smiled, for a moment caught up in the
prospect. Then grew grim again. Took a step forward out
of the narrow stall, shuffling past his minister to the sink
over the dead dog's head. "But is this more horoscope
dreaming?" he demanded.

"No, my Führer."

"I banned such things," he said, falling into his
comfortable, lecturer's manner, "as you know, because the
average person, with an ordinary will, can become depen-
dent on the prophecies. This is very bad."

"Yes, my Führer." Goebbels nodded, one hand still
gripping the edge of the stall.

"No man can escape his fate, granted . . ." His head
was trembling a little now as the excitement of ideas
coursed through him. "But the historical man directs the
very power of the stars for historical ends." Nodded,
carefully not looking into the dulled mirror. A fine coating
of plaster dust from the bombardments covered it.

"Quite right," Goebbels said, limping a half step closer
to his leader. "And so this is precisely my point: we have
done it before. We have confounded them all before."

Hitler splashed water on his deeply lined and puffy
cheeks. When he straightened, it trickled down and beaded
onto his collar. His yellowed, uneven teeth showed when he
said:

"Do you remember the night after we took power, Joseph? The world trembled! Germany flashed like a drawn sword . . ." Smiled and nodded. "Our boys swept the streets clear. You could see the will of the times in lightning strokes!" Clasped his hands before himself. Forgot to wipe his face. The water droplets clung to his mustache and shook loose when his lips moved. "Yes . . . the spirit wanted to heal the world and cleanse the poisons in the blood . . ." Nodded. The wet hairs glinted in the harsh light. "But all the best are gone now, it's true." Smiled. "But so are many of the worst . . ." Braced his hip against the rust-stained sink. A tremor shook his neck and left arm as if an electric wind passed through him.

"My Führer, we are still striking at the enemy. But few know the means at hand." He glanced over his shoulder, unconsciously. "Himmler felt that—"

The Führer clenched his jaw and was suddenly shouting, face contorted and purplish, sprinkles of water flying. "I have condemned him to death!" he pointed out. "Traitor! Traitor! Filthy Judas! . . ." Puffing and trembling. Goebbels held his arm and patted his shoulder to soothe him.

"Yes, my Führer," he said, "but he still can be useful. After he does what we wish . . ." He shrugged. "Exactly as you taught me."

The Führer was appeased. Nodded and looked sly. "Yes," he said, "very good." He began to cough violently; hacked and spat into the sink. Stood there staring for a few moments, then suddenly knelt on the cold tile stroking the frozen-jawed head of the long-muzzled dog. He was weeping. "Poor, poor Blondi . . ." he whispered. The beast's dull stare rocked slightly, the stiffened legs quivered. "What have they done to you, my poor one? . . . eh? . . ." Stroked. "I never have forgotten Max . . . did you know that? Some bastard stole him from me. I was on leave. I brought him back from the front with me. I taught him all sorts of marvelous tricks. I loved that dog, he was my best companion in those days. Some civilian bastard offered to buy him but I refused. I was annoyed . . ." He stayed on his knees, hand not stroking now, just trembling slightly. "We were going back up to the front. I called. He didn't come. You should have seen me frantically searching up and down the railroad yard. That bastard stole him! I

knew it. The filthy swine! All through the mud and shells
that animal was loyal to me and then . . . I wept . . . bitterly . . ." His head shook. "I tried to have him found in
later years. I had him looked for . . ."

"But the animal would have been old by that time, my
Führer."

Hitler looked up at him, as if from prayer, the harsh
light in his pale, glassy eyes.

"Not the dog," he corrected, "the man."

He shut his eyes. A mistake, because (what he called)
the green-dark was there again, instantly this time as if a
window had opened in his forehead, and he and the naked
queen were outside on the wide balcony that overlooked
the city carved out of the black mountain itself. The misty
horizon was fitfully lit by distant, volcanic flashes while the
massive buildings glowed with spots and windows showing
livid green gleams.

The royal pair, the tyrant and his mate, stood among
the impaled victims who were still dying by fractions as the
slow spikes worked through their bound bodies.

The king (who was Hitler too) leaned over the iron
railing, listening to the roar down in the city streets. He
knew what it meant. The enemy was inside. The traitors
had undermined the fortress. Disloyalty was everywhere.
The followers of the hidden-light cult had (he thought)
pissed their poison into the clean pool of the Great Race.

He whispered into the night even as Hitler was
struggling to open his eyes and escape the vision that had
spun itself from his recurring nightmares:

"I have no choice now. I will do what must be done. I
will snuff out that sickly flame forever."

(DECEMBER 1914)

Honored Sir: I am pleased and thank you for your
kind letter. I am now finally able to reply. First I must
tell you, on 2 December, I received the Iron Cross.
Thank God, there were plenty of chances. We went
into battle early on the morning of 29 October and
have been in those fellow's hair ever since, attacking
and defending. We were transported to the front in
lorries . . .

The bare planks banged into their buttocks with each jounce of the open truck. The sun was setting in a towering mass of cloud across the Flanders plains. The road ran in easy dips toward the sunset, pooled with shadow here and there. The column of trucks rolled on and on . . . They passed one vehicle stalled on the shoulder and Hitler could see the rows of heads in spiked helmets (like his own) in back, the driver out on the running board smoking a pipe, steam rising from the engine.

He glanced across the fields and saw a shattered farmhouse tangled in skeletal shadows.

Planks had been laid over the gaping holes in the field and along the road that at first he hadn't realized were shell craters. The wood creaked and rattled under the wheels. Up ahead on the horizon (flat except for a distant, long bluff), there were faint flashes and echoing rumbles. The sun hung fat and red in what he could now tell were masses of smoke. He knew it was cannonfire and his heart suddenly raced as he took in the sweeping immensity of it: the whole world seemed ablaze. The trucks rattled and banged along, the men sang steadily . . .

In the last wisps of red daylight, they passed through a village that was now no more than a few heaps of stones and charred, shattered beams sunk in shadow. Smelled a sweetish stink he didn't yet know was decaying flesh and then he noticed a dead horse in the ditch, legs stiffly out, belly bloated, eyes crawling black hollows.

The feeling of power and excitement took his breath away. The convoy rolled to a halt at the outskirts of a city . . .

At two o'clock the alarm came and we were on the march by three. The cannon thunder was stronger now. The sky ahead leaped in flashes . . .

They moved on into the morning: the first vague grays, spilling fog, and suddenly, not far behind, a boom and then a hissing howl arcing across the sky. In the distance, a dull thud . . . another . . . another . . . then more and more guns opening up behind them until the earth vibrated steadily.

". . . We're attacking the English!" the major said. At last! Every man of us was overjoyed. After this

announcement, the major, on foot, took the head of
the advancing column. Out there the shrapnel burst
overhead, tearing apart the trees like so much brush-
wood. We looked on curiously. We had no actual idea
of the danger. No one was afraid. Each man waited
patiently for the command, "Forward!" The show was
getting hotter. We heard a few had been wounded
already down the line. Suddenly several men appeared
out of the smoke, brown as clay. Six Englishmen and a
machine gun! We shouted to the escorting troops.
They marched with pride behind their catch. The rest
of us had to wait. We could hardly see into the foggy,
witches' caldron in front of us . . .

They were lying flat along a roll of the ground facing
the woods that were dancing and shattering in the bursts.
Burning fog and stinging smoke flowed across the fields.
Noncoms and messengers moved along the line of men in
gray uniforms and spiked helmets. Their long guns were
close at hand. A few men down from Hitler, someone was
whimpering with each flat, whip-cracking shellburst. Far
off to the left there was a sound of muffled screams.

He was nervous, excited, restless. There was a great
crackling energy in him that pressed for expression. He
tried to think about the historical meaning of this and his
own purpose in it, but thoughts kept fading from his mind,
leaving only a strange clarity: there was only life and death.
Nothing else existed.

At last the command rang out: "Forward!" We poured
out and raced across the fields to a little farm. Shrapnel
burst everywhere, and in between the English bullets
sang but we ignored them. I was out ahead, alone.
Squadleader Stoever was hit! Good God, no time to
think. We were caught in the open and had to rush
forward. The captain was in the lead. Our men began
to fall. The English had set up machine guns. We
crawled forward through a long drainage ditch. Every
so often a man was hit and the whole column was
blocked until we'd lift the fellow out and crawl on.
Then we reached open fields again. We ran for a forest
about one hundred yards ahead. The woods were
starting to seem pretty thin about now—only the

second sergeant was left to command the squad. Over us the shells howled and whistled; splintered tree trunks and branches flew everywhere. Grenades crashed, hurling up clouds of stones, earth, and roots, stifling everything in a yellowish-green, sickening vapor . . .

"Mother . . ." someone was screaming over the roar of explosions. "Mother . . . help me . . . please . . . please . . ."

The searing, foul smoke spilled over them. Shell flashes lit the murk among the smoldering trees. A boy, helmetless, crawled out of the vapors, eyes set side, wild. Hitler glanced over—the sergeant crouched beside him. The boy crawled, aimless, mad, on two knees and one arm because the other was gone at the shoulder joint where blood gushed and bubbled out. He went past the line of them, in their shapeless, smeared, gray uniforms, howling—the sound audible in the fragmentary lulls between blasts.

"Keep down, for God's sake!" the sergeant shouted.

The smoke folded over the ruined boy as another stood up and rushed after him.

"Down, you idiot!" the sergeant bellowed over the shrieks of ripped and wracked air and earth: bullets buzzed, shells hissed, shrapnel sang and whispered. The would-be rescuer took a few steps (just as the crawling boy dropped flat on his face, emptied of blood) and something invisible seemed to shake him and he fell to pieces. The smoke boiled, the livid world heaved.

"We can't stay here," the noncom yelled. "We may as well die in the open!" He crouched to his feet. "Come on, you assholes!" he roared.

Hitler freed his mind of abstract thought. The battle seemed to flicker remotely. He sensed he was being forged and tested, that energy was pouring into his spirit, felt the wind of divine wings of fire and vengeance. Men were dropping, spinning, as the army gathered itself, cheered (his own voice ringing too as if drawn out of him by an outside power) into the crashing, ringing, spitting, reeking inferno, and charged. This was war! They were riding with death, drawing in the terrible strength of death, the irresistible dark hand reaching among them all, laying each

soul bare, snuffing or passing on . . . He was carried
forward as if on a tide and didn't hear his raw voice raving
in the midst of death as he leaped over a headless man with
boots blown off; passed several soldiers in a row, tangled
together as if embracing, in a broken heap . . . out of the
woods into the open fields where the sickening smoke
thinned . . . bullets whizzed and whined, chugged into
the earth—running men would suddenly flip over, stagger,
twist, crawl, curse, howl with pain, and suddenly sit silent—
as if carefully watching over their own death—as he ran on
panting but tireless.

Again we went forward. I ran as fast as I could across
meadows and turnip fields, jumping ditches, over wire
and hedges. Then someone ahead was shouting:
"Everybody in here! Everybody in here!" A long
trench was under my feet. I jumped in. Others
followed, left and right. Beside me were Württembergers; beneath me, dead and wounded Englishmen.
Now I knew why I'd landed so soft . . . An unbroken
hail of iron whistled over our trench . . . Our artillery opened up . . . again and again shells burst in
the English trenches ahead of us . . .

It was as if the mud and clay had come to life. The
English soldiers, bunched and twisted together in the
bottom of the trench, seemed to rise from the earth, stiff,
bloody arms outstretched, ripped and gashed lumps,
missing faces. Some moaned and struggled sluggishly to
get out from under the heavy boots of the Germans who
were crowded in as the air and earth above were ripped
and chewed by endless bullets. One man, flat on his face,
seemed to be trying to crawl into the ground, pale hands
scrabbling hopelessly at the black muck.

. . . the English swarmed out like ants and then we
rushed them. We ran into the fields like lightning and
battled hand-to-hand and threw them out of one
trench after another. Many raised their hands to
surrender. Those who wouldn't were knocked down
. . . We reached the main highway. To right and left
was a young woods. Forward we went, straight into it!
We chased them out in swarms . . . we went on

through a withering fire. Man after man fell. Our
major came up, calmly smoking with his adjutant,
Lieutenant Piloty . . . He ordered us to assemble for
the attack! We had no more officers and few noncoms,
so we ran back to get reinforcements. When I returned
with a troop of scattered Württembergers, the major
was already dead, his chest shattered. There were
corpses everywhere. Now just the lieutenant was left.
We boiled with anger. "Lieutenant, lead us at them!"
we all shouted. On the road advance was impossible.
We struggled through the woods. Four times we went
forward and were driven back. Only myself and one
other man was left from our entire detachment. At last
he too fell. A shot ripped away my left sleeve but by a
miracle I remained untouched. In four days our
regiment of 3500 men melted away to 600 . . . but we
were all proud of having licked the enemy. Since then I
have been at the front the whole time. On 2 December
I finally received my Iron Cross. I am now carrying
dispatches. There were eight of us and after the first
day there were four . . .

He went up and out of the trench as if shot from a
sling. The excitement was electric. The mass of them
charging, cheering, a gray shadowy wave on either side of
him as the bullets began to spatter and then pour: a dead
man lay over the wire and Hitler and others tramped over
him, a human bridge, then tore on.

He had a vague impression that this was like walking
through the rain as a child: the first scattered, fat drops
that you avoided, ducking and twisting, waiting for the
inevitable one that would splat on you. He tripped, got up,
crouched on, sliding into the next trench, seeing the brown
uniforms rising up, coming at him, amazed at how big they
seemed with their bayonets and muddy boots, and he
shouted with a kind of vicious terror and lunged as the
lines met, swinging his clubbed rifle against the brownish
blur of them, feeling totally naked, pounding faster
. . . faster, frantic to strike. His rifle butt rang off a
Tommy's helmet as the man lunged with steel and missed.
When he fell over a clump of barbed wire Hitler smashed
his pale, round, blood-streaked face again and again,

snarling with wild fury, unaware of his own voice raving in the din:

"You swine! . . . Swine! . . . Swine! . . ." Until there was no face at all and he pulled away thinking of squashed cherries. He staggered to the side just as a pistol shot missed his head, and not even trying to fire back he charged like a drunken man at the leveled gun, but the enemy was swept away by a grenade blast behind him. Then the British were falling back and he caught up with a lanky fellow who was limping heavily, and at the limit now of his own breath and strength he managed to stick him in the kidneys with his own outflung bayonet, then dropped, wracked by panting, to his knees as the soldier struggled on, hand pressed to his side, then fell into a shell hole, tried to crawl . . . stopped. He felt a tug at his sleeve and saw it had been ripped away. A fellow German beside him started to speak over the din, shuddered, and then blood spilled from his mouth and he bled words.

Hitler turned around. His eyes were glassy. Dirt and lead sprayed everywhere. The shocked gray line was starting to retreat. Was melting down like (he thought) sand figures on the beach when the surf sweeps over them . . . two men bent at the waist . . . another, running, seemed to kick his leg off away from him . . . hopped absurdly after it before he fell . . . a helmet flew up and there was no head under it . . . a blinded boy ran screaming in circles, tripping, rolling, staggering . . . it seemed every inch of ground was being chewed to shreds. Men fell and were hit over and over again. Frozen to the spot his eyes darted wildly around. He felt if he moved at all he would die. A man fled, entrails dragging behind him. Blood collected in pools like rainwater. The fields were dimming in terrible twilight. Gunshots flashed. Men screamed and begged for help and pity. He thought, for an instant, of the sausage shop where he'd worked, the grinders endlessly chewing the flesh and bone, and he realized he might go mad now at any moment and at the very brink something (he later told one of his surviving comrades) seemed to grip his soul and tell him:

You cannot die. This is nothing. Feel nothing.

And he thought he felt it enter him. Vastness, silence and power, entered him. He stood up as if to leap from the earth. Looked around calmly as the twilight shadows

washed over the battle, as the reddish-gray light blotted at
the heaped and tortured forms, blended them into the
landscape.

He didn't run this time. Held his gun at his side and
walked, almost strolling back, even as bullets whizzed and
mortar blasts began to blossom in flashes that were instantly
swallowed up by the dusk.

He stepped over the dead and dying, who seemed part
of the dimly glowing earth until they moved or groaned.
There was such a vast and terrible beauty here, he thought:
Greenish, sputtering flares going up all along the line. The
firing was falling off to sporadic bursts now . . .

He had not been deserted. He had breathed death into
himself so that it was part of his being and so, he knew, he
was safe, untouchable. He'd been tested and the rest would
follow because the miracle had happened; the angels were
given charge to watch over him and his destiny so that a
new age might be born.

He paused a moment before entering the German
trench that now gaped at his feet where the survivors
crouched, dim shadows in the flickers of the falling flares.
He looked back at the rapidly darkening desolation; a
strange world totally purged of all shallow values, all petty
hopes of everyday greed, lust, and philosophy. In this
world you were alive or dead and had to surrender all the
talk and idle daydreams, you had to face the fangs of truth:
you were a fleeting movement of breath and shadow.

He gazed out over the ruined battlefield like a prince
surveying his father's domain. Drank this moment to the
dregs.

Each insect life could be squashed in an instant but the
power went on whether they lived or died; the flow of the
race itself, and not the individual hopeless insects who
otherwise had no meaning to their futile struggles . . .

A few pale faces were looking up at him from the
slashed ground. He was dimly outlined against the faintly
luminous clouds of smoke that blotted out the stars. A
falling flare reflected, glittered coldly in his inward, dreamy
eyes. He smiled thinly under his newly pointed mustache.

"What's the matter with him?" someone wanted to
know.

"Don't ask me," another rejoined, weary and cynical.
"Maybe he likes bullets."

"We all like bullets, don't we?" Yet another came back with, to some guffaws. "Or else we're in the wrong place."

"Never mind, comrades," Hitler told them, putting one hand on his hip, the other holding the rifle. He wondered how to share the truth of this moment with them. Doubted it was possible. "The spirit of Germany can never be destroyed."

Someone giggled, a note of near hysteria in the sound from the days of strain and madness.

"He's the spirit of Germany," the giggler said, "don't you foolish sons of bitches know that? Bullets bounce off his ass."

"Shut up over there," someone else yelled, muffled by the dank earth. "Let a man sleep."

"You'll sleep soon enough," another invisible soldier put in. "It's waking up gets to be hard."

"Aye," someone said, a Bavarian accent, like Hitler's own.

"Shut up, Goddamn it!"

Hitler climbed down into the deep earthwork and settled himself comfortably against the soft, mucky far side. Freed his canteen for a drink.

"When do we get to eat?" someone asked, down the curve of trench in the deep darkness.

"Gnaw on this," someone answered him, "you son of a bitch."

Hitler paid no attention now. He lay back with his eyes open watching the flare light on the massed, black clouds; listening to the random shots, deep thuds when a stray shell hit back somewhere . . . voices in the distance, perhaps British, murmuring.

I am sorry, I must close now. Day after day we are under heavy artillery fire. In time, that shatters the strongest nerves. I think frequently of Munich and here we all have the single hope that the enemy will soon be ground under once and for all. We want an all-out fight, no matter what! We hope that those of us who have the good luck to go home after this will find it purer and more purified of foreignism. That by the sacrifices and sufferings which the soldiers go through every day, that through the wash of blood that flows here every day against an international world of enemies, not only Germany's foreign enemies will be crushed but that our inner impurities will be destroyed. That would be worth more than any mere gains of territory. With Austria the day will come as I have always said. Again I express my heartfelt gratitude and remain your most devoted and grateful,

ADOLF HITLER

XVIII
(1914)
Munich

Minna went through the bronze gate ahead of Renga. They went up the brick path through the dense, trimmed bushes toward the cheerful blue- and gold-trimmed townhouse. The sun was steady pressure, the August air still and hot.

"She expects us for lunch," he was saying. His gray-green uniform still had fold creases across the back and he walked stiffly in his boots.

Minna was staring at the yellow dazzle of banked flowers across the lawn.

"Yes," she murmured. "I'm really grateful . . ."

"Needless."

Her silky white blouse shimmered like a snowfield. Her expression was calm and slightly too remote.

"I couldn't go back to my parents' house," she said. "I just couldn't face it . . ."

"I understand."

"It is very nice of you both to let me stay here."

They'd reached the brick steps and paused there in the heat and brilliance. She tilted her straw hat to shield her eyes.

"I'm sorry," he said, "about you and Kurt. Perhaps it will work itself out soon." He felt sympathy but was

preoccupied. He'd spent the mild morning watching countless thousands of soldiers crunching west on a suburban
road until the dust they raised billowed like smoke over the
hot, still cornfields. And he'd heard the casualty lists were
incredible . . .

"My God," she said. "Work it out . . . What do you
really think of him?" she suddenly asked.

His brow tensed minutely.

"I like him, Minna." Shrugged. "He's an intelligent
man."

"Ah . . ." Her eyes were remote again. "That just
means his brain works. That's not what I worry about."

"His heart?"

She was looking around at the soft grass, the dense
colors.

"What a lovely place," she said. Sighed. "I don't really
know what to do . . ." Held her long, soft hands lightly to
her cheeks. "He dragged me into dirty cellars . . . you
wouldn't believe . . ."

"Pardon?" He touched her arm, concerned. What was
this? Studied her face.

"Ach, Rudolph," she whispered.

"Dirty cellars?" Was it a figure of speech or some sexual
quirk?

"Those people . . . I had to get away, you see . . .
Come to think of it, I'm not so sure his brain does work."
She glanced at him, then back at the sun-rich grounds.
Some birds were gusting from one tree to another.

"Which people?"

"His friends . . . that group of cranks . . ."

"The *Thule Society*?"

She nodded. Kurt had recently tried to interest Renga
in attending a meeting. The war had made a response
unnecessary.

"They meet in cellars?" he wondered.

"Sometimes." She shrugged.

"What happens there?"

"Disgusting things." Shut her eyes. The image of the
day shook in golden violets decaying into black. Blinked the
brightness back. "Kurt talked himself into it . . . I don't
understand how . . . It's so lovely here. This is much
bigger, but when I was a child our grounds seemed like this
to me . . ." Sighed again. "My God, the things that go on

in this world!" She drank in the lush light, the heavy ripeness, the fullness that was already brimming. She wanted to take off her shoes, stockings, stretch out on the grass and drift away . . . *Oh God,* she thought, *I want something . . . something . . . just to hold and cherish . . .* She could have wept.

She turned as Eunice came out and stood there in a sleek lacy billow of houserobe. At first she thought she'd seen her somewhere and then realized she looked like someone . . . from long ago . . . tried to recall it . . .

"My God," Eunice was saying, "you're wearing it." Staring at Renga's uniform. "My God . . ."

"What can I do?" he asked her. "Eunice, this is Minna Fragtkopft."

She nodded absently, still staring at him. Minna said something and the contessa held out her hand.

"Excuse me," she said, "but it just . . . how do you say? . . . *came home* to me. The war is suddenly real."

"Yes," he agreed. "They told me when I have to go." He saw the men, streaming without end into the dusty summer.

She shut her eyes.

"Don't say it yet," she told him. "Not yet . . ."

Erika, Minna realized. *She really looks like Erika Dammerung* . . . She felt suddenly relaxed. That was a good omen. Her once best friend from childhood. Stopped straining not to think about Kurt for the moment. Looked around at the heavy green trees. Watched the birds circle and fold down into the masked branches.

Blinked away a memory, a flick of dimness: the shadowy, dusty stone basement room littered with broken furniture and strange, sheeted objects, the pale faces in the circle, the gross woman naked in the center drooling, babbling obscenities, voiding her bowels in a spasmodic gush, and then the memory of running out through the stone-gray passages . . . Blinked it completely away or else she'd have to think of Kurt.

Watched a bright, yellowish fluff sail out of the tree and wing across the searing, steady sun.

While Eunice just looked at her lover and didn't speak. Took his hand and brought it to her lips. Pressed it there . . .

XIX
(APRIL 1945)

Frank Astuti was trying to aim his rifle as the burp-gun burst chewed along the wall toward his head and he winced because he knew it was too late and anticipated the impacts that would rip his skull apart, smash bone—and then he realized (in the same suspended moment) that the crazy-looking Negro had already thrown his club which had been spinning end over end across the few feet to the squat SS man and was just hitting his arm so that the slugs suddenly spaced and struck on either side of his face (hot fragments stung his cheeks) and then his own gun was bucking over and over as the black-uniformed soldier seemed to run rapidly backward, flipping his gun in the air convulsively, fluttering his arms as if he meant to do something urgent, and then the clip was empty and time rushed back and the enemy was gone as if by magic; the strange Negro (whose legs, he now registered fully, were pale white, bony) in the steel helmet was staring at the hedge across the foggy yard.

Astuti got up carefully, shaking a little, and headed over there, cramming another clip into the Garand rifle. His eyes kept tracking around, automatically. The German's boots were sticking out of the hedge.

Astuti suddenly realized the bizarrely marked black and white man was the professor under a coat of soot. He gaped, then started as the old woman peered out through the half-parted double doors.

"What the fuck? . . ." he asked, shaking his head, staring around through the thinning fog. "What happened to you? *Madònn'* . . ."

"Thou hast a weapon of great magic," the duke declared thoughtfully. "And hath saved me from these base servants of the devil. For this I bear thee great gratitude."

He stooped and recovered his club. The woman craned her head out to listen.

"What the fuck happened to your fucking clothes?" Astuti wanted to know. "I don't talk Kraut," he added.

The other blinked at him.

"I know not thy speech, good sir," he said in a form of Middle German.

"*Che fa!*" Astuti cocked his head to the side. "*Madonn', tu sei 'pazz', capish?*" Gestured with disgust.

"Eh?" the naked duke reacted. "Is this not a foul form of the sweet tongue of the south?" he wondered in an Italian not used for centuries.

Astuti grunted.

"Now you talk book Italian. I had it in school." He went on in the best nondialect speech he could manage, assuming the oddness of Renga's language was due to his own ignorance. "But where are your clothes, sir?"

"Ah, a thousand thanks for reminding me, good sir," Renga suddenly whirled around and caught the door before the woman could dart inside again. "I need a decent garment, old crone, to clothe my nakedness." Pushed past her inside. She cowered away. When he came out, tying a white and blue flowered housecoat around his lean, stringy limbs, the American was crouched, staring into the mists and listening intently.

"Belike I must seem a moor," the duke said to himself, peering at his face in the window glass, a substance that amazed him a little. *A land of magic, altogether,* he decided. "Thou must help me, sir," he told Astuti, "with my quest."

"*What?* You're a fucking lunatic, you know that?" As he spoke in English, this failed to find its mark.

His odd companion was already heading for the road under the brightening sky.

"Where the fuck are you going now?"

The duke turned and frowned, stood there in absurd blackface, SS helmet, and flowered woman's housecoat.

"What sayest thou?" he asked in Italian.

"Where art thou going?" Astuti answered with a question.

The duke pointed to the wall of the stone house.

"To find him," he grimly declared.

Astuti turned, glanced at the Hitler poster on the wall; which seemed all burning eyes and dramatic shadows. By the time he turned back, the lean, older man was heading for the road, not even having to look behind to be sure the other would follow.

Astuti stood there, blinking, thoughtful, raging a little too, because there was never any choice. Here he was, lost behind enemy lines (assuming there were still lines), even in favors with a maniac—having saved one another's lives at least once apiece—who'd just invited him to kill Hitler. The guy was crazy all right, but educated. Maybe in the secret service . . .

Just because he stains himself black and puts on an old lady's clothes and thinks he's King Arthur, what the fuck, right? Play the cards that are dealt, like my old man always says. They're the only fucking cards you got anyway, nine times outta ten . . . This might turn out to be a big deal.

I remember I seen that movie where New York hoods catch fucking Göring or somebody. Why the fuck not? He started walking. *You never fucking know . . . in this world you never know . . .* Unslung the canteen and swallowed a slug of metal-tasting warmish water. *Anyway,* he consoled himself, *I gotta see what this* gidrool *does next or I'll be strangled the first time I fucking try to tell the fucking story . . .*

(1916)
At the Moltke's

He looked too thin, Madame von Moltke thought, and his dark, steady eyes were haunted. She knew the look too well. She'd seen it often enough in the past two years of war, the young men with a strange old age.

Renga was moving uncertainly down the garden walk toward the veranda where she was standing in the thin, late-afternoon autumn sun. The wan light worked through the red-gold leaves on the old trees around the wall enclosing the lawn, dried flowerbeds, and elaborate marble statuary. The air smelled of slowly charring chestnuts and turned earth.

As he mounted the stone steps to greet her, she saw how baggy his uniform was. His long hand reached up, took hers, and kissed it.

"Lieutenant Renga," she said, "good to see you."

"Madame," he replied, "this is the first chance I had to come."

She nodded and then tenderly touched his cheek. Behind him a scatter of leaves spun and skittered down as the cool breeze veered.

"I have your last letter," she said. "From the Somme."

He shut his eyes and briefly nodded. Said nothing and she let it pass. They never wanted to talk about battles.

"I heard about our loss," he murmured, after a moment.

"Yes," she said. This was something now she didn't want to discuss. Her husband was dead. She saw the grave in her mind: the withered flowers in a green metal vase; the yellowing imperial flag; the harsh gray stone . . . "and have you seen Eunice Malverde?"

He shook his head.

"She's in Italy," he replied. "Unfortunately we're at war with them." *We*, he thought, amused.

He clasped his hands behind his back and stared past her at the glass doors where the paled, fading afternoon was reflected, the light blue sky, the bright shimmer of trees above the wall.

"I have been writing down . . ." she said, paused, then, "certain things."

"Yes?"

She laboriously eased herself into an iron lawn chair. Adjusted her fur wrap. He thought she looked terribly old now. Her eyes only were a glint of fire in the stiff, layered wrinkles.

"Do you want to say anything about the war?" she asked.

He wondered why. Shook his head. She wasn't looking at him.

"No," he said. His eyes were far away. Studied nothing.

"I am writing down," she said, "the words of my husband."

Renga's eyes came back from the shades of battles and mists of desolation. After a silence, he said:

"Which are?"

"What he told me when he was dying. What he still tells me . . . I was with him at the end."

"Ah."

"Did you know what happened to him in the first days of the war?"

"I heard he was ill for a short time."

She shook her head, looking straight before her at the mellow, golden light on the grayed grass.

"He was not ill, Rudolph Renga," she told him. "Only his spirit."

"Yes?"

"He had what, I suppose, they could call a vision."

He smiled ironically. Glanced down at his shiny boots, then back at her seamed, set face.

"We are all of a kind, then," he said, not really amused.

"He told me, Rudi, that he recalled a former lifetime on this earth."

"The general believed in reincarnation?"

"No. But he told me this, notwithstanding. He said he fell over the map table and remembered himself in the Dark Ages." Her face showed nothing. Her hands vanished into the fur across her lap. "He said that the men of that time, the good and the evil, were being reborn in this century because of what they had done in the past. The terrible world they had helped bring about." She sat, unmoving. "He said that the worst man of all was already alive and meant to be master of the earth."

Renga almost laughed this time. Then pursed his lips. It sounded absurd. Tapped his foot a few times, nervously. At the front he had lost touch with the drama of mystical mysteries. Heard dry leaves scraping over the stone paving.

"Whom?" he wanted to know. "The Kaiser or the Russian Czar?"

"No," she said, dry and firm, "an unknown man. A soldier."

Renga grinned.

"Well then, Madame," he said, "we're safe enough. We'll be down to twelve-year-olds before this war is done. The whole middle of us will be missing. Just the old men and the children will remain." He half believed it.

"This is no joke, Rudolph," she said. "My husband saw the war would be lost by Germany. That millions would die for nothing."

He felt a chill. Sighed. The brittle leaves spun in little whirlwinds along the gray brick walls of garden and house.

"They already have," he said.

A long pause while the wind shook the trees a little and shredded the washed-out sunbeams.

"He said they were all guilty," she continued, almost whispering now, "for loosing the beast from hell."

His eyes closed and he thought for a moment he'd see it again: the black, flame-ridden form rising in his mind, blotting out the landscape. Discovered he wasn't afraid anymore. The trenches had changed him. No horror, he believed, could ever surpass reality.

"Why did he go on with the war, then?" he asked a little bitterly, remembering it.

"Was there a choice at that point?" She part-turned her head as if to appeal to him. But didn't quite. Except for her lips and eyes, he was thinking, she might be dead herself. "He hoped to win quickly and spare . . . he had to hope, don't you see? . . . What would you have done? . . . He had no choice but to hope, my poor husband . . ."

He nodded. The wan light was reflected in the glass opposite him. The sun was sinking behind the trees.

"He said, at last," she whispered dryly, "to tell you, Rudolph Renga, that the beast would drink the blood of generations. And grow beyond measure . . . that it would become a man . . ." Renga sighed and said nothing. ". . . he was sorry, my poor husband . . . he wept, at the last . . . his face was like wax on the pillowcase . . . he tried his best, God keep him . . ."

Renga blinked rapidly. Shivered a little as the sun went down and color drained from the dying day.

She labored to her feet. He helped her, automatically. She patted his arm. Her face remained set as though for eternity.

"There's something else," she told him. "I have a letter for you."

"From the general?"

"From the contessa. Your contessa. An American friend brought it into Germany."

From her, he thought. *After two years . . . from her . . .*

Contessa Eunice and Minna were sitting on a knoll by the canal near her villa. They were barefoot in the warm, southern autumn evening. Their white dresses were ghostly. Across the fields some farmer's wife was ringing a dinner bell . . . a child's voice was calling . . . a dog barked . . .

The absolutely still water was stained by twilight where

the earth and sky seemed to be melting together. The misty glow of their clothing overlapped.

"Are you hungry yet?" the contessa asked.

"Mn." Minna was noncommittal, distant.

"Such weather . . . it must be already cold in Germany."

"Yes," Minna responded, staring.

"Do you hear anything from Kurt?"

"Does he know where I am?"

"He must. I sent Rudi letters through Swiss and Americans. Of course, maybe they don't see each other." She sighed. "I pretend there's no war sometimes. I live better that way. I pretend he's just away somewhere working on his research . . ." She shrugged. "*Ma,* what can you do?" Shook her head. "He's such a good man. He tries so hard . . ." Sighed. "At least we give each other company. Italians who are rich don't have so much family, you know."

"Yes . . . But it's rather strange . . . I mean, I'm in your power."

"How do you mean, *cara*?"

Eunice was looking at her friend.

"I would be interned and put in prison here if you—"

"What nonsense! This is Italy."

"Still . . ."

"Don't say such things."

"Well," Minna said, smiling to herself, "I don't really mind being at your mercy." Stared. "Being here is rather like . . . like living in an enchanted place, a garden. That sounds foolish, I know, but I've been reading books at night that I used to read as a child . . . My God, life dies out from under you! . . . So fast . . ."

"*E' vero.*"

"Anyway," she said, eyes gleaming like the still water in her face's dimness, "I've been uprooted from my life and that makes you like a child . . . You know, I have no responsibilities here, really . . . as if I died out of my life and appeared here."

Eunice was trying to focus on the elusive softnesses of her face. Minna had a quality, she realized, that drew you into something promising depth, richness, exquisite tenderness, and (despite her sometimes acid tongue) soothing.

"*Sì, Io capsico,*" Eunice murmured. "When I'm on a

long holiday and have nothing even social to do. *Sí*."
Touched her friend's hand where it rested on the ground's
blurring.

"I don't even think about Kurt much. But I know . . ."

"Yes?"

"I know I'll be stuck with him again . . . sooner or
later . . ."

"Ah."

"It isn't even very sexual." Her voice too was pale and
still like (Eunice thought) the waterglow. "But . . . how
can you help certain things you feel?"

"I don't know, Minna."

"I disagree with him and I hate him sometimes . . .
he disappoints me . . . but . . . but . . . but . . ." She
shrugged in the vagueness.

"This I know," murmured the contessa.

Minna leaned into her so their shoulders touched.
They were a single paleness now. The water was ghosted to
nothing.

A few days later Renga was outside a command post in
a deep trench on the western front. He stood on a narrow
wooden walkway, leaning in against the sandbags, peering
just over the top across no-man's land. He felt the strange,
familiar tension of the front, the electric atmosphere where
you carried your life like a glass filled just over the brim.
The front was a total existence that absorbed men and (as
he'd discovered) left the world behind the lines a bright
illusion . . . drew men back to its darkness where each
breath was a miracle, where nothing could ever be taken
for granted except death.

He looked across the dark wasteland that was never
really still. A false sunset glowed beyond the enemy lines, a
reddish flickering. Star shells kept going up . . . red . . .
white . . . green . . . very high up the big shells rumbled
over and boomed down miles behind the forward lines
. . . machine guns went off, muffled, sporadic . . . sniper
shots cracked . . . men crept to the latrine ditches . . .
dozed . . . died . . . crawled out to string barbed wire in
the lurid halfglow of moon and mist and fire . . .

He clutched suddenly at the sandbags, hugged the
wall, as a howitzer shot (he knew the ripping sound) hit fifty
yards down the line. The fragments droned away into the

night. He slowly straightened up again. Suddenly thought about Eunice. Her letter was tucked inside his boot. He'd read it several times. He remembered saying good-bye at the station in Nice. They'd expected to be back together in a few months at most and now it was over two years. He remembered the last time they'd made love. She'd stunned him, marked him. He remembered over and over again. Between her and the war, there was nothing left, he realized, of his old life. It was a shadow of a long-lost time. Those days lived only in the secret places of his fragile existence, the soldier's inner solitude where memory is a window out of unbearable, blank desolation in which oblivion matches his every step, and Renga believed now that he truly understood the medieval painters who drew a death that was personal and followed you through your sunlit garden, stalked you in your canopied bedchamber, sat, skeletal, to share your evening meal . . . dug earth with the farmer . . . rode with the hunter . . .

He'd given a letter of his own to Madame von Moltke to pass on to his love, if she could. He hoped it didn't seem foolish and too bitter because the war was in his words. Nothing would ever be same after this, if he lived. He smiled wryly. The general had said he would live. That he had an important destiny. But it was easy, he had to think, for generals dying in bed to talk about destiny. Shook his head. Let the memories flow on . . . found himself thinking about the last days with Eunice. The rich, sweet summer nights—talking with his heart open—discovering her, the curves of her flesh, scents, strengths, and the turns of her past, the touches of light and shadow within her.

"Lieutenant," someone was calling him. He glanced down into the dim, crowded length of trench. A sniper's bullet spanged and whined nearby. Someone cursed, muffled in the wet dirt.

Renga recognized the sergeant at the entrance to the dugout.

"They want you inside, sir," he told him.

Renga nodded and jumped down onto the duckboards that semi-floated in the bottom of the trench.

On to more miserable business, he thought. *I need to get drunk.*

He pushed through a burlap hanging into the dank, cavelike, timbered and sandbagged short tunnel. The air

was cold and stank (though he barely noticed) of kerosene
and footsweat and mucky earth. The Flanders mud was
soupy clay and clung and clogged like no other in the
world.

The captain was just looking up at him when the earth
soundlessly leaped, cracked open, and blinding red went
utterly black. His last impression was of flying free, high in
dimensionless softness and peace . . .

XX
(1916)
Italy

Contessa Eunice Malverde was eating lunch with Minna
Fragtkopft at the long table in the informal dining room.
Minna was at the other end, her back to the floor-to-ceiling
windows that looked out over the white houses of Florence
and the dusty-looking green rounded hills surrounding the
city. The autumn sun was already dipping low and the
buildings were streaked with shadows.

The honey-yellow sunshafts glowed in Minna's hair.

How lovely Thou art, the contessa thought. Sighed.
Sipped her chilled white wine and studied the other woman
in the blur of highlights. Minna's long, graceful hands both
held the stem of her glass like, the contessa fancied, an
Oriental. So delicate.

She's still uncertain, she thought. *Poor, shocked thing . . .
this is all so new to her . . . well, to me as well . . . such dis-
coveries . . . such depths . . .*

How long had it been? A week now. She'd been here
no more than a week. It turned out she'd never gone back
to Germany at all. She stayed in France, working at the
Sorbonne. In the library. They'd exchanged letters and
finally she'd come to Italy for a visit.

The contessa smiled, faintly.

My God, she thought, *such a visit!*

The second night she'd finally admitted it to herself. She'd brought Minna bath salts as she was already in the steamy tub and the maid was asleep. They'd talked and she'd scrubbed her back for her, looked into her pale eyes and seen she was weeping, and had held Minna while she sobbed out two years of loneliness and despair. Kissed her cheeks and then her neck and soapy-smooth shoulders. Finally her delicate, scented mouth, tasting salt and something like mint. Felt herself go faint with longing. It had happened once before. In school, once before, but nothing like this. The exquiste softness and perfume, reaching under the hot water and touching flesh that was like a fairy tale, feeling the other sigh and, helplessly, unfold.

But there's nothing like these surrenders, she reflected, *to the forbidden mysteries.*

It was a strange, aesthetic lust, she decided. Nothing really resembling the shadowed burnings Rudolph ignited within her. It was, somehow, she was sure, the difference between northern springtime and hot southern summer . . .

Ah, Rudolph, my love, may God protect you and bring you back to me.

"It is very Italian, very Latin," she had told Minna the first morning, lying coiled together under the silken bedclothes in the subtly brightening room, in the grayish first light seeping around the massive window hangings. "At the covent school, you see, it was very common. When we were little girls and so on. They make boys seem so . . . so terrible, so sinful, you see?" Minna had just held her and said nothing, face on Eunice's stomach, her hair a vague gleaming as the light slowly gathered and sketched the forms in the room, the paintings, chairs, dressers, urns. "I was really about thirteen, *cara.* Anyway, it was nothing too much."

We just go day to day, she was saying to herself. *That's all we can do.*

"Would you care for more wine, Minna?" she asked, wanting, really, to hear her voice, gauge her mood, her thoughts . . . Was she upset?

Minna shook her head, looking out from the dusty sunlight.

"What happens to us?" she asked.

Eunice put down her glass and stared a little.

"We go on," she finally responded. Raised both her hands and gestured in a kind of shrug.

"We go on."

"We live . . . what else can we do?"

Minna didn't reply. Looked away now.

Eunice wanted to get up, to go to her, but kept herself still.

"What else can we do?" she repeated.

XXI
(1916–17)

There was no body, no form, and nothing moved anywhere in a stillness that was not silence because there was no idea of sound to measure it . . . after unmeasured time there were hints like dawning, grayish, gleaming . . . then a tall shape, willowy, swaying as if in a wind of flowing light. Became engrossed in it's water-shifting being . . . wanted to remain there forever, drinking in the shadowed illumination and soundless music . . . and then the light was a voice saying: "Go back and keep this peace within you. You have much to do."

Suddenly the dim glow was lighting the dark and solid earth as the almost figure faded, and Renga was himself again staring at mud. He felt a terrible weight and pain as his lungs strained and body tried to move. He felt a wash of agony beyond imagination. Couldn't scream because his flesh was mud to the eyes; mud gripped him solidly and filled his mouth and half his nose. He wondered, abstractly, how much of himself was intact, tried to re-form himself from the sticky goo and finally, smothering, managed a single nostril which, whistling, drew air . . .

And then there were only fragments: hands, voices around him as he was separated from the cold, foul mucky earth that seemed to fight to keep him. Freed by agonizing inches, mouth sucking, spitting glop, trying to scream . . . rocking as he was carried by the hands, hearing the meaningless voices . . . and the pain . . . the infinite, unending pain . . .

Then numbness that was a sweet bath of peace. He gradually became aware of rows of beds, whitewashed walls, the big crucifix, the quietly flitting raven-black and white sisters with their studied, soothing voices and the reek of chloroform and ammonia.

One morning the leaded-glass windows were parted and the breeze was warm and rich with spring. He shifted his faded body and tried to sit up for the first time. A young, round, red-cheeked nun fled across the quiet ward to his bedside and seemed surprised that he was really back.

"Take care, soldier," she urged, adjusting his pillow. "Not too much all at once."

"The air," he whispered, "do you smell it?"

His sunken eyes brightened, reflecting the yellow light that angled in the windows over the rows of wrapped and motionless men. His hollow cheeks were sallow; face all nose and bony brow. He felt a flow of waking strength as if his cells were drinking in the new season.

"We were worried about you," the nun said, holding his pulse.

He breathed deeply, as if for birth. The air was a sweet shock. His body stirred inwardly. His hands marveled at the smooth feel of the bedclothes. The bright air was a gentle passion.

He touched her hand with his long, bony fingers. Squeezed with amazed affection.

"It's so wonderful," he whispered.

She smiled.

"Yes," she said. "Have a care not to overdo it."

He was blinking.

"Don't you see?" he went on, excited but peaceful as a child, "everything is wonder . . ." Moistened his dry lips. "Wonder . . ."

He barely noticed when she went away, watching now the fanned sunbeams tracking slowly across the white wall and tile floor. Watching floods of dustmotes spinning,

defining the neat strands of brightness. He reached up and
poked his fingers into the streaming light, smiled at the
warmth and how his hand seemed to hang suspended there
with the arm in relative dimness. He made shadows on the
wall, bending the fingers. He watched, rapt, as the shapes
changed: an animal with horns . . . now a devil . . . now
a fat woman . . . now an angry man gesticulating . . .
now a pair of lovers.

He frowned faintly, suddenly remembering more of
his past life like something seen through a pool of water.
Murmured "Eunice" and saw the earth exploding, gray
hordes of men tossed and falling in a rain of blood and fire.
And then was suddenly asleep in a dream where everything
seemed not lit, but formed of sunlight: a glitter of brook,
green hillside spotted with yellow flowers . . . a castle on
the slope, vague in the shimmer of afternoon haze . . .
the knight in silver chain mail (who seemed so familiar
whenever he was asleep), a squire in blue at his heels,
strolling toward the gate . . . Shadows moved slowly on
the fields . . . entering the yard a beautiful woman looked
up in surprise and delight from among her maidservants,
holding a yard of red silk sewing and then the knight
glanced behind. The squire was pointing down the hill into
the valley where the shining thread of water creased the
bluish pinewood where something seemed to move just
within the shadows . . . a dim glint . . . a darker blot,
blurred . . .

XXII
(APRIL 1945)

He felt full of confidence, for the moment, limping down
the stalely reeking bunker passageway. The nurse (Feldbach) passed him and saluted.

"Heil Hitler," she said automatically. Her eyes were too
bright, almost hysterical.

He barely flipped his hand up in reply. Limped past and veered into the conference room. Flicked on the hooded table lamp and stood there, supporting himself on one hand while the other shook continuously at his side. He stared down at the netword of streets, found the Reich chancellery. The bunker was more or less underneath it. He studied the Russian positions, a mere few hundred yards away now and closer in places. He pictured the unending Asiatic masses pouring down on him. Still, if Goebbels were right, all that was needed was a final supreme effort here, hold them off just long enough for the enemy leaders to die, and let the ensuing chaos create a politically fluid situation. He nodded. Was already working it out: call a truce, then secretly mass whatever forces were left. Make a private peace with the Western powers (the American General Patton, for instance, hated the Reds . . .), then smash—united if possible, alone if need be—into the Bolshevik army and drive them back . . . back . . . and exact a terrible toll, a toll never before dreamt of! The thought excited him and he nodded. Shut his eyes to better see it. He'd been foolishly soft and merciful up to now which was why he'd nearly failed in his great task. Well, there'd be an end of all weakness! This was how they repaid him for his humanity! Well, well, there'd be no second chance, not for a single child or hundred-year-old woman!

All I need is breathing room. Just a little more time.

The first man in modern history with the will to remake the world, totally. He shook his head with fury and disgust. To re-create the line of truly divine rulers instead of the degenerate cowards and fools who had brought the earth to misery and gray mediocrity. He had opened the channels (like the legendary kings) to the invisible spirit and intelligence (something only a handful had the dimmest conception of) and failed. No, not yet. Frowned, and ground his teeth. The fools who took him merely for a politician or conquerer . . .

He nodded, then had trouble stopping his head.

He could see it, eyes thightly shut: millions of Russians driven into the freezing sea by an iron ring of tanks and cold-eyed, pitiless men.

He stared at the map again, pale slightly puffy hands in the chill circle of light, braced on the table. He would

gather himself for a final effort. Gather the will, call them
again, call them down to help. He'd believed they'd
betrayed him, left him to perish, but once again he'd open
his body and soul to the remorseless will of the world . . .

He went back and locked the steel door. Dragging his
foot he went to the far end of the room and stood facing
the gray-green concrete wall. Then he went carefully down
to his knees. Clasped his hands as if to pray. Began
murmuring in a monotone, over and over:

"Cometomecometomecometomecome . . ."

Then he floated over glittering wastes of snow where
the dead were locked in frozen blood, where his steel hands
were swarms of tanks, where his mouth was blazing
cannonry, rending, pounding, pounding, melting the foul
hordes to shreds and smears, to howling phantoms
whipped away to nothingness by the gales of his will . . .
And then his head flashed, stung: he'd tilted into the wall,
had fainted or dozed, and with terrific strain levered
himself back to his stiff, aching knees . . .

(1918)

"It's coming," the man beside him said, tense, crouching close to the mucky, crumbling trench wall. They were
all boot-deep in the clay mud. "Any time now."

Hitler glanced around the dark trench, fitfully lit by
star shells falling out in the black, barren wasteland
between the lines. Saw the young recruits in baggy uniforms that could never be cut down to a proper fit over the
gangly, adolescent limbs; their pale, waiting faces, looking
around without speaking as the big shells went over,
rumbling and muttering, and the smaller shrieked and
hissed. They never learned, he reflected, they could not tell
the little, deadly, whispering daisy cutters that came suddenly and ripped them to shreds from the monsters that
dug deep before exploding and kicking up tons of relatively harmless muck that was only dangerous if it landed on
top of you. He'd seen these boys bunch together under fire
and die like huddled sheep. He shook his head at the
thought. They died for little purpose. The training, he
decided, was at fault. That was clear. Germany had not
been spiritually prepared for this war. He could see that
now. Their defeat was inevitable. And necessary. They

would have to begin again, from defeat and chaos. They would turn to him, he thought, because he carried the flame of their strength in his breast. It would not flicker there and everyone would know that.

"Any time now," the man, a beefy veteran, repeated.

Hitler grunted and headed into the captain's dugout. It resembled a mine tunnel. He blinked against the greasy oil light. the orderly handed him a packet of documents which he tucked into his dispatch case.

"Good luck, Corporal," the captain remarked, glancing up from the map on the table.

Hitler clicked his heels, which surprised the man. There was very little parade discipline at the front. Except for the new faces, naturally.

"Thank you, Captain, sir," Hitler said.

"Give him tea," the officer said, "before he goes."

Hitler felt uneasy in the pit of his stomach.

"Can you still hear the English lorries over there?" a lieutenant wondered as the orderly handed Hitler a tin mug of steaming turnip tea, which everyone hated.

"Yes, sir," was the reply.

For weeks now they'd heard the trucks coming up to the front, one clear sign of an imminent attack. There was no hope of deception in this war, he reflected, but, on the other hand, that left it a real fight and the better side had to win, barring some unforeseen treachery, naturally.

He was shifting his feet, waiting for the tea to cool a little. Took one scalding sip. Heard his mind (or a kind of voice) say:

Get out of here now.

And he turned, putting the mug down on a crooked shelf and darted through the curtains into the sloshy trench. He stepped up onto the firing ledge to keep his feet dry.

Inside, the lieutenant raised an eyebrow to the captian.

"He's an odd duck," he remarked.

The captain was drawing a line on the map. Grunted.

"He does his job," he said.

"The men don't like him much," the other said. "I hear he refused promotion."

The captain reached for his pipe, slouching on the backless stool.

"He said he liked his job," he explained. "Simple. There are men like that."

"He's odd all the—" the lieutenant had started to say when the monster shell hit and the concussion ripped the whole section of trench apart.

Hitler was suddenly in the air and then rolling over a tangle of screaming recruits. He got to his knees.

"Barrage!" the shout was going down the line. "Barrage!"

The whole sky was flashing red, like a dozen summer storms at once. The dugout was gone. Utterly. There was a gaping pit of darkness now. Smoking bits of pulp and uniform shreds were spattered everywhere. One of the boys was gagging, desperately wiping bloody meat from his eyes and hair.

Again, he thought, *I've been spared again* . . .

Then the shells began to hit everywhere at once, walking over and around them into and out of the trench. The earth leaped and tilted. Blinding bursts. Mad shadows. One recruit was plunging in a circle, screaming, tripping, and then he vanished in a flash. The men were still scrambling into the dugouts. Hitler lay there in a welter of severed limbs and tangled guts.

He scrambled along, arching, twisting, creeping on his belly as the trench gradually melted down around him . . . passed a man howling and butting his head into the mud wall, over and over . . . another sat up in the wild light, gripping his hands to hold his torso together . . . several times Hitler was blasted flat by concussions . . . he clutched the dispatch case strapped to his arm and plunged and crawled madly on through the reeling, stinking terror . . .

Ages seemed to drag past . . . he ran, twisted and bent as if invisible hands guided his movements . . . and then the flailing shadows and flame showed the command post dugout and he ducked inside as a blast went off at his heels, and a fragment numbed his foot but didn't penetrate the thick bootsole.

He looked around the timbered cave. Dirt spumed down from the shells hitting above. The enlisted men and officers were pale, eyes too bright, faces a little sunken and too-finely etched.

The major squinted over at Hitler. The candlelight

shook shadows around his strained features. A few men were trying to play cards but concentration was impossible.

"How in hell did you come through?" the major demanded.

Hitler was a little pleased with himself.

"On my two legs, Major, sir," he replied as a direct hit shook the cave, and suddenly men were cursing and striking out with trench spades as a swarm of fat, scuttling rats broke for the entrance. The soldiers raged and struck in frenzy but most of the creatures flopped and zigzagged out into the seething night. "Dispatches, sir," Hitler announced.

"I can't say if you are the bravest man among us," the major considered, "or merely the most insane. In any event, these papers are of limited military usefulness until the storm lets up."

The earth heaved. Everyone staggered. Dirt poured down. A young recruit began to scream. A burly noncom shook him by the shoulders and slapped his face.

Hitler found himself a place by the sandbagged wall and settled down. The man beside him stared. He was gaunt with dark eyes and a jutting chin. He jabbed his thumb to point across the fetid space.

"They can't take it," he said, "these new faces." Held a canteen out to Hitler. The alcohol stung his eyes. "Go on."

Hitler shook his head. Grunted. The other man pitched his voice to the lulls as the thundering rolled over them.

"What do you think?" the fellow pressed, sipping from the canteen.

Hitler shrugged.

"Our counterattack will come in time," he said.

At the far end the major rolled up his map and lit a cigar. Sat there bareheaded, puffing. The stocky noncom who'd subdued the recruit was squinting at Hitler.

"That's a great comfort to us all," he rasped.

"If we can break through here, in Flanders," Hitler declared, "the war can still be won."

Somebody in the group groaned with disgust.

"Well, well, excuse us, General Ludendorff," the square-faced veteran said, "we didn't recognize you."

There wasn't much laughter as the pounding went on.

The new men looked around constantly, nervous, claustro-phobic.

"How long will this go on?" a pale, full-lipped boy asked.

The noncom winked at him.

"Not too long, son," he said. "We'll be saved by the general's counterattack soon."

"What did he say, Myers?" asked another private.

"He said not long, Franz."

Hitler murmured to the man who'd offered the drink: "Could it be there's a Jew out here?" He smiled, sarcastic. "I wonder how they trapped him"

"I've seen a few in the line," the other responded. "We had a Jewish officer for a while. He was shot dead on the Menin road."

Hitler unconsciously hummed a snatch of song. The words ran through his mind. He'd heard it sung in a beer hall behind the lines: *Everywhere his Jew face is grinning, Except only in the trenches* . . .

"It is just as well," he said, "that they're not at the front, for the most part. It might, otherwise, cost us the war." Then he settled himself down for a nap while the endless barrage went on and on . . .

He did sleep because when next he opened his eyes grayish dawnlight seeped into the fecal sweat-stinking hole. He thought someone was wounded. Then realized one of the boys was sobbing, beating his fists into the earth. A companion (the Jew, Myers) held him by the shoulders from behind.

"I have to go outside," the boy kept saying, "I have to see someone . . ."

The shellbursts were like a muffled drum. There were no echoes. The mud was churned up and rained back continually.

Hitler sat up, scratching the lice bites between his legs and under his arms. He crept to the doorhole and parted the canvas curtain. Peered out. Stinging, yellow-green smoke seethed everywhere in a foul fog.

He cautiously stood up and scanned the area: cratered, lifeless fields where a forest had been shattered; fountains of muck leaping as each shell hit dully. The earth was so churned soft now that (he knew) there was less danger from the blasts unless the shell practically hit you.

He ducked back as a series walked down the mushed and crumbled trench toward him. The soldiers' ears popped and hurt as one hit just outside and ripped away the hangings. The boy screamed in the brief lull and spilled out the exit. Hitler caught him and tossed him back where he tripped over outstretched feet and rolled on the packed earth, crying out:

"Mommie! . . . they don't care, Mommie! . . . oh, help me . . . please, Mommie . . ."

Pounded and clawed the wall.

"Truss him up, for God's sake!" the major raged.

At twilight Hitler took another look. The dull thumping had gone on steadily all day.

"How many shells do they have over there?" someone had asked.

"It's the Americans," another had answered.

It was raining now. The gray sheets mixed with the masses of smoke. Nothing to see. Even close hits were dim orange smears.

He hunkered back inside and settled down again. Some men were sleeping. The mad recruit lay tied in a corner. He rolled unceasingly against the wall, staying in the space of a foot or two now. He was totally hoarse, though his mouth still formed cries.

The corporal beside Hitler spoke again, grim and cynical.

"They mean to cut the wire," he joked.

"They should use clippers," returned Hitler with a smile, "and spare the cannon." He glanced around the foul, dank cave. The major was crouched close to the greasy lantern, writing. "If we hadn't hesitated at the Marne," he went on, "things would be different today. The French were beaten at that point."

The lean man shrugged.

"What does it matter now?" he wondered.

Hitler trained his gleaming, magnetic stare on the other soldier, who found himself fascinated by the intensity smoldering in the long face.

"It matters," he said. "For the future. Whatever happens out here, in the end, Germany will have to recover all her power in order to triumph in the coming days. There's a larger issue at stake here."

"You mean afer *staying alive*."

Hitler smiled.

"Yes," he agreed. "After staying alive."

The dugout shook under a near miss. The major's lantern rattled.

"But what are the 'larger issues'?" The man sat up cross-legged, lean, strong with serious eyes. "My name, by the way, is Hess."

"Hitler."

They nodded.

"Tell me more." Corporal Hess requested.

Hitler folded his hands across his chest.

"At some point, maybe I will," he responded.

Hess grunted.

"God, I'd like to get sent back," he said. "But I wouldn't go home again. The people back there . . ." Shook his head. "They don't understand anything. I pity and envy them their innocence, you know, Hitler."

His companion nodded sagely. The earth shook slightly as the impacts drummed on outside.

"That's right," he said. "They have to be rudely awakened, sooner or later."

Hess shrugged.

"Let them all come out here for a few days," he suggested. "That ought to do the trick."

"The war is a hard school, but those who graduate will have a soul impossible to daunt."

He'd raised his voice over the barrage and ended speaking into a sudden lull. The grizzled, square-faced sergeant looked up from cracking lice with his bloody fingernails.

"Well, well," he called across the miasmic chamber, "that's the best one I've heard in a while. Good for the soul. That's a new one."

Hitler glanced at the man and fell silent. Frowned.

"Hm," he muttered.

"We ought to tie you up with him." The stocky man jerked his thumb at the bound boy.

Then the floor leaped and the air was full of fumes and dust. Men screamed and shouted. The lantern went out.

* * *

By dawn they had finally dug themselves out. The bound youth and some others had been suffocated by masses of earth. Those near the entrance managed to tunnel back into the trench. They were all black from head to foot when they finally stood in the gray, foggy rainlight and realized the barrage had lifted at last. It was only falling on the rear lines now.

Hitler's teeth flashed in his mucked-over face.

"Attack coming," he said.

They peered over the shattered parapet, straining sight into the smoke and fog that blew over the uprooted and leveled barbed wire.

"Nothing yet," said Hess. They lay behind their rifles now, waiting.

Then new shells, obscenely gurgling as they came in.

"Gas!" someone shouted. "Gas!"

A warning clapper sounded. The cry went down the line.

"Gas! Gas-s-ss!"

The men strapped on the grotesque, stifling masks. The lenses quickly steamed up and added blurring to blurs.

The shells hit and popped liquidly. The deadly greenish vapor mixed with the fog and smoke and flowed over the tense troops. Each soldier wondered whether his mask were sound, or if he would die hacking and spitting up clots of bloody lung. They crouched and gasped each stale, hot, used-up breath and waited . . .

Hitler blinked, rubbed his lenses. The enemy was overdue. The technique was to use the gas only at the last moment so the troops had to suffer in the masks. The greenish-yellow stuff oozed and clung and collected in the craters and crumbled trenches. He kept his head up as high as possible to stay under the unending spray of machine-gun bullets that chewed and chopped at the line. Men were hit and screamed muffled and horribly in the choking masks. Some, in agony, ripped their faces free, burning for air and then gagging to death on the seeping poison.

Hitler concentrated on controlling his breathing. His bad lung always hurt a little as it was . . .

Just as the gas was settling the light shelling stopped too, and long, uneven lines of men (well spaced to minimize casualties) seemed to take shape out of the foul convulsions of fumes and fog.

He was very alert now, waiting for the moment to yank off his mask, breathe deep, and fight. The machine-gun posts were already opening up here and there, chopping into the advancing brown uniforms.

He felt a strange beauty in all this: blurred mist and mud, seething clouds of death, men beside him, demonic in goggles and dangling snouts, while the enemy labored like mud creatures to reach them across a sea of churned, greasy slime where to fall into the soupy bottom of a shell hole meant almost certain drowning. After the battle hundreds would be found, just helmets showing above the scummy surface, maybe hands clawed, outreaching toward lost air and hope . . .

He watched them struggle like ants (he thought) in molasses. And now the Germans were all shooting at the nearly stationary targets. A soft drizzle was falling. The men stayed bent but nearly upright as they died, now. The living troops crawled and slipped and glopped forward while machine guns swept freely over them. A wall of bodies was being sculpted as new men struggled into the death zone. But the German forward lines were so thinned out by the days of bombardment that the British were actually breaching the trenches here and there.

What stubborn courage, Hitler thought. He took his mask off and others did likewise. The air stung and stank but was safe unless you were in a hole.

Someone shook Hitler's shoulder.

"Fall back!" he shouted. Moved on. "Everyone fall back to the next line!"

Hitler fired a last shot at a struggling Englishman about thirty yards away. Saw him stagger and sit down on the mud, clutching his side.

"Enjoy that, you pig," he snarled in frustration. He wanted to shout something, a black sound that would kill. A curse that would eat these sullen, persistent attackers who refused to stop. A word that would smite and eat them with poison and steel teeth. He stood up, swaying, eyes a glare of fury as he stared into the agony of a gashed, boiling, burning, bleeding world. He felt he almost had the sounds, the doom, felt giddy, about to shriek them, somehow, when a hand gripped and pulled him from the parapet, slugs slapping muck inches from his face.

It was Corporal Hess.

"Come!" he cried.

"You fool!" Hitler responded, spitting rage. "I never retreat! I was about to kill all of them!"

Hess blinked.

"Come on, for God's sake." He yanked Hitler who hesitated, then followed him into a communications trench that connected with the rear lines. They made good time over the shattered duckboards and scattered bodies.

Slogging just behind Hess as they circled the rim of an immense crater through the smoky drizzle, Hitler slipped, swayed, clutched for Hess, missed, and went over, sliding on his back to the bottom on slick, running mud until he vanished into the greenish mist collected at the bottom as if (the imaginative Hess thought) he had fallen into the hole to hell . . .

He stood there staring down, helpless, shocked, thinking:

My God, the gas . . . the gas . . .

XXIII
(APRIL 1945)
Northern France

"How do you expect—" Frank Astuti demanded in Italian and in English too, "How do you expect to find anybody? You don't know where we are. I don't know either, right? *Capisco?* Shit!"

The Duke-Renga was marching a few dozen feet ahead of him along the twisting dirt road that wound across the open fields and cut through spurs of pinewood. It was about noon and the mist had burned away. For the moment there was no sign of war except for a distant muttering of

shells and the drone of what he couldn't know were planes.
He half-turned to answer his companion.

"Peace, friend," he said in old Italian. "We need fear
nothing on that account." He smiled, marching along, tree
limb over his shoulder. "God will guide me."

"Holy shit," was all Astuti could manage. Stared with
inexpressible emotions at the flower-print housecoat on his
companion's back. "You're looking good there, you crazy
fuck." Shrugged. "Fuckin *mameluke* . . . he's out having
lunch someplace and I'm following right behind. Sure. God
guided him right to that fuckin old lady's robe here, so who
can tell?" Shook his head. "As soon I find the fuckin
division I cut loose from ths loony bastard."

They crossed a meadow, followed a clear, bright-
running brook for a while, and came out of a tangle of
berry bushes into the smoldering remains of a little
deserted village. German equipment was scattered everywhere: a shattered truck, blown-out field guns, packs,
empty gas cans, a pile of tattered army boots, broken and
bent rifles.

The buildings had been recently flattened. Astuti read
the craters and knew it was the work of planes. The Fifth
Army hadn't been here yet.

He squinted up into the powdery blue sky. Waves of
bombers were going over, high, rumbling deeper into
Germany.

"This is a strange, tortured land," Duke-Renga said.
"Nameless machines litter the earth. Great evil birds pass
overhead."

"You're right on target, buddy."

It was quiet and warm in the sun. The embers popped
and crackled softly. Astuti decided to take a break and sat
down on a low wall between two broken buildings. He
sipped from his canteen and watched the lanky madman
(as he half-believed) in the housecoat mount the stone steps
and vanish into the cool shadows of what might have been
the town hall.

Inside, Duke-Renga blinked in the dimness cut by a
few stray lines of light from the sagging, shifted roof. He
took the building for a church and was searching for the
altar.

"I need Thy help, O Lord," he murmured. "Lead me to the murdering devil."

Not merely, he thought, *for mine own vengence but because the devil means to restore the age of dark magic to the middle world and breed cruelty and intrepid demons.*

Something at the far end of the smashed hall caught a random sunbeam and mirrored a blinding shimmer. He blinked. Walked toward it, not quite thinking yet that it might have a meaning fallen to his prayers . . .

He went over and suddenly Rudolph Renga was himself again and was standing there, reeling, looking wildly around at the strange room, then staring at the bright, bare broadsword hanging on the wall in front of him. A suit of armor lay in a heap beneath it. He numbly read the bronze plaque:

GIFT OF THE BARONESS VON LINTSTEIN
TO THE VILLAGE OF LUMPPE

Where am I? he asked himself.

Obeying an impulse, he took down the blade and held it at his side, vaguely surprised by its weight. He headed back for the entrance where daylight gleamed fuzzy and bright.

He remembered the battle, the shellblast and then only brief flashes: the dark road . . . smoke and fire in the woods . . . swirling fog . . . reminded him of dreaming . . .

He stepped into the light and recognized Astuti sitting on the low wall facing him across a littered yard. Overhead, bombers were still going over. There was gun thunder in the distance.

"Now you won't need that stick anymore," the American said, seeing the weapon.

"I keep blacking out," Renga said.

Astuti frowned.

"What's this shit?" he wondered. "You can talk English again?"

"I keep blacking out . . . Where are we?"

"You don't know?"

Renga looked around. Leaned the sword against the wall the moment he really noticed it in his hand.

"Germany," he said. "I—"

"Touchdown," Astuti commented. "I think you're out of your mind a lot."

Renga kept trying to stay focused on the warmly bright landscape. The memories or visions or whatever kept superimposing images of another time and place (or resonant fantasy) over what lay before him. He kept seeing dim, green-lit stone corridors, stairs, distant movement as if people walked with dull torches through an immense fortress . . . seemed to follow some dark-robed and armored warriors down a wide, shadow-swallowed staircase, keeping far enough behind them to be unnoticed, slipping quietly into the stronghold of doom itself . . .

He blinked and shook away the vision.

"You must help me reach Berlin," Renga suddenly said.

"Berlin, huh?" The soldier was very sympathetic. "Absolutely. I was going there myself, you know what I mean?"

"I must try," Renga said, desperate, thinking about the terrible facts, the things he knew, the horror no one wanted to hear about. He'd tried to tell them . . . tried to see the Pope in Italy . . . generals . . . tried to contact Winston Churchill . . . "They think I am insane," he murmured.

"Oh, no," said his companion. "Who fills their heads with bullshit like that? You're no more nuts than a waltzing mouse, Professor."

"I have to try because it was passed to me and it would be better to have died than not to try."

"I have had a sign from heaven, sir." He picked up the sword. Ripped the air with a vicious cut. Then, tossing away the robe, he marched back inside.

Astuti stood staring, waiting, debating whether to get away now. He found, for some reason, he still couldn't leave the madman, even without rationalizations.

When the duke stepped back into the mild sunlight he glittered in chain mail and light leg armor. He'd replaced the SS helmet with a pointed knight's model with a bar for a faceplate. It resembled a modern football mask. He'd sheathed the sword and looked (the American thought) bizarrely impressive.

"Now," he declared, "I stand ready for what must be done!" He was greatly pleased. "I regret there is no like suit for thee."

(1918)
Italy

Eunice rolled over. The silky sheets whooshed softly. The bedroom was dim. Bright, red-gold leaves showed at the tall windows in the thin, late light.

She rested her hand on Minna's sleek, bare hip where she lay facing away. She gently stroked almost the bare length of her leg. Touched her softly rounded feet and stroked back up again, a kind of questioning in the movement. Heard her faintly sigh, a vaguely resigned or helpless note in it. She turned and lay on her back.

Her taste was still on Eunice's lips. She inhaled it with each breath. She moved her long fingers over her lover's groin and rested her hand firmly between her legs. As if it set a seal on something. Minna looked at her from the pillow. Said nothing.

Eunice felt, even after all these months, as if her hands filled with silken electricity whenever they touched her, as if their souls leaked together.

Just the fact that the other made no move to resist, even slightly, made her almost giddy with desire. Her softness, edgelessness . . . sometimes she bit hard into her then hungrily licked and kissed each mark she left as if they were sweet fountains in the flesh.

She leaned up over her lover now, searching those sea-colored eyes that seemed to glow and hint at unending depths . . .

Sometimes she wished they could live without ever having to even speak words, because the purity of what she felt was smudged by their conversations.

"I . . ." she started to say.

Minna didn't quite pout her mouth. Didn't quite look away.

"This is a dream," she murmured.

"Ah."

"It is more real when I sleep than when I am awake." Eunice nodded.

"Yes," she agreed, without meaning it, because she understood why the other might have to say these things.

"I find myself in a place from long, long ago . . ." She shut her eyes.

"Yes?" urged her lover.

"A strange place . . . unlike anything familiar."

"A house?"

Minna turned so her lips were close to Eunice's breasts.

"No," she told her. "A countryside with no sun . . . bright but gray and misty . . . like pictures in a book, now that I think of it, which we had at home. Imaginative paintings of prehistoric places where dinosaurs roamed . . ."

"Cavemen?"

"No. Slender, attractive people . . . so real to me . . . cities . . . and a secret place where I go and it is as though the sun shines only there except it is not the sun . . . so real . . ."

"What shines there? Fire?"

Minna shook her head. Eunice cradled her now and kissed her shoulder. Her scent was spicy and delightful. She wanted to make love to her again except she sensed a distance and held back.

"Not fire. No . . . Light in the earth . . . no, in the rocks, something in the rocks in this secret place that shines like the sun and everything else is always gray except for the trees and flowers . . . but the sky is always gray . . . so strange and yet so real . . . and I am sent to this terrible building . . ."

"Who sends you, dear Minna?"

"I don't know . . . I am told to go and it's a palace or a prison, I cannot tell which, carved under a volcano because there is lava like rivers all around and black stones and men with spears and swords . . . I have to go there and the light . . . it's like a jewel sealed up in a locket around my neck . . ." She sighed. "Why am I talking about this?"

"I am interested. Italians take dreams very seriously."

Minna shrugged.

"So vivid. I want to give the locket to this dreadful man . . . I think he's the ruler of that place . . . I'm afraid of him . . . I don't show him the locket, if that's what it is, and he keeps me, makes me have sex with him and this other woman I think is his wife and I try to tell them things about the secret light but they laugh and then later they are angry . . ." Shook her head. "Time is so strange in dreaming . . ."

"Yes. And in waking too. But what is the final result?"

"I don't know. They take me somewhere deep and dark . . . under the palace . . . down into the earth . . . there are others with us . . . I can't really remember much there—I think I wake up because there is pain . . . much pain . . ."

"Poor softness." Eunice leaned down and kissed her foot tenderly. "Poor sweet one. No pain . . . let there be no pain in any of your dreams."

(1918, A FEW WEEKS AFTER THE END OF THE WAR)
Italy

Renga had walked from the station in the little town, and it was midafternoon by the time he strolled through the ironwork gate and stood looking up at Eunice's villa. The sun and air felt good. Crisp and good. The autumn colors lingered, that warm winter, the bright leaves against the white stucco. The clear, sharp shadows.

"Home," he said, thinking:
Anyway, it feels like home . . .

He knocked but no one stirred inside. He smiled. It was meant as a surprise anyway. Tried the door and it swung soundlessly inward. Most of the drapes were drawn and no lights seemed to be on downstairs. As if the day and season had been shut out, denied.

He listened. No voices or kitchen bustle.
The cook and the rest must be out at market . . .

His steps were muffled by the rugs and carpets and hangings as he went upstairs. He smelled traces of perfume and yesterday's cooking.
The place needs fresh air . . .

What a contrast to the brightness and vigorous atmosphere outside. The house was neat and clean enough, he vaguely realized, but felt sealed off almost like a sickroom.

His heavy boots (he still wore his faded uniform) seemed swallowed by the deep pile in the corridor. He paused at the bedroom door at the end. Smiled again. Had a feeling she was sleeping. Italians napped, he recalled, amused.

Opened the door quietly. No light there either. His eyes were adjusting; the bright afterimage from outside had almost faded. Stronger smell of perfume and wine and food and something sweeter and stranger, yet familiar. A female scent like nothing else on earth.

What, he thought, *what?* . . .

A room muffled by curtains and silks and carpeting, a single thread of day angling in high up where fabric parted on an ovesized window. And then he perceived soft music, a gramophone, tinny and whispery. And when he registered and then focused on the movement, the lingering brightness in his vision made it seem, for an instant, as if he stared into a dream of some fantasic fairyland where perfect female creatures danced in joys past man's understanding . . . another world, long lost and hopeless, and they *were* dancing, both of them, close together and naked, soundless over the rugs, the music a faint, lost sweetness that was roughened and blunted by the crude machine that called it into being . . . yes, and he understood. Of course he understood. He was shocked and yet he understood, even as they stopped and looked at him. The dream melted around them as he almost wept and almost laughed but did neither, because he now understood the sealed dimness of the house, the room . . . all of it.

"I am back," was all he said. "Back from the war."

(1918)
Pasewalk Hospital—Germany

Hitler lay in darkness. For weeks bandages covered his eyes. For weeks he woke fitfully from dreams and sights that flowed endlessly past him. He saw lost times and often-incomprehensible scenes. He saw ancient forms of the earth; saw lizards and fanged creatures, vicious and furious almost beyond understanding; saw man-shapes that were not men, stalking a world made dark at noon by volcanic ash, lit only by the flickering of flames, man-shapes with dark wings and eyes of fire sometimes flying heavily into the heavy air or perching, grim, furious, on the barren

rocks; witnessed a war that went on for ages across the
surface and above the obscure earth between harsh,
winged killers and a paler race whom (he knew) would have
been exterminated if the clouds hadn't finally begun to part
here and there so the healing sun could shine on the arid,
burning earth. The sunlight drove back the old lords even
as they hurled molten stones and breathed corrosive gases
at their enemies, drove them down under the earth to hide
from the sun's brightness. And then he beheld a new race
rising to dominate a world of hot, bright mists and swampy
earth, a mix of the old lords (who had by then become
stunted, stealthy, wingless wizards of the underworld) and
the surface people . . . he watched a child of that race
grow up into powerful manhood, fearless and agile in
comprehension, dominating his companions, defeated only
once in a serious mock-battle of wills and blunted spears
when his brother (Hitler heard their names too: Relti the
elder and Ner the younger) disarmed him at a feast-day
tournament, felt keenly the frustration and humiliation of
that day and felt the vow to never know defeat again, to
rule over all the others and pay back his brother . . . Hitler drifted on through Relti's strange life as if an unending
surf of dreamlike time swept him along: witnessed Relti's
schooling with one of the great priest-masters of the secret
tunnels beneath the mountains, masters with eyes of cold
fire who could match their breaths to the wind, smash open
the earth at a shout, blast enemies with unseen spears of
willforce . . . watched young Relti cross an inches-wide
bridge in a vast cavern overseen by the chanting elders),
balancing his way, naked, supple, to the flattened peak of a
spire of rock that rose thousands of feet from the depths of
a pit where lava lakes and streams glowed like coals, and
stood there, perched above the abyss on a surface barely
wider and longer than his feet . . . He clasped his hands
before him and shut his eyes as one of the priests released a
supporting rope and the slatted bridge went slack and
hung from the cliffside stranding Relti about twenty yards
out and half a mile high . . . Hitler felt the experience
and the power that came to preserve the boy, the power
that would give him invisible wings to return to safety
. . . and he knew (as the dream flowed away to vaporous
imagery) that the youth left the caves, armed with his will

and the knotted winds themselves, a magician warrior who would live and rule for centuries . . .

Hess had come to see him and now stood in the crowded army hospital that reeked of camphor and disinfectant. He was near the cot where Corporal Hitler lay, eyes staring and tracking empty air, hands clenching and unclenching the yellow sheets. He was smiling from his long, sallow, gaunt face, smiling with such glee and inexplicable triumph that an orderly had just stopped too and was squinting at the patient with uneasy puzzlement, hesitating, not sure (Hess concluded), whether it was agony or madness showing in that fierce, blind stare . . .

There was a buzz and murmur outside and it passed in the door. Hess heard it coming behind him, closer and closer . . . then the words themselves that shocked him though he still stared at Hitler and was the only one who witnessed his actual response as the voices said, in tones from despair and rage to relief and peace:

". . . over . . . over . . ." "What?" ". . . yes, by God . . ." ". . . war is over . . ." "Germany surrendered . . ." "No, never!" "Yes, it's true . . ." ". . . just announced . . ." "My God, my God . . ." Weeping too. "We have been defeated . . ." "Thank God it's all done at last . . ." "Defeated . . ."

And Hitler, at that moment, struggled to sit up, blind eyes rolling as if he could see, a look of victory and glee and stern purpose on his face, the lips speaking without sound, Hess was almost sure but never dared ask if he'd silently mouthed; "Thank God! Your words are fulfilled!"

PART II

XXIV
(1918–19)
The Eastern Front

Alfred Rosenberg was limping slightly, footsore from following the winding lines of German troops marching and straggling home from the eastern front in their shapeless, gray uniforms. The lines stretched away into the evening's blur as they crossed the cold, flat Prussian landscape.

He looked around the somber stone village. A few hard-faced inhabitants, old men and boys, stood on the sidewalks and stared at them. The soldiers were strangely silent: just the grinding of the boots, on and on . . .

Rosenberg, in his baggy Russian suit, could go no further for the moment. He'd fled a long way. He fell out and sat with his back to a tavern wall. A few soldiers were already there, nursing their aches and complaints.

"At last," the private beside him said. "You got rid of these damned rags first." Plucked at the front of his army greatcoat.

"Don't despair," Rosenberg reassured him. "Germany will rise again."

"You think I give a damn for that?" The man was incredulous. "I'm a shoemaker. I want to go home. To hell with the Kaiser and the war."

Another man muttered approval. The rest seemed, to the former Russian citizen, totally apathetic. One lit his pipe and puffed in silence as the columns tramped past like shades from some voiceless Hades . . .

They didn't grasp what had happened, Rosenberg realized with a thrill of fear. They had no idea of the terrible menace at their backs he'd barely escaped . . . and it was coming: all the vicious filth that had destroyed

Russia was seeping into Germany like, he thought, an overflowing toilet . . . into the whole world too, if it wasn't halted somehow.

His hand reflexively went under his coat and felt the roll of papers there. His eyes narrowed as he looked around suspiciously because he had the facts at last and what *they* would not give to silence him and burn the precious documents! Soon he'd be able to name the poison and the poisoners . . . Why not? He was already in Germany, after all. He stood up, hesitantly, hand still under his coat as if in parody of Napoléon. He kept blinking. No one was paying any attention. Still, he blushed and was ready to sit down, fully meant to, and then found (as if an outside force had squeezed the words into his throat) himself speaking:

"Listen to this," he suddenly said to the men around, nervous, emphatic, pale hands darting and fluttering, suddenly feeling that what he said now would somehow spread like a clean wind before him, that once he spoke the effect would be irreversible. "I've just come from Moscow. There's a plot to destroy the whole of Europe . . ." A few looked dully at him. One smiled. But he knew that what he now said would be embedded in the soul of a nation, and he went on with increasing energy. "The Bolsheviks are coming to Germany! You have to know this. You have to fight them!"

The smiling man looked up from cracking lice between his blunted, chisel-like fingernails. An old-timer, bearded and scarred.

"Fight?" he wondered.

Rosenberg nodded vigorously.

"Precisely," he declared.

"Anybody here ready to fight?" the old soldier wanted to know. The man beside him, rubbing his bare, sore, acrid feet shook his head, laughing.

"I saw it happen," Rosenberg insisted, excited, head bobbing. He was waving a pamphlet. "And it will happen here! The Reds and Jews will grind you in the dust!"

"That's funny," the old soldier said. "I thought I was already ground in the dust.

Chuckling.

"Are these German soldiers?" Rosenberg asked.

A burly noncom with drooping mustaches looked up sullenly.

"That's right," he said, "and these fine gentlemen here spent their best years in the damned line. So you better shut your mouth."

"The Jews have done their work well," Rosenberg muttered.

Somebody threw a helmet which glanced off his leg. Another made a break-wind noise with his mouth.

"You should read this." He held up the pamphlet. "Did you know that in 1848 the chief rabbis of Europe met in a Swiss cemetery and plotted the enslavement of mankind? Did you?"

He backed away and ducked a filthy, wadded sock that left a trail of foulness in the air behind it. He stumbled back into the rutted road and fell in with the endlessly marching troops, the ghostly dark-gray flow draining back into the heart of Germany.

He glanced at the booklet in the vague light before neatly folding it away. "The Protocols of the Elders of Zion." He pictured the scene: the chill windswept tombstones under a full moon; the black-cloaked rabbis in wild beards; bent beaks, crouching, nodding, *davaning*, clenching and unclenching their bony, pale, rapacious hands, eyes alight with malice and slyness while the demonic leader exorted them in words reported, it was said, by a Christian who'd hidden himself nearby in an unfilled grave.

"We shall create unrest, struggle, and hate. We shall poison relations between all the world's peoples. By envy, hatred, struggle, warfare, even plague and starvation, we shall bring the world to such a pass that they will willingly submit to our domination! We shall seduce and ruin the youth and not stick at bribery, treachery, treason, so long as they serve our master plan! We have the weapons of boundless ambition, burning avidity, a ruthless need for revenge, relentless hatred. From us emanates the specter of terrible fear and total terror! We are the chosen, the true men."

(1918–19)
Southern Germany

Kurt Fragtkopft lit the candle on the long table in the
cavernlike hall. The rafters were hung with barbaric
banners; shields, swords, and pikes dressed the gray stone
walls. A sign in gothic capitals proclaimed: Knights of
Teutonic Splendor. A dozen knights gathered around the
table behind beer mugs and cheese: old men, ex-soldiers,
young men.

Kurt was seated beside a pale youth in a cadet's
uniform. The fellow's hair was shaved behind in the
Prussian style. He wore steel-rimmed glasses. His soft,
white hands occasionally fingered his vague mustache.

All eyes were on the speaker, his burly face (thought
Kurt) like a ripe grape wearing a horned Viking helmet. As
Kurt's attention wandered, he noticed the ensign cadet had
turned his way, eyes lost behind the glare of his spectacles,
mouth virtually a lipless slash. He recalled a terrifying
religious teacher he'd had as a boy. The slash was faintly
smiling.

"Pretty dull," it whispered.

Kurt agreed.

He frowned and let his mind wander while he didn't
listen. He'd heard Minna was back with her family. He'd
almost made up his mind to visit her and see what ought to
be done. During the war there'd seemed no point in
pressing the issue one way or another. He'd let himself get
over being hurt, furious, and insulted the first year. He
didn't really face that he'd let his pride dominate, because
that was easier than trying to really understand her. He'd
kept busy with the Thule organization: amazingly, some
unnamed higher-up had kept him from active service. He'd
stayed at the university, in uniform, with no actual military
duties apart from writing a few papers on "Race and
Germanism" for the general staff. He'd realized, with a
certain inner swagger, how powerful his associates actually
were . . . He felt he was finally on the real inside track,
the rest would follow.

Somewhere in there he'd decided to forgive Minna her

middle-class absurdities. She was just misguided. He actually missed her, he realized. He'd been sleeping with a
nurse lately but there was nothing to it, *nothing*, he thought,
long-term there . . .

Raised his eyebrows and glanced at the prim-looking
cadet and exchanged another sly smile with him. Sighed.
Checked the seemingly frozen clock on the side wall . . .
tapped his fingers.

After the meeting ended the two of them chatted.

"Germany," the fellow was saying in a wry, flat, boyish
voice, "has to go back to her deepest roots, don't you think?
Before she can hope to recover full spiritual strength."

"A bone," said Kurt without really concentrating, "is
always stronger at the mend."

The other nodded. Round glasses flashed the torch-
flames. Delicate hands twisted the beer mug on the damp
boards.

"Well put," he agreed with strangely empty enthusiasm.

Kurt had been sent here to monitor this group for the
Thule people. Every week he went to a different meeting of
some patriotic or occult society and made a report. He
looked for potential recruits but this crew, he'd decided,
were hopeless. This dreary youth dressed as a cadet for a
defunct armed force was a perfect example. What was he
doing here listening to old windbags prate about folk-
magic . . . What nonsense!

He was about to drain the mug of pilsner and make his
excuses to his pallid companion. He was thinking about the
nurse, remembering the other night in bed together. *She's
got her points,* he thought.

"I feel," the other man was saying, "we must apply
scientific methods to the development of a healthy nation.
Don't you agree?"

Kurt blinked.

"Scientific?"

"We must get people to breed intelligently."

He blinked and forgot, for the moment, the nurse's hot
blue eyes . . .

"Why?" he asked sharply, looking for a certain slant of
response now. Maybe this flimsy fellow had more to him
than was apparent.

"To recover the best racial strains," was the reply. The

glasses flashed again. "That's why I come to these silly affairs. I'm hoping to meet men with like views."

"I see. Well, there's two of us, then."

He held out his hand and felt the other's smooth, almost fragile grip before the slim fingers fluttered self-consciously away back into his lap.

"I'm Kurt Fragtkopft."

"Heinrich Himmler," said the other.

XXV
(APRIL 1945)
Northern France

The duke and Astuti were in a deep pine forest. The narrow dirt road was padded with brown, fallen needles. The dusk was like smoke. Except for distant, wavering airplane vibrations and muffled thunder that was not thunder, they were suspended in a warm, sweet-scented peace.

Astuti was reminded of a fishing trip. He used to go with his cousin Johnny. They'd pack fresh mozzarella, Italian bread and wine. That was living, he thought. Johnny went with that Spanish or Cuban broad. What was her name? Cubans were hot. It would be nice to get laid again sometime and have a decent meal.

He'd almost forgotten (in his reverie) the nut with the sword wearing a woman's housecoat over armor, who was just now crossing under the dense branch roof in the invigorating silence and stopping under a massive tree. He squatted down with his back to the bole.

"What's the story?" Astuti asked, then remembered to switch to Italian: "What now?"

The duke was gathering chips of wood and sorting them.

"We must now take omen," he replied, shaking, then

tossing the chips onto the rich forest floor and studying them closely. "And plan our course."

Astuti nodded sagely.

"Uh-huh," he said. "Right." He cocked his head and watched. "You are asking little pieces of wood where to go?"

"Yes," said the older man.

"Sure," Astuti agreed. "I woulda done it myself in a minute." He sat down and unlaced his boots to air his feet. "It's a bitch that you're so sane, Professor." He stretched out, hands under his neck. "It's also a bitch you don't play cards, è vero?"

"As a matter of fact," Renga said in English, "I play five-card stud, among other American games."

Astuti raised both eyebrows.

"Welcome back," he said.

"Yes . . ." Renga leaned gingerly against the tree trunk. "It's like falling asleep. I feel well enough. Do I fall down in a fit? What happens when I—"

"You start talking nuts. In Italian. Fancy Italian."

"So I'm not . . . out cold, as you say?"

"Nope." Astuti sat up and lit a cigarette. "You claim you're a fucking knight or something and you pick out weird things to wear. Look at what you got on, for instance. Some style, eh?"

"My God," Renga muttered, holding his face between his hands and rubbing as if to clear his mind.

"But you got some idea, irregardless, you know what I mean?"

"Hm?"

"I mean, now and when you're long gone: you want to go find Hitler which ain't too realistic."

"Hitler," he murmured. "But . . . My God, so I'm not dreaming it." His eyes were a little wild but aware. "It's as if I'm asleep."

"Oh yeah?" Astuti responded with moderate interest.

"Why are you staying with me?"

The young American sucked in a long pull of smoke. Coughed. Stared at the cigarette, reproachful.

"Don't ask," he said. "Don't fucking ask, okay?"

Renga was trying to get his bearings.

"Where are we?" he wondered.

"Ask me because I fucking know." He sighed and

wriggled his toes in the loosened boots. Shut his eyes. "I been following you. You're the German, ain't you?" Shook his head. "I figure, if we find Hitler, you know, it would be a large thrill. It would make my week. Want a smoke? Why do you think you're a knight anyhow?"

Renga shook his still-stunned head.

"Obviously I'm being guided." He thought about the tide and how it finally had him in its flow. He was quite helpless except to go with it. "I cannot explain it to you now."

"Oh, no?" Astuti's sarcasm was like a mace blow.

"I think you'll have to follow me as you have been."

"Sure. Except you don't know where the fuck you are, right?"

"I will . . . I'm going to pass out again . . . It's happening again . . . I . . ." He leaped up, holding his face and swaying in the sourceless twilight. ". . . ah . . . help . . . follow me . . . I'm guided . . ." Leaned on a tree.

The soldier went over, feet noiseless on the padded earth.

"You still here?" he asked.

Renga sighed.

"It passed. But it will return."

"Maybe you should lay down."

"No. It's all right. It's the tide. My fate . . ."

"To be nuts? Were you always nuts or did you snap at a certain point—you know?"

Renga really didn't hear now. He was caught in a strange borderlight between two worlds: saw the dark underground, the lurking, shadowy, glitter-fringed images; a flaming pulverized city under a boiling sky; armies of millions, what looked like Hitler on his knees somewhere praying to a blank wall . . . and then he was weeping himself, murmuring:

"Eunice . . . Oh, Eunice, I loved you . . ."

Seeing her in a thousand lights and times at once, all one sad sweetness, a single sob of all things forever real and forever lost . . .

And then, as Astuti took his arm, Renga was gone and the duke was back.

"What means this, sir?" he asked in old Italian.

"I ain't sure I really missed you, buddy."

"Eh?"

Did you finish talking to the pieces of wood?" He pointed to the divining chips that the duke had tossed on the earth.

"We follow this road, fellow." Clapped the soldier on the shoulder. "At dawn we go on. If we succeed there's great reward for thee. If satisfaction at doing God's work be not enough, then the treasures of that black fiend will suffice thee, I think."

"Treasures?"

"Aye." He turned and seemed to be listening into the semidarkness.

"Maybe there's something to all this bullshit, Astuti thought. Them Nazis robbed half the world. Him being nuts don't mean anything. Shit, Hitler's nuts and he did all right. This gidrool was probably a Nazi himself. There's more here than meets the eyeball, signore.

"I do not care so much, sir," he told the duke, "concerning worldly goods. I go with you willingly."

"Well said, fellow." Went on listening.

"Why the fuck not?" Astuti reflected in English. *I swear,* he was thinking, *By Saint Antony and the blood of a potato I'll give half of what I get to the Church! Depending, you know, on the actual total, naturally.*

"What noise is that?" the duke asked.

"Which what?" Astuti cocked his ears.

"It smacks of sorcery. An army of giants, mayhap, dragging great chains."

The soldier heard it now.

"Holy shit," he muttered. "Tanks. Whose?"

"Well," the knight was reflecting, drawing his broadsword and striding toward the now clearly audible grinding, clanking, and blatting of exhaust. "We shall try one magic against another. Come, Astuti, and I pray thou are astute in thy craft of war as was thy wont before."

"Hey-hey, are you crazy?" Checked himself. Was lacing his boots. "I forgot, you are." Slung his pack, grabbed his rifle, and stooped nervously into the dimness after his companion. "Wait . . . wait up. will you?" The knight's figure a misty, fading shape on the scrawl of road. "Wait the fuck up . . . Holy mother, he's gonna fight fucking tanks now!" Hurried. "Wait up!"

(1919)
Northern Italy

Renga shrugged his shoulders after watching the two of them gradually surface in the underwater twilight of the bedroom as his eyes adjusted. The war had brought him to face this with a mere shrug. Before the war, God knows how it would have felt to walk in on this . . . Before the war . . . But his youth was already lost. The battlefield never really fades. It can be ignored but not forgotten. So he stared silently at the pair of them, Minna turning herself behind the contessa, both watching him, startled and still entwined, the whispery dance music still playing on the brass gramophone.

"Well," Eunice Malverde finally said, a little breathless, "Rudolph's come back to us at last, Minna. Welcome, Rudi."

8 July 1919
Herr August Kubizek
Rosenstrass 11
Vienna, Austria

My Dear Gustl:

I am sorry to have been so remiss in my correspondence. Events move quickly here in Munich. Have you seen Paula? Is your mother well? Germany has reached a decisive hour. The Red Jew government presently in power has sealed its fate. Many of us soldiers have never surrendered in our hearts. We have formed the free corps, small armies joined by a common fanaticism into a common goal: destruction of the Reds! Soon we march! Soon Jewish Bolshevik blood will run in the gutters! The elections that brought their damned regime to power in Germany through one of the greatest betrayals in history, will be repudiated by the German people. Men like Ernst Röhm, a war hero, will lead their men against the exploiters and oppressors of the nation. And we have secret support in high places. All Reds are known to us and will be dragged out of their ratholes soon and treated accordingly. I am working, in my own way, while still in the army, to bring justice to traitors. I will keep you up to date, whenever possible.

Yours faithfully,

Adolf

XXVI
(SUMMER 1919)
Southern Germany

Kurt Fragtkopft watched the spidery shadows of the two bicycles zipping over the white concrete road and, magnified by the low sun angle, flicking across the forest leaves that glowed the color of worn gold. The warm, scented wind was steady in his face.

Himmler twisted around to look at him. The round glasses flashed in the shadowed features.

"It isn't far now," he said. The spindly legs in baggy shorts pumped the pedals.

Kurt's own thighs were getting shaky. It was good that the valley floor was level here. He hadn't ridden so far since childhood. He grimly convinced himself it was good for him.

"You know," Himmler said, falling back so they were riding side by side, "I recently counted and found that I belong to seven organizations. It alarmed me, I think."

"Really?" Kurt tried not to pant.

"Yes. I suppose I'm a joiner." The round lenses kept blinking the light. Kurt found it hard to really see much, let alone read those pale eyes behind the glasses. It wasn't just the blur and shatter of reflections. The eyes were always lidded, and reminded him of some small animal, though he never could think of which one. "You know, my friend, I would give them all up for a chance to be in the army again. I feel cheated. I missed action by a hair."

"Yes?" Kurt was noncommittal. From what little he'd seen of the battlefields he wasn't sorry to have missed it. "I don't think it was so romantic as you imagine."

"Perhaps not, but there a man can find his soul and see what he's made of."

"Is that always so desirable, I wonder?" He wasn't sure how much he really liked this man. It was vaguely awkward. Himmler kept pressing semi-intimacies on him. Baring his soul, in a sense, and the trouble was it wasn't that interesting. Perhaps, he thought, he was just too middle-class. His ambitions seemed strangely disproportionate.

"You know," Himmler was saying, "I'm in love."

Kurt concentrated on his wobbly front wheel.

"That's fine," he said. He was suddenly worried.

"She's a wonderful girl, Kurt."

Thank God, Kurt thought. *It's a female.* Then laughed at himself for his sudden apprehension. *That would be too radical for our friend Heini.*

But, after all, he was friendly with the bulldog-faced boy chaser, that army captain . . . what was his name?

"I'm afraid my suit will fail," Himmler confided. "But I'm now taking dance lessons. I find it very challenging."

Kurt smiled. *Perhaps I was right to worry*, he said to himself.

"Ballet?" he asked.

"What?" Himmler grinned. "No, no, nothing like that."

A closed, bright car whooshed past, leaving a fine, smoky dust.

"Ah," Kurt said. Then: "Damned drivers!" Wiping at his eyes with one hand.

She told me I ought to relax more. I know she loves to dance and so who am I to argue with a beautiful lady?" Grinned with awkward rakishness.

"Very chivalrous, Heini."

"I try my best."

The vague dust shimmered in the golden twilight.

"Of course," Kurt agreed.

"The ideals of knighthood are still in the finest spirit.

Little today compares with them." He pointed ahead. "Here we are."

Kurt made out a cornfield and beyond it a squat, turretlike structure, archaic, mysterious in the gathering mists of evening. He could easily picture armed warriors watching from the slit windows and crenellated roofs.

They entered a side lane. Soft dust spurted around their slow wheels.

"I've been fascinated, you know," Himmler was saying, "by what you've told me about the hidden powers that rule destiny. But I'm firmly a Catholic, I'm afraid."

Kurt shrugged.

"The two positions are not necessarily irreconcilable," he remarked.

"I don't know . . . but I underwent quite a crisis of faith, Kurt, when I joined a student society last year."

"I noticed the scars on your cheek." He could see his companion was quite vain on this point. Watched him permit himself a faint smile.

"Yes," he said. "You know, the church forbids dueling . . . but . . ." He grimaced. "It was quite a problem for me." He twisted around and this time his eyes showed clearly through the glasses. Kurt thought there was something boyish in the look. "I love being in church." The tires were crunching over loose gravel now. "*She* attends regularly. This pleases me quite a bit. The *modern* woman, in general, I might say, is not entirely to my taste."

They hit a rutted stretch now passing the field of standing corn. Kurt saw the troops lined up in the vague twilight haze. Their ranks seemed to float over the uncertain surface of grass. With the ghostly castle behind he thought they could have been shadowy men from another age. Unclear banners were planted all around. Only a few seemed to have guns: some brandished clubs and even swords and hunting spears.

Coming closer he saw the uniforms didn't match; the helmets spanned generations as did the men themselves. Poised before them was a chunky officer in a fitted captain's uniform, hands on hips, barking a speech:

"That's Röhm," Himmler said as they stopped the bikes and listened together.

"Tonight," yelled the captain, "we march into Munich. The Reds who try to resist us we will cut down without mercy!" Röhm was calm and firm. Kurt could see why he was such a respected leader with his bullet-mutilated nose. "The fatherland is in deadly peril. You will all do what is necessary." Many of the men saluted. "Groups like this have sprung up spontaneously all across the nation. Despite the treachery of 1918—the November criminals—the fighting spirit still lives in our people."

He stumped away and the men started piling into two battered, ex-army trucks. Kurt half-turned and noticed that Himmler was arguing with one of the other officers.

"But this is too stupid," he was saying testily.

"Nevertheless," replied the other, "these are orders. You must stay behind."

"Orders?"

"Orders. You had better learn to respect orders if you hope to achieve much, Herr Himmler. You're a bit of a rebel, I think."

"What nonsense. Look, I—"

"Orders." And with that the officer went to the trucks.

Looking at no one as the machines ground and rattled away, raising dust, Himmler said, flat, baffled, and hurt: "I miss everything. I missed the war . . ." Pouted, clenching his awkward hands into fists and punching at the dimming air. "I always miss everything . . ." Stamped his rather (Kurt thought) delicate foot in the dust.

The night was wild with sound and flaring lights: gunshots, crowd howls, distant crashing and scurry. The city streets empty . . . then suddenly alive with struggling groups in shadowy clashes. Kurt smelled oily smoke from some burning building out of sight and heard the fire engines in the distance.

He followed Himmler who kept running ahead excitedly, revolver gripped at his side, craning his neck around, glasses flashing the shifting light now and then.

"Does anybody know what this is all about?" Kurt wanted to hear.

"What?" The other man was grim. "You're joking, naturally."

Kurt wondered how he'd gotten into this. Heinrich had convinced him this was a historical moment no one dared miss. The president of the republic was a Communist. The rightists had already shot his wife to death and were after him now. The Reds were supposed to be starting their revolution tonight.

"I haven't seen mobs of Bolsheviks yet," he muttered.

"That's because the army and the free-corps men, like ourselves, are striking hard and fast!"

Just so I don't get my whole ass shot off tonight, Kurt thought, just realizing he might be in serious danger out here. His nerves tensed every time he heard distant shots . . .

They crossed a huge, bare square lit by harsh, spare lampposts. Kurt saw a spindly young girl running in silence, just her feet clack-clacking on the wet cobbles, shadows tilting and whipping as she passed in range of the lights and then was gone into the darkness of buildings. People were indoors tonight, he realized, with the lights out.

Suddenly shooting, screams, roar of motors. Kurt and Himmler ducked behind the central fountain which spurted feebly from a gaped fishmouth. A black car screeched up on jammed brakes, swayed to a halt, back door flapping wide (the fender almost scraping against them), and then a tumble of flopping limbs and billowing clothes as a lump of man splashed into the fountain. Kurt saw the dead face, mouth, a raw gape of darkness. Then someone pale, round-headed without eyebrows peered from the front window and then Kurt saw a V-shaped head in a back behind a glint of gun-steel. The door slammed shut and roundhead said on the heels of the one in back who first cried:

"Thus to traitors!"

Others were crammed in there and Kurt felt the guns aimed and his heart raced in the face of death, the round mouth in the bald face saying:

"You two there! Reds?"

Himmler waved his gun and Kurt nearly shrieked and ducked, expecting instant destruction.

"Germans!" Himmler piped in his wavering, reedy excited voice. "Germans, loyal to the Kaiser and the army!" He was obviously in his glory, Kurt noted, just to be able to say that.

The round one:

"It's unsafe, comrades, to wander like this. The damned Red battalions are everywhere." A thick hand

jabbed at the fountain where the body turned in its
shadows and the spreading stains of the dark that spilled
from it. "There's one of the dogs!"

Kurt saw Himmler lick his lips and not quite turn to
look as he responded:

"Good justice, comrades."

"Better keep within," roundface suggested.

And then the car was gone in a whirr and rush.
Himmler tugged Kurt who was staring at the slowing,
spinning corpse in the water.

"Come," he said nervously, "come." Strange excitement showed.

A few streets later, ducking close to building walls and
doorways, crouching along in reflected fireglare, low
clouds glowing like coals, they heard screams ahead, raging
shouts, and gunfire.

Then, around the next semi-surburban bend (where
city-style buildings sat in vacant lots and fields) there were
barracks and a big, isolated concrete building Kurt vaguely
recalled was an army headquarters.

They crossed the street, Himmler stripping off his
overcoat to show his cadet uniform. They passed the open
gate, the sentries unreacting.

Lines of men stood under floodlights, armed troops all
around them. The army was purging communists; the Red
government, legal or not, was about to be broken by its own
forces. A single figure (Kurt at first assumed was the
commander) was striding slowly, grimly down between the
lines as if reviewing the weaponless soldiers. Kurt squinted,
saw a pale, brooding face, a full mustache, and eyes that
(even at this distance) seemed to concentrate the harsh light
into colorless, fierce glow. Coming closer Kurt saw he was
wearing an enlisted man's uniform, plain gray. As he
crossed against a floodlight his shadow flared out over the
men and swayed on the building wall. A group of officers
walked behind him as he pointed to one man . . .
skipped . . . then another . . . skipped three . . .
pointed . . . and the first man started to run, feet crashing on the cobblestones, and he'd almost reached Himmler
and Kurt when a single rifleshot cracked and he threw his
arms wide, seeming to embrace the air before toppling on
his face. The other men who'd been checked off were being

dragged away to the concrete wall where firing squads were already formed. And then Kurt recognized the face, bony, pale, concentrated: the man from the meeting who'd sat with the dwarf, now pacing on in cold brightness sending men to their instant doom. When he'd reached where they stood, one of the officers was saying with unconcealed condescension:

"Very good, Corporal Hitler. Your work is done."

Kurt was afraid, but he knew it wasn't just the guns and the screams and bullet-impacts and pleadings at the wall. He kept staring at the corporal and his mind told him that he had just a pale ordinary face with strange eyes, just some kind of spy . . . betrayer. He noticed Himmler was staring too, probably (Kurt imagined) wishing he could play some dramatic part in all this, out in the center of things with life and death hanging on his actions. Saw Himmler's glasses flash the flat, artificial light again.

(1919)
Munich

The colonel had a strangely naked face. Pale, laced with fine scars. His back was arched, one gloved hand on his hip, the other gesturing with a cigarette, his monocle flashing at Hitler who stood there with eager, restless eyes watching this perfect Prussian, not thinking he was either absurd or impressive. But now, each time fate opened the next vista before him, he was awed by the massive certainty of its inexorable machinery. He felt fear: somehow he'd be stopped short, frustrated yet again. So he watched uncritically and anxiously as the razor-slim soldier faced the office window watching the heavy rain patter and pattern the day's deepening grayness.

"So, Captain," the colonel said to the third man present, blocky Röhm, master of a virtually independent army of ex-soldiers who'd refused to accept the peace that left them jobless, "you feel we have here the best man for the work?"

It was an unnecessary question, of course.

"Yes, sir," Röhm affirmed.

"You worked for us," the colonel said without actually

looking at Hitler who was already nodding, impatient to say yes. He had a general idea of what they wanted. Röhm had let him know that much. "You were, I believe an . . . informer?"

"Yes, my colonel," Hitler snapped back, instantly afraid he might have overdone the enthusiasm. He felt he had to seem confident, not too obsequious but disciplined and trustworthy.

One Prussian eyebrow arched a fraction. The colonel's disturbingly hairless face didn't quite confront him or Röhm who sat just outside the gray window-shape of light. Hitler hoped he wasn't leaning forward too intently. Rocked back slightly, watching the bare features, glints of the monocle, gestures of the cigarette as if the smoke were writing.

"We support a political party," the commander informed him. "Does that surprise you, Corporal?"

Hitler pouted his lips into firm grimness.

"The army, Colonel Mayr, sir," he announced in his deep, hoarsened voice, "must be a political instrument by its very nature. When the nation's leadership is degenerate then the most virile and capable men must act." He clenched one forceful fist before his chest as if to strike himself. All nervousness was instantly gone. He had trouble checking the flow into further speech. He noticed the colonel was finally looking directly at him. He saw his own intense, long-nosed features in the round glass. He'd trimmed the mustache and irrelevantly wondered if it really looked more impressive. Röhm had suggested it. Fashions were changing. "Fashions change," his verbal momentum continued, watching to see if he still held the other's attention. "Fashions pass away and peacetime politics is but fashion; nevertheless, the eternal struggle of peoples never ceases. The army is the lifeblood of the state!" Managed to check himself again, shifted his momentarily fixed, far-seeing gaze. He sensed the power and smoothness of the instrument he was becoming.

Mayr had raised both eyebrows. Nodded slightly, glancing at Röhm.

"Well, well," he said, with amusement but no scorn, "this sounds like just the man. The very one, I think." Nodded. "The very one."

* * *

Hitler stood in the narrow, green-walled room. Through the steel-grate slit windows he could see the drill yard, the gray sheeting rain, frothy puddles, and he thought how like a prison it was. He turned back to the mirror above the sink, wiped water over his eyes and cheeks. Kept smiling. Couldn't help it. It was really happening . . . at last . . . at last. Sucked in a deep breath.

Started to leave to go back to Röhm and Mayr then whirled at the door, shaking his head at himself, darted back and flushed the toilet without quite looking at what he'd nearly left there.

At the door he clenched his fists at his sides and shut his eyes.

"I swear," he whispered, "I will be worthy. Even to the end." Stared up, half-saw, half-sensed the almost figure, almost form, as if wavering there. "I swear!"

The floor suddenly blurred and tilted. The greenish walls became a swirling fog. The stall door slammed into him. He knew he was falling, clutched at the rushing green that he didn't know was the toilet wall, and never felt his shoulder crash into the lid, cushioning the impact, because the lurid fog had parted and he seemed to be in a harshly glowing chamber cut low into emerald-colored rock that he knew was deep under a mountain fortress. The greatest fortress on earth.

A supple, slightly bulky in the torso, fierce-looking man with a spear strapped crosswise across his naked back stood facing him, head near the jagged roof. The greenish gleaming seemed intensified by the warrior's hollow, pale eyes. The face was like a wide V.

Hitler (though that was not his name in that place) knew him well: Lord General Rog of the Lemurian Skull Riders. Felt satisfaction seeing him. A small pool of dark fire bubbled in the cavern floor between them where Hitler sat cross-legged. It was molten rock caught in a dark bowl with a metal lid hinged open.

"Yes, Master Relti," the general was just saying. Their arms were very long with jutting, flexible joints.

Relti, Master of Kings, was staring into the red intensity of the dark bowl watching the shapes inside it change, straining to read those changes as portents. He was afraid. He'd been forced to doubt for the first time in the decades of his iron rule. And to fear too, even there, in the center of his fortress city, defended by force and magic. Because his old enemy was alive and seeking him while armies of traitors and weaklings and cowards threw themselves in futile desperation against the ringed defenses of his capital.

"There are betrayers everywhere," Relti said.

"But not—"

"Even among the Skull Riders, loyal Rog. Even there. I can trust only a handful. The shapes have shown me that much," he said, pointing to the bowl.

"They must all be slain, Great Master."

"There are powers and terrors and weapons undreamt of by my enemies. I will free them from where they sleep." Because he didn't fear all their armies or even the rebels within the walls so much as the one he sensed was near him again. Moving closer. Watching, waiting. "I will seek counsel of the woman in the pit. An evil thing is come, Rog, a slinking worm who seeks to destroy me and all I have achieved."

"I will slay him, Lord."

Relti gestured impatiently. The fireshadow portents showed nothing more. He frowned.

"He is of great power himself and cannot be slain by mortal means," he explained.

Rog nodded.

"Yet, he cannot be your equal, Master."

"He is near . . . I feel him. I hate him. I have always hated him."

"But—"

"Be still." Relti's arched eyebrows knitted into his nose. "He is my brother, Rog. My brother. And he has set the foul cowards and weaklings to destroy me. He is the cursed secret annointer of the 'New Race.'" He snarled, eyes wide and full of the blood-glowing embers and slow shadow. "The 'New Race' of womanlike soft-swords. Men who are not men but women's chattel. He has created them and set them to destroy us all and suck away our vital strength and manhood!"

Rog fumed and ground his small teeth together.

"Death to them, Master," he whispered. "Death to them."

"I must go under the earth and awaken the Lord. The unmaker who sleeps in the egg of night. I must fulfill what must be fulfilled." He leaned in closer to the bowl of molten rock, the greenish glow above creasing his face while his hollow-seeming stare filled with sullen red smoulder. "I must risk the world before my vile brother drags down the greatest glory in all memory and lets in the impure, twisted creatures massed at our gates to stain our perfect people!" He nodded. "I must risk the sleeper." His words were shadow and fire. "Better that the earth is charred to a cinder than that our enemies fill the world with their pallid spawn." He sat up. "A male with a half-hard prong is worse than a woman. I will pass through the dooms to the bottom of the world."

Leaned back over the bowl of flame until the heat beat into his face . . . and then Hitler was blinking, feeling hands shaking him by the shoulders, and a voice he didn't yet know was Röhm's saying:

"Adolf, for God's sake, this is a great moment for you and here you are with your face in the bowl."

"He seeks me," Hitler said without knowing he even spoke. "I see his eyes. I see his eyes . . ."

"Whose eyes, Adolf?"

Hitler blinked and was himself. The image was fading like the memory of a dream.

"Eyes?" he asked Röhm. "I must have struck my head." Röhm grinned.

"That's what comes," he quipped heavily, "of drinking from the toilet."

XXVII
(1920)
Munich

Renga was standing by the long, pale car, stooped against the cold rain to see Eunice in the back seat.

Here's my life, he suddenly thought. *I'm married. I teach. I'm childless. Nothing much ever happens . . .*

"I heard from Minna," she was saying from the dim interior.

"Ah." He wondered why he cared so little. The three of them had lived together for a while . . . before Minna went back to Germany. To her family home. He'd accepted their strange life like a dream of long, southern summer days . . . champagne in the garden at sunset . . . cold suppers . . . country walks . . . a lush, perfumed, vacant life where the past lost its black vividness . . . all the continuations of his past drifting until her uncle had gotten him this post in Germany and they married rather than float away from one another.

"Another letter." Eunice said with a shrug. "She's back with the fanatic."

"The husband, Kurt?"

"Yes. She's trying it again. She's a child, no? A . . . desperate, poor child." She leaned her face nearer his face. "So, enjoy your class."

"Yes," he said, straightening. "I'll see you at home."

She was still looking at him thoughtfully as the long car hummed away into the drizzle. He sensed she'd lost some feeling for him. Not exactly respect . . . He wondered if it would prove fatal . . .

He went up the slick gray steps to the campus. He frowned, going inside his building into the smell of wet clothes, steam, stale air, and damp wood.

Something's lost, he thought. *And won't return . . .*

He watched the class without real focus. He was more conscious of the rain pittering at the high windows behind him. He paced as he spoke. The blackboards were scrawled over with disjointed words and strange diagrams from the preceding lecture. He vaguely wondered what was taught in the room before he used it.

". . . therefore, *belief* is alien to true philosophy. If you hope to inquire into reality, you can't hold your prejudiced beliefs up before your eyes. It will twist your vision, because once you believe, you can no longer freely explore." He tented his fingers and stared up at the colorless, peeling ceiling. "The mind wants to sleep in the false security of belief, so it really hardly matters what it is *believing,* you see. In evil, in good, in kings or presidents. Do you see how dangerous this is? To *believe* means you don't know the truth; you are just hoping, blindly."

One red-haired, fish-belly-pale boy had his hand up and Renga nodded.

"Sir, Professor," he said, "does this apply as well to religious matters?"

"Well, what do you think?"

"Is not God and truth one thing, sir?"

"Can there be as many truths as there are religions, young man?"

Amusment in the room.

"I am a Lutheran," the boy said, deadpan, and there was terrific hilarity for a few moments.

"Don't *believe* in God," Renga told them. "That means you know nothing. To deny God is also belief. Both sides rest smugly in unproved conclusions."

A dark, thoughtful boy spoke up.

"But what else is possible?" His eyes tracked back and forth. "Just skepticism?"

"Is life nothing more than *believing,* which means not knowing anything for certain?" Renga leaned at them.

The dark student struggled with it.

"How horrible you make it seem," he said. "Yet that's what all our civilization is built on."

"Yes," said Renga. "Isn't it."

"But what can we trust?"

"Yourself. Not me. Not anybody. No experts. None of that rubbish. Test everything . . . even your own mind. That most of all. Tear down the little defenses it puts up to the vast mystery of what we don't know. Open yourself up to the tremendous unknown all around us, yes, and within us too . . ."

Do I do this myself? Where are these words from? He was watching a tall blond youth with water-blue eyes. *I must do this myself or . . . what a hypocrite you are, Rudi.*

"You'll find out everything," he said. Was suddenly pleading with them as if an overwhelming feeling, not all his own, was straining to be born here. "Only, in the name of heaven don't follow anybody!" The students, he realized, were surprised by the turn this lecture had taken. He was now feeling a great sorrow, the sorrow of all the ages that had flowed into this moment, all the pain, fear, darkness, and all the unending wars among everyone, man, woman, child . . . the tribe, church, nation, said "do this, kill them," and they believed and did it and the pain went on and on. "Don't accept anything just because others do!" he cried out. "Stand alone! Find out the truth yourself! Otherwise you're dragged on into the endless misery of the world! Do you see this?"

The tremendous feeling was fading now. He smiled faintly at himself. Opened his hands to them.

The crazy professor, he thought. But he felt better than he had in years. Listened to the rain rushing steadily outside. Hardly noticed.

XXVIII
(1945)
At the German Border

Astuti charged into the pine brush, ducking around trees,
calling out now as the tanks crashed, scraped, blat-blatted
closer and closer.

"Hey!" he yelled. "Where the fuck are you, you nutty
son of a bitch!" Branches whipped into him, stinging. "Wait
up, you fucking nut!"

And then a tremendous black shape, splintering sap-
lings, was suddenly over him, the screaming metal ripping
at his ears. He was in the middle of them and knew it was
now senseless to run if there were troops filling the gaps
between machines.

He ducked behind a massive trunk as the machine gun
spewed at him, tracers thrumming past, chewing wood,
smashing, whining . . . and then the part-armored lanky
warrior from some lost age (or schizophrenic professor
from this one) lunged past him, crying out:

*"In the name of our Lord Jesus Christ I adjure thee to
destruction, thou weapon of Belial and Meloch!"*

"Holy shit!" said Astuti, reflexively aiming his Garand
rifle. With the duke leaping aboard the tank he couldn't
toss even a token grenade at the ripping treads. So he let
off a clip at the vision slit above the machine gun and then
registered the dim forms of the following troops. (*Fuck*, he
thought, *SS!*) their black outlines fading into the darkness.
Holy shit! Mama mia! As the knight flashed his sword—one,
two, three—into the slits in the steel as if it were a gigantic,
visored helmet, like his own, Astuti heard muffled screams
as the machine gun spasmed, and he sent his next rifle clip
into the soldiers who were already ducking and spinning
for cover.

Hail Mary, kept repeating in his head. *Hail Mary
. . . Hail Mary . . .*

And then, reloading again, he saw the tank veer into a
huge tree and shatter the trunk as the knight jumped from
the back of what he didn't know was a machine and not the
armor of a devil, in a whirring flash of sword strokes. One
soldier flopping down as the blade sparked through his
helmet.

"Jesus," Astuti muttered as the hundred-foot pine was
crunching over the tank. The other panzers had started
firing blindly all around into the dark forest. Bullets from
the SS hummed and cracked around him. He didn't dare
poke out to fire back. Heard a scream in German. The
duke apparently had hacked another. He shook his head,
crouched close to the wood. "He's cooked now." And then
the blotting mass of branches swooshed down like a flail
over all of them ahead and he was already running and
reached the tank just as the turret popped open. He stuffed
a grenade inside and, as it went off with a hollow *punggg,*
ran down the trunk of the pine in time to see the strange
knight stand up among the dim branches that had flattened
the SS squad. He sheathed his blade calmly, satisfied. The
other tanks were crashing away into the woods. He shook
his head.

"All right," he said, "I believe in fucking miracles.
Period."

"Art thou unhurt?" asked the other.

"Yeah . . . Yes, *signóre.* But just tell me how you
caused this thing?"

"What is their magic to God's? Am I not a white adept
of the white circle?" He clapped the American on the
shoulder and then drew his sword again and slashed his
way clear of the massed branches. "My true test will come
when I face the dark lord himself. Meanwhile, we will
together scorn these base minions." He smiled, now invisibly. The stars were out. "Unseen power is all very well, but
to strike hard blows, ah, there's nothing so satisfying."

"No," Astuti palely agreed. "I ain't arguing. I got no
doubt you're right. Oh, yeah. You're right."

"Behold how they flee."

"They met their fucking match." The nightfall con-cealed the soldier's rather complex expression of lips and eyebrows as he spoke. *Maybe it was fucking magic,* he thought at length. "Why not?" he said to himself.

(1920–23)

Munich

"You said things would be different," Minna Fragtkopft reminded her husband. She seemed tired, hair bound up tight, a few stringy strands flicking the electric light in the gleaming kitchen.

Kurt was gobbling a piece of sausage and heading for the door.

"But aren't they, Minna?" Smiled his best smile.

She pressed her long chapped fingers to her pale cheeks. The shadows from the free-hanging bulb hollowed her features, seemed to be consuming them. He blinked uneasily at the effect.

Why doesn't she keep herself better? She looks middle-aged, he thought.

"You're still a bastard," she informed him.

"Minna . . ."

"What woman are you off to see?"

"Minna, please." He shook his head. "It's a social party."

"Ah. Will they be raising spirits?"

"Minna, it's a perfectly dull affair."

"Affair," she repeated.

"What?" He was at the door.

"And all your groups and strange—"

"My dear Minna," he cut in, "by your own admission your recent past has not been altogether . . ." He tilted his head back and forth.

She looked at him with cold hurt. Her face seemed bone and darkness.

"I put everything behind me," she said. "I came back to you."

"Minna, for God's sake."

She stared.

"Oh, go on, get out of here," she told him. "Go on!"

"I will talk with you later, my dear," he said, quickly

going out, chewing the blood sausage, "—when you're more reasonable."

Minna went into the kitchen and stood staring at the dishes in the sink. She felt drained, bloodless. Her lower back ached. Glimpsed her face reflected in the dark window. Didn't quite look at it.

Here you are again, you fool, she thought. *Here you are . . .*

Bit her lip. Remembered the home in Italy, Eunice playing the piano in the house after supper while she drifted around the lawn, barefoot, breathing, seeing, hearing; all thinking a single, wordless thought as if she floated shoreless. And now she knew her life was always haunted by images of lost things, things never in the present . . . all her life . . .

"Why don't I kill myself?" she said aloud.

Remembered a vivid, incomprehensible dream: herself (it seemed) wearing a sketch of clothing in a warm place, breasts bare, on her knees in a dim tunnel or cave, a low, menacing place; she seemed to be pleading with a black-robed man with a hypnotic stare full of dark smolder, his face long and bony, V-shaped. She sensed he was a ruler (herself a slave) in that inexplicable world. She was offering him something . . . a bit of jewelry on a thin golden chain . . . a supplication in the dream silence for him to touch it, take it . . . and then, as he reached out for the softly gleaming, locketlike heart-shaped bit of gold with one long-fingered hand the terrible woman loomed out of the shadows (this part recurred and recurred over years) and ripped her open with a silvery dagger and (in this version) flung the bright neck-chain away into the greenish dimness and in the silence somehow told the man that the jewel was magic poison that would, cureless, eat his strength away. The silvery blade kept glinting as he ripped into her heart and the scene dissolved in terrors . . .

Later Kurt was almost drunk, chewing and puffing an oversized cigar, laughing too heartily. He saw a lot of blurred but familiar faces. A foot-stomping polka was raging and swirling around the big room. There were silken half-tents set up under banners and hangings meant to suggest the *Arabian Nights.*

Himmler weaved over. His silver turban had slipped to

the side and part of the wrapping hung athwart his nose.
He kept blowing it away. His glasses flashed. He bowed
slightly and giggled. His hands were smeared with cream-
puff stuffing. There were flecks of it on his dark robes.

"Kurt, my friend," he said, "I've met a wonderful
woman."

"This is someone else?"

"Yes. She's quite remarkable. She goes to communion
every week. Can you believe that?"

Kurt shook his head.

"It's hard to believe, Heini." He knew his friend was
not the least bit cynical. He was (with the exception of some
priests) the most ardent Catholic he'd ever met.

"Women today," Himmler was saying, puffing at the
silken strand, "are weak in the morals, I think."

"How true," Kurt rejoined. "And I can't say that gives
me cause for complaint."

Himmler frowned. Shook his head as he swayed there,
trying to shift the ribbon of silk from his eyes.

"Morals are at a low ebb in this country," he said. "We
must re . . . re-establish sound beliefs." Nodded heavily.
Behind him the polka was pounding. A heavyset woman,
spinning on her partner's arm, careened into Himmler's
back and he staggered a few steps. Peered around, brows
knit. "What's this? . . ." Kurt saw how drunk he really was.
Unlike him, he thought. "She's an angel, my friend . . . I'm
unworthy . . . such a blunderer . . . a dumbhead . . .
unworthy of such a woman . . . But I will work very hard
and try to be what . . ." Nodded heavily. "I intend to make
her mine, my friend . . ."

"What happened to the last one?" Kurt wondered.

Himmler shrugged his hands loosely.

"She had some funny habits," he confided. "Funny
ideas . . ." Shook his head, then giggled. "Too modern for
me . . ."

"Ah," said Kurt. "And you were too something for her
as well, I imagine." He chewed the cigar and sipped his
drink.

"No matter . . ." Himmler lifted a glass of wine from
a table and inhaled it in one gulp. "No matter . . . I love
her dearly . . ." Shook his head and puffed at the pale
strip, glasses flashing the cheerful lights. "Religion purifies
life. Man must believe with his entire soul, and only then

may he dare to love. I have a number of thoughts on the subject . . ." He reeled closer to Kurt. "Everyone thinks I'm so easygoing, you know, that nothing really upsets me. How wrong they are, Kurt, my friend." Slugged down another glass of wine. "When I talk to the farmers at these party meetings, each time I've very nervous, you know. But I say to myself, Heinrich, you better amount to something, you better stand up like a man or life will pass right by you . . ." Weaved. "That's what I say . . ."

Kurt nodded.

"I think the party is gaining ground," he offered. The cigar was out again. The juices stung his tongue.

"Too noisy," Himmler responded, peering around, wiping his hand at the silken distraction now.

"I mean the National Socialists, Heini."

"I blunder but I'll never give up. I missed the war . . . but . . ." He whirled around. "Did you know my godfather was Prince Heinrich von Wittelsbach? Hmm? He died in battle as a good soldier should. Röhm was a hero. And Hitler too, even if he wasn't an officer." He took off his glasses and rubbed his small, pale eyes. "I was an officer . . . but I missed the battles, you see."

"Yes. That's too bad, Heini."

"I'm getting a farm. I put down the money." He wobbled closer and took Kurt by the shoulders. The dancing flailed past just behind him. The music screeched and thumped wildly. "I'll bring my sweet wife there to live . . ."

"I thought you just met her tonight?" Kurt was grinning. Got the cigar relit and puffed the biting smoke.

"When I read old German tales I see how purely people lived. I see beautiful cottages and noble castles and everyone content at his labor. Beautiful, green fields and flowers."

Kurt was fascinated by the dancing. The whirling seemed to pull at his mind and this amused him. The foul cigar went out again but he kept puffing, swaying slightly with the music. He sensed he was nearly as drunk as Himmler who was still babbling. As the couples whizzed by, the room seemed to lift and heave around and around, the faces blurring past seeming strangely agonized (but he knew that was absurd), as if caught hopelessly in the movement, fantastic costumes fluttering, robes, veils, glit-

ter, whirling in the thundering circle, trapped and lost
forever. Kurt blinked these notions away, body moving to
the gathering rhythm, sucked the tobacco, and tapped his
feet.

(undated)
Herr August Kubizek
Rosenstrasse 18
Vienna, Austria

My Dear Gustl:

At last I am knocking at the door! I have
joined a political party and you will, I think, hear
of us before much time passes. Germany is mor-
tally sick. The mark will fall. Unemployment
increases daily. The treaty of Versailles has left the
nation bankrupt. The French and British suck
German lifeblood. In a sense, it was better that the
war was lost because now our people are learning
how to hate. Only through hate and dedication
will the people's honor and dignity be restored.
We will fight back! A great leader must come soon.
I hope to pave the way for his coming like a John
the Baptist. I will speak in the streets and fight in
the streets! A new baptism of blood is needed
now!

As ever,

Adolf

(1920)
Munich

This is the hour, Hitler was thinking, pacing nervously
beside the speaker's rostrum (a long plank table) in the
stale, smoky, noisy beer hall. The long room was jammed
with a drinking, arguing, singing audience.

He found he had trouble putting his fears and this
moment into historical perspective: his mind told him the
future was assured, but his nerves had him in a sweat. This
was worse than the front line. How would this audience

react? Would he blank out in the middle of his speech? There were hundreds of hostile Reds out there.

Hess was beside him, saying something encouraging, patting his shoulder.

He thrust his hands into the deep pockets of his yellow trench coat and tried to convince himself that even if he failed tonight there'd be other chances. But he knew better. Too many eyes were on him and the secret portents made it clear that tonight was the turning point, one of those moments that could not be repeated. He wiped a pale hand at his forelock and paced. Breathed deeply, suddenly wanting to go outside, say he was ill. Someone was talking. He registered his own name and then hands were helping him up on the table as his insides sank and went cold. His brain churned like storm fogs. His points slipped away from him. Sweating, sick, dizzy, he tried not to look at the pale rows of faces floating in the grayish artificial twilight.

A month before, he'd been sitting across a round table facing the nude fat woman under a dim reddish glow in the velvety, muffled room. She breathed in erratic, flopping gasps, eyes rolled back, Eckhart slouched beside her, eyes unblinking; beside him sat the mustached captain with a pocketful of cigars, and others he'd seen before at other meetings. The woman's fat hands flipped and thickly fluttered on the black cast-iron tabletop. She grunted, almost (Hitler thought) oinked, nose running steadily, the mucus a serpentine gleam trailing over her vast, undulant breasts.

Then she was shrieking and shaking as if, he thought, she were in the American electric chair. The flabby body heaved and the table squeaked.

"Answer," insisted Eckhart. "Answer!"

"Fuck o shit o filth, God cunt and sick suck smell . . . Christ Tao and hole and hope and hate . . ."

"Answer!" Hitler suddenly heard himself roaring in fury, fear, and disgust, feeling the pitiless, cold, clear presence of truth and time straining to find a doorway through that stained and bloated flesh; straining to touch him again. "Speak to me!" he thundered. He didn't notice Eckhart smiling with satisfaction as his pupil took command of the séance.

"Hagan and Sulla," the drooling mouth mouthed. "You are and were and will be Hagan and Sulla . . . You cannot be destroyed until the last end betrays you at the peak of glory! . . . Shit piss angel sweet mother's shit! . . . Aiiiiiii! . . ."

Hitler swayed back and forth, hands reflexively crossed over his chest. His eyes were ice and fire.

"Is that all?" he whispered, hoarse.

"From your ashes the future will spring! . . . Aiiii! . . ." And she flopped from her seat and thrashed on the dark floor.

And his nerves had twanged like burst strings. He saw a greenish-glowing whirlwind rising from the gross woman. Felt himself falling as the spiraling cone seemed to reach for him . . . touch his mind which then spun with it . . . he was being sucked out of himself and poured down again far, far away . . . and suddenly he was looking up at a naked, completely hairless woman, slender, elastic, squatting (as if to evacuate) on a spire of rock, a stalagmite, her long-toed bare feet gripping the smooth sides, suspending herself above the needle point that if she slipped would impale her through the loins . . . Ritual . . . She was singing, lilting, candles set around the damp wall of the cave melting down in unwavering green flame.

And he was King Relti again . . . the lord of Lemuria . . . about to sacrifice his ordinary life for the power to save his race from the outsiders, the betrayers, the so-called children of the light whom (he believed) had been hypnotized by his brother, Ner, and set against him to weaken and poison his people out of spite . . . spite . . . well, he'd see . . . he'd see whose hate and will would prevail . . .

Relti looked up at the seer, the woman of the pit he had told Lord Asu he'd consult, while she chanted and hummed above the spike that symbolized her doom if her vision or her balance failed.

"Descend, O King," she sang. "Down to the place of he-who-sleeps . . ." Her nude face was a V of fierceness. ". . . let his strength enter you and make you the destroyer who will consume the hearts of our enemies . . . you will descend and be changed until you are yourself the sword and yourself the armor . . ."

He stood there, arms crossed over his chest, eyes intense and full of the green fire. Nodded.

"Yes," he whispered. "Yes."

She sang sweetly on:

Our enemies, O King, have poison in their hearts and loins, verily their seed is a hot poison and they would fill us with their seed and have our people conceive monsters and deformations until our true beauty and intrepid force is spoiled and we become slaves besotted by their sickly-sweet seed, O King . . . O King . . ."

"Yes!" he cried into the shadowy, stone darkness. "Monsters! Cowards! Twisted, dull, obscene, shrunken, gross, stiff dwarfs!"

He shook with fury and fear. Here was confirmation of his worst imaginings. His stare ignited. His will-strength gathered in his belly and firmed his hate and resolution. He would free the sleeping one. The terror of terrors. He would return from the terrible depths and crush the new race like bugs under his feet!

He and the priestess rocked and swayed and howled now in reinforcing, ritual, harmonized hate . . .

Hands crossed over his chest he stood on the beer table and raised his eyes in prayer to the spirit; his blanked mind panicked. He sensed his helpless need was opening him up as never before. For an instant he felt his soul naked and about to be sucked and blotted away, but better this than to fail . . . to fail . . . so he called it into himself, begged it into himself above the nondescript crowd sunk in tobacco haze, resistance, and indifference . . . he called, pleading, and his eyes suddenly filled with glare and strange light and the first row of benches went quiet and the somehow-reverential pause spread through the packed hall under the dim, raw electric bulbs.

Speak, he was asking, *speak!*

And then his voice burst from him in a shock of ringing thunder, the alpine-capped guards at the far doors turning to listen instantly, the motley listeners coming erect for a moment without opinion as a voice without words pulled at their minds setting a spell it took seconds to shake off, as the sound became:

"The traitors, cowards, and betrayers of Germany

won't say so but today two worlds are struggling for existence: the ideals of the national people and the ideals of the intangible international as exemplified by communism. It began at the moment when the Jews obtained citizenship in European states." He raised and cocked one fist, then slammed it into the other as if an electric current spasmed through him. He was totally relaxed and concentrated. The words found themselves. "The political emancipation of the Jews was the beginning of a madness: a people who were not part of our race and blood but were a race and blood unto themselves! They took root among the nations and that blood called out to itself and, in time, the whole world became their nation!"

That was, he distantly realized, close to the truth and fit. "Little by little the stock exchange began to run our national economy. This alien institution is almost entirely controlled, one way or another, by the Jews." He took a buoyant breath. The hall stayed silent. "In England and France, for instance, the Jew was able to hide himself so well he was taken for an ordinary citizen! And for this reason anti-Semitism in those countries has no elemental force. And *this* is what allowed democracy to dominate there! Only there, could a form of government be set up where genius and individual energy could be dominated by a dead mass. So it was child's play for the Jews to use this, to set up seemingly opposed political parties that all served the interest of this invisible group!" He smiled. There were a few catcalls in the rear. No problem yet. "That's why you have two parties: after one makes a mess of it—then ring in the other!"

Laughter. Lots of nods through the gray driftings of tobacco smoke. Here and there a heckler was shushed to silence.

Outbreaks of applause. Cheers here and there. The cold force still filled him and seemed to sharpen and stimulate his mind.

Divine force had not deserted him but had flowed into his soul at his desperate call. There was shouting and scuffling out there among the blurred figures in the smoke-grayed hall but he paid no attention.

"How long can this process of race betrayal go on? It will not cease until from out of this chaotic mass one man suddenly rises up, seizes the leadership, joins with other comrades, and fans the rage of the people into an all-consuming flame of hate against these exploiters and criminals who have never founded a culture of their own but have dragged hundreds of other cultures to destruction!"

His arms hammered the air, his voice drowning out the yells and battling and confusion sweeping through the rear of the meeting.

There was a commotion at one of the doors. Someone yelled in pain.

"The Jew spreads his 'revolution' like a disease! The Jew controls the food traffic and so brings about starvation. Why? So the ferment, the suffering, the need for revolution will not end! Because in world chaos this talentless, abominable race maintains its strange power over the world! The Jew wants war and causes war! He needs ignorance and promotes that!"

He shut his eyes in ecstasy, fists raised to heaven. Most of his audience waited, rapt. Most of the fighting was outside now: blows, shouts, screams . . .

"We shall fight them across the entire world!" he roared. "We shall gather our strength and strike them down! Aryans and anti-Semites of every nation must join in this struggle against the Jewish race of exploiters and oppressors of all peoples!"

XXIX
(1921)
Berlin—an Apartment

"The man has something," Göring was saying, the fluffy covers tucked around his chin. Flames filled the huge fireplace facing the bed. His wife sat in a chair. She wore a velvety nightdress.

"Germs?" she wondered.

"No, no," he protested. "I'm serious."

"So am I."

"This is a new kind of fellow, I think." His plumpish, strong hand picked an incongruously dainty pastry from a tray. As he chewed, the white sugar stained his cherubic lips. "The others mostly make me sick. Where's the spirit? Where's the Germany that made the whole world tremble? Weaklings groveling in the dust!" Wiped his mouth, smearing the stain. "But this Hitler, he's got energy and sense."

"And what will he do, Hermann?"

He rolled his eyes and sighed.

"I'm sick of peace," he muttered. "Say what you like, it makes weaklings.

"In place of dead men? Or cripples?"

"Never mind that talk. The point is, we need strength. They're turning this into a backward nation of Reds and human nothings! The Allies have chewed off our balls. The rich are still rich, naturally, but *we're* smooth between the legs!"

"Hermann, you're not in the barracks now! Mind what you say."

"Never mind that. Hitler makes a damned sound point or two. We're not finished yet, by God. Gather a few of the best men together, stick at nothing, and see what happens! That's his best idea. The war never ended."

She sipped a cup of coffee, not quite looking at him.

"I think you ought to stay out of all this . . . politics."

"Woman, it's more than politics. It's survival." Finished the last crumbs. "You ought to hear him speak. He stirs the heart. Then cooler, wiser heads will ride the storm to victory." Nodded.

She set down the delicate cup on the night table. It clicked softly in the china saucer.

"Stay away from all this, Hermann," she told him. "You want too much. I know you. Keep far away from all this."

He seemed intent on the flames: the bursting logs, raining sparks, the snapping and confusion of smoke.

"We'll wipe the grins off their faces," he muttered. "We'll show the bastards something."

(1921–22)
Near Munich

"The world has driven us together," Hitler was telling Röhm and Hess as the touring car smoothly swayed through the bluish-green-shadowed hills where white-washed houses flashed across neat farm fields. The setting sun was mellowing gold.

"Ade," said Röhm, "what a confession. So at last the facts are out!" He grinned.

"Eh?" Hitler frowned. Noticed the driver up front was half-suppressing a smile. "What's the joke?"

"Joke?" Röhm was sly.

"I'm serious."

"I'm glad to know it." He patted his companion's knee with thick, gloved hand.

"The great fish," Hitler went on, "swim in deep water. And, as the tide recedes, the small, weak, and slimy spawn struggle and perish near the muddy shore."

"What the hell are you talking about?" Röhm demanded. "Why, I thought you were finally admitting the truth."

"Truth?"

"That you're really one of us." Grinned. The driver controlled his face as best he could. "A different sort of man. Not just the enigma they make you out to be."

Hitler felt self-conscious. Frowned with his pale, hungry eyes.

What nonsense, he thought. *Sex is a necessary factor but why complicate it with men's great hairy behinds? Women at least are soft, for the most part, and made for surrender.* He generally tried not to think about these things. Late at night, sleepless or brooding through some formless, rainy afternoon, naturally such ideas surfaced. Inescapable human nature, he'd reflected more than once.

"Why, Ernst," he quipped heavily, "you know I'm consecrated to my work."

"So?" Röhm gruffed. "Is your asshole included?" He enjoyed his friends sudden unease, the nervous hands

flicking here and there, brushing and touching hair,
trousers . . . then tugging at the goatee no one liked.

"You fellows," Hitler came back, "think everyone else is
the same. Were we all like you, the human race would have
come to an end ages ago!" Relaxed instantly, pleased by his
idea. "I'd be out of a job!" Grinned.

"Excellent point!" Hess interjected.

The car was grinding to a halt off the road at an
encampment. The deepening sunbeams slanted among
rows of tents and thin trees. Hitler blinked. A shirtless man
was tied to a tree. Another uniformed man stood near him
holding a horsewhip.

"Here we are," Röhm said, "at Free Corps Hörner."

The men were, Hitler thought, wolfish, scarred, in-
tolerant-looking, and grimly watchful. He liked them in a
nervous sort of way.

These were soldiers who'd refused to surrender: the
Free Corps fighters who'd kept their uniforms and fought
in the wild revolutions after the war, who lived like modern
pirates, aided by sympathetic rightist powers in the state,
snatching booty from political enemies in open and covert
battles.

"What was the man's offense?" Hitler asked.

Major Hörner had come over and stood by the car,
thumbs hooked under his wide belt.

"Röhm," he said, "who's this fellow?"

"Adolf Hitler," the captain said.

"Ah. The big mouth." The major grinned. Hitler
didn't. "We don't have much manners here, Adolf," he
added.

These are men to be reckoned with, Hitler thought. *They
haven't forgotten the war . . .*

"I was at the front for all four years," Hitler said in a
voice of firm thunder. He stood up in the car, hands on
hips, looking the men over as if they were on review. He
liked that their eyes betrayed their hatred for the soft,
meaningless peacetime world. Here were men ravenous to
sink their teeth in the enemy's throats, men who'd had
enough, who instinctively hated the blind, creeping,
poisoning degenerates whose limbs were slow decay, whose
bodies were fat with plundered gold, whose civilian heads
were soft with cowardice. He could show such men the true
face of the Jew who'd stolen their victories from them! His

arms jerked up as if by invisible strings, and Röhm thought:

These lads here will kick in his round ass if he's not careful.

Hess watched the men nervously, then gradually relaxed.

Hitler's voice crashed out at them, into them, as if the spirit was again filling him with sound and the contemptuous major, the cynical, wolfish troops meant nothing, because the vastness of his mission dwarfed them—and they reacted as if they felt it too:

"At the front there was no time for soft thinking! No bowing and scraping. No aristocrats or fat bankers. You couldn't buy courage with gold or some fancy title."

Röhm sat back, amused and amazed as the men gathered closer, came out of tents, stood up from eating and drinking, even the one with the whip looking over, pausing, as the tremendous voice crashed across the field. The lank figure in the yellow trench coat, absurd mustache, and pointed beard seemed to grow with each choppy gesticulation. The sinking sun flung his furious shadow over them.

"In you men here, that spirit of true comradeship still lives! You know it's simple. Yes, and now we have what the Jews and Reds call *peace* . . ."

He paused to drip scorn. ". . . What do you think of this peace, comrades!" he boomed, and they all answered as if the same force that gripped him had entered into them, and Röhm suddenly realized that his own lips had moved too in wordless reply as if against his will. Their answer was a raw sound. "One night as I carried dispatches from our forward post to another . . . what a world that was! Here and there a mutter of big guns, a spurt of machine-gun fire . . . the distant howl of a shell, rough voices singing in chorus over hidden fires, men playing skat in bunkers . . . millions of men gathered there in the electric excitement and purpose of a world where hypocrisy cannot live!"

There was a muted response.

"Where courage is commonplace, where sacrifice and every highest virtue fills every day! As I stood there that night the cannons began a great barrage and the heavens were lit as by lightnings and the thunders spoke and I thought instantly: 'This is our language, this is the voice of

Germany and they fear us, they hide from us, and, in the end, we'll break them to pieces!' "

The men were stirred. He wiped his lank hair from his eyes. For an instant he thought he was going to faint again. Flashed that he was addressing a line of strange-looking, half-armored, half-naked warriors with ax-shaped faces holding spears and, somehow, he was telling them that the enemy had entered the souls of even the most loyal, that the enemy poison was too subtle for their powerful wills to get a grip on and made a Skull Rider's very strength a liability, even within the great citadel itself defended by the lightnings of power . . .

Hitler shook away the giddiness.

"And I say it to you here and now that war is never over! War is life! The victory of our people has only been postponed and soon as a man arises with a skull of iron and fists of steel"—his own were clenched before him, eyes rolled ecstatically upward—"the decay will be rooted up and swept aside!"

Röhm found himself on the edge of his seat. The voice seemed to catch at his heart and brush aside ordinary thoughts.

"There will come a reckoning because we Germans understand how to hate and never forget or forgive! Our enemies will crumble once their minions are dragged out into the streets and their empty skulls smashed like eggs in the gutters!"

And the men found themselves cheering as if it were already happening, voices gusting from them as he stood there, fixed, violently still, arms terrifically folded.

Flashed again, wild and whirling images like the unfocused tatters of a dream: winding greenish-glowing passageways . . . a line of warriors at his back . . . a woman, a young boy, a seeming dwarf, a giant warrior with a wrestler's paunch, all moving together down a sloping spiral into the heart of a fortress mountain that he somehow recognized . . . other fighters stretched out behind him and a few captives, rebels brought for special purposes . . . and further back, out of their sight, the girl . . . he knew her too and knew that Relti the king and the others didn't realize she was following them, slim and pretty and graceful even for a Lemurian, the most supple race of all mankind . . . an image of Relti kneeling between her legs, a blur—a mistress? She looked so much like him except her nose was perfectly straight. She was following two turns of the tunnel behind . . . not-quite-stealthy, images of Relti kneeling and kissing her body . . . memories or visions upset him . . . The king was moving past the inscribed stone walls that flickered ghostly runs and blots of sickly light . . . moving down in shadow and the girl with her hands clasped before her as if in prayer . . .

Then Hitler was in the scene and his Relti voice was rumbling:

"It doesn't matter if the whole fortress falls to the traitors because, when I come back, it will make it easier for me to find them and slay them. I will seal the walls and block the doors. There are secrets only the dead priests share with me."

He didn't quite smile. Didn't have to.

And then he was just Hitler again, blinking, shaking his head, looking beyond the fascinated troops as if into the mists of time itself . . .

XXX
(1923)
Munich

Kurt Fragtkopft watched the pale face across the table. The single overhead lamp underscored the features in stark shadow. Some insect circled and pinged against the metal hood. He didn't look at the other men in the circle because the pale, luminous stare held his attention. The face was fuller now but still tense and restless. He hadn't seen him since that night in the drill yard with Himmler, when they'd watched this gray corporal point and send soldier after soldier to the wall. Now that intense man with the almost-comic brush of mustache had become a well-known and feared rightist political leader. But only a few, like Kurt, knew he belonged to the Thule Group.

Kurt tapped his fingers on the wood tabletop. Hitler's eyes made him uneasy.

It will take radical surgery, he mused. *So fellows like this fanatic were needed. Minna cannot see this, naturally . . . the New Man needs ruthlessness together with the guiding mind of a universal genius . . .*

Alfred Rosenberg sat beside Hess. He had joined the National Socialist party not long after Hitler. He had found an avid audience for the forged "Protocols of the Elders of Zion" that he had brought with him when he fled the Russian Revolution. And he was now working on a book that he believed would establish the philosophical mission of the party.

"I felt it again," Hitler was saying, eyes a hinted glow in the shadow hollows, "when I spoke the other night."

"You seem tired," Hess said, concerned. Hitler shrugged. "But your health is important."

"What can I do?" Hitler asked pettishly.

"Herbal tinctures," Hess suggested eagerly. "I can recommend—"

Hitler grinned.

"Yes, yes, Rudolph," he said. "I know your views on that subject."

Haushofer leaned back out of the light glare so that his head seemed to vanish. Kurt stared at him now. Waited for his advice. He was senior and, it was said, the most advanced adept among them.

"Wolf," Hess insisted, using Hitler's nickname, "herbs can do wonders."

Hitler smiled and nodded. Rosenberg leaned in closer.

"My investigations indicate," he murmured, "that the Jews are working against us through Rudolph Steiner and his crew."

Hess pursed his lips, eyes darkly alert. Brushed away a coil of cigar smoke. The ex-captain with the rakish suit and mustache was across the table beside Kurt. His temples were gray now, long face pinched in as he sucked smoke and exhaled.

"What are they up to?" Hess wondered.

"Invisible spying. Attempts to weaken our ceremonies."

"How can you be sure?"

Rosenberg smiled and touched his nose with a stubby finger.

"I go into deep trance," he explained with obvious vanity. "I can see everything then. But never fear, our masters are stronger than theirs."

My father can beat your father, thought Kurt. The way these people sometimes talked, well, you had to screen a lot out to stay objective. Noticed a shadowflicker where the flying bug was zipping around the bulb.

The smoking captain was nodding.

"Get them when they're asleep," he advised, smoke gouting as if the words took cloudy shape. "Strike at their minds then. Give them nightmares to stop their hearts or make them crazy!"

Rosenberg nodded, taking in this sage counsel. Looked at Hitler who was just rumbling:

"It's easy to tell me to rest, Hess, but I don't always like what comes into my room at night."

"You sleep late anyway," his friend persisted.

"Why do you think?" he snapped back. "I'm afraid to shut my eyes before dawn."

"You're in no real danger," Haushofer assured him. His heavy-nosed head popped back into the light. The big veins beside his nose visibly throbbed.

"Also easy to say," Hitler commented.

"You've opened yourself," the quiet old man went on, gnarled fingers flicking the harsh light in a languid gesture, "these are inevitable side effects."

Kurt noted sweat gleaming on Hitler's stark, pale forehead. A shadow suddenly flashed over all their faces, beating, sudden, startling, and Kurt jerked back in his seat, heart racing, thinking:

It's here! My God, help us!

And then saw the moth bumping frantically around the rim of the hooded bulb, rattling faintly against the tin.

"Your will is well developed," Haushofer added. "You need not fear."

Hitler grunted this time. Frowned.

Being taken over? Kurt wondered. *Or just being taken over entirely? Thank God it's not me chosen for that part!* He tried to picture the forces, powers, their terrible, superhuman vastness. He knew they presided when this man spoke, this hollow-eyed chosen vessel. Kurt felt he'd rather obey their wisdom than know them intimately. *Thank God it's not me.*

"Will we all, eventually, see the masters?" Rosenberg wanted to know. His hands gestured as if eager to touch something.

Hitler's burning look was on him for a moment.

"Don't be in such a hurry," he suggested. The sweat gleamed and trickled down his face. His finger swept nervously at a dark lick of hair.

The lean captain nudged Kurt in the side. He chewed the cigar. Whispered in smoke:

"Always the kittens want to play tiger."

His ceramic-blue eyes winked the light as the moth shadows flicked over their faces again and again.

Minna had called it nonsense and yet everything they'd predicted was happening: the war, the revolution . . . now this man rising out of the faceless gray masses, this man to whom destiny had whispered from childhood. What, he would have asked her, filled that slouching breast with unaccustomed thunder, storms, and lightnings? What filled this raw-faced, nervous fellow, nothing in himself until Creation herself found a voice through him!

"Well," Hitler was asking no one in particular, "what about this putsch?"

"You have to act on your own," Haushofer said, "for the most part."

"I gave my word I wouldn't make a putsch." Hitler smiled, sarcastic. There were a few chuckles.

"Now's the time to strike," said Rosenberg fervently. "With you at the head, all will fall before us."

The captain nudged Kurt again. Relit the cigar in a sudden flare of smoke and fire.

"The field marshal must agree," Hess put in.

"He will, he will," insisted Rosenberg. "And then we march on the damned government! With the greatest leader of the war marching—" glanced at Hitler— "side by side with us!"

"But will it succeed?" Hitler leaned toward Haushofer, eyes anxious, feverish.

"You'll have to follow events," was his reply. "You cannot put aside this cup." Smiled at the reference. Kurt licked his suddenly dry lips.

"But . . ." Hitler began.

"Don't be afraid," Haushofer said, "you'll survive more than this before the end. You won't be deserted."

Hitler nodded. His big pale hands gripped at the water-gleaming, dark tabletop. The insect flickered and beat inside the lamp hood, ringing dully. Hitler seemed deep in thought.

"I won't weaken," he finally rumbled. "Don't worry about that." He suddenly straighted in his seat, lips grimly set. His gaze, Kurt realized, rested on no one, and what he said wasn't really for them either as he whispered: "I will never turn aside."

Kurt left first, thinking about getting home in time for supper. The cool, damp air felt refreshing. He paused on the sidewalk and considered getting her a present . . . What? . . . flowers? . . . some pastry?

The door rattled and Hitler, Hess, and Rosenberg came out together. Kurt liked Hess somewhat but the other two made him uncomfortable. And the crude politics left him cold. He sensed Hitler was quite indifferent to him, as well.

"Hello," said Hess, holding his palm out. "A little drizzle?"

"Not much," offered Kurt.

"Ah," said Hitler, "the ass-beater."

"What's that?" Kurt wondered.

"Bavarian for schoolteacher," Hess explained.

"I had one teacher I liked," Hitler said, folding his hands in front of himself and not looking at anyone directly. "He turned my mind to history. The rest were fools and mental swindlers."

"You cover a lot of ground, sir," Kurt said.

Hitler shrugged.

"I'm sure you're a good one," he mumbled uncomfortably.

"Where do we eat?" Rosenberg wanted to know.

"You mean where are the dead animals?" Hitler laughed and shook his head.

"We can go to Stupfel's," Hess interceded. "You can get puddings and so forth there, Wolf." Kurt realized that was Hitler's nickname. Found it an interesting choice. Was suddenly curious and found himself walking along with them, crossing the wet, cobbled square. The pale streetlight gleamed. Traffic scattered.

"One thing," he began.

"You want to come along?" Hess asked Kurt, glancing at Hitler.

"I . . . Not really . . . but I'd like to ask something,"

"You see," Hitler remarked, "I said he was good. A professor who doesn't yank you by the hair when he wants an answer."

Rosenberg chortled.

"You're hard on people, Wolf," he said.

"Just some people," Hitler agreed.

"But why, then," Kurt began. A passing car flung shadows around them.

"Why what?" Rosenberg queried.

"The Jews. Why the Jews? It doesn't make sense to me. They're essentially harmless. Do you really believe that conspiracy business?"

"Do I?" Hitler watched him.

Rosenberg puffed out his cheeks and said:

"The Jews are a clear and present danger. How can you be so close to Karl Haushofer and the rest and say—"

"They may represent a mediocre race, perhaps," Kurt cut in, looking at Hitler; "but the conspiracy is absurd and, in effect, you—"

"You?" Hitler asked. "Is that me?"

"We then, Herr Hitler—"

"Call me Wolf, in the street, if you please, Herr Professor," requested the leader.

"Yes. Wolf. Aren't we using, then, the same methods we accuse them of?"

"Yes," Hitler said.

"But—" Rosenberg began but Hitler motioned him still. Another car went by and the shadows fanned and flickered around the empty square.

"Are we that cynical?" Kurt asked. "Is that worthy of the powers we represent?"

"Politics is the surface," Hess interjected. "You ought to know that, Herr Fragtkopft."

Hitler stopped and stood facing Kurt, eyes penetrating, level, ferocious; and for a moment the teacher was afraid he'd be struck down. He felt sweat on his neck.

"The Jew," Hitler was saying, "is a *symptom* of mortal illness." Everyone had stopped. "Present when there is decay and weakness. Nothing in himself. Trivial in himself.

Like a tiny microbe. Trivial but deadly!" His voice suddenly
rang. Kurt's skin tingled. "The blood has been poisoned.
All blood is impure. It matters nothing if there's a calculated plot, you see? It's too late for half-measures now!
This is the meaning of my mission. The blood must flow
and be cleansed and any means, *any means at all*, is
sanctioned by the power of God and the glorious soul of
the race!" He trembled slightly in the wake of his own
words.

"Yes, yes," enthused Rosenberg. "That is higher law.
And in the eyes of the law the Jews are damned and guilty!
All around us the nations sink into degeneracy." He
gestured to Hitler who'd started walking again. "This is the
voice of destiny." Rosenberg nodded. "I'm putting all this
in my book, Professor Fragtkopft. I'd like you to see the
manuscript at some point. We are, I believe, approaching a
climax in history."

Hitler twisted his face back to look at Kurt as they
reached the far curb. A family was just coming out of the
restaurant behind him: a massive father with a big mustache, his wife, and two boys in sailor suits with round,
bright blue eyes. The mother looked uneasily at Hitler
slouching there in his yellow trench coat under the lamppost.

"Even if we perish," he said quietly, "we know we'll be
reborn. Our secret knowledge is our advantage over the
others. Our enemies will never understand us."

"Even your friends," Kurt suggested, "will have some
little difficulty."

Hitler smiled. The woman glanced back, keeping the
two children close to her skirts as they went on down the
sidewalk past the cheerful shop windows. Kurt kept watching them as (he thought) Hitler went needlessly on, saying:

"So we can boldly sacrifice our lives on this altar
because God has given us the strength and opportunity and
dedication. Being understood will come later."

Kurt watched the family vanish into the darkness
beyond the corner as they stepped out of the last slice of
light.

XXXI
(OCTOBER 1923)
Munich—the Feldherrnhalle

My God, if this fails, then what becomes of me? Hitler asked himself, standing alone in the men's room, both hands thrust into the pockets of his coat. *What a risk . . . what a risk . . .*

The grimy slit of glass touched his grayish, pale face with colorless light. He was oblivious to the urinal stink. Outside he could hear voices echoing in the beer hall. He faced the cracking, yellowish tile wall, fingers clenched around the revolver in his right pocket.

Prophecies are all very well in dark rooms but I still can fail, yet, what's the sense of waiting. It we win we can have it all now and not wait another ten years. He'd never forgotten doing the horoscope with the little dwarf Pretzle in Vienna at the little bookshop. The reading had agreed with other, more recent predictions: he had a chance now, his last for about a decade. *There's nothing to go back to if I fail and they throw me out of Germany.* That thought was edged with panic. No hope of citizenship. What could he do in Austria? Go back home, to Linz? A failure. Get a job in the sausage factory. *I'll shoot myself in that case.* He pictured the scene: in front of everyone he'd mount the speaker's platform for the final time and announce he'd been betrayed. Predictions worked but there were always errors in anything where humans meddled. So he'd be betrayed, in the end. He'd always sensed that. Nodded to himself. *Perhaps the Christ story is a fundamental Aryan legend. The superman letting his blood be shed to atone for the shame of his polluted race.* Here were issues he'd like to hammer home instead of miserable, superficial politics!

He stared at the blank wall over the urinal.

"I go to my Golgotha, if need be," he whispered.

What a world waited, a world rebuilt totally. Every lie would be smashed and the fragments swept away. In the end, the mystic union of blood with blood, the mystic vision of the divine powers struggling to be freed from countless Jewish centuries of materialism! How could he tell them so they'd see that even a good, sincere Jew, even an innocent child, was a deadly germ? *The Jew is a quality in all of us, our stain, muck in the blood.*

(1945)

In the Bunker

Eva Braun was naked. She was exercising on the rug in the dim lamplight that was a yellowish stain reflected on the green walls. Hitler sat in his baggy, gray undershorts on the edge of the bed. His legs were bony but still muscular. His torso had gone somewhat flabby and his belly pushed out under the bare-shoulder army undershirt.

He smiled, watching her, as if she were a child. She moved gracefully, watching him for approval. She did some floor turns on the dull rug until her head was between his knuckly bare feet. Her skin glowed and she panted slightly.

Then she swung around and was on her knees between his legs. He shook his head slightly but leaned back to oblige her. Lay flat on the bed staring up at the ceiling. Felt her hands and then her soft, hot mouth. Not much stirred in him.

He shut his eyes and the green-tinted underworld was all around him again. Tried to open the lids but they seemed glued . . . and then he was in the mind of the tyrant just as Relti stopped before a black-metaled, grated, massive door. The rest of his entourage gathered behind him. The huge man with the paunch leaned down to whisper to the dwarf with outsized feet.

"Maybe I would have served better to stay above and fight the traitors," he told him. His eyes were slightly protuberant and rolled uneasily. He was a general of the Skull troops.

"That is possible, Rog," said Relti, not turning. "Yet, it may be that what comes forth from below must slay all on the surface." He didn't have to look at his man's face as he shrugged, then turned his full attention to the door. There would be no handle or lock. He understood that. The first door; the first test of his quality.

He pushed with his inner force. For him it was simple, and the metal frame swung back, silent, steady.

The queen had come near and stood just behind with their son. Just ahead of the warriors and the dwarf with the too-big feet.

"What is this, Mother?" the boy wanted to know.

"The chamber of the dead," she told him. "You may fear them without shame." The dwarf snorted and shuddered, bug eyes staring. Rog fell back beside the queen wishing he didn't have to stop there.

Looking through the doorway they watched the king striding steadily inside; for a moment, his robe filling out almost like wings, his son thought.

"Mother," he asked, "who are those?"

Because inside a reddish-black smoke seethed and a crowd of people seemed to be moving up through the hot mist as if taking shape from it.

"Be still," she said. "Do nothing to attract them. Your father must command them. Or we are destroyed."

Rog moaned under his breath. The Skull troops moved, wavered. Back at the first bend the young woman following was just edging her eyes around the corner as Relti marched into the billowing haze among the shadowy, lurching, stiff crowd of the dead, bumping each other, steps scraping, uneven, on the stones; arms clashing, rhythmless. They were packed shoulder-to-shoulder. More seemed to be stumbling up from the recesses of the chamber, pressing forward, shambling, replicant.

"Learn from his voice," the queen whispered to her son.

"Obey!" Relti thundered, his voice seeming to roll and re-echo into vast depths. "You are my limbs and move at my will!" He raised one fist and turned it in the air and the dead hulks lumbered to the right, reversed it and they swayed the other way. "You are my fighters and slay whom I will!" Crashed his fist into this chest, chin uptilted, and a forest of dead arms flailed up in the reddish blurring like iron drawn by a magnet, stiff from the shoulder, lifeless limbs thrashing up and down, joints and flesh creaking horribly, like immense, galvanic laboratory frogs . . .

Hitler pulled back. Shook his head, blinking hard.

Visions, he said, *worse than dreams* . . . He refused to
worry. It was just other worlds, after all. And his soul had
been opened.

He looked between his legs at Eva's bobbing head.
Tried to feel something.

(OCTOBER 1923)

Feldherrnhalle

He suddenly realized he was hungry. And calm. He'd
get bread and cheese later, he decided.

He turned and slammed out through the door in a
spasm of energy. He was ready. No more doubts! This was
destiny and to destiny he submitted. Out in the hall he saw
Göring looking grim, Hess excited but measured,
Streicher's bald head gleaming.

He ran, pale, feverishly nervous, afraid and confident
at the same time. Gestured *Now!* to Göring and leaped up
onto the platform, hardly aware of the speaker turning in
surprise, glasses flashing the overhead light beam that
floated Hitler's face out of the shadows as the revolver
seemed to jerk itself out of the coat. Hitler barely registered
the blasts he fired into the roof that rattle-echoed and
brought the hall to instant attention. Next he felt the
irresistible energy seizing him, slamming aside weakness
and hesitation: only blind courage mattered because the
transformation could only take place in combat, the change
that would resonate mysteriously in the Ayran soul. Even
defeat, he suddenly knew, could be victory!

He was already speaking, a hysterical tremor in the
thundering, stone-hard voice:

"The hall is surrounded! Resistance is useless!" Outcries. Clamor. "Be still!" he roared, voice breaking. "If not,
I'll have a machine gun set up in the gallery!" *All stupid
confusion has to end,* he thought.

"What does this mean, Herr Hitler?" the speaker,
General von Lossow, demanded.

The other heads of the present government on the
platform were on their feet. There was Kahr, the Bavarian
dictator, fists clenched at his sides.

Hitler waved the gun around, jerky.

No going back over the Rubicon!

"Shut up," he yelled into General von Lossow's startled, cynical face. "The government has already fallen!" he lied. Stared at Kahr next, eyes wild. "The army has risen and is marching on the city under the swastika banner!" Then, waving the gun, he cut out Seisser, Kahr, and Lossow and led them off the platform. The crowd was getting ugly. Someone tossed a beer mug. There were hoots of protest here and there. Göring leaped up on the podium, waving his hands and grinning.

"Don't worry," he shouted, "we have only good intentions! Anyway, you can be happy, you have your beer!"

"Put on an act," Lossow murmured to Seisser as they followed Hitler into an empty back room. With the door shut, the hall outside echoed like a seashell. Lossow winked at Kahr while Hitler was talking.

"I've formed a new government with General Ludendorff," he was saying, feeling the emotions of the moments well up and seem to gather in his throat and chest: excitement, wild hope, fear. "I am now the government, gentlemen. You will have the highest posts in this government. Well, are you with me!" Silence. The three leaders just watched him. "I realize this is a hard decision." He held up his gun. "But whoever will not join our people to serve in this hour of need has no right to existence!"

Don't desert me, he was thinking, asking the unseen presence. Trying to somehow feel it again. "You have one choice: fight at my side, conquer or die," he told them. "I have four shots in my pistol and only one for myself!" He pressed the barrel against his temple. "If we fail."

"Shoot me, then," Kahr muttered, shrugging his short arms.

"You gave me your word of honor, Herr Hitler," Seisser pointed out reproachfully. "You promised you wouldn't make this putsch."

"Never mind that."

"Never mind? You stood in my office and swore to me—"

Why wouldn't this worm be still! What did it matter? What trivia of confused minds . . .

"This is war!" he cried. "Against the greatest evil in history! We are forming a truly German government to root out the evil!" *Don't desert me please help me win I'll never ask anything more, I swear!* Addressed to the unseen force.

"You don't win a war with words of honor. You don't win a world with rules!"

Most of the subsequent hours were always a blur to him. Things raced past, hasty conferences . . . shouting from the platform . . . cheers finally from the crowd . . . tremendous feelings of victory and hope . . . standing in the street with the great general Ludendorff, bowing, clicking his heels, saying:

"Honored Field Marshal, this is an historic moment. Today we march to victory!"

And then failure gnawing at him again, constantly, because the regular army stayed neutral and the police were waiting. Kahr and the others had slipped away in the crowds after giving him their oaths. Hess went with an armed squad to find them and drag them back. Events raced on past his control in a whirling blur. The brownshirts gathering, crashing in massed ranks behind him into the heart of the city. Göring asking Ludendorff, "Will they fire?" and the old, stern warlord replying: "On me? Never." And then facing the barricades, the lines of armed police. Thinking finally: *This is premature . . . premature . . . never mind, the very battle itself will be the victory. I can't let myself die now for nothing at the head of a rabble. The field marshal is insufficient insurance.* The gray line waiting across the square, the glint of rifle barrels. *Have faith.* But it was a mistake. The pale faces behind the guns, the aiming eyes, the tramp of feet and shouts behind, feeling horribly naked, gripping the arm of the man beside him. *Have I been betrayed?* Closer . . . closer . . . *Have I been betrayed to die here for nothing? Speak to me! Help me!* he almost shouted at the sullen tin-bright sky. And the silence was a knell. And then the flashes of the guns, the ripping sounds, thuds and screams, and he was somehow down on the pavement dragging the other man in a soldier's pure reflex and felt a wrenching pain in his shoulder that he first took for a bullet impact . . . blurs, firing, shouts, a machine gun rattling. As he pulled himself to his knees, a flash, of Ludendorff marching straight into the gun barrels which opened to let him pass and Hitler thought, furious, frustrated, *I should have gone on!* And then he was racing for the car, holding the door open, and then he flung himself into the back seat, tears burning, the unfired pistol still in his pockets. *Too late . . . too late.* The gray streets zipped smoothly past.

None of them can be trusted and it's beyond my strength to hold everything together. I'm finished I quit let them get someone else. These fools. Cowards and nincompoops! Let them go back into the gutters where they belong! I give up. I'll go back home. To hell with them all. The tears fell freely now. He knew the driver was looking at him in the rearview mirror. Good. *So what. Let them all find out what they've done to me.*

"Where do we go?" Emil Maurice, the driver, asked. But his leader didn't respond. Stared. Wept. "I think the police will be looking for us."

Hitler's lips kept working. There was a little foam at the corners of his mouth.

You betrayed me . . . you deserted me . . . How stupid all predictions and omens seemed now.

"They'll chase me down like a tramp," he said, choked up, furious. "What do I care? Everything's finished."

"No. You'll find a way, sir. You always find a way."

"I'll shoot myself."

"No. Just tell me where to head now."

"Failure proves me unfit to live." His hand lay pale and still on his lap. Emil Maurice waited this time. Hitler's tears stopped. He sighed. *Don't be hasty again,* he thought. *This loyal fellow may be right.* "Go to Himmelstrasse fourteen," he finally instructed.

"I tell you, this is the man!" Alfred Rosenberg insisted, staring inches into the bleak eyes and sagging, wide but angular face of Karl Haushofer; the behind-the-scenes master of the *Thule,* an occultist. A philosopher whose influence extended into high finance, government, and the army. They stood in the perpetual dusk of the hallway outside the courtroom. The little man didn't look at Rosenberg directly, his chill, pale gaze on the marble flooring. He kept tapping his foot and shaking his head. "I tell you this with all my heart," Rosenberg virtually implored.

"This corporal who made that ridiculous putsch? I doubt it."

"*Doktor* Haushofer, I beg you, just meet with him after the trial."

"This farce? They'll slap their wrists." He tapped his gold-tipped cane on the resonant flooring. "If you're far enough right, what harm can you come to? The biggest interests *want* to favor you." The cane cut the air. "But do

you really think the savior of Germany and the harbringer
of the coming race would make that ridiculous putsch?"

"Please, sir. I swear I'm right. Hasn't your son told you
that—"

"My son? He's a bigger fool than you."

"The Great Ones commune with him even now. And
with your help," he whispered, "the master of all might be
called."

Haushofer's eyes stared as if at unseen glaciers and
glittering snowfields.

"Does he think such things?" he asked quietly, not
glancing at the people passing in the corridor. "He's an
initiate?"

"Yes," affirmed the other. His hands moved nervously.
"He knows Christ was a swindle."

"Does he understand it is *all* reversed?"

Rosenberg nodded.

"Basically. He has his own views but they are very close
to the truth. As if he knew from some more-direct source.
And the sheer force of the man! That you have to see to
understand."

But Haushofer was already stumping toward the
double door and into the courtroom where Hitler (as if this
had been rehearsed for the benefit of this little old man)
had just leaped to his feet, shouting over the state's
attorney:

". . . and, therefore," he boomed, gutturals rattling
the tall, leaded windows, "a dictator is not compelled, he
wills; he is not driven forward, he drives himself forward!
You ask me if I'm immodest to think I could govern
Germany? When a man knows he can do something he has
no right to modesty. The army we have created is growing
from hour to hour! The day will come! The old flags will
wave again! There will be a reconciliation at the divine
judgment and from our bones and graves the voice of that
court will speak. For it is not you, gentlemen, who
pronounce judgment upon us. That judgment will come
from the eternal court of history! You may pronounce us
guilty a thousand times but history will acquit us!"

Rosenberg was watching Haushofer's face. His expression showed nothing but the eyes showed everything,
absorbed by the awkward, stiff figure, the gray ghost that
suddenly seemed to tower and strain the huge chamber

with concentrated energy, a limp banner suddenly cracking and snapping in gusts of strong wind.

Haushofer leaned forward on his cane, intent, seeing the speaker and the crowd at the same time, nodding slightly, with an almost dreamy expression.

XXXII
(1929)
The Southern German Countryside

Maybe I've been mistaken about what I've heard, Renga thought. *Perhaps because I haven't believed in anything in so long I distrust too freely.*

He looked back across the sloping yard at where Eunice and Minna Fragtkopft stood with Madame Himmler near the rustic little house. The sun was setting across the misty valley, beams slanting into the gathering mists.

The two women had corresponded over the years and, finally, since Kurt was "doing so well," they'd driven out to spend a weekend. Renga's life was quite routine. He taught philosophy, still spent the summers in Italy, and visited mostly her friends. They'd lost their only child after a few months. He wasn't sure if he still believed that the war had destroyed his inner vision. He used to think that if he'd gone on with his peaceful but vigorous spiritual studies he might have become more like a Rudolph Steiner instead of a dry, half-hearted lecturer.

Only thing about these Nazis like Kurt, he reflected, *they have extraordinary energy.* He remembered the day Hitler had tried to sell him the paintings in Vienna. Smiled and shook his head. *If I hadn't met the great man I might be more impressed.* Still, he'd agreed to come out and talk to Himmler. Kurt had (among other things) assured him that the party's anti-Semitism was not terribly serious and would be discarded after they took power. He said too many important Nazis considered it an embarrassment and strange quirk of Hitler's.

"The men are out back," Madame Himmler called down to him. "Heini's showing off as usual."

"Yes," said Renga. "I'll join them presently."

"We don't get many visitors," she went on to all of them, shaking her blotchy-red, drinker's face. "Where is my husband?"

"You said behind the house," Eunice put in.

"Where is my Heini? Hah. He's here and there . . . all over the place on his silly bicycle, making speeches. The party this, the party that . . . I have to run things here, but that doesn't bother him much."

"You learn to accept," Minna was saying as Renga strolled behind the house. Her voice was flat, resigned, thought Renga. He wondered how much Kurt knew about their relationships during the war, when Minna was in Italy. A long time ago. He wondered too if Eunice actually showed age clearly as Minna did but, because he saw her every day, it was just that he failed to notice the imperceptible onset . . . God, but where had the years gone? . . . Floated away . . .

He'd put on weight, slept calmly, drifted through his routine, comfortable life . . . Amazing to reflect on all the ominous portents that had dissolved like mist . . . He wasn't really unhappy either. He used to wonder whether Minna was too delicate to survive, yet here she was, still putting up with Kurt. He seemed to have been working full-time for these Nazis for years now, lecturing and so forth. Telling everyone, he supposed, as did Hitler, that the nation was about to fall to pieces. Well, absurd as they seemed, he thought, at least they were dedicated to action. Renga felt pale and sluggish by comparison . . .

The smell and sound were unmistakable as he came closer. The sun was just above the low, barracks-like structure. The two men were blotted into the shadow. Renga shielded his eyes. Kurt was waving, he thought, and something pale and fuzzy-looking seemed to be struggling in Himmler's hands; then squawked and flapped wildly, catching the last piece of setting sun and kicking mad shadowflutters over the house and tall pines.

"Heini!" his wife called from behind the house, "we're serving cakes in three minutes!" Then to the women, fainter: "If he's not gone, then he's with those birds." Then a door shutting.

Himmler was soothing the struggling hen as he came up to Renga and Kurt.

"How do you do?" he said, extending his free hand. The sun was going deep red. His glasses caught the last gleamings.

"Heinrich Himmler," said Kurt, "Rudolph Renga."

"What about the bird?" asked Renga, smiling.

"I don't introduce this one," came the reply, "it's a sad specimen." He displayed the toeless, twisted leg. "You see?"

"Poor creature," murmured Renga.

"If I may say so, Himmler demurred, "that's sympathy misplaced. This unfortunate averages the rest of his kind down to a lower level."

"You sound as though you blame it for its misfortune."

"Not at all." Himmler smiled, professorial. "But I must think of all the rest of my chickens. I can't let this affliction be passed along to them."

"So it's the soup," said Kurt. "It comes to the soup sonner or later, in any event." To Renga: "How have you been, Rudolph?"

"Fine enough, Kurt." He studied the other's features in the blood-colored glow. Decided he was very puffy in the jowls, for one thing. Minna had mainly looked strained as if perpetually sleepless.

There was a time when I feared sleep myself, he recalled.

The sun had just dropped out of sight, and the pale evening tones seemed to rise like mist from the woods and fields.

Himmler tossed the crippled chicken over the fence. It flopped into the obscurity with the others.

"I thought you were going to kill it?" Renga wondered.

"No," Kurt put in, "Madame will."

Himmler sort of shrugged.

"I'm no good at that sort of thing," he allowed.

Later they were gathered in the darkness under the stars drinking brandy and coffee around a rustic table. Renga was amused that his host called it his "board," as if he were a Saxon lord from the Middle Ages.

"I think it's fair to say that Rudolph here is a philosopher of the secret doctrines," Kurt said, turning the conversation.

"Oh so?" commented Himmler.

"When we met," Eunice said, "he was so intense, I used to think, *Maria*, this one will see God's face."

"That was before the war," Renga murmured. All he could see were vague glints of Himmler's glasses, his wife's rings, and the ghostly white cups on the table.

"Basically," the host said, "all doctrines agree, without realizing it, beneath the surface. As the Führer points out."

"Who?" wondered Eunice.

"Adolf Hitler," said Minna, voice expressionless.

"Ah," responded Eunice, "the head of your party. But I shouldn't think he'd be interested in such things." She could feel Himmler bursting to expound and disagree. "Such a man of action."

"But quite the reverse, Contessa," he said eagerly.

"He's not a man of action?"

"Yes, of course. That above all." The glasses flicked the stars. "But he's probably the deepest student of these matters in the world. What do you think of that?"

"This agitator?" she wondered. "Are you serious, Herr Himmler?"

"Totally, Contessa."

Downslope the chickens suddenly stirred and squawked wildly.

"What's that," wondered Minna, "a fox?"

"No," Himmler said.

"It's Marga," Kurt told her, "correct?"

"She's not here," affirmed Eunice.

Then, as the birds resettled and roosted, there was a brief, shrill gurgle out in the darkness and Renga remembered when he was a boy seeing his father slice a rabbit's throat and how the creature had thrashed and bubbled, and he felt the child's terror and the thing's pain in himself, ripping at his nerves.

"The mission of the party," Himmler was saying, "is not at all what most people think."

"That's quite true," Kurt put in, across the table. "I've met Hitler more than once. This man *literally* means to create a new world. He's studied the spiritual side of the race question very deeply. That's why I wanted you to come here. I feel you're the type the party, the *inner* party, desperately needs to counterbalance the, well . . ."

"The agitators," Himmler helped out, chuckling. "The blockbrains."

"So there's a religious angle to all this," Renga murmured thoughtfully.

"In a very real sense," Himmler agreed.

"Are you aiming to become the Pope, perhaps?" Eunice wanted to know, sarcastic and smooth. "How interesting."

Frau Himmler passed the table on her way back to the house just as Kurt was lighting his cigar and the matchflare sketched her outline in rosy fire. The bird-shape flapped in her hand, the neck too long and twisted. He noticed her husband didn't actually look, his glasses full of the flame, and then the dark blotted back and she was saying:

"Anyone want more cake? Just say so."

"My God," whispered Eunice close to Renga's ear, "she's just strangled that poor chicken! I wonder she didn't invite us to watch?"

"Hitler will take power," Himmler said. "Make no mistake about that. It's inscribed in the stars."

"Ah," said Renga, leaning forward, "this is certainly a new politics for the twentieth century."

"Forgive my ignorance," Eunice put in.

"Are you certain you're not reading mere dreams?" asked Renga.

"Well, Heilscher, for one," added Kurt, "has seen these things."

Heilscher? Renga knew the name. A famous seer. Some called him a black magician like the Englishman, Crowley. *But what has he to do with the Nazis . . . or would that be a stupid question?*

"And Chamberlain too," added Himmler, "predicts the coming savior of Germany."

"Is he still living?" Renga asked.

"He lives in Bayreuth," said Minna. "He married one of Wagner's daughters."

"Is that the man with epilepsy?" Eunice wondered. "Who fell down with the Kaiser Wilhelm . . . the night we met, Rudi?"

"Yes," her husband answered.

"What do you think of these things, Minna?" Eunice asked.

"A good National Socialist wife," said Himmler pedantically, "leaves such matters to her husband."

"Is that a good idea, Minna?" Eunice persisted.

"If I left all the thinking to Heini," said Frau Himmler, "they'd foreclose the mortgage."

She had silently returned to the table.

Kurt relit his cigar and the rosy matchflare drew all their shapes from the night and pulsed as he puffed as if they struggled not to fade and, then, with the match out, were gone behind violet afterglows. Himmler had made a sour face but said nothing to his wife.

"Mn," murmured Eunice.

"This is some party," Marga Himmler remarked. "Nobody's even singing."

"You see, Contessa," Himmler explained, "the man of the coming race will have a better brain. He won't be confused by words and ideas. He will—"

"Why don't we all sing?" his wife suggested.

"There follows mind reading, levitation," said Kurt. "Everything becomes possible."

"Well," said Eunice, "if your Herr Hitler can do all this, no doubt he'll win the elections."

"It takes more than magic, Contessa," quipped Himmler, "to win anything in Germany."

"Nobody wants to have fun," Marga complained. "You might as well have a séance if you're going to sit in the dark like this."

For an instant Renga wasn't sure if she was serious.

"Yes," said Eunice to Minna, "you could get that fat woman who soiled your rug. She was a great friend of Kurt's, I understand."

"Never mind that," Kurt responded, irritable.

Marga leaned close to Renga's ear, whispered. Her breath was thick and sweetish with alcohol.

"Pay them no mind," she said. "They like to talk big."

Himmler was excited.

"The fact is," he insisted, "a new age is dawning. The old magic is emerging again. The day of Jewish materialism is finished!"

"Must you Nazis always drag in the Jews?" wondered Eunice, with distaste.

"It's nothing personal," Himmler stated. "A pure matter of genetics, I assure you. As with that crippled chicken."

"You mean, *signóre*," she said acidly, "to have your wife strangle them for you too?"

"Look," snapped Himmler, "it's a spiritual matter. The

Jewish people were created at a time when the earth's spiritual energies were at a cyclical ebb. Their souls are, therefore, incomplete." He shrugged in the darkness.

"But that's really idiotic," Minna said.

"I should say," put in Renga, "that we're all certainly mixed together at this point, like it or not. Look at the Jewish mystics, or at Christ, himself, I—"

"You're making what's holy," Eunice said, furious, "depend on . . . *Madònna*, on breeding like chickens!"

Kurt lit yet another match, and it showed she and Himmler were both on their feet across the table from one another, his glasses full of flame, her eyes slitted.

"You must have a pure vessel," he cried, "to carry pure water in!" As the match died, his image spasmed in afterglow. "All must breed and die until we produce the perfect individual. Then, with the last Jewish taint washed from the blood, each man will be immortal!"

So it spreads, Renga thought. The shadows were back, the fanged clouds rising from boiling chaos . . .

"*Che se dice?* commented Eunice. "but have we wandered into an asylum?"

"See here—" mollified Kurt, "this disagreement is needless. Just a matter of semantics."

"The devil you say," Minna murmured.

"Do you listen to this?" Eunice asked her.

"No," she replied, "I don't listen."

"Neither do I," added Marga. "Let the men talk, my mother always said."

Renga was remembering Hitler sitting across the cool marble table under the window full of snow and ice, the almost heatless sun spilling over them. Remembered the pale face, the troubled, burning, bluish eyes. *It spreads* . . . He found himself standing up, groping for his wife's hand. He felt the night too close around him. His heart was beating hard.

"Just a lot of talk," Marga insisted, blurring the words a little.

"Let's have some beer," suggested Kurt.

If I only had Hitler's force, Himmler sighed within himself, *I could win them over* . . .

"Listen, Rudolph," he tried, "we need men like yourself because the real work will be behind the scenes. While millions cheer, we—"

"What real work?" Renga wanted to know.

I have to practice to be more effective, Himmler thought. His mind wandered, as now Minna and Kurt were arguing. He searched around for a good joke to soften the tension. This Renga seemed nice enough. It was sometimes so hard to explain things you saw so clearly . . .

"Contessa," he began, thinking how Hitler would have gripped both their hands, eyes burning with destiny, and said: 'Follow me!' "Contessa, I—"

"I'm sick of your big ideas to change the world," Marga was suddenly saying, swaying a little, "meanwhile, the party pays you nothing! I think Hitler and Göring keep it all . . ."

"Oh, please," her husband sighed.

Renga just stood in the darkness holding Eunice. The terror seemed to have receded. He decided that Hitler would probably get himself elected someday and reform the postal system . . .

Behind the house Kurt and Minna fought on in raging murmurs. Now they seemed to be coming closer again.

"How else did Göring get so fat?" Marga wanted to know.

"My apologies, Contessa," Himmler managed to get in.

"I've had enough," Minna was repeating. "I've had enough."

"You've not done so badly. I make a good living."

"You think that's all you have to do? I know what the hell you're up to!"

"Up to?" Kurt sounded surprised.

They were near the table.

"Minna, my dear," broke in Himmler, still trying to be firm with someone, "I feel—"

"Oh, keep out of it, Heini," his wife told him.

"With your *women*," Minna hissed at Kurt, then mirthlessly laughed.

"What nonsense," her husband responded. "What total nonsense."

"Oh," she said frustrated, "you fool nobody. You never did. And I'm surprised you don't blame the Jews for your bad marriage."

The day will come, Himmler was thinking, *when we can simply point and say: "Add your shoulder to the wheel there!" No more of this nonsense then* . . . He kept nervously biting his lip and trying to think of the best thing to say.

"The thing is," he said, coming around the table by feel

and finding Renga's shoulder. "The thing is to meet the Führer and have him set your doubts aside."

"I met him already. In Vienna."

"Really? How fortunate. But, you realize, his philosophy has since been—"

He was cut off by Minna shouting:

"You once had brains, Kurt. Now there's shit in your head!" And she stormed away into the darkness.

Marga tittered.

"A common male defect," she declared.

"I really must apologize again," Himmler interjected. "Really, I—"

"That's all right," Renga said, disengaging himself from the small, soft hand.

"We must be going, in any case," Eunice added.

"Yes," Himmler murmured, "naturally."

Kurt was chasing Minna. Their voices raged behind the house again.

Maybe the party ought to forbid marriage, Himmler was thinking. *Even if I don't win all the arguments, the thing is to keep improving . . .*

XXXIII
(WINTER 1929)
Munich

Rudolph Renga blinked several times when Himmler stepped out of the long black Mercedes into the thin, wintry Munich sunlight. The gleaming black uniform shocked him. Made him think of a sinister scoutmaster. The glasses flashed bleakly; the mustache stirred in a wisp of a smile.

Renga was uneasy: the uniforms, crashing boots, drums and pipes in the distance. Why had he bothered to come? Curiosity, he supposed.

Kurt had called him, and Renga had been standing in his study, the brassy receiver to his ear, staring out the leaded window into the garden where the afternoon was shattered into blue-white dazzle on the iced trees and stainless snow. In the distance the golden dome of the campus chapel flashed.

Kurt had first apologized for the scene at Himmler's. Renga hadn't really cared particularly. He'd been obsessed lately with the fact that he was a forty-year-old professor, an oddball who was tolerated because he supported nobody's university politics and so was always someone to win over.

Renga listened for a while, assured Kurt had had nothing to reproach himself for . . . finally got to asking how Minna was.

"Minna is fine, Rudolph. We understand one another, after all."

"I'm pleased to hear it."

Watching a shockingly red cardinal gust to a stop on the crackling glare of snow, pecking at invisible specks.

"After so many years," said Kurt.

"Yes." Renga really wanted to get back to the papers waiting on the littered desk. He was puzzling over Grail clues again. He felt safe behind his books once more. Nothing too dramatic had ever happened, after all, since the war. He'd been sleeping well . . . put on flesh . . . had a friendly partnership with Eunice.

There was a theory that the Grail was a substance, an element whose intense radiations beat into the soul with such avidity that superhuman powers developed. Something fallen from the stars. Kurt was still talking.

". . . so, my dear fellow, I have no middle-class views, to speak of. Let the past sleep, eh?"

"Yes, naturally." He wondered what he'd just missed.

"Whatever Minna and your wife were to one another . . ."

How did that come up?

"Friends?" he tried.

"If you say so. That's a dead issue, in any event."

"Yes."

"But it shows me you're not so aloof from life as you seem. You're one of us at heart, Rudi."

"Mn?"

"Come on. You were there with them after the war. I'm not so dense, my friend."

Renga was amused, watching the bird: a stunning crimson crashing whirr, blurring up through a glittering bush in bright tinkle-shatter, flashing up across pure blue . . . gone . . .

He recalled the two women putting their pale, silky robes on in the evanescent bedroom about a dozen years past. He'd just walked in on them, home from the war. But nothing much had happened after that. Minna had gone to her family; he'd gone to Greece with Eunice. In retrospect, it never had seemed real . . .

"Anyway," he said, "what is really on your mind, Kurt?" He'd turned away from the brilliant window. The violet image of it flashed and staggered in his sight.

"We're getting very close to taking power, Rudi."

"So I understand." Even Renga couldn't live without hearing that much news, try as he might.

Poor Minna, he thought.

"The nation's falling apart, as predicted. Hitler will save Germany."

"Yes?"

"I insist you come and meet him. I want you with us. I've always wanted you with us."

"Yes. But I still have no urge to hit Jews over the head."

"Oh, forget all that crap. Once the party's in power all that nonsense will be done with." Kurt sounded irritable and bored.

"You're sure?"

"Of course. That's one reason we need men like yourself."

And Renga didn't say *no* because he was thinking: *I'm over forty and I haven't once tried to change anything, so at least* . . . The idea vaguely formed that perhaps he should talk to Hitler face-to-face, see if that man who'd once sat across the table in winter light had really found something out he wasn't showing to the world . . . Was there really a mystery there or just a shadowy surface . . .

So he went . . . and here he was.

Himmler was about to say something chatty when a pale-faced aide hurried up to him. The parade was coming, the massed feet clumping over the cobbles. Renga hated parades; the noise, crowds, mechanical behavior. People could be so blind and dull, no wonder leaders developed contempt for them. If you cared for humanity you hated crowds, because there were no people there, just sound, fury, ripples, and heaves of blind reaction . . .

"My God," Himmler murmured. The aide looked grave. Renga stared at the blond, pale-eyed man with long generally beaked features and a cold slash of lips. Himmler seemed abstracted. His fingers played with his thick belt. The aide studied Renga for an intent moment with (Renga thought) suspicion and disinterest at the same time. "Excuse me," Himmler said and climbed back into the open car. The parade rounded the near corner with a window-rattling crash. "Reinhart," Himmler said as the aide loped lithely in beside him and the car pulled away, "this is very serious."

Renga watched them go. He'd accepted Kurt's invitation, he admitted to himself, with some vague idea of talking to Hitler, of trying to influence him in some way . . . Shook his head at himself . . . What an idea!

(Later)

Always get Heini to do the dirty jobs, Himmler was bitterly telling himself as the girl walked ahead of him into the comfortable apartment where she and her famous uncle lived. He was wearing a dark suit today with a gleaming party badge in his lapel. Kept blinking behind his round glasses. His eyes hurt from the afternoon sun. He was glad the apartment was dim.

He could see she'd lost whatever awe famous political figures used to generate in her. He watched her gracefully sit down on the plain, gray couch and cross her long, pink-tinted bare feet and adjust her silky housecoat. Her fine blond hair caught a slant of sunlight (that just creased over the neighboring roof) and seemed to fluff into rich fire. *She's a big woman,* he thought, without attraction, *for a girl of nineteen* . . . He cleared his throat. *Let me do the dirty work* . . .

"He's not here, you know," she said neutrally, "if that's what you came for."

She wasn't so hard-edged before, he noted. *It's living in the city. An abnormal way of life that gradually represses the spirit . . . man needs the clear air, the sights and sounds of wood, streams, and open fields* . . .

"I came, my dear miss," he began awkwardly, "to speak with you, in fact."

She was suddenly watching him intently, cynically, he half thought. Did she imagine he might be interested?

"What a surprise," she said, recrossing her legs and lighting a cigarette. Puffed the smoke between them, as if in defense.

It's probably already too late to preserve her from a life of dissolution . . . The smoke stung his eyes. *What a miserable affair* . . . He kept recalling fragments of the text. Heydrich had made a copy, naturally:

> . . . I long to lie at your sweet feet, dearest Geli,
> in my unworthiness to kiss them again, a slave to
> your young beauty as Siegfried was enslaved . . .

"Why don't you speak, then?" she asked, smoke spilling from her nostrils. She wriggled her toes on the plush carpet. The robe didn't close entirely and his gaze kept straying to the narrow, pale, and shadowed V. He shifted in his seat and rested both hands on his knees. "Well?" she concluded.

You can't have sex all over the place, he thought.

"Perhaps," he started, "it would be better for everyone concerned if you went to, say, Paris. I—"

"He won't let me go out of this house!" she snapped back. "He tore up all my clothes." She snubbed out the cigarette so hard it crumbled. The bright hair shook with her vehemence. "He's pretty strange, you know. He's pretty crazy!"

"He's a great man, Angela."

She smirked and shook her bare foot. He could feel the faint vibration in the legs of his chair.

"Sure," she told him. "You ought to see how great he is. You know what he likes me to do?"

Himmler's ears went hot. He didn't really want to hear it. He was fascinated by his line of thought. For an instant nearly forgot why he'd come there.

A great man's vices are as inevitable as an obscure man's, he thought. *Domehead Streicher is right about one thing, at least: morality is totally relative. Though I suspect that when true racial instinct takes over entirely, behavior is governed by inner laws that are absolute for all Aryans, others for Jews, Negroes, and so on.*

"Angela," he was saying, "that's needless." He shook his head, solemnly. His hands held his knees together. "What *is* important—"

"He makes me get up in the chair, with nothing on, and—"

"Never mind such talk!" He blinked behind his glasses.

"No doubt you and your little spies know all that already," she returned. "You peep in keyholes. That's what Maurice says." The leg thrashed on under the sheer silk; the graceful foot bobbed.

"Your lover," he said, suddenly harsh. He didn't look directly at her now. He felt more comfortable on this ground. Facts, facts, facts—without conflict or sentiment.

She slit her eyes at him.

"Spy," she said with a hiss. "Why the hell don't you get out of here?" She reached for another cigarette. "I wish *I* could, I tell you that."

"That could be arranged."

"Sure." She lit a match.

Except she'll talk her mouth off her face . . . she'll put it in a book, for all we know . . .

He stood up suddenly, looking just past her head, the shimmer of golden hair. The lowering sunbeam bothered his eyes.

> . . . your body, the long legs, so smooth when I
> look up at you and feel your fair foot upon my
> body, I lie there, slain by love, looking up to the
> divine parting of your flesh . . .

My God, we cannot have that!

He blinked at the brightness obscuring her. She took a glass from the coffee table that had been sitting untouched since he came in. She slugged down the drink.

"You're eighteen years old," he murmured reprovingly.

She didn't look at him.

"That's right," she replied. "And guess what?"

He waited, thinking how something had to be done. "What?"

She poked her belly.

"In here there's something," she said.

He stood stiffly, shifting his weight, hands at his sides. She puffed the cigarette and swung her graceful leg.

Always the dirty work . . . always . . . he mentally muttered.

Hitler was already in the full marble dimness of the apartment-house lobby while Hess and his driver Maurice were parking the car. Near the elevator gate he jerked around when something stirred darkly behind the pale daylight fanning in through one of the leaded, Gothic windows. A moment later his sight adjusted and he was staring at a blanched pale woman in dim clothes (he thought she might be in mourning) whose eyes were big and fitfully lit and, somehow, terribly hungry.

"Paula," he said, hesitant.

"Yes, Adolf. I've been waiting."

"My God, why didn't you say you were coming to Munich?"

"I wrote you. But nothing came back."

He leaned stiffly and kissed her cheek.

"I've been up to my ears," he apologized. "This has been a critical time for the party." She watched him with almost-luminous intensity.

"Certain elements have been trying to take control. A few heads have had to roll."

In fact, as he knew, politics was quite stagnant at the moment. Prosperity seemed to have reached a peak. He had put on a few pounds. He kept insisting it would all fall to pieces soon enough. Some people said he didn't seem totally convinced anymore.

"Ah," she murmured, not overly interested. The door rattled as Hess and the bodyguard entered the far end of the echoing lobby.

"Certain elements," he rumbled, "misunderstood my methods. They want bloody revolution." He chuckled. "They imagine I've gone soft." That was true. The old fighters wanted more street fights. "We'll take over the government with mathematical certainty. By elections. We use the very means of democracy to—"

"Adolf," she cut in, quietly intense. Hess and the taller man paused a few steps away. "What about your niece?"

A pause. He folded his arms. Avoided her stare.

"What about her?" he responded. Glanced at the featureless outlines of the two men. Heard the elevator clanking down.

"Are you getting married?" she went on.

He sighed.

"The long arm of the bourgeoisie reaches out," he muttered, rueful.

"Never mind that talk," she said. "This is serious."

"I haven't seen you, dear sister, in I don't know how long." He shook his head. "Must we quarrel?"

"We're not quarreling," she insisted. "I don't know what's happening to you, my brother."

"Ach, Paula, for God's sake."

Above her shadowy clothes her luminous eyes searched his face.

"I've been dreaming again," she said.

He frowned, still not quite facing her.

"About me?" he murmured.

"Yes." The lost, frozen, deserted city, herself fleeing, desperate to find him, sensing terrible danger in the darkness where unseen terrors moved like ghostly wolf-packs . . . forests of dead arms reaching up through the icy snow . . . her brother lost, blind, wandering the empty wasteland . . . her panic to find him, save him from the dark . . .

"Well," he responded uneasily, "I have my own dreams, anyway."

"Notwithstanding," she whispered.

He heard Hess clear his throat. Didn't look around.

"Why don't we have dinner later on?" he suggested.

"I have to get a train home." The ghostly pale midnight emptiness closing in . . . the dead in rows up to their necks in snow, frozen tears flashing on their faces . . . she ran, fell, called his name in the hollow, unanswering night. "Why don't you tell me what I want to know?"

"Must I?"

"No." She still stared into him, gripped both his arms. "Please."

"Please. Please what, Paula?"

"Please!" Gripped into his flesh until he winced. "Marry her . . . do something . . . save yourself."

"Save? From what?"

"Please, my brother."

Her hands bit in. She stared into the hollow night of dreams and cold. He saw she was weeping slightly.

Upstairs he looked left and right before stepping out of the elevator. He put Paula out of his thoughts. Went down the carpeted hall with Hess and Emil Maurice. He'd decided he'd speak to her again. She was needlessly upset . . . He unbuttoned his yellow raincoat.

"We'll settle with all of them, in time," he said. Went into his apartment alone. Hess stood with the lanky-faced bodyguard who was scratching the tip of his chin with grave concentration.

"Well," the Deputy Führer said mildly, "you have also taken good care of our Angela?"

Maurice nodded slightly, not meeting Hess's eyes.

"Mn," he emitted.

"He trusts you with his whole heart, Emil."

The ex-wrestler nodded. Inside, a woman's voice (Geli's) was shrilling. It went on for a while and then was flattened by Hitler's unmistakable thunderclap. Then silence . . .

"I think," Maurice said laboriously, "she feels . . ."

"Yes?" Hess was soft, conciliatory. He was famous for quiet reasonableness. Even opponents believed him to be a good restraining influence on the Führer.

". . . that she feels cooped up." He shrugged his wide shoulders. "I think."

"Naturally."

The door was suddenly wide and Hitler's cold-eyed flushed face seemed to fill the whole space as he yelled back into the dim interior. Hess glimpsed the frilly drawn curtains, grayish light gleaming on an empty polished chair with a strangely underwater quality. Geli's sobs sounded from around the bend.

"Never!" he raged. A gob of spittle sailed down the hall and was lost in the misty twilight of the room. "A thousand times never! In here is where you stay!" He banged the door shut and glared at his bodyguard. "She keeps inside."

Maurice nodded, avoiding his master's look, thinking: *You too they have poisoned you too* . . .

On the way down from the apartment, in the slow elevator, Hitler was trembling. He felt the trembling rush down his spine from his throat and something like sexual excitement burst between his legs and the greenness was there again like a film over his eyes and he thought:

Another attack . . .

As he reeled a few inches to the right and bumped his shoulder into the elevator wall . . . saw into a vast, flat space, acres of underground set with stalagmites that had joined the low roof with the smooth floor and seemed to have been intricately and obscurely carved and blurred with ages . . .

He shook his head and came back to the present, wondering about the vision. He knew it was important. Something, he believed, from a lost life trying to warn him, perhaps . . .

XXXIV
(1945)
In the Bunker

He'd dozed off at his desk, lulled by the steady rumble of still fairly distant shells. He muttered and moaned in his sleep as the greenish-black pictures formed in what he knew wasn't quite a dream:

In the tunnel on the intricately carved and ages-worn flooring, the party of Skull Troops, General Rog, the big-foot dwarf, his wife, son, and captives had stopped to eat and drink. The spearmen in their black and red light chain mail, short skirts, and shirts stayed close together, almost openly huddling away from the mass of stiff, lurching figures that closely followed, rattling and rustling, half obscured by gouts of sooty fumes as if their dead flesh smoldered.

Relti's son had come close to him, looking up. His father was distracted, kept chewing his lower lip. Noticed the boy but at first said nothing. The boy, by custom, had to wait.

The dwarf, making a wide circut around the dozens of close-packed, animated dead, slunk back along the wall, retracing their steps for a little distance. He told himself he was making sure no one followed them. He knew he wasn't going to desert his master. But he wanted a breathing space. Which of them didn't? The cold smoke from the dead choked him and he coughed hard enough to hurt.

"Yes, boy?" Relti finally asked his son, looking at his queen who was standing across the tunnel from him, apart from where the troops and terrified captives squatted on the chill stones.

"Father, why must we go into this place?"

"We must."

"It is a dreadful place."

"Are you afraid, boy?"

"I don't like it. I think something will happen to you here."

His father smiled, thin, long lips creasing without parting.

"Perhaps it will," he said. "Fear is no shame in this place, boy. Do you fear them?" He pointed at the smoky dead leaning and swaying together in a scrimmage-like mass.

"I don't like them, my father."

Relti touched the boy's shoulder, firm but not untender, in his way.

"They are tools," he told him, "of power. Power is all that matters. Without power we are destroyed and made nothing—slaves like them." He gestured at the captives, strung together by thin, cutting, wirelike bonds.

The dwarf, in the smoky dimness beyond the restless dead, shouted something.

"What do you say?" called back General Rog.

The dwarf struggled back, dragging someone small and slender. A woman.

"She was sneaking after us," he said. "I caught her."

The queen looked nasty.

"The whore," she said, not loud or quietly either.

Relti recognized her. His favorite concubine. He no longer trusted her and had left her in the palace. She'd been corrupted by the rebels, he believed.

The dwarf dragged her, in his surprising grip, to her lord.

"They don't get by me," he said.

Relti looked at her. She was almost too lovely. His wife had often claimed she was a bait sent by his enemies to ensnare and weaken him. But his wife, of course, was hardly unprejudiced. Almost too lovely. They all had high cheekbones but hers were delicate and perfect. Her wideset grayish-blue eyes showed a mix of some outland blood that was exotic and always fascinated him. Her body was supple and strong and curved to perfection. He never could look at her without desire. Even there, in the depths among the doomed and the dead.

"You disobeyed me again," he said.

"I love you," she said.

"Ha, ha," said his wife, not coming any closer, head still and tilted slightly back.

"You disobeyed."

"My lord," she said, "this is a terrible place. And these things will ruin you. I love you, my lord."

"Yes," he said.

"All your great power," she said, "should be turned to understanding."

He didn't quite smile.

"A woman will tell me what to understand?"

"No, Lord. Just to love."

"Love." He gestured with his head and the dwarf released her arm and drew back. "Should I leave here and seek the hidden light? Were you sent to help me manage my power?"

She was weeping, just a little. She knew it was hopeless but tried anyway.

"In all this darkness," she murmured, "we have need of light, my lord Relti."

His eyes went far away. He stared at the smoky swirling where the dead packed and shuffled and creaked together, waiting to move on. He didn't notice (or didn't care) as his wife moved nearer, erect and silent, pushing her son behind her, right hand beneath her robe.

"You have been poisoned too," he said to the girl. "You have been sent by those who would undo all I have done. The power must be preserved and passed on forever. Else we are pale worms slowly dying in the slime of a riverbank. Power fills and makes puissant this"—he raised his arm—"useless, perishing flesh." Pointed to the dead. "Even there is the truth of all things!" His rich voice rumbled and shook the stones. "Those empty husks are yet filled by power! It is all that may cleanse the unclean. Even your weakling love may be burned into purity by it!"

"Whore," said the queen and struck from under her

robe in an arcing blur, her amber eyes bright with fury.
"Die!" The dagger ripping the delicate perfection of the
young body and ripping the green vision, Hitler (or maybe
the king too) screaming himself awake in his chair, hands
spasming over the maps on the desk, crying out:

"No! No! Elel, I love you! Elel . . . no . . . no . . ."

And then just sitting there thinking about Geli. Blinking, hand trembling in his lap. Geli naked, haunted,
watching him from the bed . . .

"Ah," he sighed. "Ah . . ."

(1929)
Hitler's Apartment

In the elevator the colorless, cracked brick steadily
passed the brass bars.

"What can I do?" he asked helplessly, staring.

"Well," his friend hazarded.

"Ach, Rudi . . . Rudi . . . What can I do?"

"Marry her?"

"My God . . . you too? A man like myself has no right
to marry." He chewed his lower lip, hands thrust into his
pocket as the cage creaked slowly down. They bumped to a
halt and the bars scraped back. "I am tempted, as I was
telling Himmler . . ." Smiled. "He was here today, I
learned. I must have upset him." Shook his head. "You
know, Rudi, I used to think he was queer like his pal
Röhm."

"Are they pals?"

"Who knows?"

"How are you tempted, Wolf?"

They were now crossing the dim lobby toward the
ironwork door. He glanced into the shadows where his
sister had surprised him, as if expecting something to
emerge again.

"To do just the reverse," Hitler said, "of what I should.
To retire to the south with this girl." Nodded, once. "Take
up my artistic work again . . ."

Hess hesitated, hand on the door handle.

"Are you really tempted?" he wanted to know, watching his friend closely.

"Hess, I cannot." Set his lips, feeling the inner twinge,

the old sadness, loneliness across a gulf of misunderstandings. "That sort of life is not for me." His eyes were faintly misty. "Not for me."

His friend started to speak as they went out into the fuzzy brightness of the street . . . and then said nothing more . . .

Himmler was almost asleep. He'd stretched out on the cot at headquarters to rest and meditate. He felt he needed guidance . . . tried to still his thoughts and let his consciousness reach beyond himself . . . carefully controlled his breathing . . . tried but his brain rattled on as he sagged and rose between sleep and waking . . .

The perfect way to elicit information from prisoners is undoubtedly mind reading . . . I must bring this up . . . it should be possible to influence enemy leaders and troops by the use of concentrated spiritual suggestive force . . . the Führer has indicated as much in private conversations . . . "A race of master adepts will be the irresistible soldiers of the future," *he said . . . such an army of magicians will have to emerge from the SS . . . obviously . . .* He sighed. Told himself to concentrate now. Try . . . stop wandering . . . *I need help!* Tried to hold the image clearly in the darkness of his head: the firm, wise king Heinrich I. *Help me, please! . . . must I make this sacrifice for him? . . . have I the strength for it? . . . Speak to me. I beg of you . . . speak! . . .*

Sleep lapped at his consciousness. He tried to hold himself just at its border . . . yes there it was, a tremor in the grayish dream twilight . . . a commanding figure floating in mind's dusk, a wordless voice sounding:

It's not dry yet.

Himmler was motionless on the cot, half-drenched. He knew the voice understood his question though he was unable to speak or even think words now.

Nothing is dry yet.

Then he shuddered fully awake. The gray room was empty. Dim daylight vaguely fanned in around the drawn shades. He stared at the blank ceiling and played over the message.

Yes, he thought, *thank you for answering me . . .* He understood the meaning. Nodded grimly to himself . . . *not dry . . . yes . . . the cement of our movement could still fall to pieces . . .*

"The world is at stake," he muttered. "I have no choice . . . " *The true sacrifice is never known!*

Let others win glory on the open battlefields, his was the nobler and the harder task. For, he reflected, John the Baptist always lost his head while preparing a thankless way for the Messiah. No doubt there were always such men as himself behind all the great ones of history. Yes . . . an interesting idea, he decided.

"And now it's time," he whispered, alone in the gray room, glasses laid aside, pale precise eyes fixed on the blurry, featureless ceiling.

These are the dramas, the tragedies . . . someday, perhaps, an Aeschylus or a Wagner will be able to express the somber agonies of Hitler, Geli Rauble, and Heinrich Himmler . . .

He didn't want to get up yet, though untired. His mind went on: he imagined the SS order as it someday would be, millions consecrated, fearless in a world he helped make possible . . . a pure way of life . . . beautiful children, glorious women filling the vast, open places of the world . . . clean colonies of noble farmers and woodsmen . . . a world of castles and honest, toiling peasants living in harmonious balance with nature . . . *The Jew's power sprang from the cities because they could not live honestly with nature—so we'll have no more cities.*

Somewhere along his reverie he stood up and went outside into the dusk, wrapped in a gray raincoat with a slouch hat tilted over his smallish head. A drizzle now misted down. The cobbled streets were slick. After a while the streetlamps came on and gleamed on the sidewalks. He gradually picked up his pace until he was striding rapidly with determination. He passed rows of shop windows where the rain showed in the light, billowing the hollow shapes of the wind.

He nodded to himself from time to time, whenever he reaffirmed that he would make this sacrifice for the sake of the world to come. All around, he felt the dark chaos and blind, dead pathways. The New Order which binds men together and makes sense of time and empty, endless space; saves men from the desolate, chill isolation of being a tiny, fragile human speck squeezed in a few years to nothingness by the indifferent machinery of the universe. Here was purpose and deep meaning that no rosy-cheeked slut of a girl was going to stain . . .

He didn't think about anything as the elevator rose until he had a sudden fear that he should have taken the stairs. Well, it was too late . . . He'd have to risk everything. Be bold. This was a soldier's job. Though he'd missed the battles, he told himself, he was, none the less, a warrior.

King Heinrich would act just this way, he thought. *My duty transcends any personal considerations* . . . He smiled thinly. Adolf Hitler himself would never know the secret debt he owed. The unsung deed . . . you had to be hard as steel to be worthy of greatness . . . History could never know, true, but history would feel this act . . .

The gate stuck, part open, and he had to yank it all the way. Discovered his hands were sweaty. His muscles felt watery, somehow. Was annoyed with himself.

His heart pounded. A woman was standing there holding an umbrella. He studied her face fearfully, irrelevantly, as if the details of middle-age creases and rouge and flowery hat mattered to him. Though he was weak, details were sharp. His mind felt very clear. He felt like his nerves were jerking his limbs when he moved. Averted his eyes in strange embarrassment.

"Are you getting off, sir?" she asked.

Now I've been seen . . . that's bad . . . For an instant he wanted to go back down. Try again another time. Yes . . . that would be wise, except his body had already jerked him past her, tipping his wet hat and bowing metronomically, saying:

"Yes, my good woman."

He hurried on, fighting not to look back. His peripheral thoughts raced on thinking she had some significance, knew something sinister. And next he was looking into the craggy features of Emil Maurice, the bodyguard.

This is stupid . . . I should have prepared . . .

Heart racing, he drew himself erect and aimed his chilly eyes at the big, bluff man. He had a peripheral feeling that the floor might open beneath his feet in a moment. Kept willing himself on in little spasms of purpose.

I'm a warrior . . . I must act as one . . . I must act . . .

"Yes, Herr Himmler?" the man was saying, repeating. "What? . . . ah . . ."

. . . the decisive act carries all before it! . . . I should have sent Heydrich . . . no . . . no . . . You're a warrior . . . this is the front . . .

He discovered he was actually hungry. The idea of having food began intruding on his attempts at concentration.

"The chief is out," Maurice said.

"Naturally." Kept his eyes chill. Felt a little better now. Talking seemed to help. His sweaty hand gripped the revolver in his deep pocket. "We want you to take charge of the street entrance." *Very good idea* . . . He kept his mind on the details of the problem and that was helping considerably. *Step by step* . . . "I, on the other hand, will take charge here." He was already working out the story for later. Blinked behind his chill glasses. *He's unsure* . . . "Because there is some danger of Reds coming here to kidnap her. My men discovered the plot this morning."

"They found out the chief lives here?"

"This is not hard to discover. They're a deadly enemy." *Now, command!* he told himself. "Go now," he said firmly.

Emil Maurice nodded, vaguely saluted, and headed for the stairs.

"Heil Hitler," Himmler called after him, then tried the knob, already cursing himself: How could he have overlooked a simple thing like a key? He knew he couldn't face ringing the bell and having to get her to let him in again . . . and next a swelling thrill of destiny as the door swung silently inward. Unlocked.

Step by step, he said in his mind, *detail by detail* . . .

She was still on the sofa, bare legs draped over the arm, curling and uncurling her toes. He blinked the icy sweat from his eyes, hearing with uncanny clarity the rain on the windowglass, the creak of boards under his feet, his heartbeat as she swung her legs around, mouth moving, starting to sit up . . . *A little closer,* he thought . . . whoosh of chemise, a cloud of cigarette smoke . . . a car honking in the street, the distant clanking of the elevator, her words coming as if she were suspended in a muffling mist. *Now the gun* . . . everything in the mist . . . *Aim carefully* . . .

The pistol sight at eye level, her body a pale blur beyond it, her voice in the blur too . . . the gun jumped in his hand and he saw no effect and then she was on her feet . . . *Concentrate* . . . his mind as if a guiding voice spoke through him, sustained him, now unaware of body, sound, or time passing. The misty rush of her came at him and at the next shot (he heard this one) she stopped, arms lashing at him, then backed up to the couch and sat down, awkwardly. He stood watching her face which was suddenly clear, frowning as if trying to understand some point, as if about to say something, and then he wanted suddenly to stop time, reverse it, help her, take back the forever-lost moment . . .

"For Germany," he said, voice cracking like a teen-ager's.

She writhed now, flung her legs back and forth, gasping and looking at him. He kept licking his lips. Then she spoke blood; he watched it spill over the pale bodice.

Die, he was thinking, *for God's sake why don't you die? Please! It's done . . . it's done . . .*

He tossed the gun into her lap where the seeping wound was blossoming. Turned, took two steps . . . *You did it . . . it's over . . .* then whirled back, flinging down the note that he knew he should have made her write, obviously . . . obviously . . . well, too late for that. Looked at her face again: the open mouth dribbling blood and he bent over as if punched in the belly and seized by invisible hands behind the neck, then bolted for the door, thinking if they'd heard the shot he'd say he was outside and came in and found her like that . . . *Nothing to fear . . .* gagged again. *Done . . . done . . . done . . .*

And then knew he'd never make it, dropping to his knees, stomach slamming, snapping the vomit like a scream in a single, violent spew, clutching the wall, pale, shivering. Then heard her groan and was chilled with ghastly fear: perhaps he still could save her? His mind speeded up again: *Nonsense . . . she's lost . . . and strong like King Heinrich . . . like the Führer . . . be strong . . . don't make sounds just don't make sounds . . . just die, please . . . just die and we'll start over as if it never happened . . . please . . .*

The burning foulness was in his nose and throat and mouth. He kept spitting on the carpet, snorting.

My God, I can't stay here . . . my God . . .

Scrambled upright along the wall and plunged for the door. Make sure to lock it. Out into the hall. Empty, thank heaven. Started to run, then made himself walk for the stairs. Tell Maurice he'd had word the threat was over for the moment. The Führer was out of town. Send Maurice home . . . yes . . . Stay with the details. His head was clearing as he went down at measured speed. Tell Hitler he sent Maurice away because he feared something unfortunate was developing between the girl and him . . . Details . . . that was the secret. And it was over. No going back, anyway. Took deep breaths . . . Send up an SS guard and let him discover the suicide. The Führer was safe and clean, that was the point. It was over and he'd come through like a warrior.

XXXV
(1945)

The river seemed as wide as a lake. The evening sun spattered the wind-chewed surface with fading gold chips. Astuti and Duke-Renga were peering through a hedge of low trees across sloping green fields, some already broken by the plow, incongruous and eternal in the eye of war. In the distance, masses of smoke blurred the horizon and earth into one uncertainty. Intense greenish flame flashed where (Astuti reasoned) some kind of chemical dump must have been hit. All explosions were dull and distant and might have passed for thunder echos.

"This has gotta be the fuckin' Rhine, buddy," the soldier reflected aloud. "And the fuckin' Fifth Army ain't crossed here. There's fuckin' *islands* in this river, for crissake. This is some fuckin' river. And I don't see no fuckin' bridge." He blew his nose into the ground, holding a thumb to a nostril. "I don't see shit, in fact, Mr. Duke. The Krauts must all be dug fuckin' in."

"So we have come this far," Renga said, in English. Astuti glanced at him. The professor, in his strange tatters and armor with the longsword slung at his hip and the battered SS pot on his long head, looked grim and shaky. He had a wild stare that the American had seen in the eyes of men too long at the front; eyes seared by dark and fearful sights.

"Welcome back, ace. Where you been?" He fumbled a broken cigarette from the mashed pack in his helmet webbing and got it lit, blowing smoke that the freshened wind sucked instantly to nothing. The wind rushed and rattled the silky new leaves and puffed concentric waves in the wild grasses and flowers that dotted the slope with soft shocks of gold.

Renga sighed and stayed there, resting on his knees as if in prayer. He rested one sunburnt hand lightly over his forehead as if afraid the skull would crack.

"Where have I been . . ." he said.

"That's what I asked you. Fuck, my feet hurt. You know how far we walked since you—I mean the other one—fucked up Schicklgruber's tanks back there?"

"His name was never that."

"What?"

"It was always Hitler. Not Schicklgruber."

"Yeah. We must of come twenty miles. The thing is, I'm with the truck infantry. We ain't supposed to fuckin' march so fuckin' much, you know what I mean?"

"God, God, sustain me in this," Renga whispered, pressing both hands to his gaunt, chapped cheeks. "I found a dying woman in a terrible place . . . a girl . . . I . . ."

"A broad?" Austuti sucked at the smoke, his stubby fingers cupping the butt. "Where was that? You see, I accept you now. You're normal to me. I fuckin' talk to you like anybody else."

"In hell . . ."

"That's what I mean."

"They murdered her . . . like my wife . . . I've been down to hell, you see . . ."

"I don't doubt there's lots of broads down there, doc." He shrugged. "The army must have crossed way west of here. That's what I figure." Smoked. "Fuckin' Patton, that cocksucker, must probly be eating dinner in fuckin' Berlin right now."

"Because she tried to bless them . . ."

"What's that?"

"They killed her because she tried to bless them. It's just like the later Christians, in a way . . . and other things . . ." He looked around now, awestruck by the subtle beauty, the pure tones of the fields, the glitter of water, the sun now going red and green behind the horizon clouds. He was greedy to drink it all in because he expected at any moment it would be taken from him and he'd be groping again in dim, foul corridors in the underworld where he'd bent over the slim girl who'd been stabbed in the back by Relti's queen (though he didn't know that), the blood bubbling from the corners of her mouth as she'd gasped a warning:

". . . the Destroyer . . ."

"What?"

". . . Relti the Destroyer . . . he goes . . . to free . . . the sleeping one . . ."

"I do not understand."

"The one . . . will eat the world . . ."

"Then it will choke him, I think. It has choked me."

Her eyes seemed troubled for a moment and he was desperate to soothe her.

"All is well. Peace." He softly touched her forehead with one hard, scarred hand. "I was one of them, you see. Now I am free. I will slay Relti. I should have done it when we were children."

Her stare was on nothing now.

"It matters little . . . we must all come . . . to the light . . . at last . . . at last . . ."

And she was gone.

Renga stared across the Rhine at the boiling smoke and distant flashes of flame.

"We'll have to find a boat," he said. "All the bridges must have been destroyed by now, I imagine."

"You imagine pretty good, Professor," the soldier agreed, sucking the butt down to a hot stub, slightly searing his full, chapped lips. "Where do you think you are, when you're not around here?"

"Hm?" Renga thought about it. "I . . . I am following someone . . ."

"A broad?"

"No. A . . . an evil man."

"Like Hitler?"

"Yes. He looks strangely like him . . . I think . . . but it is my brother; I am following him through caves . . . tunnels . . ." He was rapt now, caught in the memory of the vision. "But there can be no such place . . . It must be a dream or insanity . . . I broke a cup . . ."

"Insanity, huh?" Astuti commented. He didn't quite smile.

"I am getting closer . . . there's a terrible pit and then a tower where a great, evil shadow waits on top . . . on top . . ."

"I'm sorry I asked," the American said as Renga reeled, holding his head. And then he was the duke again, still talking except the subject had shifted slightly as the language went to Italian:

"And so I shall, with God's help, find the evil one, hide where he might."

And Astuti:

"You too, eh?" Then into his own Italian: "Ey, do you know King Arthur? The Round Table, right?"

"What? Nay. I have heard tales of him but he were dead long by my days."

"Your days. Where do you think you are now?"

The duke grinned.

"Here, with you, foolish one," he said.

And then Renga came back, though Astuti was still speaking Italian:

"So you're a knight but after King Arthur." He was stumped since he'd heard of no others, and to him all those centuries were squashed together into one vague period. "What year is it?"

"What?" Renga wondered. "Come on. I have a little rest now from the madness and we cannot rest here."

They were almost to the river when Astuti noticed a squad of Germans filing down from a line of small, undamaged-looking houses. Maybe half a mile off.

"Hmun," he grunted.

The sunlight was only hitting high on the hills now. Soft shadows filled all the hollows and overflowed into the fields.

"How beautiful this world can be," Renga said.

Astuti cocked an eyebrow.

"You got a fresh approach," he commented. Then: "Holy Shit!" Renga was just about to ask what his other personality was like, but automatically looked where Astuti jabbed his finger at the sunset across the river. And then became conscious of the buzzing roar of the Messerschmitt that was coming straight in at them.

"*Gott*," he said.

"I didn't think the Krauts had no more planes." And then bullets were fraying the earth, slamming past them, and he flopped down flat, shouting, "Get the fuck down, doc!" registering almost subliminally (by stance and attitude) that the duke was back.

The duke stood unmoved as the slugs cracked and hummed around him. He folded his arms.

"Excellent," he said, in his Italian. "This dragon will fall to us and its blood will anoint us with good magics."

The German squad (still in the middle distance) had paused to watch the plane bank to set up another pass. He'd obviously spotted Astuti's uniform and assumed there were more Americans in the trees, because on his way in again he let off a burst into the undergrowth. Tracers zipped and flailed the ground.

Astuti crawled into an unplanted furrow and made himself small, poking his rifle at the oncoming aircraft in futile defiance.

"Trapped out here like a fuckin' rat," he said.

Thinking how the Germans only dared show themselves at twilight now because America ruled the air. Then he realized whichever troops were left around here would be turning up pretty soon, so that even if the plane failed they were in serious trouble.

The upright (and somewhat comic) figure of the duke, now brandishing his sword, must have infuriated the pilot because he bellied down to within a few feet of the slopeless field aiming, Astuti could see, to clip the madman with his propeller blades and probably save on ammo too.

"Duck, you stupid fuck!" yelled the American, getting his feet under him in one motion, angry, despairing because he had no choice, diving to tackle and save the civilian, seeing (in horror) the shark-faced plane leaping toward them, dust spraying around the furious blades. And then missing, landing on his face because the duke had actually charged (the Germans on the hill were just watching now in God-knows-what amazement), howling his war cry into the mounting blatt-roar of the engine that seemed to fill the whole world with mechanical snarling, the plane too close to shoot now, and, next, a sparkling flash as the duke's swordstroke arced into the plane's wooden blades and one flew off (the impact spinning the lanky duke into smashing somersaults across the furrows), which was enough to jerk the wings into a fatal tilt nearly taking Astuti's head off when one dug in and snapped and the Messerschmitt pinwheeled and crunched to a shattered halt.

The duke was already up and following before the soldier could clear his senses.

"Come, Astute one," he called. "The creature's power is ours."

By the time time the American arrived at the flameless wreck (the pilot looked like New-York-cut steak, he thought), the duke was bathing his face in engine oil that had cooled somewhat spilling over the ruined fuselage.

"Its blood is hot from hell and foul to touch," the duke told him. "Yet I think we should both drink some." Jerked his head up at the gaping cockpit. "See that poor fellow there, half-eaten by the thing. Well, he was this monster's last victim."

"Drink?" Astuti wondered.

"It will confer great power and tireless strength."

"Drink that fuckin' oil," he said in English. "What do ya know?" Shook his head. The twilight was going gray. The Germans were coming fast now down the slope and into the field. "Draw me a quart, Duke."

"What do you say?"

"I'll pass, Duke. I'll pass this time."

XXXVI
(1931)

The party offices were empty. Hess passed the long table and then went upstairs to the back offices. The papers he wanted were there. He opened the door and was already running into the room and then, awkwardly, stopping, halfway to Hitler who was facing the window full of gray-

ness. The water-scribbled building and sky in dissolving
lines down the long glass. Hitler's reflected face frowned
there dimly, ghosted in, eyeshadows like holes in the
melting world.

All Hess saw was the pistol, grayly glinting, cocked,
neither pointing nor not pointing, at the big head.

"My God!" Hess cried, "what are you doing?"

Hitler didn't turn. The gun stayed where it was. His
voice was shaky.

"It's all right, Rudi," he rumbled. "If I meant to do it I
would have done it. A man like myself doesn't hesitate
when something's necessary . . ." Shrugged. "I *almost*
meant to do it."

"Because of Geli?" Hess gripped his shoulders from
behind with both hands, looking at the reflected face, faint,
shadow-chewed.

"Because I see what my life will be . . . Rudolph?"

"Yes, Adolf?"

"I've sold my life away. It's too late to turn back . . ."

"You see?"

"You've helped me and I'm grateful . . ." He didn't
move in his chair. Hess stared into the reflected emptiness.
"We've worked together like brothers . . . You know, I
was never a child in the usual sense of the word . . ." Hess
had a strange feeling that the ghostly, hollowed image was
actually doing the talking. "Without greatness the world is
dreary, and even as a child I felt that . . . it often
depressed me. I felt greatness like a force demanding to
reveal itself to the world . . ."

"You've said as much before," Hess murmured.

"Have I? I think maybe I talk too much, Rudi."

"Your genius shows itself as you widen your scope. I've
always realized that."

Hitler nodded slightly. Didn't stir under the firm
hands.

"Yes," he said. He seemed to feel somewhat better. "My
enemies like to say I was driven to this life by failing to get
into art school." He chuckled. "What an idea! I enjoy my
critics. They give the brain a rest from having to be
serious." Hess straightened up. He could see Hitler was
going to be all right again. "But greatness," the Führer

sighed, "bends you to itself." Hess kept his hands on his friend's shoulders but was self-conscious now. Licked his lips wondering if he should move away . . . "But then, when I imagine quitting the task, I say to myself: 'Well, Adolf, what then?'" He chuckled bass, brief. "The muddy little people are in for a surprise. Before I'm done they're going to have to be great or perish!" Smiled. "I'm here to be the scourage of mediocrity. Or else the world will slip back into the sewer and stay there!"

"Yes," agreed Hess. His hands felt sweaty. He finally pulled his hands aways. Hitler seemed not to notice. "There are thousands of artists," he said. "But only one Hitler, I think."

The Führer was scratching his chin with the revolver barrel. He was in good spirits.

"History may say," he suggested, "one was enough, eh, Rudi?"

Hess laughed. Hitler pointed the gun at the vague reflection that the rain churned and melted. Squinted thoughtfully.

"Angela was my last hope," he said.

"But—"

"I know, know. It was no hope at all. It was always too late for me." He set his jaw, holding the gun aimed steady. "It's not easy . . . not easy . . . I'll wall my heart with iron!" he whispered. "I swear I will! . . ."

Hess knew he was crying, though the tears were lost in the rippled emptiness of his sketchy face. For all he knew, he meant it.

XXXVII
(1931)
At Home in Italy

Renga was trying to sleep. The room was stuffy. The pillow, lumped and wet with sweat, dug into his cheeks and made his neck sore. He'd sighed and tossed and struggled through brief dream fugues until the endless hours ran infinitesimally into the dawn and now, in the first, irreversible grayness, he tried again, covered his head with the pillow as much to stifle away Eunice's soft, regular, irritating breathing from the next bed as to blot out the dim light . . .

And then the light went sickly green as if (he didn't exactly think) chlorine gas were somehow burning in the interstices of the ragged rock walls where he was picking his way down into the mountain under the besieged fortress.

He'd just reached the inner gate that opened into the forbidden area where only the chief priests and the royal family were permitted. *Where,* he thought, *they permit their foul and debased rites . . . lightless and degenerate . . .*

He remembered when they'd played together by the river in the great city, himself nine and Relti twelve, himself taller and thinner, his brother wider with a slightly beaked nose broken in a stone-throwing fight two years before, when he'd ordered the leader of a rival group of boys to do what he told him. Relti was now pointing across the slow, warm river at the ruler's palace, all spires, long rainbow arches, and massive, fernlike trees reflected and blurry in the water. They were both barefoot and wore grayish tunics and held short, boy's spears.

"Next I'll be a warrior," Relti had just been saying, "and when I come to be a full man I will be King."

"Ha, ha," he'd responded. "That's funny."

His brother had squinted at him. Annoyed. He'd poked his speartip into the fine sand.

"Our father is poor and a fool," he'd said.

"Because he's poor we—"

"I will be the greatest warrior of our people and so I will be King because that is the law."

The younger boy had been puzzled.

"What law?" he'd wondered.

"The old law."

"Who said?"

"I was told."

"Who told you?"

"Be still, Ner."

"We're gong to be priests, you know that." He'd brushed back his fine hair with one long, supple hand.

"You're a fool too Ner." Relti kicked the sand and frowned at his spearpoint. His eyes smoldered. His brother was surprised by his sudden force. "It is the law. I will be the greatest fighter and slay the king and take his power. you will bow—"

"You're dumb, Rel." He'd walked away along the bright glitter of beach as the sun briefly showed a full disk behind the virtually perpetual overcast. He'd poked the butt of his spear down and used it like a cane. The delicately huge, swamplike fronds swayed overhead. "Priests aren't allowed to be warriors because—"

"Be still, you little toad," his brother had shouted at his back. "Grandfather told me that priests were once the best fighters before the women's laws came . . . the king is like a woman, he said, and—"

Ner didn't turn back. He was watching one of the two legged dragons, green with a red horny crest, stalk with awkward power down to the water's edge about fifty yards ahead. They rarely saw them this close to the city. Next year Rel would be old enough to hunt one. A rite of passage, he knew, of which some of the elders and priests disapproved, saying it had only made sense when their people still lived in jungle caves and hunted to survive.

"Look at that Gan," Ner had said. The sudden brightness intensified the violet-greens of the steamy rain forest.

"Grandfather said I could be King," Relti yelled, nervous, frustrated.

"He's old and crazy. Everybody knows that," Ner had called back.

"Be still, you beetle! . . . You shitlump!"

Ner had realized his brother's voice was suddenly too close and was already turning as the spear-shaft was arcing down. He got one arm up to save his skull. He felt the supple bone bend and fracture. The pain shocked him for an instant.

"Rel," he'd gasped.

"I'll kill any fool and damned woman-boy like you! I'll kill any damned one!" He had stood there, the spear trembling in his grip, eyes wide. "Any damned one!"

(1933)

"Even if you were to stop here," one of the women at the reception was saying, silk dress rustling as she raised the cigarette holder to her lips with studied elegance, "you will have achieved a great deal, don't you agree, Herr Hitler?"

Her face . . . all the faces were pale blurs to him. He kept smiling, nodding, but had little idea of what was actually being said to him. This was the high moment of his life. He was waiting for the last assurance, the official word. He was too excited to focus his thoughts.

These pompous aristocratic monkeys, he said to himself. *Where's Goebbels? He's a fanatic, at least, though he doesn't fool me for one minute . . . none of them fool me . . . they imagine they'll run things through me, well, let them imagine . . .*

Because the National Socialist German Workers Party was the second strongest in the nation. The economy had collapsed and the shouts of "Hitler was right!" rang in the streets. In a few moments the nearly senile president Hindenburg, the old war hero, would appoint him Chancellor of Germany. Once he had the post the SA and SS would have a free hand. The police would be his. And soon the rest of the state would follow.

Some people were waltzing. Uniforms and jewelry flashed.

"Even if you were to stop here," she was still saying, "you will have achieved a great deal, don't you agree, Herr Hitler?"

There was a feeling of victory in the glitter, swirl, and roar of the party. Heads turned as he answered her:

"No. I do not." *It took so long but at least it's here . . .* He wasn't looking at anyone directly, eyes raised and glowing. "To stop at any point is death. Nature exists in continous flux and development toward perfection. National socialism reflects nature. If man or a movement stands still, putrefaction sets in at once."

"As in the case of the Jews," someone put in.

There must be some word by now, he thought nervously. *Where's Goebbels? . . . Damn it . . .* He was staring at the huge candelabra across the room.

"No," he contradicted, eyes full of the sparkling, artificial illumination. "Even the Jew has a kind of mechanical response to nature. An imitation of progress, in fact." He frowned, grasping for an image to express it. The perfect formulation that would reveal the nature of these people forever eluded him. "As a deadly disease may mutate from stage to stage, growing as it destroys the healthy tissue around it. Thus, while it is never precisely stagnant, it is never anything but disease!"

He barely was aware of the nodding, thoughtful heads around him. He was very tense . . . and then Goebbels was grinning up at him, pumping his hand.

"It's done!" he exulted. "It's done, Chancellor Hitler!"

Hitler shut his eyes with relief and ecstasy. Felt energy pour through him. His legs, for a moment, danced to the music of themselves. He looked warmly around at everyone, the glitter and excitement.

They've opened the door, now let them try and close it! They liked to look down on me but it's to me they must come in the end . . . That friend of the Wagners, that Chamberlain, he was a true prophet . . .

He remembered, a few years back, walking across the hushed, rich lawn, the twilight air silver-violet, the old stone house a depthless blot against the shimmer of sky. Walking, Wagner's son and daughter flanking him, then leaving him under the soft, summer trees (the thought that these were the very grounds once paced by the great composer intoxicated him) where the frail, old man was sitting, slightly twisted, in a wheelchair, his linen clothing and lapsheet a shapeless paleness. The old philosopher and teacher of the Kaiser was waning. His eyes seemed hollow, like a cat's, fugitive . . . They spoke for a while about nothing much, then Hitler said:

"The racial mission is not over, sir."

Chamberlain stirred slightly, his breathing sighs.

"It seems we all failed . . . there's nothing much left to say . . ."

"No, Herr Chamberlain, that's incorrect." He bent close to the fragile, lined face hinted in the dying light as if (an imaginative onlooker might have thought) to drink the last fitful gleaming of the old man's life. "The power has been given to me, as it has to others in the past. A new youth will arise. A youth of steel. The decay of the past will be swept away."

"Ah," breathed the old man, head rocking slightly back and forth. "Ah." His legs began to slightly though rapidly vibrate so that the chair creaked as if a motor were running. One skinny, pale hand clutched at Hitler's sleeve. Plucked feebly. The voice was a whisper, shaken by the steady vibration. "You bring me . . . new hope . . . new hope . . ."

"Never doubt it, sir. The old gods are stirring in the blood."

Now the rest is easy. The little outcast from Austria, Chancellor of Germany! Yes, yes, now we get to work!

He looked at everyone and no one as they crowded in to pump his hand, half-aware he was saying, over and over:

"Now . . . now I have them in my pocket . . . now I have them in my pocket . . ."

He reeled, giddy, though he'd drunk nothing but water. For an instant the strange light filled his head. For an instant he saw the misty, mysterious world of his dreams and fainting spells superimposed over the bright, festive ballroom: grim, slender, cold-eyed, V-faced warriors and graceful women gathered in some incomprehensibly solemn ceremony in a hall of dark emerald, bowing to the leader he recognized, the one called Relti, who stood over the crumpled body of another who lay bleeding on the steps of a low dais (which might have served as a throne) and was just lifting (in the vision none of them moved, so that it might have been a painting or a stopped frame in a film) a thin, spiked crown and setting it on his head. Bright blood drops showed on the cold, harsh, dark metal shape . . .

Hitler blinked hard but the image remained.

XXXVIII
(1945)
In the Bunker

Hitler went into the bathroom and washed his face over and over with tepid water that smelled like clay. He carefully didn't look in the mirror. Muttered to himself from time to time. Dried his face and leaned against the wall, nose and forehead taking the weight. Muttered:

"Show me . . . let me see something . . ."

Shutting his eyes and waiting for the picture to come because now he needed that . . . needed anything that would take him nearer dreaming . . .

And the images came and he regretted it at once, but it was too late, and the bilious underworld absorbed him again . . .

The procession had stopped now in a vast chamber that appeared to have been blown out of the living rock by some volcanic cataclysm. The greenish illumination was dimmer here. Relti stood at the lip of a pit that had a narrow ramp cut into the sides, corkscrewing down into darkness.

He stared down. Something huge and shapeless, a slow heaving of shadows suggesting limbs, heads, horns, as if a single beast with many necks threshed the darkness of the pit. He knew what it was. He had to overcome it and absorb its power. He had to accept it if he was to continue. He knew that by the time he returned from under the world he would be changed forever. He would buy the strength to war without end against the enemies. Without end.

"Bring the prisoners," he commanded, not looking back. He felt the terror of his followers. Even his queen, he knew, would want to flee, strong as she was, for a female. And his son would be ready for greatness after this journey.

The Skull fighters dragged two young boys and a middle-aged woman to the edge of the shaft.

"Accept these lives for toll, O lord of the bottom without bottom!" he intoned.

And then the pale, slight figures were already sailing down the pit, seeming to be sustained in slow motion by gusts of shadow reaching up as if greedy claws clutched at them, the woman's last words still vivid, crying out as they tossed her over:

"You will fail! The light will find you deep as you bury yourself!"

Fading as she fell, swallowed by the silent, gnashing blackness, and for a moment, his son, fists clenched, controlling his feelings as he'd been trained, imagined her last words were somehow written on the dusky air in faint streaks of dying gold . . .

Hitler jerked his head back from the damp, chilly wall. His nose hurt. He'd been pressing his face that hard—as if to penetrate the brick.

"Enough of this," he muttered. "I'll be insane soon enough. No need for preliminary hallucinations."

Except he was sure they weren't hallucinations and he really wanted to know the outcome but was afraid of it too—as if it could really matter to him now. As if he didn't really know.

(1932)
At the SS Castle

Himmler took a deep breath. His pale, naked body prickled with gooseflesh in the damp cellar. He was part of the circle on the stone floor. He wasn't looking at the others, Rosenberg, Drecklicht, Fragthopft, Hess . . . Everyone was panting.

"Very well," said Drecklicht, "once again."

They all linked hands except for a hooded man (otherwise naked too) who entered and squatted in the center of the circle, holding what seemed a cat-sized animal, all trussed and swathed, in one hand. It wriggled feebly. Kurt saw there was a portrait photograph under it, laid on the floor. The face was hard to see in the uncertain candlelight. Suddenly the man's other hand seemed to sprout a steel talon which Kurt didn't register was a short knife until the blade had flashed through the creature's neck (he was trying to stay detached, scientific, about this, because he understood the theory behind the ceremony) and the pale bandagelike cloths were staining, fat, ruby drops gathering, and then the acolyte shook the strangely silent, spasming thing and spattered the picture.

Kurt was now singing the chant with the rest, gripping Himmler's small-boned hand on his left, fingers cold and sweaty, and Rosenberg on the right . . . then he finally distinguished the pale features in the picture, the brush of mustache, blood drops gathering like poison dew around Hitler's mesmeric, hollow-looking eyes.

I see now, Kurt thought, *it makes sense* . . . The burst of death energy was being focused to protect the Führer, the image acting like a lens. *Yes* . . . *the thing is to stay completely objective in these dangerous territories* . . .

(1933)
Munich

Renga stood at the window beside Eunice looking out over the city, watching the torchlit, shadowy masses pouring through the dark streets. The mass voice was a muffled, unceasing, oceanic roar, swelling over and around the deep drumbeats and band-blare.

"It's hard to believe," she commented.

"Is it?"

"That Kurt's friends are masters of this country."

"No," he said.

"What do you mean?"

"They have a million brothers," he explained.

She stared.

"Also, in Italy," she murmured. "But they don't scare me so much there. *E vero.*"

The stirring below swirled through his unfocused sight, dots of flickering on shapeless, hollow darkness. He was trying not to imagine himself into anxiety. Leaned on the sill of the open window, feeling these human convul-

sions pull at him as if to draw his soul into the shadowy
creature down there whose heart was the beating drum,
whose thoughts were blaring brass. He kept trying to
picture their country home among the brilliant, sharply
tilted Italian Alps countryside. Told himself they'd stay
there for good. He'd pick up his real studies once more,
forget the years between, the war and waste . . . He
refused to pull away from the view, as if to defy the vision
he dreaded, the shapelessness freed by the leader's thundering, ceremonial violence, frenzied, stony vitality like a
mountain dropped into a dark sea, waves crashing onto
every shore on earth because the sea was the united
darkness of all souls everywhere and Hitler spoke to all
nations. So, thought Renga, if Christ had spilled his blood
to soften the stone mind and heart of earth and touch the
flickers of sweet pity in everyone before he too was buried
under the terrible tide of believers (because God is always
the first victim of religion as truth is of science), so Hitler
would spill others' blood to drain away compassion.

His hands clutched the sill as he faced the night where
the mobs roared inarticulate and inexplicable triumph
. . . and then he could hear the wordless thunder over-
loading the loudspeakers, meaning swallowed in reverbera-
tion, the stone rage, need, fear, loneliness, despair, and
revenge . . . *revenge!* . . . revenge for all frustration, all
bitterness . . . revenge and gigantic, shapeless triumph!
No need for words! The raw soul spoke like dreaming.

He twisted his face away, trying to think about the
sweet countryside, the shade trees leaking golden afternoons. His books . . . the flower garden along the walls
. . . twilight suppers, quiet conversations, the wash of
peace across the grass . . .

"I cannot believe what I see," Eunice said. "*Dío* . . ."

"But you must," he murmured, eyes shut, face turned
down and to the side, hands still gripping the sill.

"I saw some of them today . . . dragging an old man
by his beard, making him lick the sidewalk . . . *Dia mia*,
what a thing! So horrible." She clasped her hand before
her. "These are Kurt's brothers, you tell me? Eh? I
screamed at them, the filthy *cannibali!* One hand went up in
unspeakable disgust and outrage. "They laughed, the
bigmouths! 'Get ready!' one told me, 'this is just the start.'
Just the start, eh? *Gli animale!*"

Renga stood up straight. Turned his back to the window.

"He doesn't know what he's let out of the cage," he muttered.

"It was horrible."

He dreams, Renga thought, remembering Hitler's eyes, *and these are the things he dreams . . .*

"What can we do?" she asked, standing at an angle to him, focusing on her own faint reflection in the window-glass. Her glowing fleshtones partly blotted out the night and the city. "We have to . . . fight back."

"No," he said, "we have to go away." Didn't move. "They're taking over the college too."

"I called Minna the other day."

"Yes? Is she leaving Kurt for the hundredth time?"

"Don't be sarcastic. It hasn't been easy for her. She's tried, you know."

He shrugged.

"Life slips by," he said, "while you're half-looking."

"Is that an answer to anything?"

"No." Turned to her, his dark eyes intent and still. "Do you think I'm satisfied with myself, Eunice?"

"All right, Rudi. Let it pass."

"I'm getting to be middle-aged soon. I just want to have a life . . ." Shook his head. The crowd roar swelled and boomed. Then the rasping voice blasted again. "What have I done with myself?"

"You're a decent man," she told him.

He sighed. Raised his arms and flopped them back.

"Is that my epitaph?" he wondered. "What about Minna?"

"She wants to fight too."

"Good. She can beat up Kurt."

The roar smashed the night like a giant's fist, rattled the windows.

XXXIX
(1945)
At the Rhine

The German squad was coming fast across the twilight
fields. When Astuti looked back from the river's edge
they'd already reached the crumpled fighter plane that the
duke had miraculously chopped out of the sky and now lay
(he imagined) like a shattered insect.

"Fear not," the duke told him, "we are now defended
by the dragon's magical blood."

"Yeah. Dumb of me to forget that." He loosened his
carbine and walked, looking back.

"A magical craft will now carry us to the far side," the
duke assured him. "I have seen the vision of it."

On the downslope to the river, the shadows were
deeper and they were wading through brittle, waist-high
rushes that grew right out into the dark current.

Astuti's companion was still going through a phase of
rapid fluctuations between Renga and the knight.

It was Renga who actually tripped over the anchor line
from the flat-bottomed rowboat that was half beached on
the crushed reeds.

German voices (past the plane and still coming, though
above their line of sight now) were shouting.

Renga was on his knees, staring at the shadowy water
while Astuti commented vividly about the "magic fuckin'
boat." Because Renga was remembering the hidden place
in the misty hills of a lost world where Ner (or himself) had
gone to find the rebels Relti called "Betrayers of the Race."
He clearly seemed to see the huge, fernlike jungle, immense, wet, pale flowers, and delicate pale birds under a
dull sky. Seemed to stand beside the lovely woman who
held up a cup to the grotto rockface where the golden light,

in that sunless world, spilled slowly like thick liquid from a cleft into a rich pool at their feet. Like a dream world. The cup was carved of pure white diamond. It held the liquid light. As if the sun were hidden in the earth and they'd tapped into a squeezing of brightness.

"Drink deep, O warrior," she told him.

He almost had, except the black-armored Skull Troops had charged out of the thick undergrowth that closed in around the rocky hilltop. So he'd been followed. So it was his fault these people gathered here in secret hope would be destroyed.

The killers were supple and quick, lithe as ferrets. Everyone there was falling to spear and dagger. So fast, so fast . . . Ner was barely able to save himself, falling with the cup in his hands as he tried to protect the girl, smashing it between his bare torso and the rocks, a shard breaking off inside his chest muscles just above his heart. He rolled and got his thin whip-sword free and fought, but it was too late for her. She sat, eyes open, back resting on the rockface where the light flowed like honey, spilling over her, washing away the blood that welled around the thrown dagger pinning her graceful neck to death. Her deep, lovely eyes. And he wept and slashed his way clear, thinking how he'd find his brother, dancing over the bodies of the rebel worshippers, snarling with hate, spattered with blood, driving back the fluid killers with the fury of his will and blade . . .

That was memory within the vision of the lost world. Next he was drawn fully in again and found himself, as Ner, once more in a narrow tunnel, descending into the bilious underworld light. He was now limping slightly. He'd had to fight his way past the sentries at the surface entrance, and a spear-haft had cracked across his knees as he put his point through the warrior's head.

He was inside the fortress now. Relti, his brother, he told himself, was going to die . . .

He came to a triple forking. One passageway sloped down, one up, while the last ran level and was brightest and most tempting. He squinted at where it lost itself in greenish phosphorescence.

Ner paused, resting on his sheathed sword.

"Where are you, Rel my dear?" he whispered, "I long

to see your face again. And," he added, "more than I long
for the light to shine upon you."

He said *light,* but his mind saw his sword's brightness
slashing and then redness like fire mixed with blood. He
felt the stroke; paused in his stride, imagining the impact of
his blade.

He took a deep breath.

"Brother, I come," he said and, without hesitation,
headed for the right-hand passage that rose sharply,
believing it was a blind and a message too, because what
rose most steeply always fell the fastest . . .

(1934)

At Wagner's House

Goebbels and Himmler were alone together behind a
bush, standing in a flowerbed. Lilies were pale around the
SS leader's bright boots and hid the propaganda minister's
twisted foot. The sun was setting behind the stone house
where Richard Wagner had lived. Hitler's voice was a
distant, muttering rumble on the far side. A woman
laughed in a pause, then he spoke and laughed.

"Well," Goebbels was saying, eyes tracking restlessly,
"you agree this is absolutely essential?"

Himmler's pale, strangely naked face showed nothing.
He squinted behind his glasses. The hedge shadow gradually rose to cover them as the sun tilted to the horizon. A
dog was barking now and Hitler's voice called to it. The
barking shifted rapidly, then returned . . . again . . .
again . . .

"Yes," the SS chief said at length. Nodded. He was
wondering how far to trust Goebbels. But, he felt, he was a
better ally than some. Göring wouldn't butt into this
business, and Hess would follow, in the end. And it was
clearly in his own obvious interest to weaken Röhm's SA
and leave his own organization dominant. He was im-
mensely proud of his men: he was getting the best blood,
the seed of the future . . . Here now was a way to purify
the party. The essential evolutionary principles had to be
maintained or else all the rest was senseless . . . the bad
chicken had to leave the flock . . .

"The Führer is an instrument of divine will," Goebbels

was saying. Looked avidly at the other man. "It's for his sake this must be."

Himmler studied the bony, intense features, the restless hands. He wondered how much he really knew.

"Yes," he said. The woman's voice (the dead composer's daughter) said something about ducks and geese and Hitler laughed again. "I agree."

"Good."

"He already suspects treason, I think."

"Still, to turn him against that fat queer Röhm will take some doing."

Himmler kept his arms straight at his sides. Squinted. He considered how much to tell this voracious intellectual. *Bad race,* he thought, *look at the bone structure . . . not to mention the foot that no one ever mentions . . . crafty like a Jew too . . . God knows what poisons have clotted in his blood . . .* He felt a surge of secret power behind his carefully expressionless face. Not many would even dimly grasp the real purpose of the SS. Certainly not this fellow.

"It can be done," he said with quiet confidence. "Everything is ready."

They all talk about divine will, he thought, with slight contempt, *but really they can't see past brute physical methods . . . right before their eyes when the Führer speaks they can sense the invisible forces, yet they just talk and talk . . . it amazes me!*

He smiled to think what most party members would say if they witnessed some of his daily rituals. What children they were!

"Very well," said Goebbels. "We'll send in hourly reports to the chief on the progress of the SA mutiny until he has no choice but to take action." He part-turned away, squinting sidewise to watch the face that seemed blanched by the black cap. "It's for the chief's own good," he needlessly added, revealing his haunting distrust and uncertainty. "We must lift these burdens from him." Himmler didn't even have to nod. Across the wide lawn they could hear the resonant, raw voice again. No laughter this time. "History will thank us," Goebbels concluded.

The next day, the morning sun threaded through the blinds and gleamed on the smooth, barely bearded face and seemed to burnish the coppery blond curly hair that fluffed on the pillow. The young man slept deep and easy.

Röhm lay on one elbow watching the slim, elastic muscles wink along the golden-pale torso with each long breath.

He was letting his desire build slowly, enjoying each little postponement, relishing the awkward strength, the rich lips . . . whenever he wanted, he simply had to reach his hand slightly. Smiled with relaxed satisfaction . . . a moment of tranquility . . . thank God things were better than they'd been in years . . . after all that fighting at least there were a few rewards: a sweet boy like this, good friends. There was Adolf's worst mistake: he denied himself too much, far too much. He's really one of us, he just can't face the truth . . . the sweet truth . . . Smiled and lightly brushed his fingers, traced the young man's thigh and genitals.

"You, Mere," he said, "it's afternoon."

And then, as the bright, ceramic-blue eyes popped open, the door shook and rattled, voice in the hall shouting. Röhm sat up, burly, hairy, startled and already furious as the lock gave way and there were black shadows and faint silver gleamings filling the doorway that after a moment's squinting out of the sunlight and shielding his face he saw were SS men. He leaped up on the mattress, the boy watching silently from the pillow, as the troopers shouted:

"Good morning, queers!"

"You!" he raged. "Your names! Give me your names, you sons of bitches!"

The boy pulled the covers up to his face, hands clenched pale near his chin. The blocky commander was still raging when Hitler burst past the two guards, sending one staggering into the dresser, spilling glasses and bottles that seemed to keep falling and shattering for an incredibly prolonged shocked moment as the man frantically, hopelessly clutched at them and Röhm noted that Hitler had pinned his Iron Cross to the breast of his leather coat and then the hoarse voice flattened all other sound in the narrow space like a thunderclap:

"You filthy traitor! It's all up with you!"

"What?" cried Röhm in shock standing naked on the rug now as the SS gripped and yanked his arms back.

"I arrest you," screamed Hitler, "in the name of the party!" Spittle flew. "Traitor!"

No mercy, he was repeating to himself like a chant to drown out everything else. *No mercy . . . no mercy . . .*

"But . . ." Röhm protested, trying to get loose and follow his old friend into the hall as he whirled and strode away, holding his fingers pressed to his ears, shaking his head. Outside there were scattered yells and gunshots . . . "But I am loyal to you! . . . Wolf! . . . Wolf! . . . Listen to me . . . in the name of God, don't let that little *Reichsheini* destroy me!" He saw Himmler's face in his mind, the bloodless pallor, eyes feelingless as the glinting glasses themselves. Hitler was gone.

"Get your clothes on, faggot," one SS man said, a red-head with uneven teeth. The other, dark-faced, laughed. "Look at these disgusting pigs." *What nonsense,* Röhm thought, *what nonsense . . .* A shudder of fear. *He'll never really hurt me . . . oh, those dirty, conniving pigs!*

Himmler was sweating. He leaned against the cold brick wall and felt his heart race. Blinked. He'd put the lights out in the damp office and dim, gray, dirty light gradually filled the gritty, barred windows.

A series of shots *bung*ged and echoed in the courtyard. He took a deep breath.

Why was I cursed with these nerves? I've tried herbs . . . special foods . . .

He steeled himself again. Pictured the scene outside, the group being marched from the cells, the execution squad waiting . . . heard the tramp of boots now, a voice shouting commands.

The will must dominate the nerves . . . King Heinrich would never have behaved this way . . .

Pressing his lips tightly together he flung himself in front of the glass, just as the rifles came level, the pale-shirted men against the gray wall blurred, melted into the gleaming dawn that leaked down into the airshaft. Then the sharp crash and his body shuddered as the men seemed snapped and spun (as by windblast) against the stone, flopping down . . . except his eyes had shut themselves tight again and he was raging in his own darkness at his own reflex.

Röhm looked up from the cell bunk in the harsh daylight. The gritty greenish bricks were at his back. The two SS troopers and Hess had just come in and were paused, awkward, waiting. Röhm was in his underwear, massive. His hairy feet were flat on the chill floor.

"Well," he said, "has the Führer ordered my release?"

"No," said Hess.

One of the men held out a pistol, and when Röhm's hands didn't lift from his knees he dropped the heavy weapon onto the mattress where it bounced once, dull-gleaming.

"My God," Röhm said, "I can't believe this nonsense."

"You better," Hess said. "The Führer offers you this alternative."

"Look, let me see him. That's all I ask. Tell him I must see him." He sat perfectly still, belying the energy of his words. Didn't look at the gun. Hess shook his head. "I won't shoot myself, Hess. You tell him that too."

"It changes nothing," Hess responded.

"My God, I helped him . . . I created him . . ."

Hess turned and went out. The SS men stayed. Hess heard Röhm's voice from the corridor.

"Without me there would have been nothing! What a nightmare of nonsense . . ."

The second SS man watched as the other retrieved his pistol from beside the prisoner's motionless thigh. Cocked it with a startling click.

The second SS man was in a cold sweat. His heart raced, hands shook, knees half-melted, and he wanted to go to the bathroom. He could smell Röhm's bodysweat.

"A nightmare of nonsense," the SA head was repeating, staring. Himmler had ordered him here. Insisted on it. "Kurt," he'd told him, "those of us who were not in the war must learn to be objective about death. We missed the blood initiation the Führer and others had. There's nothing much to death. I've seen that. A spent sack of flesh. The soul goes its way, so objectively there's nothing to fear. We have to look on utterly unmoved, you see? Utterly unmoved."

So Kurt watched as the first SS man took point-blank aim at the pale chunky man on the bare mattress who didn't look up, lips still moving. Kurt's stomach knotted. *Like a pig!* he thought as the half-naked body spasmed and kicked into death, flapping hands at the blunt hole in the chest, sobbing broken breaths, struggling almost (he thought) as if in labor with it, to bear it . . . then he smelled the spilled bowels and for an instant believed they were his own . . .

XL
(1938)
Berlin

Hitler faced the tall window behind his immense desk in the immense chancellery office. Fog beaded the glass and churned in the light spilling out from inside. Beyond that the night was inpenetrable.

He kept his hands locked behind his back, watching the reflections: the Austrian president Dollfuss, chewed by darkness and fog, standing back from Göring and Hess who were closer to the wrought silver lamp. Dollfuss looked at no one. His voice was almost expressionless. Biting.

Hitler didn't have to listen to know what he was saying. *Should the weak eat the strong?* he was thinking. Waited until the voice stopped. *What does he expect from me?*

"The Führer sympathizes with your position, Herr President," Hess said.

"You are certain of this?" the slight man responded.

"Herr Dollfuss," said Hitler, clearing his perpetually rough throat, "I have given my word of honor concerning Austria."

"Yes, Herr Chancellor," Dollfuss agreed. He didn't say 'Which word of honor?' yet. Didn't have to.

"There you are," added Göring. "National socialism doesn't need force to win. It will triumph *morally* over the world!"

Hitler winced slightly at this effusion. He couldn't see if the Austrian leader reacted in the obscure glass where his own image was a featureless outline.

"Do you wish more assurances?" Hess asked.

"No," the grim man said. "No more. The same one."

"Do you want me to say it once more?" Hitler wondered.

"No."

"Well, then?" He let himself frown though he felt only weariness. He was hungry and there was no end to these scenes. Pointless scenes. Thought about a cheese and spinach casserole. And after that he could meet with Speer and discuss his new drawings. He was redesigning his hometown of Linz. Decided to be firm with his architect about the need for a golden-domed bell tower in the heart of the city . . .

"In writing," Dollfuss said.

"What?" asked Göring, eyes widening.

"Put it in writing and sign it."

Hitler was already smiling, nodding at the swirling fog and shadows.

"Whose name would you like on it?" he said, with a chuckle.

"What difference would it make?" wondered Dollfuss, expressionless.

Hitler nodded with respect.

This one is tough, he thought. *Too bad he represents the dwarfs of a dying empire . . .*

(1938)

Vienna Again

The moon was high, the night clear.

It's begun, Hitler said to himself. *And nothing can turn it aside . . .*

He was barely conscious of the crowd in the *platz* below. Swayed on his feet. Felt tremendous energy pouring up through him from the heart of the vast earth.

It's begun . . .

He had just entered Austria in triumph. The country had come into the Reich virtually without a struggle. Dollfuss was dead. Too bad. The SS had botched things there. He'd been furious with Himmler. The man might have been won over to the New Order.

"Germany," he was thundering "is one blood! . . ."

Vague, wavering, so that at first he mistook it for smoke gathering from the thousands of torches until it towered, swirling up into vaporous substantiality, hinting a face, voracious, hollow eyes . . . felt the jewel-hard thoughts that were his own words too . . .

His voice gusted over the crowd in giddy triumph and vindication. Each shadowy emptiness was suddenly filled with himself. He felt them all melting together in the mysterious torchglow: the light and dark flowed into the great face, all into one, single, lordly, intrepid expression . . .

Walking down the steps later, arm outstretched at the packed shadows in the great square, he flashed back to standing there on a chill, dreary winter evening years and years ago, in his ragged, cast-off clothes, shivering, staring at the dim crowds swarming home from work, the meaningless, mechanical murmur . . . his loneliness . . . how he'd stood there, fiercely imagining, and it was as if no time had really passed but that the two scenes had melted together and the dreams of youth had formed into flesh and stone.

He nodded. Breathed deeply. Went on down the steps and into the waiting car.

I consecrate myself again, he thought. *I shall never relent!*

He was giddy, bathed in sweat, collapsed into the soft cushions and muffling interior, the voices around him remote and blurred. As the car fled through the dark streets he watched images, more vivid than any cinema, flash and flow: with closed eyes he saw dark, burning landscapes, vast civilizations . . . lush paradises and bottomless hells . . . struggles that ripped the world in fire and blood; winged beings of fire and brightness warring while misshapen, mucky creatures clambered from seas of slime and mounted on one another to reach into the unstained sky . . . watched, body quivering from time to time, rocking back and forth from half-consciousness to semi-sleep . . . falling down . . . down . . .

XLI
(1945)
In the Bunker

Hitler had drifted from the bathroom and now sat on the hard edge of the bed.

"I don't want to sleep," he whispered.

He lay back. Stared at the ceiling. It was getting easy to sleep, finally. Too late, he thought, to do him any good.

Somewhere, drifting, listening to the distant booming of the Russian shells and American bombs, his eyes shut and he was walking down the tapering spiral that circled around the inner side of the pit, the almost-dwarf man with the big, shambling feet that kept hitting into one another pressing close to him like a troubled dog, saying:

"Master, is this the last terror?"

And the king (Relti) answering, distracted because he was focusing all his will-force into holding back the many-limbed, multiheaded, bestial, shadowy form that, seething with malice, had swallowed the sacrificed prisoners and now swirled around them as they descended, still followed by the clashing dead, with the smokiness fuming sullenly around them as if their empty bodies were sustained by smolder. The dead he'd commanded and led from the chamber of mists.

"Calm yourself, Bol. This is an ally and helper."

(1939)
Munich

Renga looked up from his coffee as the SS soldier sat down at his marble table in the pale, late-afternoon city light. The buildings were dimming, vague across the wide square. He blinked at the haggard, ashy face that it took moments to recognize because now there were jowls and puffy eyes.

"Kurt," he said, "what a surprise to—"

"Never mind that. Where is she?"

"I see you have been promoted."

The waiter was hovering near the black and silver shoulder.

"Where is Minna?" Kurt Fragtkopft repeated. Grim.

"Why . . . I haven't seen her in some time."

That wasn't true. She'd been at the house a few nights ago. She'd come into Renga and Eunice's apartment with a woman friend. The friend had sat quietly by the French windows that opened over the rooftop: a tall, short-haired, intense woman. A Jewess. She hardly spoke while Minna and Eunice debated with Renga about political action.

"And what will be accomplished?" he had wanted to know. "Should we overthrow the government? Like they did?" He sat at the uncleared supper table, the candlelight glinting on his gray hairs. He supposed only women would have the brazen purity to try it.

"No," his wife had said. She stood across the room in a frilly shimmer of pale blue and cream silk.

"What then?" he asked. "What are we talking about?"

"Jews," Minna added, glancing at her dark-haired, silent friend seated beside her.

"Ah," he had responded. "I see."

Eunice sighed.

"Do you, Rudi?" she'd wondered.

Because he wanted to go back to Italy with her. Kept imagining the house, the lush garden, the sweet walks by the unrippled canal that cut across the fields. Because he knew that sooner or later they'd get him into it. Too deep for choice. "I have to help you, then," he'd said. Drummed his fingers on the thick cloth. Stared at Minna, plump but haggard, hair knotted tightly back so that she seemed in pain. "But you realize it's a few drops of water into the sea?"

"Yes," Minna said. "Better than nothing. Which is all Kurt offered to do. I tried him first, you see."

He had nodded.

"Naturally."

"He won't lift a finger. Forbade me."

"What did you expect from an SS man?" Eunice asked coldly.

"I fought for his heart," she replied. "But lost."

Our lives, Renga had thought, *are mist* . . .

"What about love?" he wondered.

"Yes," said Minna, "but there's not enough. Hitler won. He ate my husband's heart."

Renga sighed. The silent Jewess had glanced out the window and then back at her friend with stoic pity.

Minna's partly mad, he thought. And had suddenly sensed he would be too, eventually, inevitably. But not enough to escape, just enough to suffer.

"We will do what we can," Eunice declared.

"I want it back," Minna said, staring. "From Hitler. From him." The eyes were blasted bright, terrible. "I want it back from him . . ." She had rocked slightly. Stared . . .

Kurt licked his lips. His tongue was very red. Then he produced a cigar and lit it, sucking and chewing smoke.

"Don't lie to me," he finally continued. "I know she and your wife are mixed up in something. And I'm not the only one who knows these things."

Renga studied the sleeve of the hand that held the cigar up to the puffy face, noted the SD insignia. *Sicherheits-dienst*—the SS Security Service. Heydrich's men.

"Is this official, then?" Renga was watchful.

"Don't be an ass," the other hissed impatiently. "If it were . . . Minna is still officially my wife. And she's mixed up in something."

"In what, exactly?"

The officer's eyes were restless behind the clouds of bluish smoke. The waiter finally inserted himself.

"Some coffee, *Herr Standarten Führer*?" he inquired.

"*Pernod*," Kurt said, looking at Renga, "Don't you know?"

"What?"

"What they're up to?"

"No."

Kurt looked about ready to spit.

"If I were not involved in this, you'd change your tune pretty fast, Renga," he said. "At the SS *hauptamt*."

"I was not aware I was singing," Renga said dryly. He was both worried now and disgusted.

"Minna is mixed up with fanatics," Kurt said. The waiter set down his drink and left quickly. "Jews . . . Reds . . . malcontents of every description."

Renga studied his coffee cup, the pale glint of china.

"Everyone doesn't have to be a Nazi, do they?" he inquired. Didn't look up. Kept remembering Hitler's face across the table in Vienna, the colorless cheeks and hollow eyes in the unsparing wintery light.

King Adolf the First, he thought.

"They're undermining the state, Renga," Kurt told him. "Treason is treason. And in this country it's suicide." Whispered. "You don't imagine the Führer is going to make the same mistakes the Republic made, eh?"

"Naturally not."

"He can be pitiless, when necessary."

"Only when necessary?"

"You should have joined us." Kurt tossed down his colored drink. "When you had the chance."

"But I didn't join. I don't join things."

"Look, I despise politics personally. And so does the chief himself." Shrugged. "It's a necessary evil."

"So much is necessary."

"Someone had to do something about the world. What a waste of evolution to let the yellow races and the Reds divide it between them."

Evolution, Renga reflected, with contempt, *the same fears, greeds, sacrifices, and hopeless hopes . . . all through history the same . . . maybe even the same people recast over and over again . . .*

"Someone's always doing something about the world," he responded. "That's the trouble."

Kurt relit the cigar and puffed heavily.

"There's always resistance to anything truly great," he said and stood up, scraping the metal chair back.

"I agree," Renga said, still not looking up from the lacy gleaming cup on the polished table. He was tired. Wondered if he would dream even in a nap, because every night he was wandering through the lightless corridors under the immense castle, lost, following hints of footsteps and echoed voices, winding and wandering deeper and deeper into the massed rock of earth and obscure dimnesses . . .

"Minna and your wife will be found, you realize. I can't protect them." Kurt exhaled a massive puff of gray-blue vapor, eyes remote now, cold. "And where will you be? There's no room anymore to be neutral. And I'll have to protect myself, you understand?"

"Naturally."

"I looked you up today." Gestured incompletely. "I leave it in your hands. I don't want to see anyone needlessly hurt."

"Then, I think, you made a wrong turn back there."

Kurt puffed and exhaled, the smoke mounting and slowly unfolding in the almost-windless air.

"I warn you," he said, "they'll be found. It won't be pleasant."

Renga remembered when they'd come into the classroom a few years back, while he stood shocked, the brown uniforms filling the doorway then crashing and scuffling in the aisle, some students watching, some protesting, a few seeming (he'd thought with pale horror) pleased as they dragged three Jews out. Then Renga finally reacting as if his body had been caught in a hiatic spell . . . and then he was fleeing after them through the parted students into the hall, the last skinny, puffy-faced boy struggling among the bulky brown shirts, his face already weeping blood, other professors at their doors, watching, one shouting: "They cannot do this legally! They're not the real police!" and then Renga gripped the boy's flailing arm that desperately seemed to beseech him, rushing through the strange vacuum of his shock and outrage, then pulled, set his heels as if to drag the Jew from the grip of a natural catastrophe like a flood or avalanche, as if the brown figures were merely symbolic of force and as unaware of him as crashing stone—except his shoes skidded on the tile, and as the mass jammed through the main doors they veered and he was snapped away like a child in a game of crack the whip, sailed, went down, and spun into the far wall hitting hard enough to leave his head ringing . . .

* * *

He watched Kurt striding rapidly across the square into the dimming day, black boots winking over the cobblestones.

I have to find them, he thought. *If he knows, they all know . . .*

XLII
(FALL 1939)

Deputy Führer Rudolph Hess stood by the glass doors that opened onto the terrace. The silver moon hung above the greenishly fading sunset, a yellow crease that seemed to hold the jagged mountains in hushed suspension. Fire lisped and hissed in the massive fireplace. He saw Hitler's shadowy outline on the hollow night.

"We've come this far," he rumbled. "We will go on to the finish."

"But how do we explain the war . . ." Hess began and broke off.

"Is there a choice but to fight it, Rudolph? I can't bluff Stalin out of Russia. If we don't fight, the Reds will wear down the West. There are two religions that matter: the senseless materialism of Marx that makes all men equally meaningless, and ours which calls mankind to dream in the sacred spirit, to rise to towering genius!"

A silence. Hess was thoughtful, still staring, still afraid, restless.

A log popped in the fireplace and a single coal arched over the enclosing screen like a shooting star. Hess turned around to face his friend. "You have to sacrifice everything," Hitler continued. He touched Hess's shoulder. "I've seen the face, you realize. I've seen the actual face of greatness, Hess." Because his sleep was never sleep. Because he'd sit up and work on grand architectural designs or talk all night—his inner circle actually drew lots to see who would have to stay awake until dawn, though he never knew that.

After each day's sunrise, he felt, the worst danger was over, and he would reel to his bed, eyes burning, head throbbing, and ease himself down as if through a literal surface into the churning images and melting scenes . . . and he'd shudder away in a silent scream, over and over . . .

Even in the grayish light he'd twist and grasp, convulse his pillow, sweat into the sheets, flash, vibrate, but because it wasn't dark he could pull back from the greenish, shadowy images that waited behind every dream to terrify him . . .

"Yes?"

Hess looked away, startled, as a soft voice called from beyond the fireplace and it was a moment before he recognized Eva Braun backlit in the far doorway.

"What are you two doing in the dark like that?" she wondered, with affected petulance and amusement. "You look like a pair of 'warm brothers' maybe." Laughed.

"Well, Eva," Hitler shot back, "that's out of the question. All the party fags went in the purge." And then even Hess was chuckling.

"I wanted to see you, Adolf," she told him.

He walked over to her. Hess stayed discreetly behind.

"Yes?" he queried when he reached the doorway. He could see down the hall into their bedroom. Her flesh was plump and firm and she was young. He smiled. Sometimes he had her stand nude in dim lamplight while he watched from another room, standing in the darkness, replaying the familiar image from his youth, the one he'd seen from the summer yard through the opened window. It was like something from Wagner, he thought, the image, voluptuous and innocent, enhancing, enriching the moment. "You're overdressed," he said. "It's warm in here."

She knew what that meant and was pleased.

"Oh, Herr Chancellor Hitler, is that so?"

He understood that she felt important when he wanted her. She was a good girl, he reflected, and she listened well. The trouble was (and he knew it), he always had to list her virtues as if to reconvince himself, and that made him uncomfortable and slightly guilty. What could he do? . . . She wasn't—he almost thought "Geli," but he never let himself actually name the name.

There was excitement now. The image was clear and golden. He would come into the room while she stood perfectly still and kneel at her feet and kiss them, run his tongue along the clean, bare toes, then suck them tenderly. His breath came a little thick and short suddenly. Yes, work his way by sweet inches up the strong, young legs.

"Hess," he said without turning around, "women are absolutely necessary." He took Eva by the arm, puffing up the silky peasant sleeve. "But some are more absolutely necessary than others." And walked her down the hallway over the deep carpet.

"Ach, Wolf," she murmured, girlish, parting her lips.

"You really look too warm in these clothes," he half-whispered to her, feeling a little giddy.

Himmler sat up in bed. Blinked into the colorless blur. It seemed to be dawn. There was a strange silence pressing in on him. Something was in the room. He felt a presence. His mind raced in fear but seemed far away from his body which seemed frozen. Couldn't even shift his eyes. Tried to speak . . . nothing . . . shout . . . nothing . . .

Heinrich, he tried to cry, *help me, Heinrich!*

And then he was trembling, sweating, fully awake, the room suddenly pitch-dark again. The nameless, watching something was gone.

"Heinrich," he muttered, crushing the covers around himself. The draught from the parted window was chill.

Everyone, he heard, and couldn't tell if he were thinking or dreaming, if the voice were within or without. *Everyone who might damage us has to be destroyed* . . . He feared there were great gaps in the defenses. He had to seal every crack, exterminate each threat while it was still a germ . . . yes . . . new ideas were suddenly flooding in and he suspected the spirit of the long-dead king was inspiring him. He had to intensify the mind-reading research. He'd have to do another memo. The SS would, naturally, take the lead here. Henlein was in Tibet that very moment, searching out forbidden occult secrets. The fully telepathic superman would hold subject races in perfect thrall. Not even faintly inimical notions could be developed in secret. What a purity that would allow! A clean society without resistance or confusion. So far, the experimental interrogations via telepathy had yielded mixed results. But it would just be a matter of time and uncovering the best racial types for the job. The truth was, everything could be bred into or out of mankind. Once that idea was completely digested and taken to the limit then nature was at your disposal. He nodded to himself. *We have invisible enemies and these will have to be blocked by invisible means and so even these attacks in my sleep will be stopped . . . We will war for men's dreams,* he thought.

The phone was ringing as he flicked on the light and set his steel-rimmed glasses over his nose. The first silvering of autumn dawn now showed at the windows. Around six, he estimated. Took up the phone.

"Yes?" he said.

"Herr Reichsführer?"

"No," he quipped, "you're reached Winston Churchill."

"Eh?" The voice was startled, then cold. "This is Heydrich, sir."

"Oh? I thought it was Roosevelt. What is it, Reini?" He yawned.

"We got hold of a certain party."

"Ah . . ." Yawned again. "Which certain party?"

"Hanisch. The former tramp. He went back to Vienna, it seems."

"Ah. The author." Himmler was sarcastic.

"He's finished his writing career."

"Very good news, Reini." Hanisch had written articles for the foreign and German press before the party came to power, recalling the days in the Austrian flophouse with Hitler.

"I feel we should expand the list," Heydrich said.

Himmler walked into the bathroom with the phone. He ran cold water and dabbed some on his pale, strained, sketchy features with his free hand. The cold light filled the sink mirror.

"Reinhart," he said, "you're always expanding everything."

"Nevertheless. Anyone who knew the Führer in the early days is a potential liability."

"You always want to overdo things." He stared at his pale eyes.

And it always ends up on my shoulders, he thought. *This one can't endure himself unless he's getting ahead . . . he has no real belief, just a gaping hollow within.*

"I think I am correct in this case," Heydrich's voice said, metallic in the tinny speaker.

"No doubt. But we'll discuss it again, Reinhart. Thank you."

He hung up and stared at himself, feeling very depressed suddenly. As if the seeping gray in the room were penetrating his mind with chilly bleakness . . .

The list will grow and grow in more directions than you can imagine, Reinhart Heydrich, he thought.

Himmler stood there, cold water beaded on his colorless cheeks. Shivered slightly, poised as if listening.

(Nuremberg)

I cannot let it happen and do nothing . . . I saw it devour Kurt . . . it will devour everything . . .

Minna Fragtkopft saw the darkness spreading like ink in water, staining the world, as she walked through the morning streets. The image stayed with her like a remembered dream, its meaning vivid and obscure.

The medieval towers and facades of Nuremberg brightened slowly. A postman passed near her. Further on, a milk cart rattled over the cobblestones. She heard drums in the distance: tat-tat . . . tat-tat . . .

Last month he'd found her, pushed his way into Renga's house past the servants and confronted her alone (they were away for the weekend) in the library where she sat reading in a leather chair under long late-afternoon slants of mellow-gold sunlight as if she were behind a wall of soft brightness.

They'd argued, naturally. At first she thought he wanted her back, for some reason. But he didn't. He was just worried about himself. He was always guilty and uneasy around her and she knew he knew it. She wondered why he never gave up trying to convince her of things . . . What did it matter anymore? He always would say: "Because I respect your mind." But, she had long ago concluded, it was simply guilt, and fear of being terribly wrong about everything.

"Your ideals," he'd insisted that day, pacing in and out of the deepening beams that seemed sucked away into his black tunic, "are no more than what was whispered in your ear in the cradle. The same with your morals." Each time he stepped out of the glow her eyes would lose him in the contrast of shadow. "Had you been raised a cannibal you'd devour human flesh without a thought. So it's all relative, my dear Minna. All of it!" He seemed, she had observed, almost passionate about it. Sighed within herself. These things fired his blood and yet he was lost in a moment of warmth . . . her body . . . the child—there, she believed, he faked feeling. And when the child died, that had been the end for forever and all time . . . the end . . . there was no one to blame for that, she supposed, unless they'd poisoned the very air the baby girl had breathed with their discontents and indifferences. She had put it firmly from her mind as he ran on, explaining, exhorting . . .

"How did you find me here?" she finally had asked.

"What? . . . That's my function, after all. Finding people,"

"Fine work for a teacher."

"Oh, and that's good coming from a sex pervert," he'd snapped. "Where's your girlfriend, anyway?"

"Oh, shut up, Kurt." She'd fingered the book in her lap. As if he really cared even about that. He just had to feel justified night and day, she thought. "That was in the past." Remembered then like a dream . . . as if it had happened in half-lights and remote intensities . . . the quiet house; pale, glowing garden seen from the dim window where she seemed to have lain enchanted in the bedroom among grayish silks and subtle draperies and deep rugs where day and season seemed suspended into the uncanny prolongations of early childhood . . . softness and sweetness and silence . . . she never could remember a word she and her lover had exchanged as if that were dream-lost too, even when she saw Eunice again years later.

"We're building a clean world," he'd said furiously. "Without morals or confusion. Mankind will be pure, not because of some absurd religious teachings, but because its true racial and spiritual essence will express itself fully!"

"But you don't even whisper," she'd protested, shocked. "You shout it in everyone's ear! My God, how can you—"

"That's different," he'd broke in. "These are temporary measures."

"Yes, yes. Always temporary everything!" Because she

was half thinking how that sweet spell was forever lost, how Eunice, in different light, had become a firm, clear friend as if the lover had been another person altogether . . . and she saw she was being forced into a glaring, harsh brightness, dreamless, and she was frightened because she knew she wouldn't run away this time. In the shadows he'd just lit his cigar.

"Never mind all that!" he'd raged coldly. "Just keep out of politics before you get into trouble." He'd jabbed his finger at her through rose-gold sunbeams that suddenly stirred and billowed with smoke as he exhaled violently. His voice was strained, she'd noted, and brittle, and she knew then how deep it went, how he'd become more and more abstract and felt (to her fancy) like a metal sheet, a tinniness. "You have no idea," he'd gone on, jerking back the hand from the whirling, expanding blue-gray cloud, "no idea at all of how serious the consequences can be! In the New Order there's no escaping behind conventions of any kind. You have to be very, very objective."

That had been a month past . . . and she believed it had swallowed his heart and he lived like metal. *Objective,* she thought, walking, staring, hearing the drumbeats across the square, arms hardly swinging at her sides, hair knotted severely back from her forehead. She was very objective. And it didn't matter that all the politicians and rich in every nation (and their police and armies) were all essentially the same.

Hitler was more terrible because he was so vivid, and almost wasn't mad. He was feeding on their brains and hearts.

And he had just eaten Dora too: Three days ago she'd gone out to try to find her cousin who'd promised to help her escape. Minna had watched her cross the suburban street and melt into the twilight. She'd rested her forehead on the leaded glass, watched the tall, slightly ungainly, short-haired figure blurring into shadows like ink soaking into a blotter . . .

There wasn't any choice, she couldn't have stayed at the Rengas' much longer. His jaws had to close, sooner or later . . .

He's eating me too. The thought was thin, bright, nearly hysterical. She shut her eyes. That was no good because the teeth flashed. *Me too . . . Me too . . .* opened them again. No good seeing that or she'd run and scream . . .

The crowds were gathering already though he wasn't due for hours yet. She knew his ideas weren't the point: they came to bathe in his energy. And he had swallowed and destroyed them. She held back the image with a nervous shudder. Her husband was tin, he scraped and rattled . . .

She sat down at an outdoor cafe table facing the square. She was peaceful looking, contemplative. The waiter could tell she really didn't see anyone, and concluded she was unhappily in love.

She waited, keeping her mind away from the gaped mouth, the chewing . . . picturing instead the house she grew up in, the walled garden, the cool, green summer shadows under the old, old trees . . . her father playing the piano toward evening . . . the cooking and baking smells at last, late sunbeams firing the ivy on the gray wall with gold . . .

She wasn't trying to rehearse. She knew she'd speak at the right moment just as she knew she'd be able to get to him. That part didn't trouble her at all.

She sipped a coffee as the sun gradually ticked above the dark, gabled roofs. She didn't taste the coffee or the roll either. Her concentration stayed on the sharp shadows on walls and streets; flashing, narrow windows high up; the clarity of autumn air.

The big waiter was standing near her in his white apron. His arms were folded. A spotless, snowy towel was folded over his forearm.

"I'm closing a little early today," he told her. "For the Führer's speech."

Her heart leaped suddenly.

Does he sense something? she wondered.

She half glanced at him, feeling as if he could somehow perceive the little revolver in her purse. What if he picked the bag up to move it from the seat and felt the steel weight? She almost reached over and snatched it away.

"Ah," she murmured.

"I think we've got no choice. The French will force us to fight again."

"Perhaps not," she said, not looking at anything.

"War must come." The waiter was staring across the open space where people walked and waited. "Men struggle. It's nature."

"That's what my husband says."

"Well, madam, your husband is correct. But thank God we have the Führer this time!" Nodded. "He reads the future . . . it's pretty amazing, eh?"

"Yes," she palely agreed.

The drums were picking up now, coming down one of the twisting, Gothic streets that debouched into the square.

"This time there'll be no treachery at home to lose the war for us," he said.

"Certainly not," she agreed, fumbling money from her purse, holding it slanted away from him as she stood up.

"Is your husband in the army, madam? I have two sons . . ." He took the payment, ruddy face friendly and serious. "One is an officer. From my station in life that wouldn't have been possible before Hitler." He took up the empty cup. "Is your husband in the party? I joined in '34." Shrugged massively. "I would have sooner, naturally, had I heard the Führer speak. But I was involved with my business, you see." Nodded. His eyes were dark and unreactive. Fine gray hairs flourished in his nostrils, she noted unconsciously. "Still, it's the spirit that really counts. I heard him speak. It was like a flash of lightning into my brain, madam."

"I see," she almost whispered, feeling very depressed suddenly. She felt that her heart was pounding and was somehow subject to the gathering rhythm of the drumbeats.

"I felt new hope. Life wasn't so bare, suddenly." His eyes seemed to gaze into profound deeps. Age, she could see, was refining his cheekbones and brow. He gave her a safe, comforting feeling and that depressed her, she realized. "Finally," he said, "the world outside, you see, made some sense. That was a lightning flash. Hitler revealed the truth." He smiled warmly at her, blinking, moved. "He explained what was going on. I felt like a young man, eh?"

"Yes," she murmured, moving away. "Good day."

"Good day, madam," he exclaimed warmly. "Come again."

Just as Renga's hand gripped the door handle, he knew, felt his insides sag, knew something had happened though he went through the form of rushing from room to room, not even calling her name, afraid his nerves would be sprung by the sound of his unanswered voice. The long windows flashed by, harsh, bright gray with relentless daylight.

My God, he was thinking, *why? oh, why? . . . please be here . . . oh, Eunice . . . Eunice . . .*

The hall . . . doors . . . then stairs fled past . . . then out on the chilly, harsh streets . . . shouts and rattle and clatter as the shop windows (shut for the parade) fled faster . . . dim black and silver uniforms moved like shadows at the right of his sight . . .

"Why's he running?"

"Stop that man! Hey!"

"You there . . . you!"

The drumming and blare becoming part of all other sound and breath and pulse too . . . and then he was lost in the crowd lining the big square, glimpsing the marchers through the onlookers, over heads, between bodies, cutting, ducking, shoving . . . the boots rat-tatting behind him part of the crashing general roar . . . then the wild, booming cries:

"*Heil! . . . Heil! . . . Heil! . . . Sieg Heil! Sieg Heil! . . .*"

Knew Hitler would be in the first line of marchers and already (in each flicker of space) saw the woman-shape in airy lavender and white crossing from the other side, already past the line of SS and ordinary police, and he was thinking:

Too late . . . too late . . . Remembering the end of the argument the other night, Eunice waving her arms and following him:

"So, *Professóre*, you tell us, eh?" she demanded. "We don't raise a hand to stop these . . . these brutes? Is that it, *Professóre?*"

"Don't you think," he'd exploded in frustration, "I'd like to make it simple too and go knock some other fool in the head?"

"But these men are evil, *uomini malvagi!* The enemy—"

"Yes, yes, and where do we end and the Nazis begin? They're just poor bastards like ourselves. If there's a war, don't you think the Russians and French and English will loose horrors you couldn't tell from German? Will German babies and French and—"

"All right," Minna had suddenly interjected, "there's

no doubt you're right. We're all the enemy. But I won't be eaten alive! I won't be eaten by that beast!"

There's something more to peace, he'd insisted, than just not fighting. Something positive, not passive, a tremendous force that could sweep them all into sanity. The fighters had the cheap vitality that swept you along until you were too old to march or care, and then it was a distant dream and then they died. But he had no words yet . . . no words . . . there was something not part of the grinding, crushing surface movement and would not perish with it—but he had no words.

Wedging himself frantically between two SS guards holding back the swelling crowd, he charged into the street rushing for the bright, flimsy flutter of Minna's dress just moving out of building shadow into the thin clear sunlight, aware of others moving too, not chasing him but converging on her, glimpsing (through the troops and police)Hitler's face, lank hair smoldering, calm eyes, (features thicker than he remembered), and then the gun in her hand for an incredible, unending moment unfired. Renga tensed, waiting for the sound, the shock, wondering distantly why Hitler wasn't ducking or covering up—as if he actually believed he wore invisible armor or felt he had to leave it entirely up to fate.

And then the crowd crashed past Renga and he didn't know (as the flood of uniforms swallowed her) she'd just flung the gun down at the dictator's feet and was simply staring at him, eyes on eyes, an arm's length away, Hitler pushing through violently, holding the others back (her arms were already pinned from behind by Hess) and the guttural voice focusing its power on her as the parade was grinding into chaos behind them.

"Are you a Jew," he asked, "or a fanatic?"

"No," she said, smiling faintly.

"She's cuckoo," a massive man said, and she peripherally registered Göring.

"Why didn't you shoot?" Hitler demanded. "Well?"

She smiled because he had turned out to be a living man, just a person standing there in front of her, eyes too bright and lips too grim, but no devil-beast. No, she decided, amused, his mouth was too small to eat her.

"You can't do it," she told him, smiling. "You're doomed too."

He stared at her, one eyebrow raised.

"Take her away," someone said.

She didn't see Himmler's pale eyes staring without expression behind his glitter of glasses, lips pressed white with terrific fury. He'd just recognized her. The parade momentum was forcing them all to walk and back on into the square.

"She's out of her head," repeated Göring.

"No," hissed Himmler, "she's not." An inflectionless snarl. *She's the real enemy,* he completed to himself. Because she hadn't fired. He alone truly understood her failure.

Renga lost himself in the crowd. They'd soon be looking for all of them, he realized. He'd been momentarily spared, and felt the unseen pressure again that (he believed) would lift and drive him like a tide, more helpless even than poor Minna . . .

The crowd swarmed and was pressed back. He tripped on the curbstone, clutched at someone . . . missed . . . cracked his skull against a lamppost, reeled, blanked out for a few steps and was witnessing a scene, a memory of the lost world where the slim, intense warrior (he didn't know was named Ner and that in 1945 would somehow become himself, that he would lose his personality in a kind of epilodial trance and find himself living out that incomprehensible life and death) was alone, bleeding from several minor slashes and punctures. He was now alone on the misty hilltop by the grotto of the hidden light with the dead squad of Skull fighters sprawled around him, along with the worshippers. The warrior stared at the wall where the liquid light had flowed from the living rock among the soft, oversized, pale blossoms into the pool where the slender girl lay face-down, gracefully dead, perfect legs and arms starfished while her blood mixed with the lingering, fading golden hues.

He dropped to his knees. It was just water now. Stained water. The light was gone, had vanished when the chalice shattered under his body and the shard pierced his chest.

He panted and felt weary and sick and angry and despairing. Hated his brother—though Renga, in his strange remembering, didn't feel anything. He jammed his sword into the soft earth as if into Relti's flesh. Wept and cursed . . .

XLIII
(1945)

The duke had dozed off while they were crossing the water in the warped, leaky boat they'd found in the reeds. Whenever he slept he became Renga again and Renga, sleeping, was Ner working his way deeper down under his brother's stronghold as he went up a flight of slippery stairs then down a sinking bend while things scuttled and slopped, invisible in the shadows . . .

Aha, his mind said, as he spotted a glint of iron in the archway ahead. *Some fairly husky lad.* He sensed how deep, deep down he'd come. Drew his sword with grim pleasure. At last something tangible to battle.

"Come on, then," he said. "Rehearse thy regrets, giant."

Because the figure practically filled the doorway, backlit by random stains of greenish-gleaming light from the clashing, sparking as it wordlessly burbled breath and groped scraping along the walls.

It's blind, he realized.

"What are you?" he shouted. No response. "What, deaf too?"

But it obviously sensed him somehow, the thick arms groping, wearing what seemed gauntlets with long, steel talons. Then he saw that the faceplate was indeed eyeless, a single piece all around, with pinholes for whatever strange breath it drew.

It was far too wide to pass. The awkward lumbering was deceptive. He sensed the machinelike power and abstract fury of the thing sealed in silence, darkness, and hate, a fit defender of this place that, he realized, was becoming more fantastic the deeper he went down through the labyrinths and shadows, as if reality changed with

movement the way consciousness shifted into sleep. He
sensed this was all part of the dreamer's mind.

Yet, because he felt its senseless helplessness, he
backed off and held his stroke. It was a victim too,
somehow. Big and designed for evil, as it seemed, he felt
pity for its groping violence. Then the huge, ripping hands
clapped together, and if he hadn't reflexively jerked away
his head would have been ripped off.

It kept sucking breath in a wet burble. Lurched
another step closer and this time a fist snapped out and
caught his helmet a glancing, ringing blow, jarring him
back like a mace-stroke.

He slashed a counterstroke, his head burning with
shock flashes, then struck again, and then the terrible
taloned hands had him, were tearing, scraping, armor
actually crunching as the blind, soundless iron mountain
ground him with machinelike strength beyond his understanding. He screamed, chopped the hilt at the blank mask
as the stubby thing lifted, hugged him, and the claws
pierced his backmail and he felt the blood spurt. His blows
were hopeless.

. . . After a while he realized it was just carrying him
back through the archway and across the echoing space.
His head was pressed into the vast chest. He felt like a child
being taken to bed. He glimpsed faint, greenish illumination that stained the vast arched darkness like discolored
moonlight . . . and then they descended a long, steep,
winding staircase and he wondered how it could move so
unerringly. What magic guided this hulk? He understood it
was bearing him deeper into the dream . . .

"Canst thou understand speech?" he croaked at it. His
twisted neck hurt and he'd given up his futile half-swings.
"Art thou a fiend serving fiends or flesh and blood as I?"

Just gurgling breaths for reply.

*He sounds like a drain . . . at least he's not shattering me all
at once . . .*

Down into almost blackness . . . down . . .
down . . .

And then he was back on the street in Nuremberg,
staggering away from the interrupted parade that was
grinding forward again, drums and brass braying out the
Nazi anthems, hymnlike, ponderous and gloomy.

My God, he thought, trying not to break into a run. He

wasn't fleeing the SS or the crunching, gearlike, stamping soldiers but, rather, the rising tide he felt lapping at him across lost centuries, drawing him into the blackness, flame, and storm.

"I have to get out of Germany," he muttered to himself. "I have to . . ."

He had to find his wife and get out. He could barely not run. His body jerked in the spasmodic grip of his will.

My God . . . poor Minna . . . my God . . .

Himmler was still glaring as they dragged the woman away and the march awkwardly struggled back into regular motion. *My God, that bitch,* he thought, *she was always against us . . . and her husband, she had no respect for her husband . . . That filthy bitch! . . . She's no doubt working with that other one, what was his name? With the foreign wife . . .* He tried to recall Renga but the image was blurred. *I know their little game . . . they don't fool me . . .*

"They keep trying," he snarled. "How could that bitch have come so close? A few heads may roll when this parade is over."

Hitler, beside him, was sardonic and unflustered.

"Heinrich," he rumbled, "relax. It wasn't *you* in her sights."

"That wasn't the point," he snapped back with surprising bluntness. "Better if it had been me! I was wounded once for you, my Führer, and would gladly be again."

"No," Hitler declared over the blaring and crowd roar. "They might kill *you*." Laughed.

"Even the gods can fumble the ball," Himmler insisted dryly. "We cannot be too zealous, my Führer."

Hitler shrugged and saluted the crowd, left hand locked around his brass belt buckle, expression firm, almost blissfully confident.

"It'll take more than a madwoman, in any case," he said.

"Was that all she was?"

"What difference does it make?"

The SS leader was unsatisfied. He sensed more sinister forces here. Glared suspiciously at the cheering thousands, the windows above . . . even the darkening blue sky beyond the ancient roofs and spires.

That night Himmler finally fell asleep after staring at the blank blackness for hours . . . his unconsciousness was an instant, luminous churning that kept him gasping and jerking, surfacing and resinking . . . at one point Hitler, in lucent green armor, was making a speech without words to a torchlit army. He was explaining that this war was but a continuation of Lucifer's battle to bring the light of intelligence to the dark density of matter on shapeless, struggling earth. Because Lucifer was not the devil: the devil was matter without spirit and belonged to the machine-men, the worshippers of mere gold and chemistry, the blind scientist, the doctor who mistook man for a lump of electric fluids in random animation, who perceived only the dull world of the half-senses . . . he writhed in the covers and chewed into the pillow . . . Hitler in the glowing armor flung up his arm over and over as if to grasp the smoky vastness above him in his pale hand, flashing meaning from eyes and gestures as if divine wrath had taken visible form to shake the dreaming universe with vivid vengeance. Himmler twisted over, eyes popped open, then shut, brain forming words he might have actually sounded too: "The Jew is the devil! The soulless degrader and scum of history!"

And he sat up, sweating, heart racing madly . . .

A vision, he was thinking, *a true vision . . . thank you . . . thank you . . . I am chosen . . . oh . . . thank you . . . I'll do my duty . . . I'll do my duty . . .*

XLIV
(1940)
GHQ

Hitler noted that some of the generals were uneasy, even pale. He raised his eyes to the open window where the sun and spring breeze gathered among the pine trees. It was evening now in these Prussian hills. In two months the insects would be fierce, he thought in passing. There were

misty belts of swamp all around. General Brauchitsch was
objecting to something again. Hitler waited, alert for the
best point to break in. Didn't look directly at the jowly face.
The man, he decided, was getting to be one step north of a
complete nincompoop. *Amazing how men in responsible positions can have not the least notions of the real forces underlying all
that they do . . .*

He cocked his head to give an impression of seriously
listening to the general's rather bleating discourse.

*I'd like to design a uniform for the Wehrmacht more like the
Hitler Youth . . . I'd give a great deal to be able to wear short
pants again as I did in the early years of the struggle.*

Those days seemed bright and simple in retrospect.
International politics was another matter. Still, he was
grimly equal to it just because everything led to the sword
in the end. Since he'd accepted that from the start he was
always ready, while others (excepting Stalin, he realized)
dreamt of endlessly postponing what had to come. The
very existence of nations created endless battle. Politics
meant finding an excuse to strike at the weakest neighbor.
It began with the tribe and never ceased: Americans murdering Indians, trampling Cubans, Filipinos; the British
eating half the world . . . Japanese . . . Chinese . . . all
of them. He was, he saw, simply more honest and direct
having seen through the hypocrisy to begin with . . .

Suddenly he was speaking because the general had
paused:

"The final decision has been inevitable from the first,
Brauchitsch." His eyes were instantly luminous. Everyone
in the room felt the sudden energy. He waited, then felt the
next rush of ideas pour through him. "The Russians are
unprepared. Stalin hopes to strike at us when he's ready
and the blow will be hard if we wait for it to fall. Since the
purge of his generals his army is led by young, inexperi-
enced Communist fanatics. We can maneuver them to
destruction. We have to strike and strike fast!" Pounded his
fist into his hand and stood firm as stone before the map
table. His voice assumed an amazing steadiness, profound
calm. "With the French done there's no one at our backs.
The British will come to terms eventually. After all, we have
the same enemies: the Reds. The longer we wait the
stronger they grow!"

A pause. General Brauchitsch spoke into the silence

that the breeze seemed to float through the window in rich, warm gushes.

"We cannot be certain of her resources," he insisted. "It's a vast space that swallows armies whole up there."

Hitler nodded. The problem was awesome and fascinating. The world hung in the scales. Europe had to be secured before the earth could be won. And he knew too, in a corner of himself, that he needed to be totally busy. Time and silence were like a void before him . . . Chief of Staff Jodl was speaking now:

"Our intelligence reports are clear on Russian strength and production capacity."

"But," insisted the other general, "they could be mistaken."

Hitler broke in, firmly impatient.

"Intellectual knowledge is, by definition, finite and therefore imperfect," he explained. "In the end, a soldier has to trust his courage and a leader his intuition. Our enemies are confused, insecure, while we are firm and sure because we have one, single will! This is a weapon no report can explain!" He laughed. His own misgivings vanished as he spoke. He was amused and conversational now. "Tanks alone won't do it, gentlemen. Those of us who've been to the front know what can be done by naked hands and teeth, face-to-face with the enemy." He narrowed his eyes and frowned. "Unfortunately, I seem to be the only one here who's had the privilege of learning that lesson. It's something hard to grasp from miles behind the fighting." *Keep them off balance,* he told himself. *Staff officers ought to be insecure.* He smiled to soften the barb. Brauchitsch seemed unabashed. Hitler locked his displeased stare on the old soldier who failed to flinch.

"In case you didn't know it, Commander," the general stated, "I was a line officer at the Somme. I was wounded twice and received the Iron Cross, like yourself."

Hitler grudgingly changed his attitude. Nodded, looking vaguely out the window at the bright, gathering spring.

"I'm delighted to find this out," he said. "But it makes your point of view all the more peculiar." He put all the quiet force he possessed into the next words, suddenly, hands on hips, elbows thrust out as if (some of them thought) he meant to begin a peasant dance step, he winked and said: "We can win before the Russian winter. If

Napoléon had taken better care of his panzer groups he would have done so himself!"

Laughter went around the room in a gust of relief out of proportion to the remark. Brauchitsch looked unconvinced but managed a shrug as Blomberg clapped him on the back.

"Trust the Führer," he recommended. "This campaign won't be his first miracle."

The other general widened his eyes as he murmured:

"Are miracles going to replace divisions?"

The staff was drifting toward the door when Hitler said:

"There's something else." Everyone turned, surprised; this wasn't his normal style. They waited. He was grim, chill, remote. "This war will be more than a struggle between two peoples. It will be a battle of *total annihilation* between two absolutely opposed beliefs! The normal rules of battle will not apply here." He watched it as if he were miles tall, feet braced across the curved earth, seeing the dark forces pouring from the icy east, to batter down the last citadel of light and glory where they would rape and mutilate and breed the last Áryans into mongrel, mindless swine . . . *Well, Satan,* he thought, *the final dice are cast!*

The generals (even Brauchitsch) seemed half-hypnotized by what shone in those eyes and beat at their minds. Blomberg realized he was trembling slightly. "Something was in the room" he was to tell his wife, "I felt something terrible there . . . terrible . . ." For an instant, sweating, he nearly bolted for the door.

"There will be no mercy in this war. On either side. The men must understand this point." He seemed to return from the reeling heights of vision. "If Germany fails in this sacred crusade, an age of darkness will fall such as the world has never seen!" He set his teeth in fury, fists raised solid as stone. The bright air at the windows plucked at his tunic. "The Jew has sown fire and will reap the whirlwind! He has forced all this on us"—his voice burst from him and rattled the windows and the men there felt goosebumps spring out over their flesh—"but it is *he* who will be shattered!"

He was dizzy . . . black flecks spun in his sight . . . and then the veil parted again in a greenish rush and he was looking through the strange lens with strange eyes as if floating in a vast, dim underworld hall whose roof was lost in blur, seeming miles high, a sharp spire rising from a molten pool that was crossed by a narrow, railless stone arch . . . focused down on the company of black-armored warriors, the slim, intense, steely queen, her child, the potbellied general, and awkward dwarf, the half-circle of dead in their seething fumes, all ranged behind the robed king who stood facing the bridge. The dead who'd followed him from the chamber where they'd waited in endless smolder to test his will and become his slaves.

One of the dead, the leader, was just scraping and stumbling forward, the living shrinking back, a plume of strange smoke flowing behind it as if it actually smoldered.

"Speak," commanded Relti the king.

Hitler was startled, upset, trying not to be drawn in this time, trying to pull out of the vision—except he felt or somehow heard the inflectionless dead voice seeming to say:

"The enemies are strong here, Master." Toneless, rasping.

Hitler was drawn until the Relti's sight was his own. Relti-Hitler forced himself to look directly into the expressionless, bloodless face of the dead warrior before him whose eyes were lidless, unblinking, like grayish glass, nose and mouth a slash-sketch, acrid smoke curling from the withered body.

"Which enemies?" Relti demanded.

The toneless unvoice rasped, fumes shaping in its slit mouth:

"You cannot resist them without risking the touch of their color. Only the dead can overcome them. Behold." Pointed one stiff, skinny arm at the bridge where dozens of what seemed armed knights (in a fashion of armor unknown to Relti) were coming across, moving fluidly, floating as if drifting on an occult wind.

Still trying to pull away, Hitler's consciousness obtruded for a moment as he thought they looked like knights of the Round Table and that they had to be spirits and that the scene was a dream and that he was going mad from strain and overwork . . . and then lost himself again as Relti snarled:

"I see the cursed glow."

A faint golden shine pressed down almost to extinction

by the weight of shadows. He knew (and Hitler, fighting to awaken, felt) that if those spirits touched him even as he scattered them to shreds with the whirlwind of his fighting will, the color would cling to his flesh like a disease.

"The dead will defend you," rasped the shrunken thing that seemed animated by the steady gusts of its own fumings, lurching forward toward the graceful, faded, armored forms . . .

XLV
(FALL 1940)
Somewhere in Germany

"Where is your husband now?" the pale, young razor-thin man was asking Eunice Malverde, in German.

She sat, huddled in her long woolen coat. The evening wind was cold gusting down the alpine slopes. The sun was just behind the western peaks. The shadows and autumn mists pooled in the valley below them where the climbing highway was a twisted strip of faint luminescence.

"At home," she answered, staring down the steep slope. She could still make out some of the men down where the road passed within fifty yards of the dense pine trees. The road then swept into a tunnel cut through the bones of the knife-edged mountain. "He's at home." She thought of him: he was drinking again. He'd rage about the war and futility and how he'd missed what he should have done . . . and drink more. She sighed and shut her eyes. Her hair was tucked under a beret and was steel gray at the temples. She was tired. Her back hurt from climbing. She knew she'd pay for nights spent out on chilly mountainsides. *Aristocrats*, she thought, *either do nothing at all or make crazy stands . . . it's probably the inbreeding . . .*

"He doesn't want to fight?" persisted the young man. His voice seemed pale as his cheeks. His blue eyes were washed out almost to silver and seemed to suck in the waning light. His large, bony hands were gripped around a stubby machine gun.

"He doesn't have to," she said.

A bearded, bulky man leaned against a near tree trunk a few yards downslope. His rifle leaned beside him. Now she could barely see the ones near the road. *His heart was always at war,* she thought.

"Everyone has to," the young man said.

"I don't know about everyone," she replied. Tucked her hands into her deep pockets and felt the hard, surprising edges of the automatic pistol. "*I* have to." Because after what happened to Minna, and others, there was no more time for words. Not while the darkness rose everywhere and she felt like when she was a child at the seashore going out, fully dressed but barefoot, as far as possible on one of the long, sandy spits that poked into the ocean. She'd stand at the tip and look back with a thrill of fear as the incoming tide began to softly and rapidly chew away the thin strand that linked her to shore, the shore that suddenly seemed so sweet, safe, and far away . . .

"Do you hear anything?" the razor-faced young man asked, watching along the pale string of concrete road.

The bearish, burly man tilted his head back to reply:

"There's nothing yet." His German was weak, accent Italian. "Don't worry. There's time yet, eh?" His teeth showed in the last glimmers.

Eunice took slow, quiet deep breaths. She wondered what she would do when it finally came to violence. She'd try, she supposed, hoping not to embarrass herself or anyone else.

The young man angled his edge of a face toward her.

"Someone said you are a countess," he said. She noticed how his hands gripped and ungripped the weapon across his lap. The half-moon overhead brightened as the greenish-red sunset sank like a slow wave behind the peaks.

"Yes," she answered.

"And your husband is German."

"Also yes."

"And yet you joined us."

"That's not so strange. You're young, I think."

"No," he said, "not anymore." He moved his hands.

She could see he needed to talk. She forgot her own nervousness.

"Yes . . . somebody's got to do something."

"Of course," she agreed, looking in his restless, avid eyes.

"You know, I'm a Jew."

"I imagined you might be. But I'm afraid you look more Aryan than my husband." She smiled in the subtle half-light.

"That's why I got away. I had a Nazi friend." Snorted. "What the devil," he acknowledged, "he wasn't even a bad fellow. That complicates things."

"*Sì*," she murmured, thinking about the villa, the quiet landscape . . . Renga . . . Minna, poor, lost Minna . . . No one knew what really happened except that she'd vanished and had to be dead by now . . .

"How about your husband, is he a bad fellow?"

"*Che?*" She sighed, and noted, with only faint amusement that he might be interested in her. *Dim light*, she thought, *leads to flattery* . . . "No, no," she protested, "Rudi's a fine man." *To fight the beast*, he'd insisted, holding his wineglass with both hands and staring into it, weaving, haggard, miserable, *feeds the beast*. "No more talk," she'd said. "No more talk . . ."

"Ah," said the young man, looking around. "Why is that strange priest with us?" he asked, glancing up into the shadows. The stocky man cocked an ear and half-turned, still watching the valley which was quite dark now. The wind gushed through the massive old pines.

"I don't know," she shrugged. Took her hand out of the pocket with the gun.

The bearlike fellow leaned closer. She couldn't tell if he was smiling.

"The priest, eh?" he said confidentially. "He's not here to bless your dead body," he went on in Italian, "I can tell you that."

"What's he saying?" the young man asked.

She stared at where the priest was sitting, thought she distinguished the tiny glint of his cross in the dim blot of his cassock.

"The big shot sent him here," said the burly man.

She knew this meant one of Mussolini's generals, one of the plotters. She'd met him once at a reception before she stopped going to receptions. An erect, sparkling old man. Fathomless eyes, she recalled, like her husband.

"Why?"" she asked in German for the young man's benefit.

The beard moved in a head shrug.

"What do I know, signóra?" he replied then, in German: "They say he was a gypsy. But who ever heard of a gypsy priest?"

There was a single, soft whistle downslope where the men and shadows were one thing. Eunice saw three sets of headlights down in the valley, better than a mile away. The steady wind blurred over the motorsound.

"They're coming," the young man said needlessly.

The bulky man grunted and spat into the darkness.

"Contessa," he told her, "they say without this priest's help we can't kill the mustache." Which meant Hitler.

"Ah," she murmured. This sounded like something for her husband. Something he'd understand.

No one had noticed him move but the prelate in question was suddenly standing over them as if, she thought, he'd gusted on the wind. She stood up, involuntarily taking a deep breath. The little silver cross flashed under the dark face. He seemed to be looking just at her when he spoke, though she felt rather than saw the dark eyes.

"A great power," he said, "entered into that man and defends him from destruction."

"Ah," she whispered. The priest's voice was remote, calm.

"It was called to him."

"Yes."

"Come on," burly said, "we've got to get ready."

The others started moving down the rocky slope, taking up positions covering the road. The cars were audible now, the lights slashing and dipping across the night. She stood there as if held while the priest said:

"It has to be distracted or he will escape again."

"The power?"

"I don't name it," said the distant voice. "But I have seen it."

She could only really see the cross in the dense shadows where he stood. She looked away. The cars were straining up the steep turn that ended in the tunnel. Her hand had darted into the gun pocket, then jerked out again, empty. Her heart raced.

She started after the tall young man who straightened from a crouch just as the last taillight flicked into the tunnel. When she glanced back she couldn't see where the priest was; just moon-edged pine shadows.

Seen it? her mind said. *Seen what?* Except there was a chill in that.

Heard the brakes jam on not far into the dark cleft. They'd obviously come to the barricade. The idea was to close them in. But was Hitler really in there? Trapped like that? She swallowed. Felt she might float away in a moment. Spotlights and headlights splashed out of the entrance.

She looked nervously around, stopping suddenly: there was the priest, kneeling before a massive, knife-edged boulder. Seemed to be praying, bobbing back and forth in terrific, silent intensity . . .

She jerked around as shots hammered, echoed strangely in the tunnel. She yanked the gun out and aimed at nothing. And then the priest was leaping up, shouting:

"No! No! It's not here! It's not here!"

As a concentrated volley ripped from inside the blocked passage and she heard men screaming and raging. She saw vague movements, muzzle flashes . . . then more cars came skidding and ripping rubber around the bend, spotlights probing the hillside, machine guns *burrupping* . . . tall figure stagger-running through the wild shadows, coming nearer, shots spanging and sparking off the rocks, then he twisted and went down as if, she thought, jerked by an invisible wire.

She scrambled down into the lights, yells, confusion, as the wounded young man twisted to his feet, breath sobbing, clutching his hip . . . and next she had him, stumbling, groping, gasping with him back up the hillside under the trees as bullets whanged, buzzed, chugged into wood and flesh . . .

"Betrayal," he sobbed. "Betrayal . . ."

"Please," she said, with panic and tenderness, *"Dia Mia,* please! Oh, don't fall down . . . please don't fall down . . ."

Almost tripping over the priest who was rolling, rebounding off tree trunks, silent on the moon-stained earth, hands to his throat as if (she dimly thought) he were being strangled by the shadows of the gun flashes and lights, rolling, banging, as if trying to break free from terrible hands . . .

No doubt, she told herself, he was shot. But there was no time for anything now but saving this boy because some of them had to get out of the jaws . . . some of them . . .

That was her prayer too, clutching him with a strength she never imagined she possessed, on . . . up among the dense trees, rushing in pain across the muffling, sweet fallen pine needles . . .

(Berlin)

Göring and his wife were eating alone in the smaller dining room. The table servant had just gone out. He looked through the candleflame at her pale face. He was uncomfortable. The goose sauce was already repeating on him. He'd just made a decision to get more active in Luftwaffe affairs again. After the English fiasco he'd pulled back in frustrated disgust. Who needed that nonsense? After all, man was born for more than war!

That's something the "great one" doesn't understand, he said to himself. *No wonder he eats vegetables and drinks water, his guts would rot away otherwise . . .*

"He's got no blood in his veins," he suddenly said. His wife understood.

"Whatever he's got, Hermann," she told him, "he's done well for himself."

"Aah," expostulated her massive husband, banging his palm down on the table, shaking the delicate flames, "let him do well. *I* sleep at night and eat like a man!"

"You eat like three men," she commented.

"Well, well, Karin," he said, patting his barrel torso, "I need more exercise."

"You like being fat," she said coolly. "Admit it. You had trouble digesting as a child."

"What?"

"So you make up for it now," said Karin.

"Oh, certainly, certainly. I should be psychoanalyzed, maybe?"

"You should have been head of the party. Hitler may be great, as he thinks himself, but he's too unbalanced. He'll sink the whole ship someday, you'll see." She stared into her bare dessert plate where her features bent and merged into the dove china-plate reflection. "He and that disgusting Himmler believe all kinds of rubbish. You said so yourself."

Göring sucked his teeth. Worked a blunt fingernail at a chip of sinew between his front incisors. Grunted.

"Aren't we all perfect Aryans?" he asked, smiling.

"Very funny. Goebbels and that seamy crew . . . ugh!"

"Just tell me, Karin," he said, grinning, "who in hell *do* you like?" Laughed. Freed the fragment from his teeth and took a slug of wine.

"You know, the Führer slinks around"—she looked up from the dull plate—"like a . . . a pickpocket!"

"Perfect," he said admiringly. "He does slink sometimes. I don't think he can help it. Those years in Vienna." Grinned. "He once told me policemen make him nervous. Of course, he was joking, I think."

"Of course."

The red-haired, thin man reentered and served the dessert. Pale pudding.

"What's this stuff?" the Reichsmarschall asked the somber man.

"It's good for you," his wife insisted and waved the servant out. She was staring at her husband now. Intensely. "They say Himmler and that bunch practice witchcraft. Did you know that?"

He shrugged.

"They need to practice something," he offered, pouring another long-stemmed glass full of wine. "They're not good for much."

"They say Hitler's involved in it as well and—"

"They . . . Who in hell are *they*?"

"Don't you see the effect that sort of thing can have on a mind like his? Filling it with strange—"

"Never mind Hitler," he cut her off. "He's too dangerous to fool around with. The other ones I can handle. But it's no good taking chances with *him*." Tasted the pudding and grimaced. "This tastes like shit."

"Ach, Hermann! For God's sake."

"Well," he protested, "piss then."

She grinned. "He's just a nervous man with a loud voice," she insisted.

"What? . . ." Drank. "Hmmm . . ." Felt pockets of gas stir deep within his vast paunch.

"Hitler," she said. "Or do you believe what Goebbels writes about him? 'He is not as you and I!' Give me strength."

"You haven't been close to him as I have." Göring was very serious suddenly. "I don't know what he is." Pushed back from the table. "I can do what I like with the others."

"Even that little crawling Himmler gets the best of you these days."

"Dammit, woman," he bellowed, "watch what you say!" Slammed his wineglass down, snapping the stem. "I'll knock him on his goddamned ass when the time comes!" He noticed his thick, soft palm was bleeding. The crease of bright red was soaking into the mist-colored linen.

"You watch them," she was saying, "they will be the ruin of all of us!" Her lips were colorless, tense; her glare all ice and fury. "Something insane and disgusting. And you'll have stood by!"

He said nothing. Was swaying a little, and blinked at the steady draining of his blood. He pressed a napkin to the slash.

Shit, he thought.

He remembered something from when he was still head of the Prussian *Gestapo*: one of his men, what was his name? . . . Hil? . . . Hol? . . . no . . . *Ernst something or other, wasn't it?* . . . A young idealist, intense, thin face. He'd joined the SS, transferred, and there he was back in Göring's office a few months later in the black and silver uniform, hands pale and nervous on his knees, eyes starey, uncertain. *Idealists,* Göring thought. He'd believed, he said, that in the SS intellectuals would be able to "purify" national socialism. The party backbiting and petty politics had, he said, sickened him . . . *If you couldn't digest that,* Göring thought, *well . . . a pack of milk stomachs . . .* And there he was, prim in his stained virtue, in the Reichsmarschall's view, shaken and ready to cry, for all he knew. Because he had been a minister, he said, they'd taken him for special training where they did terrible things. What things? Some vague answers: a camp and then a castle in Prussia . . . So? . . . There was a medical area where dead human bodies were cut up and displayed . . . He'd been sick, naturally . . . *He never came to the point,* Göring thought, remembering . . . Living people too, all cut up. What's that? Yes, and they made him pull the organs out and touch things. Why? To teach him to lose all his prejudices. Göring was half-convinced the fellow's nerves had unstrung and had woven hallucinations into his original fantasies, but the memory of the conversation troubled him and he stood there, stanching the blood with the dove-gray napkin, frowning into the past: Ernst Gersen, Gastein . . . something close to that, sitting there, staring, too-white hands on black trousers, telling him tales about a secret order within the SS full of foreigners, even Orientals, working, he said, on what Himmler called "spiritual warfare . . ." Because he'd been a Christian, he said, they'd made him defecate on a crucifix to free him from his past. They sounded, were this true, Göring decided, like a crew of schoolboys, Freemasons, and perverts! He'd laughed but Ernst just stared. No, he'd told them, he'd almost gone mad. *Almost,* Göring thought. Religion was all going to be scientific, they'd said, the soul was like electricity and its force could be tapped by "dream power" and he said they'd actually *dreamt* a man to death . . . What? . . . An old man from a concentration camp, they'd made him die by picturing him dead . . . Voodoo? Göring idly wondered, and then tried to dismiss the man who repeated that he had been a Lutheran minister . . . What do you want me to do? Göring asked. They have to be stopped. Yes? Tell the Führer.

Göring shook his head.

"Are you all right?" Karin asked.

"Yes," he told her, keeping the napkin pressed tight to the wound.

Tell the Führer, he thought. *The minister . . . if they'll believe one thing they'll believe anything . . . what a weak belly that one was!*

"What will you do?" she pressed him. The servant was clearing the dishes.

"How the hell do I know?" he snapped back. The story, absurd and cracked as it was, disturbed him. The party, more and more, seemed to draw maniacs.

XLVI
(WINTER 1938)

Kurt Fragtkopft worked his lips uneasily, staring out at the hard Prussian landscape through the slit stone window. The sun was setting behind solid tin-colored snowclouds. The earth was stony, bare. Ice stood in ponds and crusted the streams and ditches that ran along the bleak fields the farmers had abandoned to the season.

Himmler had promoted him again. Invited him to his private castle for a "special conference." His career was smooth. That unpleasant business with his wife hadn't really hurt, thank God. He disliked thinking about it. He'd done what he could for her. Himmler told him the evidence suggested that she'd fled to England. After the war, he decided, he'd straighten things out with her. He had no idea she'd been arrested for raising a gun to the Führer. Or that Himmler had kept her in a camp for the past two years. He assumed she'd run away at the behest of her tainted associates . . .

He sighed and rubbed his eyes. He was nearing fifty. Childless. His daughter had died in the crib. That was that. A bleak fact. He was nearing fifty and all he could say for certain, to justify his sacrifices, was that perhaps, once, he'd seen misty emanations exhaled by a fat woman in a convulsive trance . . . that was all the magic . . . so colorless . . . glorious beings weren't walking in golden life . . .

Lately he loved sleep. He thought about sleeping during the day and he was spending longer and longer in bed in the morning, drifting, coming back . . . sinking . . . surfacing . . . dropping deeper and deeper for uncounted hours . . .

He sighed and stared. Well, at least he was on the winning side. That was something. And maybe there'd be

real magic yet. Maybe . . . The snowclouds seemed solid
as stone.

"Herr Gruppenführer," said a voice behind him in the
dim stone chamber.

Kurt turned and squinted at the orderly's vague outline.

"Yes?" he responded.

"The Reichsführer will see you now."

"Very good." *My friend, the Reichsführer,* he thought. *We
are on the brink of ruling the world* . . . The idea failed to
excite him. *We've all lost our wives . . . except Heinrich just
hid until Marga went away . . .* sighed. *Too bad Hitler's not a
girl, then Heini would be in heaven . . .*

He smiled vaguely and followed the orderly into the
dim, heavily carpeted corridor . . .

Later that night they were all ascending a wide circular
staircase into the castle's central tower.

How theatrical, thought Kurt.

They were all holding torches that stank and sputtered: twelve of them. Symbolic: the Round Table, signs of
the zodiac, apostles . . . *and,* he added, *the tribes of
Israel . . .*

Himmler was in the lead. He'd made everyone dress in
ancient plate armor and, Kurt thought, the creaking,
clanking, and pinging sounded like a panzer column while
the weight, discomfort, the hollow ringing in the helmet,
the simultaneous heat and chill, were past analogy.

*Did human beings really wear these outfits? Christ, this has
gone past even absurdity! These insane fantasies! . . .*

He was puffing and sweating as he climbed the
unending stairs.

Himmler stood in the circular tower chamber in a ring
with the other eleven armored men. The torches seemed to
sway them in and out of the darkness.

*Everything comes second to this . . . we will come to control
all physical things . . .* He smiled wanly inside his dark
visor. They waited in silence except (he noted) for a good
deal of deep breathing echoing inside a few helmets. He
was thinking about the meaning of blood sacrifice, partly
recalling a conversation with Hitler at the Berghof. They'd
been standing alone on the terrace in the icy, alpine night

under a vast hood of stars surrounded by peaks that were wedges of darkness into the hard glitter.

"But what, then, my Führer," he'd asked, "is the actual blood itself?"

Hitler's eyes seemed slightly self-luminous. They tended to concentrate even the dimmest illumination.

"The blood," he answered, "to the awakened eye appears in its true condition as a vital, glowing substance more like a gas . . . no . . . an electrical fluid. All the energy of the soul concentrates there, you see. Even stupid scientists admit that from the blood it might be possible to recreate the entire human being!"

Himmler had basked in the intimate pleasure of this discussion.

"So," he commented, excited, "from the blood you can tell everything. The state of evolution of race, and so forth."

"Exactly. The blood is pure power. The ancients knew this perfectly well. When you sacrifice a living creature, at the instant of dissolution all the invisible energy in the blood is released in a psychic explosion." Hitler stared across the vast mountain gulf where the snow hinted paleness as if the ice of space had congealed there. "I am convinced that eventually a man's racial purity will be determined by a simple blood-smear test."

Himmler's eyes had widened behind the frosty gleam of his glasses. He thought of the incredible possibilities for the SS in that case.

"Ah," he'd breathed.

"Therefore," Hitler rumbled, "when a victim dies in sacrifice, whether on altar or in battle, the adept, by concentration of the will and the will alone"—his hands became fists, chin uptilted as if to answer the glitter and silence of the sky—"uses the energy of the dying to strike invisibly at his enemies!" He was whispering.

"Ah."

"Now, perhaps, you understand some of what was done along the way."

"Yes . . . yes, my Führer . . . yes . . ."

Now Himmler looked at his armored knights as the two masked troopers dragged the heaving, flopping sack into the center of the stone floor. The flameshadows bent and fluttered over the shapeless lumpings of canvas that made little stifled grunts and gurgles. One of the troopers held up a silver SS dagger.

Kurt shuddered. Broke into a chill sweat. His body wanted to run. Felt stifled and terrified in the heavy metal suit. Nightmarish. Watching a medium grunt and soil herself was one thing. Shut his eyes. Imagined the child in the sack, trussed, gagged . . . In ancient days, he'd said, when a nation embarked on a great course, the vital youths vied with one another for the honor of giving their virgin blood for the glory of the race! Of course, Himmler had added (through his opened faceplate where the glasses glittered anachronistically), enemies served the purpose almost as well.

Will no one intervene? his mind desperately asked. Let someone protest and he was ready to follow in an instant! But what was the Reichsführer saying now?

"What we do may seem cruel at first, to some, but it will be a kindness to the world because the war will be shortened. That's noble enough purpose. But it is also an act of reverence in the deepest and most sacred sense. An act of worship, an absolute trust!" Kurt squinted through sweat-blurred eyes around the ring of blank steel men wavering in fire and smoke.

But he knew why, there was nowhere to go. *My God, why do I just stand here?*

He was trying to watch and yet not watch as the sack was ripped open and the long silver blade stung the flamelight. Himmler was intoning and dedicating as the blade winked down and he heard struggling flesh split and gash and he made himself see the second gaping mouth in the throat that bellowed blood and Kurt was thinking *what an ugly child* even as his stomach spilled bile into his mouth and he reeled and then knew the snout that burbled and tossed in the wild beating was a pig's . . . a pig . . . *He tricked us* . . .

And he knew why: because they'd all stood there thinking it was human. He swallowed the acrid, burning spew in his clenched mouth. He'd passed Himmler's little test, he realized. They all had. How horrible. Kept his eyes shut tight as the group began to chant tinny, wordlessly, inside the iron heads and next, as if they pulled it from him, heard his own voice ringing in his steel shell. He kept his eyes buried in his flesh as if that would make a difference . . . some kind of difference.

XLVII
(1945)
In the Bunker

Hitler let her gently tie his hands in front of him. The pressure eliminated the palsy. He was undressed, completely. He lay on his back across the gray rug. She'd hung a shirt over the light. Their bodies were pale luminescence, like underwater creatures in the depths. She stood over him, straddling his chest. He grimaced a smile. It was starting to work a little. He'd sensed it might. It always had.

She placed one bare foot on his chest. Kneaded the flesh with her soft toes. He enjoyed that.

"Suck them," she commanded, dipping her foot into his mouth. He obliged. Shut his eyes. Felt the first pulse and stir of pleasure in his penis.

"Ahh," he rumbled and then, behind his closed lids, he was caught in the green again; back in the body and mind of the tyrant Relti, facing the last, lost defenders of the tower:

The somehow-faded armored shapes floated forward across the slick stone flooring, the molten pit and spire behind them, faces (if any) sealed behind faintly glowing golden visors. Relti knew they were guardian-warrior shapes, fading with unthinkable ages, set there by the lost race who'd forged the fortress mountain to conceal a technology of magic and terror. Powers they'd discovered and regretted. Forces that could unmake the earth and spoil the young civilizations. The weapons, Relti believed, left by the gods who fell to earth, shattered and smoldering, driven from the skies in the greatest of all wars—a war he would have practically ransomed his kingdom to have seen. As a boy he'd studied the old texts and lain awake at night trying to imagine the combat, the fury and fire and desperate attacks, vast wings beating the blazing air, light-nings flung across heaven, swords of flame and madness and forever hate, the earth cracked and bursting . . .

"I am here to claim these things," he murmured over his shoulder to his queen. "The fists of the gods."

The leader of the dead still stood near him, swaying in its sluggish swirl of bitter fumes, its fellows pressing closer, creaking, leathery, crushing, rattling in a mass, moving against the faded warriors.

"We destroy the enemies, Master," the leader grated and rasped, slash mouth spilling smoke. "Forward!"

And they thumped and dragged and creaked to the attack.

"Mother," Relti's boy said to the queen, gripping her legs.

She was a little shaken herself but always kept control.

"Fear not," she assured him. "Your father is master. This is for your sake."

Relti sensed the huge, dark, multiheaded beast shape like a shadow around him, sitting on his shoulders. It had become part of him as they'd descended the spiral steps to the bottom of the pit after feeding the black thing with human souls. It was his servant and master too. Lover, friend, and disease. The beast (Renga saw it ages later in youthful nightmares) had put roots into his soul.

"I sacrifice my human form," he murmured. "I sacrifice my human hand. I sacrifice my human heart. I sacrifice my human head."

At the peak of this tower carved miles high from volcanic rock, brickless, lost in greenish-flickering whirl-winds, rested the egg of time, the womb of the sleeper, the ultimate god whom he could awaken once his form was changed. No unaltered mortal, it was understood, could ascend those unending stairs and ramps that passed into and out of the tower.

The shadow around him was like wind and whispered things. Told him what was next and what he must do. Told him how his enemies would be blotted out, pressed flat, squeezed and left empty, blown away into smoke . . .

The Skull soldiers moved protectively around him. General Rog tightened his guts, as the Lemurian saying went, and the big-foot dwarf shuffled in his bulky wake.

"Even into hell," Rog said, "we follow our lord."

"You first, General," muttered the dwarf. He was Relti's actual favorite, though he gave no sign of it, generally. He amused the king and was his "persuader" because he had a silky manner of speaking. It was said of them that he could talk a wolf into sharing a rabbit. "I will keep an eye cocked to our rear."

Relti moved forward with a dreamlike certainty. The whispers were telling him that his right hand would soon burn and crush even stone, that his right hand would be a god's hand. The hand of legend. The hand severed from the sleeping god's chief captain.

The dead now thrashed into the ghostly, golden line whose wan gleaming seemed a hopeless flicker against the harsh, green, and bitter blackness all around. The enemies of greatness, he reflected, had always existed. And they'd won the great war of the gods. But the sleeper would awaken and the final battle would begin.

"Destroy them," he commanded the dead. "Their weak gleamings sicken my sight!"

The guardians were too old, too faded. Their wan beams, like coals in a draught, flared for an instant as they floated into the seething line of animated husks and, in the fugitive brightening, the queen blinked with a troubled look; the big general seemed almost embarrassed; the dwarf winced; and even the hardened Skull fighters felt a strange touch of what they didn't actually recognize as pity, a bittersweetness, like longing, like a lost childhood morning . . . but only the boy actually saw the whole scene shimmer and bend so that, briefly, the golden glow filled everything and was reflected everywhere because the youth's already cold, penetrating dark eyes had welled up with tears for the first time since he was seven after which all tears were forbidden a male.

His father snarled, stung and furious, as the quick, stiff zombic creatures howled without sound and stamped out the last gleamings, slapping aside the hopeless, flimsy weapons, ripping the armor open, empty now, that had been filled only with glow.

"Dress yourselves, my children," Relti commanded, almost smiling now as the biting smoke swirled where the faint light had burst and died.

The general whispered to the dwarf who was just behind his massive rump:

"Are these his pets and pride now? Will we be the next cast aside?"

Relti was already rushing forward to the bridge, robe fluttering, winglike . . . raced across as if dancing . . . stopped, staring straight up the steep sides.

His son had blinked his tears away. The queen was looking at Rog.

"Worry about your own heart," she told the general.

"I am loyal," Rog said.

"Then, there's little to fear," put in the dwarf. Everything about his expression was serious except one corner of his mouth. The queen couldn't quite be sure, either way. She didn't love him. That was only her husband's indulgence.

The dead were pulling on the thin sheets of armor. Smoke boiled out of the seams. They lurched and clanked together now.

The boy watched his father, the great cloudy shape stirring like a whirlpool of shadow above the king's shoulders, start up the carven stairs around the tower. The molten lava in the moat blended lurid red with lurid green.

The king raced up the step, right arm stretched out before him, shoulder level, as if clutching at something unseen. All of them moved closer into the heat-blasts from the pool to get a better look. The now-armored dead were dipping their hands into the lavic moat and, at the touch, their steel coverings filled with furious flame; a flame that did not die once the spindly bones were charred away. Then, blazing, they began to post themselves in a circle around the tower.

Relti reached the first level and stopped on a platform there. He thrust his outstretched arm into what seemed a hole in the wall. A burst of green flame spumed out around it. He screamed in terrible agony. His queen blanched. His son cried out. The warriors sighed.

The scene dissolved and Hitler heard his voice crying out, over and over:

"No . . . no . . . no . . . I cannot bear any more . . . no . . ."

(1941)
Spring in Berlin

The room was utterly dark because of the heavy blackout curtains. He was soaking in clammy sweat. His hands clenched and unclenched and he believed he'd done something to his right arm because it prickled. The hand was heavy and numb.

I must have been sleeping on it if you call this madness sleep . . . God . . . God . . .

He flung back the covers, his body seeming to steam in the cool rush of air. Eva Braun groaned and he snarled in spite and fear, feeling isolated and helpless because he couldn't escape into sleep. Because he feared the thin barrier might somehow fail altogether and the nightmare spill into waking sunshine . . .

"My God," he muttered, jealous, frustrated. "You sleep like the dead."

"Hmm?" she voiced, and sat up instantly. "What?" she said and slumped back.

"Nothing," he grumped. "Nothing."

"Can't you sleep again?" she yawned.

"I never can sleep. I don't know why I try."

"Poor Ade," she soothed, touching him through a yawn. "You're all right, baby boy . . . you're all right . . ." Groped her hand. "But you're wet?"

"Didn't you notice it's raining in here?"

"What?" Shook her head to clear it. "A leaking?"

"What?" He sighed. "Sometimes I'd like to cut my head off to stop my brain."

"But such a brain." She was almost awake now.

"How would you know?" he asked, smiling.

"Oh yes, I'm so dumb," she returned. "But at least I get a good night's sleep when no one wakes me up."

"Want to trade places, hm? Then we'll see who sleeps."

"You were always high-strung."

He grunted. Let himself flop out flat, staring hopelessly at the ceiling where a fuzzy glow blurred in around the drawn drapes.

"I'll give you charge of the Russian front," he told her. "See how you rest after that."

She was nearly out again.

"Hm . . . yes . . ." she murmured, lightly touched his chest as she turned under the sheets.

"You accept command?" he asked, facetious.

". . . was it? . . . oh . . ."

"I have a worse enemy than any damned Russian," he muttered, frowning at the vague shapes sketched on the ceiling's blankness. "I've wiped out millions of them, but this enemy I can do nothing about."

"The English?" she part woke again.

"No," he rumbled, "the German general staff." Shook his head on the sweaty pillow. "When I was at the front an order came and we tried to obey it. That gave me a false idea of the German army."

She semisat up. Rubbed her eyes.

"They disobey you, sweet cake?"

"They lie. It's the same thing. I can't be everywhere at one time. I can't check what they tell me so easily. One man can only do so much. Not matter who that man is."

She leaned back. Stretched and yawned.

"Well," she comforted, "you'll beat the Russians anyway. You always win."

He tried to take deep, even breaths because sometimes that helped him doze off. He was half in and out of a dream, aware that one wrong thought would strand him on the weary, endless unsleeping side . . .

And then there was clear, sparkling sunlight washing with the wind over the summer garden where his mother walked, flowing in a white gown among sunflowers and sweet heat. Then the shadow slashed across the vibrant grass, the rapid, flailing shape, the old, musty maleness gripping him, and he felt himself cry out, and shuddered and sweated awake again into the silence. The gaining, yieldless day cut in around the drapes. Her light snores sounding . . .

Minna Fragtkopft sat in the hard chair, staring at the stray lance of grayish daylight that crossed the stone room that was virtually a prison cell—though it was actually the head guard's office. Sleepless, haggard, and numbly sick she waited, unfocused. It had been a year since she'd slipped through the crowd and rushed toward Adolf Hitler. A year.

They'd been questioning her again. They did that every so often. They'd taken the splint off her arm and snapped the bone again. Her agonized wrist hung limply. It would never really heal. Her fear of them was even numb. She always tried to answer the questions. But she got confused about what they wanted her to say. Sometimes she begged them to tell her. Everything was gray and unclear and now the door opened and her sagged body tensed reflexively as a black uniform came into the colorless blur of her sight.

She didn't seem to know this one. Maybe her mind was too destroyed. She wasn't sure about that either . . . wasn't sure . . . wasn't sure . . . wasn't sure . . .

She blinked at the colorless features that seemed all glinting, insect eyes.

No, she told herself, *glasses . . . glasses . . . not a bug I'm not mad yet . . . not yet . . .* These were her first formed thoughts in a while.

And then the flat, depressive voice, dimly familiar from months or weeks or . . . when ago? . . . What was it saying? Did she have to listen? Better to look at the pretty places in her mind, the drifting scenes she sometimes knew to remember . . . the wall behind her parents' house closing in the lawn, the trees in brittle autumn light . . . her sister Helga setting out the miniature teacups and plates while she arranged the dolls in their places, their children's fingers stubby, earth-stained, dresses twisted up over plump legs.

So much goes by, she was thinking, watching the old pictures. *I had such hopes.*

Pictures of Kurt coming to court her and her feeling: *he's a man, big and strong. I wonder what it's going to be like? Those things between their legs. God, what do you do with it? Helga says they want always to put it in your mouth . . .*

The dry, dull voice breaking through:

". . . you imagine I don't know there's a vast network of enemies willing to use any means to hurt the Führer? Hm?"

Pause. She knew she ought to say something.

"Yes," she managed, hoping it was right.

"What? What are you saying?"

The glass gleams came closer and she thought the insect was going to bite. No, no, just a man with glasses on, she insisted to herself.

"Yes," she tried again. Her brain was numbness.

"The Führer had divine protection, you idiot. And he has me, as well."

"Yes," she agreed, nodding, trying to recover the images. Her broken wrist throbbed. She tried to float away again to safety where nothing bad touched her.

Suddenly remembering Eunice in her arms so many years past, so supple, warm, and sleek . . . comforting . . . a night that melted into a long, unmeasured sequence of satin touches, softness like honey, oneness like wine . . . and then the morning came . . . all the harsh mornings always came . . .

"Do you wish me to encourage her to speak, Herr Reichsführer?" another voice asked in the gray blurring.

"What have your encouragements achieved up to now?" Himmler responded. "You never even found out her name," he smiled to himself. A good thing that was one of his private cards to play if needed. If Kurt got any foolish ideas . . . The glasses came closer and closer. She stared hopelessly as the voice was pitched intimately: "You imagine I didn't notice a few things, Madam? Hm?" The gleaming seemed to fill all space. "The Führer's planets were in serious affliction that day." Pause. She thought she was supposed to nod. "Naturally, you knew that. *They* knew that." He sounded triumphant. She tried to keep her eyes shut but the gleaming followed into her personal darkness. "I want the name of your group. Your magic failed, didn't it, madam? Our powers are much greater. You can join us if you cooperate, hm?"

"Yes," she murmured, finally. Perhaps there would be no more pain if she kept saying yes.

"You see," he said, as the glasses receded, "I was right. What do you think of that? Herr Heydrich? Herr-know-everything-logical brain!"

There was another dim shape behind him, a thickening of the blur. It had a cool, respectful voice that was all control.

"Herr Reichsführer," it said, "is this conclusive evidence, do you think?"

"Heydrich, if I control the mind, the body follows. So whoever controls the invisible world controls the visible easily. Our real enemies work unseen." The insect eyes came back and she saw an image reflected in them like something from a dream: a gaunt, hollowed old woman's face, cut by harsh shadows, contorted in what seemed perpetual agony. *Poor thing,* she thought. "Don't they?" the voice demanded as she stared at the burningly ravaged features. "You're just a dupe and tool of wizards and fanatics, correct?"

Watching the face she realized it spoke when she spoke and said:

"Yes." She moaned, far, far away in herself and couldn't shut her eyes.

"So, again, Reinhart Heydrich." The glasses shifted. The face was gone.

She moaned as the dark shape with faint silvery gleamings (she didn't know were uniform markings) drifted into the general blurred grayness. Now her sight was vacant and imageless again and she moaned . . .

XLVIII
(WINTER 1942)

"What more can I give?" Hitler asked the bright tin-colored slice of day at the narrow window where the snow settled steadily, faintly hissing on the barren Polish landscape.

He sat in the simple, hard-backed chair in boots and greenish undershirt. The blurry light was fading by gray degrees. He sighed and rubbed his haggard face. Listened to the voiceless snowfall. When the knock came he grunted:

"Come in."

I have to go on, naturally. The Americans will stay tangled with the Japanese for a while . . . there's plenty of time left . . . Sighed. *But we keep losing the best men because they're the bravest . . . while the cowards . . .*

"It's survival of the cowards," he said to Dr. Haase as he set his bag down on the desk. "That's our modern evolution. The only way to balance things is to bleed off the weaklings and shirkers in direct proportion to our losses at the front or else the bad blood will drown the good."

"Ah," murmured Haase, "excellent point, my Führer."

He was preparing a syringe, rubbing a spot of cotton on Hitler's upper arm.

"I'll take a proper cure after the war, Hitler thought. He knew that was a poor excuse but the shots helped a little. It was all day-to-day now. The stomach pains never left. He didn't like to think about the possibilities.

"It isn't so easy," he remarked to Haase, to take his mind elsewhere, "to change history." Smiled and heard the doctor chuckle.

"Quite a job, I'm sure," he agreed. "Not my specialty."

"They think I'm so powerful but, really, Haase, the minute I turn my back God knows what pig-doings develop!" Shook his head. "Good enough to sicken the dogs. And dogs are loyal. They prove it by actions, not by swearing deep oaths. Wagner and I both are characterized by the deepest love for dogs." Chuckled. "I wish some of my SS and generals could be replaced by wolfhounds!" Winced as the needle stung in.

I can't take my eyes off the war even for one moment . . .

"You are not so good, you know," the doctor said quietly.

"That's because I let you get started on me in the first place. Now I'm stuck."

"The fact is, Führer, the heart worries me a little."

"It worries me too, Haase." He stared at the snowy grayness outside. "I can't let it get too soft." Cleared his throat. "That's my secret weakness: I want to be soft with everybody."

Haase grunted and poked another needle into the kinked, bluish vein and pumped the drug home.

"It's a secret, anyway," he said.

"When they kick me I kick back. I do what I have to do. The Jews found that out. But if a man says he's sorry and repents his errors . . . I'm no Stalin. I want to forgive everybody. So I let people hang around who ought to be gone, you see?"

"Ah." Haase looked faintly uneasy. Nervously rubbed his loose jowls.

"Stalin's the only one I worry about," Hitler said. "It'll take more than Himmler's witchcraft to knock him out of the picture."

"Witchcraft?" The third needle went in. Hitler watched, fascinated by the gathering blood mixing with the colorless stuff in the vial before it was squeezed into him.

"The blood, Haase. That's the secret to everything."

It flows into the earth and the souls of men water the earth in battle and crops spring from this earth with which we have a union because the world is part of all the blood shed since time began . . . the blood is gathered into rains and we eat and drink the substance . . . His head felt light and floaty from the last shot. His heart seemed quickened. His depression was lifting.

"It's amazing," he said, "what vitamins injected directly into the bloodstream will do, eh?"

"Yes, my Führer," Haase murmured nervously.

After the war I'll give all this up, Hitler told himself.

He strode to the window, his back to the doctor who was putting away his gleaming tools. Flung open the sash and let the snow spin in around him. Breathed the chill. Sensed the voice out there, masked by the hissing rush of snow, almost finding a tongue in the wind telling him how cold was sucking the heat from all futile life eternally, how the final snows billowed over everything, chill seeping down through soil and base rock, deeper, until the heart of the earth became ice and the sun itself a faint chip of glitter . . .

I cannot relent even an inch, he told himself. *The first retreat is the last . . .*

"How do you feel now, Führer?" the doctor asked.

"Excellent." He still faced into the whirling snowfall, picturing how he would dispose the troops for the final battle. Then, as Haase quietly left, he imagined a gigantic painting of the Russian army being crushed, a city block long and several stories high . . . yes . . . and he'd do more than commission it, he'd stand there and supervise the actual work just as the great Italian masters did in their studios . . . yes . . . all the energy, passion, heroism, would be expressed for generations to come . . .

He stretched up onto his toes and cocked his fists into his hips.

"Excellent," he repeated to the empty room and the freezing, deserted landscape . . .

Kurt read the paper for the third time and shook his head at it for the tenth. Stared blankly out the side window as the car sped through the snowstorm. He had no idea where the sun was. Gray-white blanketed everything. They floated on in hushed suspension.

Of course he'd heard rumors about the camps but there was always exaggeration. The enemy loved to accuse

the Nazis of the most imaginative outrages while they
themselves bombed cities full of women and children into
rubble. They lied, he reflected, almost as boldly as our own
Goebbels. Despite the fact that the English started "terror
raids" against civilians they blamed the Germans, and so
on . . . Someone had said (he seemed to recall) that Hitler
had the power to bring out the worst in his enemies.

And his friends too, he amended.

Except here was a document signed by his chief and,
he supposed, his friend. A long way from cutting a pig's
throat in a castle tower!

Himmler sat, prim and pale, beside him. All the stifled
light seemed concentrated in his round glasses. His soft
hands were folded across his lap. He was wondering if he'd
have to bring up his wife. The facts would destroy the man.
Also, he told himself, he liked Kurt and wanted to protect
him. He would only use her arrest, he decided, as a last
resort.

"That's the general order," he said, "that everyone else
received some time past."

"So this has been in progress?" There was no date on
the paper.

"Obviously. And the methods have been perfected."
Himmler winced slightly. "I wish it could be otherwise but
it's not possible." Pursed his mustache up near his nostrils
and breathed through it nervously. "So I am now ready for
you, Kurt, my friend, because you're the only one of the
original group with the courage and special knowledge for
the job. Most of the others are either dead or too old."

"Hitler has left it altogether in your hands, Herr
Reichsführer?"

Himmler seemed uneasy as he waved the question
aside with a loose gesture. The gray-whiteness streamed
past the windows and whooshed over the windshield where
the wipers scraped. As the driver took a steep turn the two
of them swayed together as if invisibly linked.

"This is my burden," he said to Kurt. Cleared his throat.

Kurt was staring out at the vague shapes: a row of
sudden pine trees like cowled giants; a ghostly house . . .

Does he really expect to wipe out whole nations? he asked
himself. *Am I supposed to help?*

Glanced again at the paper where his left hand held it
across his knees, stark against the SS black.

"I don't quite understand," he murmured, reading:

. . . most of you will know what it means to see a
row of corpses—500, 1000—lying there. But seeing this thing through and, nevertheless—apart
from certain exceptions due to human infirmity—
remaining decent, that is what has made us hard.
This is a never recorded and never-to-be-recorded
page of glory in our history.

"I'm going to stand beside you today, Kurt." The pale
hands closed around each other. "You'll see, it's not so
difficult, once we get used to it." Nodded. "You see, I'm told
one can get used to it."

"Used to it." Kurt was watching ahead, startled, for a
moment, by what seemed a sinister form striding over a
line of trees which then resolved into a sentry tower with
a barbed-wire gate . . . and next the car weaved and
skidded to a gentle halt.

"It's not so hard," Himmler said. "There are a few
brutes, naturally. But I try to have them weeded out.
There's no place for sadists and perverts among us." He
leaned close to Kurt, reminding his subordinate of decades
before when young Heini the romantic had endlessly
confided in him. The glasses were full of shapes billowed
into the snow by the swirling, empty gusts. "The war and
the world will be won right here. By you, Kurt, by you!" His
soft, cool hand found Kurt's knee and gripped it.

"I feel I must refuse, sir," he replied, nervously licking
his lips. He went on into the other's silence. "I don't
. . . well, feel qualified to command such a place. I have no
background and—"

"Kurt." The sentry had just ordered the gate opened,
and the fence and helmeted, bundled-up men slipped past.
"This is unworthy of all we stand for. We are not merely
soldiers, we are crusaders against all the darkness of
history. The new age will be our age. The price will have to
be paid."

Kurt shut his eyes. If he fell from grace here, what
waited for him? No family anymore, no wife, no children . . . obscurity and poverty . . . *At my age? My God.*
Sometimes it was hard to see the connection between the
magic and secrets and the open results: the new age
seemed to have opened in the bloodiest war in history, in
burning cities, slaughtered peoples, and the same stupid

police and politicians in new uniforms, yes, while the leader stood like a dreamer on a thousand platforms and thundered in the millenium.

He sighed. There was no way back. Even without the dream, to be on the losing side would be a disaster second to nothing imaginable. What had Macbeth said, in obstinate despair? "But I am in so deep in blood that sin will pluck out sin . . ."

"It doesn't really matter to me," his chief was telling him, "if it's a Jew or Russian or anything else. The point is, the power we can release through these rituals is beyond calculation." The glasses were full of snow as if, Kurt thought, round windows looked through his head. "We have twelve locations that will be mandalically coordinated. Almost no one will have the least idea of the true purpose of all this."

Kurt pulled his eyes from the empty reflections and pictured again the great race as it might have been: the dark and golden towers, the tall magicians clothed in fire and stars . . . The barracks went past outside like shadows in the storm. Then the long car stopped.

"I don't suppose," he sighed, "you'll let me say no." Himmler didn't smile.

"Quite correct, Kurt," he agreed.

XLIX
(1945)
Inside Germany

"So you're with us again," Astuti said across the fire they'd built close to the blackened side of a burnt-out tank. The starless night seemed to press at the silent stutter of flames. He realized he was getting used to all this. That worried him.

Yesterday they'd crossed the Rhine just ahead of a

squad of middle-aged Home Guard reservists. As if propelled by unerring simplicity and total faith in what Astuti accepted as his mania, the duke had plunged to the riverbank and had all but fallen into a partly beached rowboat with oars set in the locks. So they'd pushed it off in about one unbroken motion, the American levering himself in at the last moment, splashing out until the bottom dipped away. He then lay athwart the stern while the other man rowed (in his mad world they apparently had skiffs) and bleakly watched the flick-splashes as the German bullets kept just missing. Then he asked, in Italian, if the duke actually had expected the boat to be there and wasn't really surprised when the imperious, intense man in tattered housecoat and battered armor told him that he left such matters entirely to God.

On the other side of the mile-wide river God provided an undamaged half-track truck that Astuti could drive. The duke had sat meditatively in the passenger seat while they roared and crunched several miles into the night, then slept and started again before dawn. Still no sign of the armies as they passed bombed-out, deserted villages, air-struck railways, trucks, tanks, all smoldering . . . on across the otherwise green, flower-dotted early spring countryside . . . until a flight of what neither knew were P-50 Mustangs on a roving destroy mission rolled up and over into a firing pass, probably amazed to find there were still Germans mad enough to move by daylight under the American fire and steel that had made a prison of the skies.

"We're in trouble," Astuti had advised, in English. "Let's get scarce, Daddy!" He'd stood up tugging the duke to his feet in the open vehicle. "This *gidrool* ain't going play with you and your sword."

"What are you saying?" the duke wondered.

The first bullets were already chewing along the road straight at them. Astuti was already diving, pinning the lanky, terrifically strong man's arms to his sides long enough to get clear of the still-moving armored truck that, a moment later, crashed into a wall of fifty-caliber armor-piercing and incendiary shells so that it more or less dissolved in clubbing flame . . .

They'd pushed on, keeping away from roads. At one point they'd spotted lines of Waffen SS troops slipping east through the woods. Judging from what sounded like small-arms fire to the northwest and the general concentration of smoke that way, Astuti concluded (more or less correctly) that the Third Army had broken through in a fairly narrow, wide-sweeping wedge and was racing to slice the country in half—which would account for the big, relatively quiet spaces around them.

By nightfall they'd reached flat, swampy country that made the American feel more lost than usual. They'd settled down for the night in a group of blasted armored vehicles as the mists were just gathering into a muggy evening.

Renga looked around, wondering.

"It's a dream," he murmured. "I am very close to him . . ." He rubbed his beard stubble. "I'm getting very close . . ."

"Close, huh?"

"To him . . . my brother . . ."

"Where'd *he* come from?"

Renga nodded, as if agreeing with something.

"My terrible brother . . . we are all brothers . . . Time and space mean nothing . . ."

"Until you run outta them, doc," Astuti philosophized, digging in a can of Spam with his bayonet blade.

"A moment ago I was alive ages past."

"Sure. I seen that." Poked a slice into his mouth on the tip of the weapon. "Want a bite? It tastes like what flies eat when they run out of shit."

"In a dream. Or is it?" Renga shook his head. "All the powers I liked to talk about . . . and now, maybe, I'm finally facing them . . . God, it's so different . . ."

"You're what they call a split-up personality. My uncle Dom is a little that way."

"Do you know where we are?"

"I've been following the other one of you," he said in amused wonder. "Can't you ask him?" Cut more Spam. "I trust any nut who can bring down a plane with a fuckin' sword. Believe me."

"I don't want to go back there," Renga said, letting his head loll wearily on the dark steel tank-side. "And I cannot escape . . . my whole life has led me to this battle . . . and I cannot escape . . ."

"Yeah? Like the fuckin' draft." Astuti chewed and reflected. "I know a few guys got out. There's ways." Shrugged. "I didn't give a shit. I was a young-blood punk two years ago. I knew a lot. Now I don't know nothing. But it's too late because I'm stuck in the middle of this shit." Sighed. Stretched. "What the fuck, just let me get outta here alive and maybe bring a little something back. I don't ask a lot." Spat into the fire. "*Misèria.* I was so fucking smart, right? Lemme go in the army and be a big shot. Yeah, among the little shots."

"What says't thou, loyal fellow? the other wondered in old Italian.

Astuti regarded him seriously.

"You're never dull, pop," he commented. "I think we should rest, *signóre.* No?"

Where's the other guy when he sleeps? he wondered. *Do they both sleep, or what?*

"I agree," said the duke. But we needs must press on even by night. If the enemy has sensed my presence, eyes thou sees't not will be watching. His power grows in darkness. And only in daylight might he be slain."

"You figure he's got some kind of radar on us, eh?"

"What says't thou?"

"Is there really gold where we're going?"

The duke stretched out.

"Yes," he said. "And thou shalt surely merit much reward when we have done, brave fellow." Yawned. "And bear in mind thou serves't God in this business." And then the duke was snoring,

. . . while Renga (who was Ner) stood fully conscious in the narrow tunnel where he'd been following the track of his brother into the underworld. The faintly greenish gleaming outlined the clumsy, shambling, massive mechanical giant that had carried him deep into the tunnel warren and dropped him. It now turned and scraped and struck blindly at him—no, he realized—struck at everything, windmilling tremendous steel-clawed limbs that shrieked and sparked along the walls and floor. He knew it wasn't alive, had no heart or brain to strike back at. Yet he had to pass it. Moved closer, sword braced, but a terrific swipe sent him rolling back, light armor clinking, stunned. Heard the thing crunching on, unhurried, unaware . . .

He crouched and blinked. The thing was the weight of

the world. It was almost above him when he snapped a
sword-cut that rebounded from a stubby, grinding limb. He
ducked back again. Realized if he kept giving ground he
might as well retreat all the way.

Paused. Sensed something, some movement, life, purpose, outside of his cramped reality: another world, close,
unseen, and he was a part of it too.

"Oh, Lord of light," he prayed. "lead me from here!"

In the pause, one blocky steel hand clipped the side of
his helmet and his brain went white-blank, his center failed,
and he went spinning, sailing, and he glimpsed a man in
that other world sleeping in strange costume (didn't know it
was Renga, himself), fragmentary armor and odd robes in
a moonlit landscape (the moon smaller than in this world
where it was rarely glimpsed through the eternal mists)
among massive metal hulks he couldn't imagine were
smashed-up German tanks.

Another man sat beside a dying fire, leaning on a
peculiar (he thought) club (rifle). And then a voice spoke in
his mind: "Pass the iron beast in the other world, O lost
warrior who dreams time." And he was running a few steps
past the violet embers and the two still figures (of Astuti
and Renga), straight, he had to believe, at where the
mechanical frenzy smote and chipped the stone walls of the
passageway but he now saw only the small moondisk above
hushed, wind-sweet pines and that pure light became the
inflectionless voice of silence . . . and then the impacts
and greenish, sickly darkness crashed back except this time
he was, somehow, behind the monster as it stormed away
the way they'd come and so he went on and found himself
in a vast cavern. The illumination was centered in a chill
spot high up. Distances were hard to judge and seemed
strangely distorted . . . then ahead, the cries of pain
again, pleading, women's voices . . .

*My path runs straight to hell through this substantial
nothingness . . .*

He went on, straining to see into the smeared light that
obscured more than it showed in hazy greenishness . . .

(At the Camp)

Kurt recognized Rosenberg among the black uniforms waiting for him at the bottom of the wooden outside stairs in the greenish-yellow light that spilled from the administrative offices on ground level. But who were those others? And, anyway, Rosenberg was not in the SS.

"What's this?" he whispered to himself. "Japanese?"

"Greetings, *Standarten führer*," Rosenberg said. "Heil Hitler."

Kurt saluted in silence. Pondered the oblique-eyed faces in the crisp uniforms. At their backs were the spotlight splashes from the machine-gun-tower eyes.

"Well," he said, "obviously I'm dealing with the *allegemeiner* SS."

He counted four impassive, yellowish faces.

"They speak no German," Rosenberg told him. "They're from Tibet."

"Ah."

"No one believed we could do it." He moved his puffy face closer to Kurt. "The Führer himself lost confidence." One frail hand plucked at the taller man's lapel. "But, you see, events have borne out Himmler and myself." Sniffed. "The 'extremists.'" Smiled abstractedly. Kurt realized the man wasn't actually looking at anything.

"Ah."

"The camps we were using in the north have been overrun by the damned Reds." He drew back in fury and disgust, eyes tracking the empty blackness beyond the near wire. The Orientals waited, unmoving, remote. "So we're here tonight to risk everything to win the war at one stroke."

"Ah."

"We dealt with the filthy Jew American President. Now comes the turn of Stalin and that bumbling English drunkard!" He rubbed his pale knuckles tensely together in the greenish spill of light from around the window shades. "The risk is to us too. These . . . methods . . . can destroy the practitioner." Nodded. "Great forces are unleashed . . ." Gestured vaguely.

"Yes," Kurt murmured. "This way." Led them across

the dark yard. The wind shifted and the reek of burning flesh half-choked them. Kurt cursed silently. He'd forgotten his scented handkerchief to press over his nose.

"I take it," he said, "we need these gentlemen tonight?"

"Didn't Himmler explain?"

"No. Not really. Hinted."

"Is he here?"

"The Reichsführer?" Kurt was sardonic.

"He is supposed to be here for this."

"He said nothing."

Rosenberg shook his head in a fussy manner.

"We need all the assistance possible," he said.

They reached a line of guards standing at the edge of a long, deep trench. Their shadows stood out in the harsh floodlights.

His best men, Kurt reflected. *The poor bastards . . . like me . . . drink themselves to sleep every night . . . some go mad, from time to time . . . what am I thinking? We're all mad, only some show it more than others . . . I don't care I don't have to believe anything anymore . . .*

"We have less than a hour," Rosenberg said, "until the exact moment. Do these men know their part, tonight?"

"Naturally. But why can't we use the gas chambers as usual? Shooting is the worst way."

Rosenberg was peering into the pit. Closed and unclosed his hands.

"Are you certain of the capacity here?" he wanted to know.

"If there are two things we've mastered, Herr Rosenberg," Kurt replied, "they are obeying commands and stacking up the dead."

"The exact number is important."

"No doubt."

Am I actually saying these things? Kurt asked himself.

"This is a science," Rosenberg said, staring into the darkness that pooled at the bottom of the trench. "An ancient science."

"No doubt."

"You question this, Fragtkopft?"

"What do you know about it?" Kurt heard himself snap back.

"What?" The bulged eyes blinked at him.

"Do you have any idea what I've seen here?" As

Rosenberg suddenly stiffened Kurt wanted to smash his face in. Felt a rush of sick hate and saw the other draw back from the chill death in his look. "I'm poisoned by blood, Herr Rosenberg." He stopped his mouth, cold, remote, refusing even the hypocrisy of tears because he knew if he weakened now, anywhere, he'd break everywhere. "Three years of this, Herr Rosenberg. Three years." He turned his back on the other's uncertain silence, and found himself facing SS Sergeant Höss, who saluted. *If this really means nothing,* he thought, *then my brain will break open* . . .

"Sir," Höss was saying, "do we start getting them out now?"

Kurt was staring, lost in remoteness. And terror.

"Sir?" the noncom repeated.

"Ah," Kurt whispered, thinking: *If this all means nothing . . . I'll have to kill myself* . . . Usually he felt better, thinking that. But it felt flat today. It wasn't long now, he realized, it wasn't long now . . .

"I'm worried," Höss said, "that the Jews might make trouble. This is not part of the normal routine."

The man reminded Kurt of the old Bavarian postman from his grandmother's village. What did he believe? he wondered.

"You hold onto routine pretty tight," he said, "don't you?"

"Pardon, sir?"

"Without the routine it would all be over, wouldn't it, Höss?"

The man took a deep breath.

"I do my job," he said, almost expressionlessly.

"Did you know, Höss, that despite the Reichsführer's best efforts most of the SS slip into church whenever they can?"

The man's face showed nothing.

"Yes? Sir?" he wondered.

"It seems to me being a Christian is no impediment for a good SS man." A chill, remote joke he didn't even have to not laugh at. "Go on, Höss," he said. "Get them out here. This has to begin punctually at midnight." As the sergeant clicked his heels and turned, he said after him: "We're going to put a curse on the enemy." Chuckled. "After all," he said to Rosenberg, "it was good enough to put a curse on Germany."

"What are you saying, Commandant?" Rosenberg beat his pale palms together. Behind him the Tibetans stood wrapped in their silence.

"It was good enough to give us Hitler."

"Are you losing faith, eh?"

"Faith," Kurt said, looking at nothing.

How can I get out of this? he asked himself again. So remote. *How? . . . I'm not mad enough to stay to the end . . .* Found himself strangely envying the real believers because they would go to the finish of this gigantic, terrible, and banal piece of theater . . .

He was watching the first lines of prisoners being let out. Stayed remote. The youngest in the camp. That was the order: children, young men, and women first.

"If you want this to go with any speed," he pointed out to Rosenberg, "I'll need a lot more riflemen."

"No." Rosenberg's hands kept closing and separating. He watched the ragged, frail figures being herded into the flat, hard floodlights. Insects cut and circled near the bulbs, the fluttering shadows flicking over everyone. "We don't shoot them."

"That's interesting." His stomach went numb as he remembered Himmler having the pig's throat cut in the tower. "You think we should perhaps cut all these throats?" *Why not? Why limit ourselves?*

"No," said Rosenberg. "These men"—meaning the Tibetans—"will draw whatever blood is necessary."

"That ought to be something." He turned his back again, started strolling, hands locked behind him, carefully not looking or really listening, carefully remote.

The groggy-looking, shadowy victims were being driven quickly into line. No one said much.

"We'll need you here," Rosenberg called after him, "in about fifteen minutes."

The machine was in gear. There was nothing to say. Once you have the rules then the rules rule the rulers, he was more or less thinking as he walked away without answering the party chief. Where the rules are strong the soul dies: behind the bureaucrat's window, the policeman's shield, the soldier's gun, the priest's scrolls of sin . . . everywhere . . .

L
(1942)
Dachau

The noon sun pressed at their faces. Himmler stood erect
and locked his hands over his crotch. He knew his heart
was too quick but refused to acknowledge it.

I must control my will, he thought, picturing Hitler's
stern face. *I don't accept weakness . . .*

Felt isolated among these other men. They seemed
solid, real, confident. They could have no idea of his secret
suffering. He felt chill sweat ooze between his fingers as he
rubbed them over his slick palms.

The uncompromising sunlight showed the naked,
bony, sheared men and women and children lined up along
the long trench.

I think my nerves are a purely physical problem, he
continued. *Simply chemistry that can be controlled . . .*

He knew the others (save for Kurt who was just taking
over command) were watching him for reactions. "Let *him*
see what it's like," he sensed they were saying. "Let him see
what he expects others to do."

Very well, he thought, *they like to make fun of me a bit too
much in certain circles . . .*

"We're ready," one of the officers said, looking at him.

The Waffen SS, he was thinking, *the big war heroes, they
like to call me amusing names . . .* Frowned. *I'll send a staff
memo over there . . .*

"Herr Reichsführer?"

He blinked at the sun. Set his teeth.

"What is it?" he asked. He didn't feel that well.
Thought maybe he had a flu.

"We're ready to proceed."

"Well, why not?" He smiled, faintly. Tried to send his

willpower to slow his heartbeat. Tried to lock his eyelids open. Vowed to miss no detail this time. "This is necessary," he said, for no particular reason. "What we do now is done for future ages."

The SS commander who Kurt Fragtkopft was replacing raised an eyebrow. His face was bony, haunted-looking, coldly repressed into fury.

"Do now?" he wondered. "We've been doing this every day."

"Yes," Himmler muttered, "naturally, naturally." Blinked. Stared straight ahead.

The Jews, Kurt noticed (watching as if from far away through a strange glass), mainly stood passive. Mothers clutched children. The glass turned it into a picture somehow suspending the horror . . . Some were praying, he thought. One woman was shouting something, defiance . . . they were so wasted and seemed to him almost despicably weak and hopelessly helpless, as if it were their fault. But what use was resistance? It just made a bigger mess and ended the same way . . .

He felt a distant contempt for what a human being could be reduced into. The idea that they were Jews really meant nothing to him. He tried saying to himself they were somehow a poisoned seed but all he saw were miserably naked, soiled, broken human forms and thought:

We're all like this, we've all degenerated to this . . . disgustingly mortal . . .

He felt his mind was safe behind the glass of these abstractions. Unless one of them spoke to him personally. That might be different. He held up the glass, thinking how all people of all nations had to be reduced to this and destroyed until all that were left on earth were immortal, superhuman beings.

In spite of himself, Himmler's eyes shut as the first shots cracked and sputtered, and he kept fighting them open as they'd close, so the scene registered forever in his memory as a jerky series of virtually still images: the harsh, sun-shadowed bony flesh seeming to stagger all at once as if a terrific wind had struck . . . blank . . . the tangled shapes flopping, limbs wild, back into the pit . . . blank . . . dozens still somehow standing and kneeling. The guns going on and on, shaking his nerves until he nearly shouted Stop! Stop! Stop! . . . blank . . . dozens writhing in and out of the pit, blood jetting and running as the bullets chewed and chewed like unseen fangs into the living mass.

His hands shook and he locked his fingers together, sucking deep breaths. Had a panic that he might fall down. Fought with his eyes, desperately.

"Are you all right, Herr Reichsführer?" a voice was asking.

He nodded, not trusting himself to speak. Got his eyes open again as a few noncoms with pistols walked through the struggling, suffering sprawl, firing (he noted) calmly and rapidly into skulls. Thank God for the calm. Imagine if bloodlust had taken possession of the men! The idea terrified him. What a shambles! Something had to be done about that. His brain swam. He clutched at the logic of it: cool reason had not been impaired by the shock.

Now other prisoners were coming forward wearing the absurd striped pajamas, and began lifting the bodies from the edge and rolling them to rejoin the main, bleeding, spasming horror that seemed (to his wild, sweat-blurred sight) a single creature dying in pieces.

How much blood can those skinny bodies bleed? his mind questioned.

"Herr Reichsführer?"

"Yes?" he made himself say. He'd lost control of his eyelids again.

"Do you wish to inspect the grave?"

In the darkness of his head it was worse because the first impact kept replaying, vivid, bright: one curious child crouched between its mother's legs, squinting against the noonglare, seeming to study the drilled precision of the firing squad.

"Do you wish—" the commandant began again as Himmler cut over him.

"Not necessary. I have some comments and suggestions, however." Swallowed and turned around, relieved to be looking the other way at last. It has seemed endless. Back in the pit someone was screaming, high, thin—like, he thought, a wounded horse. *This is a bad method . . . very bad . . .* Smiled thinly. At least he'd stood up to it. Except for a blink or two. So he felt almost bouyant. Took a jaunty step. On the whole, he decided, he'd stood up to it damned well. Began humming under his breath to drown out the screaming.

"Well, Kurt," he said, almost heartily, clapping his protégé on the shoulder, "this is not pleasant, but we're men, and Germans on top of that!" Kurt said nothing. Thought nothing. There was nothing to think. History was killing these people, killing all of them. The SS was just another instrument of the gods. "This is man's work. But I'm putting a stop to these inefficient methods. This shooting is no good. For a dozen reasons." He half-glanced back at the pit where the screaming had finally stopped. His eyes jerked shut again. He took off his glasses as if to wipe them. "Very . . . inefficient. I'm glad I saw this for myself."

With the glasses off, Kurt noted, his eyes were just squints.

(At the Berghof, Berchtesgaden)

"You always insult me," Eva Braun complained as he came out of the bathroom in his dark robe. His pale hands adjusted the belt knot. "Adolf," she went on, "I hate it." she flounced down on the neat bed in a flutter of frilly white. He shuffled around the room in floppy slippers, poking at papers and a stack of books, blinking behind his heavy-rimmed steel glasses that were never seen in public.

"What did I say?" he asked, closing the drapes on the glowing, grayish chill of dawn.

"You said I was primitive and stupid. At dinner."

"Did I?" he temporized.

"Yes . . ." She started to cry and he winced. "You did . . ."

"Nonsense, sweet cake," he assured her. "I was just making a point about marriage." Opened a book. Blinked at it. It looked dull. They were always sending books. As if he had time for such things. Too much reading, he considered, dimmed the fresh, intuitive powers. He'd read a lifetime's worth in the past.

She was studying him.

"This is no kind of life for a young woman," she said.

"Which, sweet cake?"

"This! I wait for you . . . months on end. And then what happens?"

"Yes?"

"Not much happens, that's what."

He came closer to the bed, holding a newspaper in one hand.

"I apologize, my dear," he told her.

"Think you can always charm your way?" She pouted. Flounced. "I'm still hurt."

"Poor Eva."

"Would you marry me?"

"Hm?" He went around to his side, stripped off his robe, and slipped under the covers in his flannel pajamas, adjusting the paper against his knees.

"You heard me, Adolf."

"You know my views on that subject." Scratched around his bristly mustache.

"But if you were free? If you weren't the Führer?"

He shrugged and smiled.

"That would be another matter." Sniffed. "But I *am* the Führer, though I start to wonder whether Goebbels and Göring are always convinced of that fact."

"I like Hermann," she said. "He's silly." She brightened. "Remember when he wore the Jewish armband to the reception?" Giggled.

Hitler grunted.

"Lucky for him Himmler wasn't there," he heavily joked. "Would have proved his great-grandfather was named Moses Göringstein."

"Frau Goebbels is very elegant," she mused, irrelevantly.

"Yesss," he drawled, turned the page, scanning.

"I hate Himmler," she suddenly said.

"So strong a feeling?"

She flounced in a kind of shrug.

"He makes my skin creep sometimes," she said.

"That's his job, pet."

"He looks like a worm."

"Well, I'll make you deputy Führer. When I have a headache, you can take over and make appointments."

"Hah, ha," she said. "You always make the same jokes."

"I'm not making a living with jokes." He smiled. "Anyway, you couldn't do much worse than poor Hess." He dropped the paper on the rug and put out his nightlight. Set his glasses on the stand. "Good night, Eva."

She still sat up on her side, in the muted glow of her lamp. Looked at him.

"Anyway," she said, "you'll probably wake up shouting again. What's the sense of trying to sleep?"

"Better," he murmured, "than screaming while you're awake." His breathing gradually steadied.

"Anyway," she said into the gathered stillness, "I don't think you'd ever marry me. Even if you weren't Führer."

He was suddenly alone in a vast silent whiteness, floating forward as if the wind bore him. Dark figures seemed to reach out of a frozen snowbank . . . men, women, children . . . frost-crusted eyes were glares of ice . . . terror rushed through him like electricity . . . he saw hundreds, thousands on thousands, locked, twisted together as he rushed faster and faster . . . *Save me!* he seemed to cry . . . and then a flash of the other dreaming, the underground terrors that were to spill over into his tormented waking by 1945 where he would be lost in green fire and dull red smoke. . . . Now he was flashing down into the underworld again and then seemed to regather himself into solid form as Relti partway up the miles-high needle-peaked tower that jabbed out of the molten moat where the dead (now in armor they'd stripped from the vanished golden guardians), in a loose cordon around the periphery, waited for the lone enemy, his brother . . . Relti sensed him back in the stone and shadows, still coming, working his way down through the defenses and dangers. The swirling, multiheaded beast shape rode the tyrant's shoulders, shadowy claws reaching into his body, his nerves. The thin unvoice shrilling warnings . . . and the pain . . . pain, jolting, paralyzing, because he felt the teeth, the thing in the hole in the wall where he'd just thrust his arm, the rows of needle, ripping teeth chewing his fingers, grinding the bones, crunching to the wrist as he tried to pull free, howling, staggering around the narrow parapet, nearly toppling back down the steep steps that curved around the ancient tower . . . and then the pain was gone and he saw his new hand: enlarged, clawlike, glittering dark, metallic-looking, heavy yet moving easily with a multiplying force of its own, throbbing with power that thrilled up his arm and lifted him into a dark, violent ecstasy, the shrill beast-voice urging him to strike the lavic stone and he did, booming down at his amazed and shaken followers who stood beyond the ring of the dead, looking up at him as he raised the new fist that darkly flashed the lurid dimness:

"This is the hand of dooms!"

Struck the wall before him and the stone cracked. The unvoice of the shadow beast on his shoulders hissed from one of its seven heads:

"This is the key! Open the door!"

Another blow split it wide and it opened. There was a chamber inside. Glowing ruby-blood-red walls. Another head (he saw and heard them more clearly now) whispered advice:

"Enter and take heart."

There were stairs swirling up on the inside here. He leaned out for a moment and shouted down:

"Wait here until I return! Let no enemy live to follow me!"

His son saw him gesture with the terrible hand before vanishing into the hole in the wall. Tears burned in his eyes again though they didn't spill down his cheeks this time.

He clutched his mother's arm. Felt it trembling. The fat general and the big-foot dwarf, trained as they were to magic and outrage (not to mention the troops themselves), were in a state of shock. General Rog stepped closer to his Skull fighters. He was thinking about the long way back to the surface. Was thinking about not just running, telling himself a calm retreat would be best.

The dwarf was sweating, ashen. He just realized he'd soiled his leather shorts. His bowels had let go, loosely. He cursed. A moment later he felt that his mind had been sharpened like a blade on a grinding stone. He cut through all fear and doubt and saw the truth before him, half-turning to call over to fearful General Rog:

"Relti is the glory of our people," he told him, starting to hobble forward, feet hitting together. "All the greatness has gathered into him. He is a god! We must all follow him."

Hurrying forward, staring up at the gape of blackness where his master had just entered the sheer tower, thinking how the master would give him strength, how he would be raised up, seeing himself with a new body, tall, slim, supple, and strong . . . imagined women pressing close to him, doing whatever he wished . . .

He ran for the narrow bridge now, passing the queen and her child who was just saying:

"Mother, he's being eaten . . ."

"Hush, boy. Be strong. He will—"

Clenching and unclenching his fists, distraught.

"No . . . no . . . he's being eaten in there . . ." Shutting his eyes so that tears were forced out again, burning, catching the molten glow seeming drops of fire or blood. "My father's being eaten . . ."

The dwarf rushing past the line of dead who stood swaying and creaking, almost shoulder-to-shoulder, shrieking (as the general was still backing away, his men automatically following him) as he crossed the bridge:

"Follow the master! Follow the master and be saved!"

And then the scene was shaking, brightness ripping through the dense, gleaming stone . . . brightness that hurt, and he was thrashing, trying to surface, aware of being someone else, somewhere else . . . face-down, clawing into the covers, trying to climb except it was downward and he thought he was screaming:

Mother, help me! . . . Aiii . . . save me! . . .

One hand knotting in Eva Braun's silk nightgown where she partly woke beside him in the big bed.

And then he was back in the gloomy, claustrophobic underworld again in the ever-repeating dream, now Relti, climbing the inner steps that wound up the inside of the tower, the big, metallic hand heavy and strange at his side, clinking against the faintly phosphorescent stonework. One of the shadowy beast-heads was curling down to tell him:

"Pass through the next door, you have the key now."

Because the steps stopped and he faced a single, huge block of polished stone that dimly reflected his featureless outline.

The block was shaped like (he vaguely thought) a female torso and about where the left breast would be was a hole.

He thrust one invulnerable finger into it. The block swung back on noiseless balance. He went in and discovered a chamber about six by six modern feet in diameter. Relti (like most men of those days) was about six feet tall. This was, clearly, the inner cylinder that went straight up the center of the shaft. The steps were cut into the curved wall and went up into greenish, fitful obscurity. To reach the steps he had to pass a slim woman-shape cast of dark metal. He examined the workmanship. It might have been naked flesh sprayed with fluid iron, he thought.

Each eyelash was distinct. The lips were set in a mirthless smile. One hand held something. A lump of stone, he decided.

Glanced up at the shadowy beast-body and swirling necks gathered around his shoulder. One of the heads obligingly coiled down.

"Take heart," he thought it told him, except that an instant later the metal figure moved, with supple, irresistible speed, catching him off guard just long enough so that her left hand (not holding the stone) slashed into his chest, razor fingers gripping deep, and (in a burst of pain beyond even a Lemurian's capacity to divert) he heard his ribs break, flesh burst, and the chill, obscene violation (as consciousness recoiled and tried to flee) as the fingers closed around his heart and his body spasmed like a speared fish held upright on the end of her arm, the smile fixed, the head tilted almost maternally as his mouth shrieked blood . . . twisted and kicked and heard his sound now, torn from him as he clutched the air over the bed, clawed blackness . . . then spun away and was on the rug, his own hoarse sounds finally waking him as Eva held him, his eyes blind and wild tracking past her face, yelling:

"Let go of my heart! . . . Let go of my heart! . . ."

And then aware of the room gray with morning (the light blinding and painful again) and himself panting, kneeling, spent.

"Ade," she said. "Calm, my dearest. Calmly. You are safe. You are with me."

"Ahh," he groaned. Shook his head. Blinked hard. Recovered himself. "Yes . . . she was coming for me," he murmured.

"She?" Eva was puzzled. "No, it's just Bormann. At the door. I was telling him—"

"Bormann?"

"Yes. I said you were asleep."

"Bormann . . ." He wasn't trying to get up yet. Sucked slow breaths. His head, back, lung . . . everything hurt.

"He woke me up," she was saying. "Something urgent, he says."

"What time is it?"

"Eleven."

He held his head.

"What does he want?" he asked.

"Something in Russia went wrong, I think."

He groaned awake. He knew it already. Knew it had to be Stalingrad. Struggled to sit on the edge of the bed. His heart sank.

"Of course," he whispered to the dream. "Of course . . ."

LI
(1943 con't.)
Italy

Renga sat in the empty house near the parted glass doors that opened into the walled, Italian garden. Vaguely he was remembering when he came back from the first war and found the two of them making love. Now Minna was as good as dead and his wife was missing . . . He hoped she'd come back here, somehow. He wasn't thinking about what he'd just gone through to get out of Germany, across France, and into Italy. Sighed and repeated the thought that the *Duce's* people were nothing like the Nazis and the worst of those were in the east.

He watched the sunglow deepen its rich violet-reds behind the shadowed wall. The hazy gleaming grayed slowly in the velvety room. He waited, hands folded across his lap.

Then the door in the wall opened, spilled a slightly brighter wash around (he instantly, regretfully saw) a tall man. Renga stood up slowly and stepped outside. The figure was a vagueness on the grass, moving hesitantly toward the dark house.

"Hello?" he said.

"Hello," responded Renga.

"Who are you?"

"You're looking for my wife?"

"Am I?"

"Or do you mean to loot the house?" Renga was sardonic, distant. Half a bottle of wine sang in his head.

"Yes, I want to see her." Renga could distinguish the silverish trim suggesting the black uniform and cap of the SS. "Is she at home?"

"I'm waiting for her."

"Do you expect her soon?"

"I thought someone would turn up, eventually." Blinked his weighted lids. Why wasn't he afraid of this Nazi? Because he realized he wasn't. He hadn't roared up with a car full of killers. That was one thing. "Do you plan to arrest her or just shoot her in the head?"

"I want to see her."

"So do I, Herr? . . ."

"Gerstein."

"So you're part of it. A nice Nazi like yourself." The wine felt thick in the blood of his face. Smiled with the thickness. "Pity, pity . . ." Swayed slightly. The wall was edged with paling sunset.

"Are you Herr Renga?"

"Who the hell knows what I am." Chuckled. Liked the thickened feeling when he smiled. "I knew the great Führer, many years ago . . . many years . . . do you think I might have changed history back there? Hm?" Laughed. "I didn't, anyway."

"I wish I'd known him," muttered the SS man. His voice made Renga picture white fire. "But had you any word of Eunice?"

"I haven't seen her in . . . my God, more than a year . . . I've been looking . . ." He imagined he could smell the first stirrings of spring. A hint of grass and changing earth . . . He didn't feel like smiling anymore. His eyes burned. "I was a teacher once . . ." Shook his head. There seemed something in the wall's darkness, something moved . . . or was it in his mind? "Things happened to my brain," he said. "There are other worlds all around us . . . within us . . . but I'm a coward. I hid myself in the whale's belly. I'm one of those cowards who hide from their real duty . . ." Swayed again. "I take it you're not like me, um, Gerstein . . . hm?"

The officer's face was very close now, palely suggested. But Renga stared at the wall where darkness seemed to move within darkness. He was drunk enough to brave it and wait.

Show me something, he asked within himself. *I won't run anymore if you show me something.* He was totally sober for a moment from sheer fervence. *Whatever horror or glory . . . please, I beg you, show me something!* Seemed to see, in the thickening night, a dark landscape opening like a door.

"You can help me, perhaps," Gerstein said. "If you wish to help." He was breathing unevenly, close to Renga.

Still staring at the opening, the other said:

"My god . . . only give me a chance . . . don't let me die merely sarcastic and drunk . . . like too many of us . . ." Had no desire at all to smile. Held himself on a line between blur and sharp.

"I tried to see the Pope," Gerstein said. "And others. None of them will open the door. They're afraid of what I bring them."

For an instant Renga considered walking to the wall, trying to pass through it into . . . but the effect, or whatever it was, seemed to end as he focused on it. Like details in a dream. He sensed it would open again.

"Afraid," he muttered.

"I'll have to give it to you. I doubt if I have much time left to do anything else." Breathed, rasped. "The word's out on me."

"Do you think she's dead?" Renga suddenly asked, touching the man's arm.

"How can I say?" His hand clenched back with quiet fierceness. "My god, what is death to me, anymore? I come from death's back gardens . . ." Renga tried to focus on the phantasmal features, sensed something remote and cold as if the man had come through that strange opening in the darkness. "I have the proof. I cannot let my life go until I show the proof, you understand?" Breathed, raspy, uneven. His fingers were gripless on Renga's wrist. "I'm sorry, but it goes to you now. Instead of her." Breathed. "You'll have the proof now. I can let . . . my life go . . . you understand?" Breathing whisper.

"Proof?"

The still hand on his forearm seemed the only substantial thing in the floating vagueness where everything appeared to be dissolving . . . and then the hand was gone. Renga wasn't thinking anything at all.

"Ah," Gerstein said, seeming far away now, lost in the draining evening, tears in his remote voice. "Don't you think I *long* to die? . . . Don't you think . . ."

And then the hand came back, pressed something on him: a roll of paper, as if sealing some profound bargain. Renga worked his thickened lips:

"Perhaps you should rest?"

"Rest?" The remote voice laughed like sobbing. "I'll soon rest, comrade. But it's yours now . . . I pity you . . . pictures . . . sworn statements . . . proof . . . pity . . ."

"Proof of what?" Renga held the scroll shape to his grip and knew somehow he'd been floated to this melting moment by the dark tide of all his days. And he wanted to drop the thing, whatever it was, because he knew his wish had been granted, he had his chance . . . wanted to drop it and brush past this strange, ghostly, distant, tormented twilight shadow and run.

"I was a minister of God," the man said, breathing in dry spasms.

"Would you like some schnapps?" Renga tried.

"I'm free now I don't have to hold on anymore . . . I tried, you understand. But we all went mad in different ways . . . I was also a guard in the death garden . . ."

"Garden?"

"Dachau. I joined the SS to spy for . . . it doesn't matter why . . . millions are dying. I came to see the Pope, but it's too late for me . . . I tried to save them . . . you have no idea . . . no idea . . . I am part of them and they're dead so I am mostly made of death . . . I wish this were just excessive speech but it's real, my bone and blood are changed . . . when I touch you, you feel it . . ."

"Millions?" Renga tried to grasp it. His eyes seemed to stick when he blinked.

"Jews . . . others too . . . we unload the trains, you see . . . the endless trains . . . and we shave the hair quickly and when they're all dead we pry the metal from the teeth . . ." Remote, uneven whispering.

"What are you saying?"

"Sometimes they scream because they know what's coming . . . don't you think I want to join them? Hm?" A whisper like the faintest fluting of breeze in the gathered stillness. "I'm made of death . . . but I had to deliver the proof first that no one wants to see . . . ah, you should hear them when they're all packed in, the agony . . . and my prayers are screams . . ."

"Wait," Renga said, "I cannot . . ."

Except he'd already melted out of his drunken range, a shape of shadow through the invisible gate that creaked once, faintly, behind him and Renga groped, hopelessly holding the scroll in one hand, trying to move through the thickness of himself like walking underwater, swaying in the deepening hush . . .

LII
(1945)
Somewhere in Central Germany

Himmler stayed in the car, staring straight ahead at the fuzzy semicircle of light at the end of the tunnel. He breathed unevenly, with sighs. The sound of bombers passing overhead echoed strangely in there. The gray vagueness illuminated his pale face, the driver, and the dim guards in black posted along the curved concrete wall.

He tapped his fingers, waiting. The officer leaned in close to him, speaking quietly.

"Herr Reichsführer, what response will you make?"

"It will all clear up, soon enough."

"But Hitler has ordered your arrest for treason. How—"

"It's sheer nonsense." Himmler stared at the formless light. "There's no communication with Berlin. Adolf Hitler, the greatest and most misunderstood man in history, will soon die a hero's death. No one but myself can possibly save Germany."

"But can you be certain he will die, sir?"

"May was always known to be the fatal month."

"But didn't the astrologers say that after this date the Führer's destiny would improve?"

"Yes, Captain. But not in this world. Goebbels had the chart explained to him. Do you think the poor astrologer would tell the truth?" Smiled bleakly. "Would you tell them or the Führer that he was doomed?" Adjusted his glasses. "All these things will be misunderstood, whether we win or lose."

"Can we win, sir?"

"We try."

A car suddenly appeared in the entrance glow. He watched the sentries pass it. Was thinking that when they heard Stalin and Churchill were struck dead he would be sitting at the negotiating table. He was trying to get the talks scheduled for tomorrow morning. He hoped General Patton would be there. "Gentlemen," Himmler would say, "this is the moment for a new alliance and the defeat of the Red menace!" He kept rehearsing his speech. Was sure he had the firmness now, the dramatic force. He believed that once Hitler was actually dead he would be able to call his spirit to guide him, the same way that Hitler himself was guided by the great power . . .

He was still musing along this direction when the other car crept up and stopped.

One man got out of the sedan and stood there, vague as the others. Seemed to be wearing a floppy hat. The captain brushed past him after saluting his leader.

"Come in and sit down," Himmler invited, "Herr Beckman."

"Excuse me," the man said, "if I don't sit. I've been riding a long way."

"You Zionists were right in the first place, I think."

"Perhaps. Will you continue to help us get people to Switzerland?"

"That's the point. I'm doing all I can. It's time you Jews and we National Socialists buried the hatchet, as the Americans say." Smiled, unseen in the dimness.

I have to protect us, he was thinking, *one way or another. I cannot bring back the dead . . . I'm not responsible for all the machinery . . .* Tried to imagine explaining such things to the foreigners if he were a prisoner. Made a mental note to get a poison tooth capsule fitted. It seemed distant and absurd. He couldn't imagine actually killing himself, after all, a hard core of the dedicated could survive in some remote area and perhaps produce the superman in some hidden stronghold . . . He decided to work up a special proposal, talk to Rosenberg and a few other experts. *There's always more than one hen for a rooster* . . .

"Do you wish me to shake your hand?" the Zionist asked.

"Well, that won't be necessary. But, really, it's time to let the past go."

"I can understand your taking that position." His voice was neutral. Himmler sighed within himself. None of this was going to be easy.

"I hope you share it, Herr Beckman."

The man's tone was a shrug now:

"How many of my people will you next set free?"

"It's a complicated issue."

"Yes, Reichsführer. How many, then?"

"Don't pressure me," he snapped. "Who do you imagine you're talking to?"

"I don't imagine, Herr Reichsführer. I'm just asking a question. Do you think I'm ungrateful for your efforts?"

Himmler sighed again. Drummed his pale fingers on his knee. God, it was going to be difficult.

"I've tried to be kind and civilized," he said absently.

"You are the best judge of that," the man said, without inflection.

"I do what I can," Himmler muttered. The machine runs without me. I can't just snap my fingers at it, you know, Herr Zionist."

"No doubt, sir," was the unsatisfying answer.

The Reichsführer was nervous and subliminally furious.

"We'll be in contact, shortly," he said, by way of dismissal. "I'll arrange the shipment." He knew their power was far from broken. The best of them had probably escaped long ago. The last hope was the experiment. So he had to recontact the Allies. *I just have to stretch out my arm west and I'll touch the nearest American,* he quipped. Reminded himself to get the cyanide capsule. To fall into the hands of the Jews would not be pleasant . . .

LIII
(1944)
In the Bunker

He didn't look at his face in the mirror as he passed it, and
then his baggy dark pants were around his ankles and he
sat down. Just the top half of his head was visible if he
glanced up, except he didn't. His left hand gripped his bare
left knee, the other shook out the map as he shifted his
buttocks on the seat-rim and waited . . . the griping,
familiar pain squeezed his intestines with, he fancied, iron
fingers.

His steel glasses reflected the gray bathroom. His
breath caught, stopped, and strained. He was suddenly
sweating with pain. Forced himself to concentrate on the
map.

He often didn't notice he was muttering to himself
until he was in midsentence. What a strain he was under, he
thought, and history would lie about even that. They'd
never see him as he was. And did it matter?

Hitler winced as something moved, deep within, and
his fingers whitened and convulsed around his knee and he
strained to expel the burning poison, chill and dizzy . . .

"God . . . I'm racked . . . I'm racked . . ." *How can
I make good decisions? . . . Will the war be lost because I was
shitting myself to pieces? . . . God! . . .*"

The lines, colors and shapes on the map swam. The
bowl rang, resonant as a terrific, hollow gob of wind broke
from him. *Like a shell from an 88,* he joked, in the moment's
ease that followed. His mind, he knew, tended to wander
increasingly. The dysentery, the medication . . . Sighed
and rubbed his knee. Fraction by fraction the pain was
starting again. His thoughts drifted . . . remembered the
third party congress, hours of speeches and saluting in

public, the long, sultry afternoon wearing away as if time were caught in mud . . . like the mud they'd crawled through in Flanders when he was young, and masses of men the color of clay and excrement, dragged themselves through a roaring hell . . . shook his head. Remembered how after hours of speeches they'd rush for the urinals. Grinned, recalling how Göring shouldered Hess aside in the field houses:

"Luftwaffe first," he'd bellowed. "If you piss as slow as you think, Rudi, I'll let it go on poor Himmler!"

Laughed, for a moment, remembering . . . Those were buoyant days . . . Frowned:

And now the great general of the air, he thought, *what's he worth? General of the hot air . . . They might as well be pigeons shitting for all the damn good the bombing does . . .*

Strained: felt burning liquid trickle, drop by drop, from him.

"Ah, . . . God in heavens! . . . ai . . . ai . . ." Shuddered and doubled forward. Tried to keep his mind on the contours and shadings of Russia and Poland, the scrawled outlines of the massed armies, dark arrows he'd drawn ripping into the Reds, into the symbolic, stupid, ugly defiance of the whole world that refused to see the glory of his mission . . . "This is the last hope," he said, as if to the walls or the mirror he didn't let himself quite look into. *If they break this time, the pursuit must be unrelenting!* "We chop the guts out of the bastards!" Hissed with new pain as another flood of poisonously hot waste leaked from his seared insides. *Aiaiai . . . We had them a . . . a dozen times . . . let them off lightly . . . man for man we knock them all on their asses but all together they're squeezing us to death again . . . ai! . . . God, it hurts . . . Americans, British, all together . . .* Sobbed in a breath. *If they break this time they'll crack open . . . this war hangs by a hair . . . All the stakes are on the table . . .* It was virtually a matter of will now. There were few new Russians turning up on the front anymore. *I can't let those blunderers alone up there, they're giving the world away . . .*

And then the pain swelled and swelled and his sight flashed and there was roaring. He was going under . . . suddenly the map filled the world and he was poised miles and miles above where armies moved, writhed over the earth and he was diving faster than falling, screaming

down into the heart of the battle that flashed and sounded
and went out in a wink and he was back in the dreamscape,
zooming through a tremendous cavern, flashing to an
instant stop within the needle-peak tower that rose like a
fang from the molten moat crossed by a thin blade of
bridge where the armored dead stood guard and the queen
and her son still waited, watching the awkward-footed
dwarf trotting up the spiral stairs that circled around the
structure, then darting into the opening Relti had made
with his unhuman fist. The potbellied general, Rog, and his
Skull Troops were now withdrawing into the corridor back
the way they'd come . . . The dwarf was rushing for the
steps that led up around the tower . . . Hitler melted into
Relti, standing in the six-by-six cylinder of a room where
the metallic, perfect female shape was holding his dripping, still-pumping heart in her left hand.

No more pain! his mind screamed.

Sprung ribs arched from his bloody chest. He swayed,
waiting for the body to drain into death and free him, still
starting to fall backward into unbelievable shock, except
the right hand of the living statue thrust forward with fluid
speed and slammed the strange stone it clutched into the
gaping wound. A flash of green flame burst from Relti's
chest. He jerked wildly around the chamber, skidding, fire
pouring from mouth and ears and the hole in his body
. . . and then the steely arms were around him and he was
being carried in her embrace up the steps that circled
inside the chamber . . . up . . . up while the green
flames filled his mind and the many-headed blackness that
rode him coiled and uncoiled its necks and seemed to sing
hooting shrieks of song in clash and triumph . . .

The glow flared up and then there was dim grayness
everywhere and he stared at a perfectly flat plain that
ended at a featureless cliff. Heard a gurgling of water and
wind, then understood it was his own breath . . . moved
his head slightly and the floor broke free and there were
walls again and the mirror above the dully gleaming sink.

Groped to his knees, pants caught around his calves, a
cold draught on his bare flanks. He took a shuddering
breath. Noted his face had been lying on the map.

"We're going to lose," he heard himself rasp, clutching
the sink and levering himself back onto the toilet. A gleam

caught his eye: his glasses, across the little room, dully glinted as if someone stared at him from the floor. "We're going to lose," his voice repeated. Held his face with both hands. Shook his head remembering all the effort and fury as chills shuddered through his spasmodic, burning insides. *God*, he thought, *right to the end . . . to the end . . .*

(1944)

At the Death Camp

The gray shapeless curtain was stuck. Commandant Kurt Fragtkopft cursed, yanked, and finally climbed up on a stool to jerk the ring free on the track. He could have called his orderly but he wanted no company.

Up on the stool he could see over the top of the fabric down into the midsummer, sun-bright camp yard. Glimpsed the lines of spindly, naked prisoners feeding into the gas chambers. He kept his eyes unfocused. Straightened the curtain so it was completely closed. He was sweating in the stagnant room. Even with the windows shut he imagined he could smell things from outside . . . he'd stuffed rags around the frames but the taint penetrated.

Went back to his desk, staring around the hot, gray dimness. Made a note to have the flowers changed: the roses were starting to rot.

Stared at the reports on his desk. Picked up and dropped the pen and rolled it in his fingers and dropped it, over and over . . . Reports: 3967 last week, this week 3890 . . .

"I could run away," he whispered . . . like others did, people he knew and had heard about . . . sighed in the stifling office. "I could kill myself." Nothing answered him. Outside, muffled, he could hear SS Sergeant Höss shouting commands in his biting, mechanical-sounding voice.

Stared . . . thought about how he should have stood up to Himmler a long time ago, refused this duty . . . and then what? . . . Blankness . . . a long time ago his wife had run off . . . vanished somewhere . . . and others too. He wondered what had happened to her? He'd investigated, years ago, but lost her in Nuremberg. No

trace after that . . . perhaps she was dead . . . He sighed
and shrugged. He'd discovered he needed her a little late.
He'd wept over losing her, now and then, but the years had
deadened it . . . He rarely thought about her anymore.
No point. Probably she was dead. He'd vowed that if he
found her he'd begin again and do things differently. But
he never found her . . .

Picked up and dropped the pen on the reports that
deadened the slight sound. Stared and sweated into blankness . . . In the beginning he would try and picture the
coming age: sit there and raise peerless towers in violet
skies and see the chiseled giants of ruthless beauty design-
ing magnificent landscapes . . .

Blinked the beaded sweat from his eyes. Stared at the
blurred, shapeless draperies where the hot light outside
beat and probed.

"I could," he whispered, picking up and dropping the
pen with slightly slippery fingers. "I could . . ."

LIV
(1945)
On the Road to Berlin

"By the time we get there, Dorian," Eunice Malverde was
saying to her young, razor-featured lover and fellow
partisan, "the German commander will have withdrawn his
troops. That's what we worked out. Then it's up to our
group to hold on against any stray Nazis who turn up."

"And then the war ends tomorrow," he said with a
hard-edged sigh, aiming the open touring car down the
straight flat road that crossed the plains of northern
France.

"It might," she said. "This is what we've worked for."

She was very tired and a little irritable. Her lower back

ached all the time now. Her hair was nearly all gray and she wore it knotted behind her head.

The fat, red sun was sinking almost directly behind them. The shadow of their heads and the car stretched ahead on the pale, dusty highway.

The Germans were falling back all along the line that had been broken at Normandy, in the nearest thing to panic the Wehrmacht was capable of.

"You really believe they'll succeed in killing him this time?" he said. Poked a cigarette into his mouth but didn't try to light it. The wind rushed around them blurring all other sound.

She stared across the flowing fields where a distant white farm cottage gleamed, then winked behind a smooth fold of hillock. Crossed her arms and tried to get comfortable.

"We've come this far." She shrugged. "There's no place to go back to." She didn't think about the past often. There was no point. It was a miracle still to be living. The relationship with Rudolph had probably exhausted itself, in any case. She believed if they'd stayed together it would have faded away . . .

"You could go to the Americans," he said, something like metal in his voice. "And then to Italy." He glanced up at a massed formation of bombers flashing rose-red in the setting sun. Fangs of steel and thunder pouring into Germany to rip and chew it to pieces. He wondered if anyone he'd known would survive. He was grateful to Eunice. She'd given him a few softly healing moments. There was never going to be more than that: no growing up or growing old. He was all done with the common process of a lost world . . .

She closed her eyes.

"I don't think about those things," she said.

"Maybe you should."

His long, pale hands closed and unclosed on the steering wheel, with cold fury and old weariness.

"Look," she said, "these are his own generals. They'll do what we couldn't."

"Maybe that priest was right."

"Which one?"

"You told me about it. That night on the mountain. When we were tricked by the SS."

She opened her eyes. The sun was gone. The shadows were nearly melted together. They were almost safe from being strafed. Later there would be enough moonlight to finish the ride.

"Who knows?" she said.

"Maybe Hitler's a *dybbk* or the devil's son. Isn't that what the priest said?"

"A what?"

"A demon."

"That's a Jewish word?" she wondered. He rarely used them. Germans were never altogether comfortable being Jews, he'd told her, even before they were murdered for it.

"Yes," he said.

She shut her eyes again. Everything was heavy and dull. Remembered the priest, writhing and rolling among the trees while the shots sprayed and spotlights flashed, how for an instant the pines and the mad shadows seemed alive, clutching at him . . .

"He was probably shot," she vocalized.

"Hm? Who?"

Her head lolled as she tried to sleep. With luck they'd arrive by dawn. They could hear distant thunder now that wasn't thunder . . .

The dust gushed up along the road shoulder as if an invisible runner was rushing past them, each step flinging up a smoky spurt. And then they registered the machine-gun banging from the dimming sky and then the bulky fighterplane slammed so close overhead the prop wash rocked the car and she glimpsed the white stars on the underwings and the barrel-fat dark body. Probably one of the bomber escorts roaming the countryside, chopping up anything that moved. Not unusual. Obviously the pilot hadn't heard Hitler was being killed, she more or less thought.

My god, in a few hours the nightmare may be over, and we die here like this . . .

Dorian kept the pedal down. She watched the stubby plane bank and roll to get back into firing position. Every detail of these moments were terribly clear.

He spotted a stand of cypresses and jerked the car off the road under the uptwisting branches as the slugs chewed and whipsawed across the road and smashed the trees to pieces all around them. She knew she screamed as the car shuddered and rang and then the plane was past again and, minus a fender and most of the back seat, the car lurched on through the trees and then it was suddenly dark enough to be safe.

Back on the road they just breathed as he drove through a shadowy dell. The killer plane was gone . . .

She held his arm and let herself tremble a little. His face was set straight ahead, hands pale and firm on the wheel. After a while she said:

"Dorian . . . perhaps there'll be something for us . . . something . . ."

"No," he said, holding the car steady into the fallen night. "There's nothing."

She pressed her face to his shoulder. Kept her burning eyes closed. Didn't think about anything. Then said:

"Poor Dorian . . . You'll see. It will all end soon . . . You'll see . . ."

That morning a certain Colonel Count von Stauffenberg with his one eye and one arm and aristocratic polish excused himself from the staff meeting on the Prussian hill in the wooden building where Hitler, because it was a sunny day (or because, some later hinted, he'd been warned in his sleep by an unseen protector) had decided to meet instead of underground.

The colonel went quietly outside while Hitler was listening to some report, staring at the map table, one eye cocked to the bright window where he could see tall pine trees, bluish, sparkling in the fresh light . . .

The bomb in the briefcase was so close to his legs he could have kicked the table support it rested against while the acid ate through to the fuse . . .

The colonel hurried through the checkpoints to his car where he sat until suddenly the frame building flew to pieces, ripped and broken generals spinning in the air, fragments raining down as the heave of smoke boiled into the pristine, cloudless sky . . .

"It's over," he murmured, nudging his driver to drive. "He's dead."

Eunice and Dorian reached the town before dawn. It was air-raid dark, naturally. As they crossed the river on the narrow bridge the high arch of the first support startled her: for an instant it seemed a towering, steel figure looming over them like a childhood terror. She blinked and rubbed her face. Realized she'd been on the edge of sleep. The river slipped past in a misty glint.

"We're here," he said, staring to see into the darkness along the far shore. There were shapes that could have been trucks, rocks, shacks, or tanks. No way to be sure. That was where they'd be if the Germans meant to hold this key point on the Meuse. But they were supposed to have pulled out by midnight. Once word was flashed of Hitler's death.

They passed inside the town's medieval walls. The first grayish hints of dawn began to define the turrets and towers. He was beat, nervous. His head ached.

"Now we'll see," he murmured.

"You heard the radio too. He'd dead."

"Why isn't there cheering and dancing, then?"

They slowed up pulling into the town square.

"For God's sake, Dorian, what's wrong now?"

"I smell my death. That's what my grandfather said." He shrugged. "I would like to have married you, I think."

"Himmler and all that crew will have been arrested by now."

"Of course," He stopped the car and shut off the engine. "But otherwise we're surrounded." Because there was just enough illumination to outline the panzers parked under the low buildings and the glint of helmets and sidearms.

"Maybe it's all right," she said.

"Sure. I can see that." Letting out his breath and shutting his eyes. "Anyway . . . anyway, would you have?"

"What?"

"Married me?"

There was an officer standing by the fender now. His silver SS trim glinted like (she thought) liquid.

"Unfortunately," he was saying to them, "your scheme failed. So I don't imagine you should contemplate marriage at this time." He didn't laugh.

"Ah," she murmured.

Dorian reopened his luminous eyes without trying to see anything in particular.

"The Führer," said the officer, "was saved by a miracle."

"Ah," she sounded again. Tried to picture it: a massive, amorphous darkness swirling and embracing the flame-eyed tyrant. "Naturally."

"So that's that," the German said.

"Whose side were you on?" she wondered. There were soldiers ringing them now.

Dorian held the pistol in his lap. He was working through his steps: a quick shot through her head (as agreed long before), then bite the barrel himself if they gave him time enough—and finish it. His heart's pounding filled his ears. He could see them all now as they subtly emerged from the night.

"What does that matter now, madam?" the officer returned.

She saw Dorian moving out of the side of her sight but she knew it was too late for that. Too late . . . She clenched her hands and shut her eyes and let her mind pray, heard the shattering windshield, the spray of glass chips whipping across her face, heard the reports as the impacts bounced him back and forth beside her while she sat and waited and thought she actually saw the tremendous shadow hovering over Hitler, straddling the horizon with a face now: lean, avid gaze, infinite, bottomless . . .

LV
(1945)

The fog was thicker, Astuti noted, than smoke, as if the earth were coolly smoldering. Far to the right there was a steady whooshing sound of trucks. He could hear the gearshifts. There was no way to tell if they were German or not. He thought about the American plane that had nearly chewed them to pieces. Decided that, looked at a certain way, one side might be as bad as the other.

The duke was a few steps ahead and seemed on the point of dissolving into the mist as if his form was a transient gathering of twilight vapors.

The son of a bitch goes on here, Astuti thought, *like he knew where the fuck he was . . .*

"Eh," he said, grinning, "maybe you got bat blood, you know what I mean?"

They were crossing a field. Long grasses swished knee-deep. The world was a tin-colored circle barely past arm's length around them. They'd passed a bullet-chewed signpost some distance back that Astuti had pondered hopefully. He'd strained the few German words he'd picked up to fit the scattered letters. ALT M EN. Spat in disgust. Something old, maybe . . . *Alt,* something or other.

His boot hit something solid in the grass.

"Wait," he called ahead. The knight paused and turned just at the limits of visibility, seeming to melt and reform as the mists shifted.

Astuti picked up a blackened, shapeless hunk of what looked like lead. Shook his head at it.

"Just what I been looking for," he announced. "A perfect fucking doorstop."

"What hast thou uncovered, comrade?"

"A wheezis Watchit," was the illuminating reply. "From the planet Mongo."

"Is this of value? Magical?" the duke asked.

"Only if you cast it away, Signore."

He tossed it high and watched the heavy lump vanish, and then the dull reddish flash and sound and impact of dirt spanging off his helmet as he dove for cover in instant reflex, then caught himself on one hand, bent absurdly as if attempting a half pushup, because he knew at once what it meant and that the sign must have read: HALT MINEN! So he cried out:

"Holy Cow, we're in a minefield."

"What says't thou?"

"Do not move! Stand there! Death in the ground!"

He levered himself upright with terrific strain and stood there staring around into the yeildless gray, thinking:

Maybe if we could see the sign we could walk straight back except we can't . . . we can't . . . we're fucked up the ass . . . up the ass . . .

"This is a fucking minefield!" Astuti cried. Then in Italian: "Do not move your feet, understand?"

The duke took this in from where he seemed to be dissolving into fog, calf-deep in the wetly smoking grass.

"More ill magics," he stated. "Yet, methinks we cannot stand and mutely wait for our troubles to pass."

"I'm glad you're so calm," muttered the other.

"Often thou mumbles in thy beard, Astuti. Speak freely, man. Explain this sorcery."

"There are things like . . ." Astuti groped. ". . . like iron mushrooms under the ground . . . yeah . . . If you step on one . . ." His hands made it clear.

"Ah," nodded the knight.

"We ain't got a detector . . . We'll have to poke the earth with something . . ." Thought. "Your sword is okay."

"Eh?"

"Fuck it," he whispered. Tried to walk exactly in the duke's tracks, sweating, expecting doom as each step sank into the deep grass. Made it.

"Thou art a worthy man," he was informed, approvingly.

"Yeah. Sure." His legs wobbled.

A dark, stinking gush of smoke mixed with pale mist rolled over them. They both choked and spat.

"A wind from hell," sputtered the duke.

"It smells like a fucking glue factory."

"We stand close to the enemy's lair." The dark foulness boiled around them, then was thinned somewhat by the veering breeze. The air remained stained. "Near the devil's hole! God has guided my feet and He will take me the rest of the way." Started walking very deliberately. "Follow me." Marched into dimness.

"Hey!" called the soldier, rooted in panic. "Hey! Holy shit!"

Clutched and caught the tail of the knight's flopping blue-white housecoat and desperately yanked. "You outrageous nut!" Raged, eyes burning as more acid, dense smoke flooded over them . . .

Renga came back for just an instant this time. The green-flecked darkness ripped in half like a torn cloth and he breathed the biting smoke and fog of Germany, hearing Astuti's complaining voice and then, in a blink's time, the oppressive underworld slammed back down again like a stone gate . . .

He was at the bottom of the spiral descent and had just entered the short stretch of tunnel that led to the miles-high and -wide cavern where the tower jabbed up from the molten moat.

He felt his brother Relti now. Felt his force like a physical pressure. He had gone about halfway when he noticed movements blocking the streaks and blobs of luminescence: figures moving toward him in the narrow passage. No way to duck aside.

His hand went to his sword hilt. What nameless creatures might they be? He waited and when they came close the movement stopped. He knew they were men or manlike, at least.

"Who goes there?" he asked, ready. After fighting the blind beast on the levels above he was unimpressed by much. Only the memory of the dying girl lingered, troubling, infinitely sad and lost . . .

"What's that?" a bluff, yet cold voice responded that he didn't know was General Rog's.

The witch-fire light fizzed and flickered, shifting heatless embers around the walls.

He could tell there were about a dozen and assumed they were Relti's men.

"Name yourselves," he requested. He felt their fear. Wondered what they feared.

"We will," Rog said, leveling his spear. "Our name is your doom."

"Doom," he said, unimpressed. He could make out their skirtlike armor mesh and insignia now. "I was doom before this. My name is Ner." He smiled with rueful, almost pitying anger.

Rog raised both thin eyebrows though the gesture was invisible in that light. He temporized at once.

"In truth? His brother?"

"I am in haste to find him. It has been many years. Many years."

"Ah. I see. You are, he has said, a great wizard."

"He has said."

Ner felt the faint pulsing warm spot in his chest above his heart where the crystal sliver was lodged. It strangely soothed him and increased his indifference to all these shadowy things, these meaningless conversations. He'd otherwise have drawn his sword and struck at once.

"Has the city fallen?" Rog asked.

"I know nothing of that," Ner said. "I must go on to rejoin my brother." He drew his weapon, without haste.

The general raised one wide hand, lowering his spear with the other.

"We have no quarrel."

"Have you abandoned his service?"

Rog shrugged.

"He needs us no longer," he explained.

"Have you been touched by the healing light?" He didn't think so but felt obliged to ask.

Some of the troops muttered. He felt them tensed, fearful, dangerous. Wished he knew why and knew it was useless to try and find out much.

Rog laughed.

"I am sick of the dark," he said, "but that is another matter. In any case, your brother, the lord Relti, is not far ahead. We won't hinder you, sir. Only the dead stand between you and him." Turned to his men. "Let him pass."

LVI
(SPRING 1944)
Italy

Renga was still drunk the next evening. Unshaven in his baggy suit he wandered around the deserted house from window to window, staring at the fields while the shadows shifted around and gradually sank into the general, glimmering gray.

He now was leaning on the glass of the French door that opened into the walled garden. An empty wine bottle was a glint at his feet.

He knew and knew and knew she wasn't coming back here. He knew it was the worst because it was always the worst . . . so he held it back, floating on the warm mist of wine, watching with blurred intentness as each shape lost first its density—trees, shrubs, stones . . . then the outlines themselves melted away . . . Kept it just a numbness, except as the dark swallowed all forms he felt it haunting the place, waiting on the stairs, in the rooms . . . it had swallowed her and memory was valueless afterglow and it was coming for him now, swirling out of the stealthy night and he was already running, unaware of the French doors bursting glass as he charged across the edgeless landscape where the last stain of reddish gold seemed suspended without even sky or earth . . . through the gate in the wall (without feeling it bang into his shoulder) fleeing across the footbridge and the last luminescence of the motionless canal water . . . fleeing at the dying sunset, drawn into a wild race that wouldn't end until something happened . . . something . . . and a long time (perhaps) later he fell down in a cushiony darkness under the thin horns of a yellowish new moon where the breezes whispered him into abrupt, utter sleep . . .

He sat up in a silvery, sourceless glow. *Dawn*, he thought. Jerked in sudden fear: a humped-up, massive shape loomed over him, things like spiked heads, long necks, squarish, lumpy, bloated body. He cried out silently as if underwater. Felt helpless, bared . . . felt rather than heard the meaning of the thing's dark voice as it told him:

Ready yourself.

What are you? he asked, wordless.

Ready yourself. You are to become a doorway from the dream. You are beginning to open.

I am asleep!

A doorway between the two worlds. The war is fought in both. Asleep.

You will enter into the door through yourself. You will go out through the door into yourself. What was will be what is. Is will be was.

Or I'm mad. What babble!

Neither of you, who are one, is mad.

Please let me wake up!

The war must be won in dreams or it will fail in waking.

He couldn't shut his eyes or move. He struggled, felt suffocated, chilled . . . the scene flickered and the shape was instantly clear in the first spears of sunlight burning through the valley mists: two mules and a monk in a wagon. The monk sat there, peering down at him where he lay in a half-grown wheatfield, the sharp tips shaking the fresh light. The monk's face was pale with very black brows, head completely bald.

"But are you all right, *signóre?*" he asked Renga, in Italian.

I was drunk, he was thinking, blinking, rubbing his face. Sat up. Winced as the shock of moving hammered in his head.

"Un," he muttered.

"You do not look well, *signóre.*"

"Un," Renga repeated. Rubbed his face. His clothes were damp, stained. The hangover pain was concentrating in his eyes.

"I was dreaming about my dreams," he said, for no particular reason.

"Do you wish a ride?"

"Yes," he replied, remembering, reaching in his pocket

to touch the roll of papers. Remembered the night: the SS ghost, absent Eunice. Looked around, drank in the new sun, the sweet, freshening colors that seemed to burn away the shadows that shaped them. She was gone . . . Tried to spit, dry-mouthed . . . she was gone and now he was supposed to serve the phantoms.

Stood up, leaning on the wagon, staring at the monk in his brown robes.

"*Signóre?*"

"Do you know what they're actually doing?" Renga asked.

"Pardon? Whom?"

"Brother, they are opening the gates to let in hell."

"Ah," the monk said, nodding, quite serious, as Renga mounted up beside him. "Where can I take you, friend?"

Renga settled back, body swaying with the jerking mules as they set off into the terrific southern sun that was now clearing the rim of the smooth, ancient hills. He squinted into the glare. He felt there was something changed, something different about himself.

"Friend?" the monk repeated.

"Take me to Rome, to the Pope."

The long, bald man was grave.

"You are troubled," he said.

Renga shut his eyes. Nodded.

"Ah," he said. The sun seemed to blaze into his head, even with the lids clamped shut.

"You're not Italian."

"True, brother."

The wheels bumped and creaked as they angled up the green slope above the wheatfields. A flight of blackbirds fountained and scattered above the bright grain.

"Do you wish to talk to me?" He didn't smile. "—Though I am not the Pope."

Renga's eyes were open again. He felt he was actually breathing in the sun's penetrating impact.

"No," he said. "Better not to hear some things."

"Ah." The grave face looked ahead. He snikked the reins lightly as the delicate-footed beasts balanced up the steeply tilted slope. "You can come and see the abbot, if you wish." Renga took the documents out of his pocket. Fixed his blurry sight on the photographs without giving the monk viewing angle.

"The abbot," Renga muttered. "No. It had better be the Pope." He was forcing his sight to see impossible images dancing in brightness and blurs like dazzling water. He tried to insist away, somehow, the flat black-and-white pictures, just shadows, not outrages of blood and ruined flesh . . . just paper shadows of humanity wasted to bony unreality, stacked, massed, twisted, lolling, and stiffening . . .

"It's a long ride to Rome," the monk said, as they crossed the shoulder of the hill. "Where did you come from, friend?"

Renga rolled up the pictures and stuffed them into his suit pocket. They were a stain on the brightening day. Like a speck in the eye.

"I came from my house," he said. "Well, my wife's. Malverde."

"The contessa is your wife?"

"Was."

"Eh?"

"She's gone."

"Ah." The monk crossed himself. "I am sorry. A pity."

"Did you know her?"

"Slightly. But . . ." He looked a question.

"Renga. Rudolph Renga. We seldom came here."

"Ah."

"I just realized how much I loved her."

The monk pursed his lips, looking across the fecund hills and fields as the sun mounted and the earth steamed with richness. *I just realized . . .*

LVII
(1945)

Kurt Fragtkopft paced along the line of victims being herded toward the mass graves. They were just pale strips and spatters of shadow under the floodlights. He looked at nothing.

So he didn't notice or turn his head the first time the voice spoke. He assumed Rosenberg was sending after him.

These assholes, he was thinking, *what do they know about anything? Let them see tonight what it's all about* . . .

"Kurt," the voice said, repeated, and he shuddered, stopped. Stared straight ahead across the shadowy compound where the wire glinted.

What? What? What? his mind kept saying. He stared along the lines of bone and shadows, cavern-eyes skull faces. They weren't supposed to call out his name. That wasn't in the rules.

"Who spoke?" he demanded, clamping his hands to his hips, facing the ghostly rows, as if that made some difference.

"Kurt," he heard again and then the face floated into focus, harshly lit by a bounce of floodlight: a bald head, long, hollowed face, like the rest, starved, shrunken limbs and breasts, legs, he thought, resembling a chicken. He stared, put a sneer on his face, watched only the details so it wouldn't bite into him. His duty now was to show firmness. They had to stay calm. There were too many of them to face if there was panic and screaming and . . . shut and opened his eyes several times. *All the same faces,* he thought, *all the same faces* . . . *no face at all, really* . . . *no face* . . . This sort of thing was absolutely forbidden. With good reason: no intimacy, however slight, was tolerable. How many men could caress the calf whose throat they were about to slit?

399

"What does this—" he began but then her flat, still, soft voice without anything in it:

"My name is Minna," she said, floating a step closer, standing very solid on her absurdly fragile legs.

"Un?" His mind didn't think. He stared. The line was moving past in shreds of glare and dark. A guard swept down with a dogwhip, driving them on. Aimed a crack at the woman. Minna. Kurt made another sound without shape, snatching the SS guard's sleeve and spinning him away, just staring at the face, putting the hints back into flesh, lips moving soundlessly as they both wobbled to where the line was lost in the packed thousands being pressed into the tremendous pit.

And then he understood what he had to do because there was always a limit and it was now passed. Without even having to think he reached for her arm and pictured first keeping her in his office until he could have her sent to safety, feeling it would be all right so long as they didn't have to really attempt to talk . . . because he assumed he knew why she'd called out at the last moment, not thinking that perhaps she'd had days, weeks, even months, to have recognized him so why wait until now, until the grave was dug before saving yourself. So he was stunned with strange fear when she slipped his grip with startling energy and he sensed there might be other limits too, long passed, and he shouted instantly:

"No! Wait! Wait!" Trying to find something to really say, seeing the features he knew in tortured parody hinted in the bald ravages before him. He felt shapeless sound welling up in him again, a sound that might fill him like a cloud and jerk his body beyond his will, as she moved to the edge of the pale shadow mass that had been smeared and worn into virtual identity. He felt her stare, steely concentration, as if the bones and shreds and lost memory of her were possessed by an alien fury like a flaming blade and he knew that besides saving her he'd have to, somehow, dull the edge or she'd slice his soul to shreds.

"Please!" he yelled, suddenly desperate to save not her but himself . . . himself. "God! Please! Please! Minna!"

He watched her as if across a gulf in a dream, reaching in underwater helplessness and silent screaming: clutching at her, missing, staggering, yelling, not even hearing her final curse, the cut that would destroy him, everything out of order now, spinning and crashing to pieces, all the meshed gears of hopeless fantasy.

"Good-bye, Kurt."

As she melted into the livid pale and dark, joining like clay to clay, traceless, seamless, gone, he flailed and flung the feeble shapes left and right, kicking and punching in terror and frenzy, not hearing groans and snapping bones, digging into them, voice a raw, wordless screaming filling his skull, pounding . . . pounding . . . the guards elbowing in behind him, stepping over the broken people writhing almost languidly in his path . . . and then he was stuck at the grave's edge, the flesh there a nearly solid wall. He pounded and ripped at the frail gestures that were human beings, screaming in a hopeless spasm because it was too late and her ghost had destroyed him before sinking back into the shadowy sea of hell.

He screamed, twisted, boomed, flopped as the guards dragged him back, beating their rageless way through the phantasmal doomed . . . and then he broke loose and raced, howling under his breath, back into the almost-seamless mass . . .

Himmler was sitting at his desk with just a single dim lantern lighting the room. The power had been knocked out during the last bombing. It was nearly midnight. Some of the phones were still working.

He waited, glasses on the dark wood desktop that gleamed like water. The air blower rattled behind him in the underground stillness.

He felt sweat clinging. His clothes were getting soaked. *You'd think it would be cool down here . . . We have to hide like rats thanks to Göring's wonderful Luftwaffe . . .* Stared at the gold-trimmed phone that glinted in the rosy flame-shadows. *It's time he has to do it now the lousy Russians animals are dancing over his head . . . the Führer won't hesitate . . .*

"God," he whispered "help us! Please . . ." The last hope was now. The last hope to save the sacred fire from the muck of history. He was weeping and didn't bother to wipe his washed-out eyes. Sweat and tears ran down his puffy cheeks as his mind pictured the bestial tide pouring through the last ragged defenders. "Farewell, Adolf Hitler, the great." Choked up. *Farewell . . .*

The door opened and Kersen, his masseur, came

quietly in and stood in the weak splashes of uneven glow. Then moved around behind his boss. This man had already saved many lives through his influence over Himmler's moods.

He gripped the pinched, rounded shoulders in his firm, long hands and began to knead. Himmler sighed and trembled slightly, suddenly stunned by his tension.

"Do you wish to lie down, sir?" Kersen asked.

Himmler shook his head, shutting his eyes, giving himself up to the ecstasy of the deeply penetrating fingers.

"Ahh," he murmured.

"What will we do?" Kersen asked, after a few moments.

"Hm?" The Reichsführer's head lolled on the high, velvet-backed chair. "Ah . . . yes . . . I understand . . . well, Kersen, don't worry, we'll soon see what's what . . ." Sighed. The servant waited, knowing he had only to prime his employer on most subjects. "I'm trying a number of alternatives. It's on my shoulders to save things now . . . ah, that's good . . . good . . ." His glasses faced him in front of the inkwell, flashing his face back at him: a pale, melting outline edged by fire.

"Is there much hope?"

"When the phone rings we'll know something . . ." Sighed as the blunt fingers worked the sides of his neck. "You better not get caught if we have to run for it. They'll hang you first of all."

"Why is that, Herr Reichsführer?"

"Because without you I couldn't have survived so long." Wanly smiled.

"They say the Führer has fled Berlin."

"Nonsense. You know he'll never do that." Sighed and lolled his head against the steady, penetrating hands.

"So if everything fails we'll have to flee west?"

"Yes . . . yes . . . I suppose so . . ." He didn't pursue that line. It led to blankness.

And next the phone went off like an explosion and he jerked forward in his seat to plunge for it, his face flicking across the glasses in a wink of flame. His breath rasped as he asked:

"Yes? Yes?"

"This is Heilmond."

"Yes."

"The bunker is cut . . . off . . ." The connection

drifted. The voice seemed to dissolve and reform into unhuman electric raving and stutter.

"What?" snorted Himmler. "Speak louder, dammit!"

". . . in or out . . . tried . . . message . . . Russians . . ."

"What! What!"

". . . dead . . . message . . . named . . ."

"Named? Named who? Is he dead?"

". . . Goebbels dead too . . . Dönitz . . ."

Himmler leaned to the side and the glasses picked up his bent, bulged image again.

"Dönitz what?" he yelled into the chaotic wire whines.

". . . named new head . . . I . . ."

"It's a lie! Do you hear? Arrest Dönitz! He's a traitor!"

". . . Reichsführer, I . . . now . . . cannot . . ."

The buzzings rattled into sudden, voiceless shrieks more terrible to the ear than human pain.

"Arrest him! Goddammit! Arrest anyone who challenges SS authority! The Führer was deceived. Bormann's work! The filthy pig betrayed everything . . . Arrest Bormann and that whole disloyal gang, do you hear me, Heilmond! . . . Eh? . . . Answer me!"

But there was nothing on the line but a howling, raging scream and he jerked the bell from his ear, slammed it at the cradle, missed, and it clattered across the desk and whispered its mechanical pain into the rug.

"Dönitz," he muttered.

"Bad news, sir?" Kersen waited behind the chair.

"Poisoned against me . . ." He groped for his glasses and set them carefully on his nose. Sat back, in silence. Outside and above he thought he heard muffled barking. One of the dogs, he half-thought, at the guardhouse. The earth vibrated slightly, resonant. Bombs or shells. Closer and closer . . . *We delayed everything too long . . . now I've got to be brave* . . . Blinked. *A man has to try his best . . . his best . . . Please help me . . . please . . .* Blinked behind the finger-stained glasses that he didn't bother to wipe. He picked up another phone.

"Get me Dachau," he said.

"Herr Reichsführer," the operator aide said, "the lines are all dead."

"Dead?"

"The bombing must have cut the cables."

"Cut?"

"Yes, sir. But I had a call coming in from Dachau that was broken off."

"What were they saying?"

"I don't know. Something was wrong."

"Yes . . . yes . . . why not?" He swallowed. Sat and stared. "Why not?"

"Sir?"

"Something's wrong . . ." He hung up. His pale fingers drummed on the desktop. Stared. Kersen said something but he didn't respond. Took off his glasses again and his unfocused eyes turned the rosy wink of flame in the black metal lantern into a vague globe that he could have imagined was a smoke-palled sun sinking behind the horizon line of desk, the blurred phones and books become trees and cliffs and dark habitations . . .

And then the knight was lost in the stinging smoke and fog as Astuti hurled himself forward, still shouting:

"What! Wait!"

Not even thinking about being blown up because if he once stood still he'd freeze. He hit, rebounded, clutching at the lanky outline who was clutching him back, desperately too, coughing, weeping, saying in German:

"My God! My God! Am I in hell here? . . ." Then English: "Where is this place?"

They fell over together in the steaming weeds, Astuti shuddering, tensed, as they hit, crackling, waiting for the blast to tear them apart . . . nothing.

"Stay fucking still, will you?" he pleaded.

"What is this place?" Renga asked again.

"Some fucking field. How do I know? I'm still fucking following one of you."

Renga breathed deeply. Kept his sleeve over his mouth and nose to strain out the smoke. His eyes ran water.

"I see," he whispered, "I see . . ."

Astuti was rooting in his pack for the gas mask. Then remembered he'd tossed it away. "The only gas the Germans got," he'd informed a green replacement, "comes from their fucking *sour*kraut." Pressed a handkerchief to his face which muffled his curses.

"I wonder if I'm getting used to this," Renga wondered.

"No comment. I don't know why we ain't dead." Coughed and spat. "The other guy, the duke, he ain't too impressed with minefields and tanks and Messerschmitts." Coughed and spat. "I figure we're on a path that the Krauts use. The trouble is, they always fucking zigzag. We gotta be on some of the zigs or zags, you know what I mean?" Nodded, sagely. Renga just sat there, holding himself across the chest. "Sooner or later we're gonna zig when it fucking zags and that's that . . ." Shrugged.

"What can we do?" Renga asked, keeping his tearing eyes shut. He wished he would black out again into the greenish dreams. None of these worlds seemed real anymore. He felt thinned and shadowy . . . *Am I the sword of the gods,* he wondered, *or merely a madman?*

Astuti crouched carefully to his feet, taking Duke's sword and gingerly probing the tip into the soft earth. He began working a path forward by inches.

"Just so we don't go in a fucking circle we'll be all right," he muttered. Held the cloth to his face. Stopped as he hit metal, carefully found the edge, and dug and pried the deadly disk into sight while Renga rested on his knees now on the steaming earth.

"It's not over yet," he whispered in German. "I wish it were over . . . I wish . . ." Nothing drew him in any particular direction, anyway. He'd failed . . . he'd failed before and was probably failing now, wherever he was . . . whatever he was . . . "I have to accept this . . . I have to accept this . . ."

He thought about the girl again, back in the dream, the other world, his (he believed) coherent madness. The dying girl, he'd just realized, resembled Minna: the girl slashed open, telling him she'd tried . . . tried . . . and he understood that all the times and worlds, real or imagined, enclosed one another and never completely died and those who were part of them were a part forever . . .

They inched along, Astuti sweating steadily in the muggy air, bent into it like some demonic farmer formed in the mists and smokes of hell, harvesting the dragon's actual crop; inching on under an invisible sky, stooping, coughing . . .

"*Mingia,*" Astuti muttered.

"You've been chosen too," Renga told him. "No one

ever hides, no cave is deep enough nor desert lonely. We are all Jonahs."

"Yeah, sure," the soldier responded, then cursed, working on into the deepening, strange twilight.

"The war on the field is done," Renga said, hugging himself and staring through his burning eyes. "But there's not going to be a victory . . ."

"There ain't? That's a cheerful thought . . . son of a fucking bitch," he said, freeing another mine.

". . . the nations are destroying the wolf that has half-devoured them but they've only done it by drinking enough poison to kill the beast as it feeds, you see . . . so everyone's doomed . . ." Because he saw that the creature was going to be more deadly as a phantom than ever as a living, fanged, snarling reality . . . "I'm supposed to strike at the ghost," he said, dry, without emphasis.

"Oh yeah?"

"That's why I'm lost . . . I can't sleep, live, or die . . . that's why . . . because I have to strike in the world of ghosts . . ."

"Uh-huh," grunted preoccupied Astuti.

So Renga wasn't afraid or surprised this time when he became Ner again and the darkening fog swirled as if in a cyclonic wind and formed into green-tinted shapes, billowed into the dead defenders now in charred armor, their red eyes burning in hollow helms, flames showing, seething, in the steel joints where sparks flew, dribbled, hissed. Relti's zombies. The dark mist condensed into the sheer tower that stabbed into the greenish underground sky. His sword was still in his hand. More machines, he realized. Dead things . . . warriors, filled with fire, shells of blackened metal grinding at him, rasping with tottering, awkward speed, chopping the air with massive axes, and he understood if he perished here he could never escape.

He moved aside from the nearest. It scraped to follow, guided by whatever strange senses, ax chop-chopping, the others shifting too, gathering around him with just enough space to swing weapons, forming a blazing hot wall of fanged iron. He ducked close and slammed a terrific slash into the nearest one's side plates, avoiding the looping ax. The metal parted instantly and streams of screaming fire gushed out, driving him back. He thought if he opened enough holes its power would drain away. He hit again,

again: fire spurted from the skeletal shell with no sign of fading. He grimly understood. His blows were making things worse because now he had the flames to deal with . . .

The queen and her son were out on the thin knife of bridge that arched over the molten lava moat. The black-ish-red glow seemed to melt in their eyes while the heated air tugged their clothes and hair.

"Who is that fighter, Mother?" the boy asked her.

"An enemy, perhaps." She freed her dagger and held it at her side as if it would really matter.

"Those things," the boy said. "They have become all fire now."

"Yes. A wonder among wonders. Great is Master Relti's power. The forces bless my husband as I am blessed by him."

"He's gone, Mother." The boy was staring at Ner's attempts to get through the line of steel and flame. He would duck down, then cut to the side. Useless. The wall of blazing dead held him back. "My father is gone."

"He will return. And with his strength we will go to the surface and take back everything that is ours." She rubbed her face, watching Ner slashing at the metal suits of flame in frustration and despair, then falling back from the furious heat. "Come," she said. "We will wait on the other side for your father."

Backed across the span with him. They both watched the warrior, who they didn't know was the boy's uncle, fall back from the hollow guardians, weary and stymied.

"Wait for what, Mother?"

"For your father."

"My father is no more," he repeated. "They are eating him inside there." He stared at nothing now, his eyes full of melting fire. "They are eating him."

High in the needle of the tower Relti was climbing straight up a chimneylike shaft. His unhuman metal fingers ground into the stone and, while his feet braced along, levered him higher and higher into now-total darkness.

Each pump of his new heart filled him with bursts of wild energy that was frenzy in his veins, burning, igniting his flesh with superhuman strength. Oh, he knew it now, knew he would slay all his enemies, smash them with the

new hand, rip them apart, blast their brains with the power
of his new voice fed by the godlike madness of his heart's
vitality! He saw it all. There was no doubt.

And then his head struck the top. Solid rock. No light.
Hundreds of feet to the bottom. While his metal hand
braced, he pushed above himself with the other and a
trapdoor opened. His mind swirled with thoughts. The
sleeping god would wake and return to the surface with
him. The shadowy beast-shape that perched on his shoulders bent its seven heads in a frenzy, whispering, invoking,
explaining, praising, raging, adoring, lusting, telling him
how the sleeper would stretch out his arms across the
world, how his gaze would melt the earth, why fires and
fogs that were slowly fading would spread everywhere
again until the stupid sun was dulled to a disk of lead . . .

Relti was just an exultant speck now riding his own
seethings, gathered into the vaster furies of elemental,
eternal violence and unending hate as the sleeper's, the
Great One's, dreams and anguish beat into him. The
undefeated lord trapped down here, raging across forever,
dreaming of a dead sun and burning world. A universe of
fumes and shadowy glow . . . of an arm that could reach
and close over all the spinning worlds . . . dreams rising
like a whirlwind or waterspout of wanting without end . . .

The seven heads of the shadowbeast were singing a
hymn of revenge and victory as Relti thrust his own head
through the narrow hole (as if to be born again) and barely
registered (much less had time to react) when a steel face
and fanged mouth closed over the top of his skull and
ripped it away with a single bite and the shadowheads
shrieked with glee and ecstasy as a molten ball was slammed
by steel paws into his head, the brain hissing into char,
smoke, and steam, and the stone heart and iron mind were
now united and Relti died and lived at once and somewhere far away Adolf Hitler woke screaming from a nap
and Eva clutched him in the grim, green-walled bunker cell
on the hard mattress and soothed him over and over again
until he could just lie there and stare at the ceiling and
tremble, the image still so vivid he feared to close his eyes
again even for an instant . . .

Ner was weary and numb. He stood there, backed up,
panting, the sword dragging his arm to his side. He felt the

fitful sleeper stirring on top of the tower. He understood
that as it was disturbed it would dream vividly and those
dreams would lap at all human consciousness. Those
dreams made weak men mad and stained even the strong
with causeless anger and strange desires. He understood
that his brother meant to fully waken that ancient terror
and risk the unmaking of the world and the restoration of
eternal night.

He had to break through, but how? Pass a wall of
armed, flaming husks clashing together, roaring (he
thought) like oil-soaked torches.

He tried running along the perimeter but they stayed
packed in a tight semicircle closing off the bridge where (he
noted) the woman and boy had just crossed. They were
packed three and four deep but were set so as not to chop
one another to pieces: there was always a little space. But
the space was too slight . . . unless . . . but he'd have to
sacrifice even defense. Step by step he realized he was being
stripped bare.

He was already unstrapping, flinging his armor away,
backing up, drawing them a little forward to spread their
ranks slightly. Finally, barefoot and in his tunic with just the
sword he believed he had a wild chance. No point in
thinking. There was no other way to his brother. Toes
gripping the smooth, greenstone floor, he danced into the
black furnace of undead killers.

LVIII
At the Death Camp

Rosenberg scurried along behind the SS line as they drove
the victims into the long pit. The eastern horizon leaped in
bomb flashes as Berlin was fused, shattered, and churned
to rubble. A steady echoing rumble under foreground
curses, shouts, orders, wails, screams, pleadings, and
chanted prayers . . .

"Quickly, quickly, it's time!" Rosenberg kept repeating, running into the SS sergeant who roughly shoved him to arm's length, scowling at the shocked, pouch-faced official. "Watch what you do, fellow," snarled Rosenberg. "Where's the commander?"

"I don't know, sir."

"He must come here, now."

The grim-faced noncom said nothing for a moment. Then:

"You better find him, then, sir. I have orders to carry out." And strode away along the edge of massed chaos where the pit was now packed solid, those underneath struggling and crying out, suffocating in the stink as bowels and bladders opened and emptied, everyone caught and twisted, crushed in flesh and bone darkness: undulant panic sealing the mass into a single suffering. Commandant Fragtkopft was somewhere in the middle levels, upside down in the terrible blackness of hopeless breath, thrashing with the rest, fused to them, clawing in hopeless reflex, climbing laterally downward with each kick and twist, howling, babbling and foaming now . . . sometimes with his wife in the sunny yard at the university before the First World War, trying to explain to her the necessity of making abstract philosophy a concrete part of everyday life . . . then somewhere in his childhood . . . then deeper, where colors dreamed and the world died into misty shadows and there was just an endless pulse and flow, directionless, everything spilling out of him, memories, thoughts, feelings, faces . . . bubbling away forever . . . without even being, he was there among shapes and movements, touchings, warms, colds, nearnesses that soothed and darks that were remote . . . he felt presences close-by, bathing him in concern, watching . . . there was nothing, just dreaming, breathing, unmarked silence . . . soothing foreverness . . .

Rosenberg had found the nearest lieutenant.

"You must empty the cans quickly!" he insisted. "Time is short! Understand?"

"We have our instructions, Herr Reichsleiter." The ax-faced, dead-pale man was smoking a cigarette without taking it from his slit lips. He stared at the fleeting flame on the horizon beyond the thrashing torment at his feet, beyond the wall of wire.

"Excellent, then," said Rosenberg.

"Yes. But the men refuse."

"Refuse? Refuse what?"

"To pour the motor fuel on the living."

The official went pale with chill fury.

"Are we suddenly so squeamish!" he hissed. The officer shrugged, staring. "Do we suddenly forget the meaning of a command?"

"The commandant said he'd take care of the difficulty at the proper time."

The Orientals in the black uniforms were waiting and watching the famous party philosopher, tilted eyes showing nothing.

"Yes? Where *is* Fragtkopft, then?" Rosenberg leaned close to him. The man shrugged again. "You're ready to desert, aren't you, lieutenant? You're a pack of faithless dogs, I think."

"Sure," said the man. "You see me running, don't you? It's too late even for that, Herr Reichsleiter."

"If the Bolsheviks get you, you won't be so philosophical." Rosenberg checked his good pocket watch for the tenth time in five minutes. "Have them place the cans all around the pit," he ordered. "These fine, moral, loyal beings will do that much for Adolf Hitler and Germany, eh?" His lips shook. "I'm an old man and I'm not ducking my duty, lieutenant."

The officer, still staring at nothing, clicked his heels.

"As you wish," he murmured, and headed for the troops.

"We'll do everything ourselves," he said to the leader of the Tibetans who nodded, silently, then spoke quietly to the others, translating.

Adolf Hitler shuffled up the gray corridor past the bathroom and stopped at the steel storeroom door. Listened to the singing inside: the shattering glass and shattering laughter.

He pushed the door ajar and squinted. Tinny music was playing, slightly too slow, out of the downwinding gramphone. The effect was disturbing, twisting what he realized was Negro jazz (where had *that* come from) into cries suggesting raw, animal pain.

Squinted and blinked into the long room: dim, green-

ish emergency lights showed one of the bunker steno-
graphers, blond and quite naked, dancing around the
couples on the floor, draped on cots, copulating or unconscious. The singers were at the far end, rocking, heads
together.

He started to speak, then didn't. Stared at the pale
shapes that struck him as being no more solid than the
greenish air itself. The whole bunker rang and shook
constantly and all lights but these flickered.

Stupid, he thought. *So stupid* . . .

The girl wobbled, the dance a mere symbol. What did
it matter? For a moment he felt the wall closing in and he
wanted to drive his tortured body into a run . . . up the
stairs and out . . . out into what? Where was he? What
place was this, really?

Someone dropped a bottle. It didn't break; chinked,
rolled down the concrete floor.

Stupid . . . *stupid* . . . *stupid* . . .

Wanted to speak again . . . to rouse them . . . He
opened his mouth. Show them . . . what? . . . Show
them how stupid . . . what?—what was so stupid? He lost
the thread. His left leg began to buck, his arm in a mild
frenzy too. He clung to the doorframe to keep from falling.

No . . . *never think* . . . *never think about what was
lost* . . . *never* . . .

The greenish light trembled, faded, and he feared he
was fainting. Then glimpsed the sleep landscape opening
there as if the walls and tangled human forms were
shadows dying away into the brain's twilight.

He turned, pushed away to stagger along the cold wall,
limping, reeling in strange panic as the generator rattled
and stuttered and the lights all went black and he almost
screamed because his mind went green.

No! I'm not ready yet! Please . . .

The light shuddered on again.

"Nightmare," he whispered, dry. "Drugs and my
fever . . . yes . . ." Found his way into his room, desperate to lie down . . . except it was Goebbels's room. *I'm just
confused* . . . *there's still time* . . . For what? He stopped
the line of thought. He was staring. *The children are able to
sleep through anything*, he thought. Because the boy and
younger girl were peacefully stretched out on the couch.
God bless them . . . He sighed and felt a little better. *All my*

genius, all my . . . all struggles come to nothing . . . He was too numbed even for the friendly old self-pity which had been for him a form of prayer, an affirmation that providence was aware and listening.

The children were so fair that he wondered again, dimly, how twisted Goebbels could have produced them, so blond, tender, and exquisite. *What a world was almost theirs*, he thought. Maybe he should add that to his last testament. His look brightened briefly, thinking about the message he was leaving to posterity . . . then he sighed and lost interest because even that was going to come up empty and numb. He'd soon be gone, wiped away to gray blankness forever. Nothing he said would have practical meaning to him, anyway.

Now the pain in his insides suddenly refocused him.

The second door opened at the far end of the room and the last child, the eldest girl, was suddenly framed there, one arm clutching the frame, tugging, struggling with her mother, and then the doctor loomed up behind (they didn't see Hitler), the little girl crying out:

"Oh please . . . oh, please, Mama, I don't want this . . . please, Mama, I don't!" Panic, tears, and then he saw the hypodermic and understood the other two weren't sleeping and shut the door in a reflex shudder. Turned away, leg flopping, arm twitching, mouth soundlessly garbling to itself, holding his will steady now with a flash of his old energy.

"This isn't the end," he muttered deep, like guttering wind in a drain. "This isn't . . . " What? Wasn't what? Otherwise, why was he spared, what had all the miracles meant?

Passing the stairs that led to the surface where shell reverberations echoed hollowly, he met Bormann and some others. He barely glanced at them. No matter. The last miracle would only come at the instant he actually raised the pistol to his head. The final test would depend on his actually pulling the trigger. Yes, that made sense. When God saw he was willing to die He would act. He smiled. The walls reeled and the strange, greenish light seeped through the false solidity of stone and steel and earth.

Bormann was just a blur, a shadow leaning down at him. He barely heard the words:

"My Führer, you must save yourself! I insist. I swear,

I'll have you carried away against your will, if need be. The
world—"

Except he'd heard "against your will" and the smoldering flame flared instantly:

"Is that so, Herr Bormann? I advised you to get on
your way. There's no time left for gestures."

"But—"

"I've said my last word on this subject." What would he
do, hide like an animal? Even if they broke through the
ring of steel they'd simply have to face the end elsewhere.
Somehow he knew he'd always expected this; now it was up
to the final miracle . . . Suppose he was captured by the
Reds and kept in a circus cage? He wasn't even trying to
focus. "My death will plant a seed that can never be
stamped out!" he cried at the grayish-green shadows.
"None of you can understand my mission! None ever did!"
He clutched his trembling arm and limped away without a
farewell, shoes clack-clacking on the cement.

The power had flowed again, the words had found
themselves. In the past he would have gone on, but there
was now nowhere to take it. He struggled through the
corridor, watching the green mists swell and fade
. . . reeled, hardly felt the wall smacking his head in a
burst of green fire . . . his head . . . his head, all the
pain possible in all the universe had concentrated there and
his screaming seemed normal speech, upright on the flat
top of the narrow spire of tower that spread out like a dish
to accommodate the giant figure of the sleeper who lay
stretched out in a dully lucent egg made of what seemed a
jewel substance . . . the froglike, fanged steel beast was
still now, its work done when the skull of the seeker was
opened and his brain replaced by a dense globe of hot
metal.

Relti exulted in his agony. The pain was power and
would sear him forever yet what could he not do now to
others! Ah, what could he not do . . .

The shadowy beast-necks wound around one another
in ecstasy. His eyes were pure red coals. The massive
sleeper lay above him on the buttressed altar of living rock
within his greenish egg. Relti took it in, looked with fearful
delight on the long, glossy black limbs of that unchanged,
ancient being whose descendants were blind, twisted
dwarfs creeping through lost caves deep in the earth.

Looked with fearful passion at the folded, leathery-looking wings, long, sharp V of face that moved slightly as it tossed in the storms of its slumber.

Looked and forgot even the name Relti because Relti had been a small thing, a mote in the infinite eye of power, a passing shape that now was absorbed into dark greatness.

He stepped forward, iron hand raised, stone heart pounding, metal brain whirling with pain and somber vistas of a remade world of perfect fighters and masters—hard, smooth—flying in volcanic clouds that covered all the sky, diving to bathe in lava lakes and streams, mating in billows of fire, driving pale, feeble slaves in masses to raise eternal monuments of black and green stone.

"What joy!" he screamed. Even his whispers now would be screams. "I come to wake you, O maker of perfection, O most high and beautiful, destroyer of the maggot-races! Scourge of the weaklings! I wake you, my only lord and love! I wake you forever!"

LIX
(SPRING 1944)
Northern Italy

Renga sat on the cart. The monk had stopped under a row of apple trees. The blossoms arched over the dirt road. The mounting sun fired the white-pink with burning gold and they sat in the scented luminescence.

The monk held up a stone jug of water. Renga gratefully splashed some into his fuzzy mouth, breathing deeply.

"Ah," he said. The changing light flickered over them, almost like watersheen. The grave, quiet eyes were watching him again. He ignored the obvious curiosity.

"If you want to see the Pope," the monk said, wry, quiet, "you better get a new suit."

"Do you think Saint Peter would have worried about my clothes?"

"Saint Peter," the monk smiled, "has been out of the job for some years."

Renga rubbed his hurting eyes and yawned until his bones shook.

"Will they talk to me in Rome?" he asked.

"No."

"How do you know?" No reply. Renga watched the blossoms tremble and sway in the warm drifts of breeze from the valley. Realized he was still vaguely drunk. Hadn't slept it all away. How strange. He'd heard of that happening. Maybe it was the champagne. "When I was a young student," he said, "I set out to find the Holy Grail . . ." Chuckled and shook his head. "Like Parzival."

"I see."

"Do you?"

"I see more than you think, brother."

Renga glanced at him.

"I was more like you then," he commented.

"You're still like me."

Renga thought about it.

"Can you make any suggestions?" he wondered.

The monk faced front now, staring along the dusty road ahead that wound through shimmers of gold and blots of tree shadows.

"I see in the spirit sometimes," he said quietly.

"Ah. Please tell me," Regna said sincerely, "if there's anything that might help."

The smaller man shut his eyes. His pale tongue worried his lower lip.

"You cannot go back," he finally said.

"That's true enough."

"Don't fear."

"Don't fear? That's easy advice, monk."

"You should never have left your home." The monk opened his eyes and stared. His tongue was restless.

"How sage. Should I have waited for them to put me into a damned camp? Hm? So they could pry the gold from my teeth?" He was suddenly weeping, without transition. "Shoot me in the head? Those miserable, demented, ignorant—"

"They won't hurt you if you . . ."

"What? What?"

"They cannot hurt you." His little, bloodless hands clenched on his knees. The tongue went out and in. Renga saw he was almost in some kind of trance. He knew the signs too well. "And you will go home, anyway."

"Never!" Renga popped his eyes. "Are you insane? Never! I'm going to your Pope or as close as I can get to him and show him the proof of what they're doing to the Jews! . . ." He grimaced. The terror of it clutched at his stomach again. "And others . . . probably my wife too . . ." He lurched to his feet; a few sweet petals dropped spinning past his face. "I have the proof, you see that?" Grimaced. "That's why it's too late for me . . . the bastard passed it on to me . . . on to *me* . . . it's the curse. Every second we stand here talking, they're dying . . . every second . . ." His hands gestured shapelessly. "You see? You see?"

"They won't listen," the quiet monk almost whispered, not looking at him. "You'll be arrested here. You must go home. God has . . ." He hesitated.

Renga swayed on the tilted floorboard.

"God? God *what*?" he demanded. His eyes now saw only the fuzzy, exquisite gold and pale, as though the air had thickened to rich color, as though the breeze itself were pure and various light.

The monk's eyes were shut. His pale hands clenched one another.

"God has chosen you . . ." Whispered. ". . . you . . ."

Renga swayed, trying to get his balance, to check the horizon or ground, but there was only the shifting patterns of edgeless color and blinding bursts of hot gold as the sun speared through. He was just drunk, his mind tried to believe. The perfume was a caressing breath and the man's voice was directionless, distant, and somewhere along he knew he was falling and wondered how long it would take him to hit because he knew the words he now heard were not from any pale, monkish lips but resonated with the force and hinting from beyond consciousness:

". . . chosen to uncover the light . . ."

Uncover . . . uncover . . . The fluffy air and perfumed brightness tilted past as if he fell underwater in a dream into golden wave shatters, pink-white ripples . . .

falling . . . falling . . . *Light doesn't choose,* the voice that
seemed his mind too explained. *It reveals everything to the last
stir and splinter and wink . . .*

He couldn't tell if he'd struck the ground or not. His
eyes seemed absorbed without distance into the flooding
wash of color and he couldn't separate his sight from what
he saw. Every current, every ripple, was lucid now. All the
perfumed light . . .

LX
(1945)
Central Germany

Jesus, am I beat, Astuti thought. He'd been probing and
digging in the minefield for hours, creeping through the
deadly ground in swirling fog. The smoke had shifted or
died away. The knight (after Renga sank again) tried to
help but couldn't understand the principle and tended to
poke too hard with the swordtip. So Astuti bent into it as
the sunless day died imperceptibly.

"When does this enchanted place end?" the knight had
just asked.

"Shit," was the illuminating reply.

"What?"

"When I get to *fucking* Hitler's house."

They'd reached a narrow, water-filled trench. The last
grayish-fuzzed daylight gleamed there.

Astuti knelt and caught his breath. Struck the sword
upright in the loose bank.

"This water stinks like a sewer. Jesus."

"Thou callest on God a great deal," the other observed.

"You ain't heard nothing, *goombah.*"

"Eh?"

"There is shit in this water."

"Eh?"

Then they rested, slept . . . and woke in moon-tinted mists.

Astuti shrugged and stood up, stepped over and started chopping at the earth again. Bombardment thunder rolled in the distance.

"Of course," he said, "I could be nuts and you could be all right. Sure . . ."

"Look," said the other, "a magical snare, it would seem." Lines of barbed wire hung suspended in the vaguely luminous fog. "We are close to the devil's house at last."

He strode ahead, snatching the weapon from the toiling soldier who rested on one knee now, reacting too slowly, almost accepting it even as the blade was flying up to smite and sever and his outcry was too late:

"No! Wait! Wait . . .!"

Because the wire was already *spang-spunging* violently back in a burst of blue fire and sparks and the alarm bells were raving in the darkness. Then German shouts. The last stroke flamed and strange glows that were searchlights moved and flowed around them. Voices cried out overhead.

"*Show thyselves, cowardly spawn!*" the knight yelled.

"That's telling them," Astuti cynically muttered. He jerked his rifle around, indecisive. His companion was through the wire and, once again, melted into the cold smoke. A siren began to grind a nerve-shattering scream into the night.

The duke trembled and Renga surfaced for a moment. Renga felt doom closing over him. Heard the shriek of doom in what he didn't know was a siren and saw the clouds and glows of hell all around. Then fell back to the greenish blackness again, dancing through the blazing armored shells, seared, his loincovering burned away, naked with just his sword now, racing across the bridge set with razor-edged stones that had gouged the boots and sandals of the others and ripped his feet to bloody tatters by the time he reached the other side where the queen and boy waited. She aimed her dagger at him and crouched behind the point.

He glanced back: the armored things were following, crunching and clashing over the narrow span. No choice but up, he knew. No choice but doom.

"Stand aside," he said, gasped. "I seek the tyrant Relti alone."

The boy shook his head. His eyes were quite mad, full of the red glow from the moat.

"Too late . . . too late . . . you cannot save him now . . ."

"Save," Ner cried. "Save."

The queen stepped nearer, blade first.

"I know you," she said. "I know you. You are the one he dreaded most. He loved you and you betrayed him."

"Loved." Ner was choking on words now. Any words.

"Your brother."

"Yes," he said. "Yes. Stand aside."

The advancing dead clanged and hissed flame at his back.

"He's past all help," the boy sobbed.

"Be strong!" his mother shrieked.

He covered his eyes.

"This is a terrible place," he sobbed. "I hate this terrible place . . . help me, Mother . . . please . . . take me home, Mother . . . please . . ."

"Weakling!" she yelled, slapping at his head with her free hand. "You disgrace us!"

Ner fled past them and up the steps that circled the tower, leaving bloody footprints. The boy had crumpled, covering his face and keening in lost, hopeless, mad terror. The queen turned and followed her brother-in-law. She was, he understood, worse than mad. She had her dagger and she followed. Behind her the dead had crossed and were lumbering and scraping toward the stairs.

Ner was too weary of it all even for rage or revenge. It was almost mechanical now. He had to destroy his brother. He felt nothing about it, one way or another. And he felt pity for the boy, trapped in his father's darkness. And for the cruel woman too, because she had never known love and he had and remembered the pale gold skin and fluffy hair and graceful limbs of her . . . and the kind eyes as she'd held out the golden shimmer of cup to him in the hidden place where she'd been stabbed and torn by Relti's Skull Riders while he fought desperately to save her and ended with only himself alive there . . . but he'd know love, more than all the sweet women entwined with him in all the lappings, suckings, pressings, and intimate penetrations of his life . . . more, he thought, much more with the pale gold radiance of the cup playing over their two

faces like watershimmer and her tender hand like heaven's
understanding . . .

So he climbed the spiraling stairs around that black
tower above the moat of hell, bloody, weary, and doomed,
and felt nothing but pity and lost sweetness. And the
twinge in his chest where the splinter of shattered jewel still
throbbed . . .

As he climbed past the landing where Relti had
entered the tower, the metal female shape lunged out for
him. Silvery, glistening, it reached clawed, gracefully
shaped fingers to tear his flesh to pieces. He backed up the
steps, slashing, the sword ringing and chipping on the
dense limbs and face. Useless. And it was fast so there was
no running, he realized.

His feet were bad and the stone was hot. The thing's
stare was a glare of crystal. So he went for the eyes next.
Smashed, slashed—chipped his blade. No result. He
backed up the steps, barely able to keep ahead. With his
armor on he would have, he realized, been doomed at
once.

"Is this all?" he asked himself. "To end for nothing?"

The lithe, massive female shape charged up with
inexhaustible, unhuman energy. He ran now, desperate,
balanced against the constant turning, the crack of the
thing's feet closer and closer as he panted and strained until
his legs seemed to be churning into metal too, dull, dead,
unresponding . . .

And so, being what he was and what his race had
always been, he finally turned to face it and strike a last,
hopeless blow (since he now believed he was going to fail
and die even if he reached the top of the spire), and
blinking, gasping the lifeless, hot air, he hardly realized, at
first, that the thing (he couldn't call it she) was running
straight on the steep turning, the nearest arm clutching
and missing him because the smooth, steel feet had skidded
in Ner's bloody prints and momentum did the rest. It went
silently over the edge. He stood there, leaning on the
curved wall, drooping . . .

Rosenberg struggled along the pit, feeling the strain in
his back as he emptied another can of gasoline over the
living, naked mass at his feet. The sudden fog thinned and
swelled around them. The line of guards faded and
thickened as the gray billows broke.

Rosenberg cursed steadily.

"Swine . . . running away . . . I'll be a week in bed after this . . ." Glared at the nearest guard who was nervously shifting his machine gun from hand to hand. "You son of a bitch," snarled the famous philosopher, "lend a goddamned hand here or I'll have you shot!" The man hesitated and the little leader stumped down the mist-flooded line, yelling: "All of you! This mutiny won't go unpunished! Help me or you'll suffer for it! This isn't Italy!" A few men were already moving forward. "That's right, spill the cans over these vermin! I'm in command here!"

The SS lieutenant called over from the far side of the pit, the floodlights barely framing his shape in the chill grayness.

"You have no actual authority here, Herr Reichsleiter," he pointed out.

"I'll show you authority when Himmler arrives, my friend!" was the retort. "Read your belt buckle. I represent National Socialist authority." He'd just reached the impassive sergeant who stood with his arms behind his back. "Well?" Rosenberg demanded. "Well?" *We're almost out of time*.

Most of the soldiers were now joining in with the Tibetans as the victims stirred and feebly struggled, wept, and cried out, the fog blending, melting, fading the writhing, bony, contorted struggles . . .

"What can you possibly threaten me with?" wondered the SS sergeant.

"You'll soon see."

"Will I? It's all over, you know. We'll all be dead soon enough." He shut his eyes. "I've done enough horrors, up to now."

Rosenberg's eyes seemed all whites.

"Disloyal, defeatist swine!" Panted, held his chest where a sudden pain ripped, and he half-staggered to the edge of the mass grave and raised his arms over his head. The Tibetans all held lit torches now. Spaced themselves from one end to the other. The last in the row were reddish stains in the blur, receding and returning as the vapor boiled past.

The sergeant was suddenly raging at Rosenberg's stooped back.

"Idiot," he cried, "that's not enough gasoline to—"

And broke off not because Rosenberg was shouting into the blanked-out sky, arms still upraised, but because the first alarm was blasting. He turned and groped into the virtually opaque night, halfway across the yard by the time the siren itself went off as the wan searchlights poked into the obscurity . . .

Hitler was opening the door to his room when Goebbels came down the corridor, the light fading and coming back . . . fading and coming back . . .

"My Führer," he said, voice a little too strident.

Hitler waited, one hand on the knob. Vague hopes of news, of some undefined possibilities, kept him there. How many times had the doctor come up with the incisive idea, the practical suggestion that saved the day . . . not like that disloyal daydreamer Himmler, for example. Yes, his mind was suddenly sharper. Yes . . . while he was, of course, ready to die, perhaps a turn of fortune was in the offing.

"Doctor," he said, trying a smile, except the cripple's voice was too tense and he knew it.

"My Führer, I salute—"

"Any news?"

Goebbels seemed puzzled. Blinked rapidly.

"News?" he wondered.

Hitler's eyes went dull again.

"Never mind," he grunted and opened the door.

"We're ready." Goebbels kept blinking, his slash mouth, jerking at a smile that never quite formed. As the bunker shook under each impact and the light died and recovered his (to Hitler) sketchy shape seemed to sink and rise from the darkness.

"Ready?" Hitler repeated, holding the knob.

"For the ceremony."

"Ceremony?"

"Yes."

Then he remembered: the young heroes.

"Now?" Sighed. Shut his eyes as the propaganda minister dropped into darkness again. Well, he wouldn't think about anything else just yet. First the ceremony, then something to eat. There could always be new developments . . . at least he didn't have to think now. He nodded once. Felt decisive.

Give the young heroes their medals. The last blood in Germany. The last form for the last miracle to take . . .

(1944)
Climbing Back into Austria

Renga's breath seared his chest. The needle-sharp, snow-bright air dazzled among alpine abysses and angles. He scrambled through the late afternoon, skidding on the icy crust down a desperate tilt toward the distant, bluish-green valley.

He glanced back. Yes, they were still coming fast: three black dots on the long shock of slope above. He heard faint shots but again no impacts.

He'd tried, he'd tried . . . and the Italian police had been waiting in Milan. But he still kept the crumpled, water- and blood-stained papers and images that had poisoned his mind and (he now believed) the world too because the world was everyone's mind imagining and dreaming together . . . so he'd tried and they'd been waiting . . . at the cardinal's house they'd shot instantly and he'd fled through a garden of coppery cypresses and pale, cool statuary, leaping over banks of winter flowers and threads of stream. Ran up into the pine-dense mountain forests . . . he'd tried . . . remembered fainting in the monk's cart and the next thing was the cool, silent room, richly gold sunbeams streaming in the slit window overhead, seeming thick enough to touch in the sparkling dust. Remembered, as he fled, the round-faced, hairless abbot standing over him, holding the deadly documents and saying, almost crying out, that the Church wouldn't dare chance a German victory, even at this late date. So they'd do nothing.

"How cynical," he'd whispered, fiercely from the pillow.

The abbot had shut his eyes and stood there, hands just trembling, rattling the papers.

"I shall send you to the cardinal."

"Yes?"

"And he will say no. You will beg him but he will say

no." The eyes had stayed shut. "I wish you had never come here, signóre."

"Yes . . . you could tear them to pieces."

"I'd have to tear my brain to pieces, in that case, too." The hands had just, barely, trembled.

He'd tried . . . climbed . . . hid . . . fled past mere pain and exhaustion because he was going back to haunt them with the ghosts and shadows of horror . . . if nothing else could haunt them. Because he hadn't yet realized what he really meant to do. Couldn't have faced it yet . . .

Now, crossing the treeline, snow sprayed in bright chippings, and he heard the hum of richochets this time. Spurted ahead, too fast, and knew it was too fast but they had the range, the next burst chipping sunsparkles around his feet . . . and then the mountain tilt spun and reversed itself . . . he clutched void . . . heard the schussing as he pinwheeled and rolled, accelerating past the spare, dark trees and juts of rock . . . then he relaxed, let go of everything as when he toppled through the sun-shimmered blossoms out of the monk's wagon. Let go like a thrilled child, sailed, cushioned past all harm, through the crystal flashing and beyond the reeling sun . . . too much speed . . . too much space . . . flashing while velocity blanked everything and, as into a dark dreaming, he plunged into bottom and blackness and the greenish-stone world, saw the wizard before the bilious egg, enraptured by the burning lights that seemed to beat and show the skullbones and fiery brain within and Renga felt the force that was dissolving the wall between worlds. And then Renga was sucked close until all space was filled with the towering terror of his dreams, the many-headed, gnashing horror . . . and then he was screaming it all away, scream-ing himself back into the icy twilight where he now lay deep in a snowbank where (he didn't see) the Gypsy wagons were already stopped and someone was slogging across the snowshadows toward him . . .

LXI
(1944)
GHQ in Prussia

The late afternoon sun angled in the open windows and lay bright and fuzzy on the maps where Hitler and the generals stood.

His head hurt. Eyes, really. He toyed with his glasses, then removed them, half-listening to some field marshal's dreary recital. He squinted at the blurred colors and lines on the maps. There had to be a way to rip them open, to crack the enemy. Tried to imagine the stroke, the breach, the irresistible, contorted violence whose external form was panzers and flooding troops . . . the map seemed to fill into solidity . . . the glasses glittered in his hand. The generals were waiting because the report was finished. The Führer stared . . . looked out the window, his mind drifted . . .

He turned and took a step away from the table and then there was a gigantic slap-impact of silence and pressure: he floated, sailed, ascended . . . for some vivid hiatus in all time and space he felt the whole earth melt into mist and bend. All the nations wavered, resisted; lost and regained shape within the infinite hollow of himself.

And next the shattered building was silently raining down all around him in masses of smoke over the shocked, ripped, seared, and twisted men, and as he drove himself upright, in ballooned and burned-away pants and shirts, not feeling the pain yet, his first thought was:

A miracle, a miracle! I've been saved! They tried to kill me again and I've been saved!

The first of the guards who reached the spot saw the Führer, his hacked, bloodied hands gripped fiercely before him, staring up out of choking smoke at the clear sky, eyes wide, looking as though he'd just had word of a great victory . . .

(1945)
At the Death Camp

The duke was peering up through the swirling fog at the stilt-legged guard tower that seemed to stride forward as the gray billows swept past.

"*Foul giant,*" he cried, "*tell thy fell master I am come to slay him!*"

"Hey," Astuti called over the siren-scream, trying to locate him, "where the fuck are you?"

"And put out thy flaming eyes!" Astuti heard to his right and circled that way, gun leveled. Someone blurred past, dark, yelling in German. Other voices took it up. The searchlights were blocked and swallowed into indistinct shiftings. And then there was the knight in flopping houserobe and gleaming chain mail taking terrific chops out of the log legs of the tower, shaking the whole structure with each blow, crying "Enchant as thou wills't, I shall hew thee down."

In fact, noted Astuti, he was nearly through the support—and then it cracked sharply and sagged.

"Hey," yelled the American, "lets get outta here! *Let's go!*"

But the duke was already at the next support. A machine gun overhead fired blindly into the swirling opacity. Voices and shots cracked all around. A pair of shapes groped into shadowy sight. Astuti fired at the mushroom helmets and they were suddenly gone. He might have hit one.

"Thy great howls will avail thee naught!" the duke flung defiance at the siren as he hacked through the next leg and then the tower went over, wood shrieking, nails popping, machine gun spitting . . . lights . . . raving alarm . . . all the way to the ground where it invisibly hit in a billow of chaos . . .

"Holy shit," the American said, trying to drag the knight away.

"Nay, hold off thy hand," commanded the duke. The

lean face was burning with fury. "I sense the evil near. I will close with it though hell itself should gape!" He rushed into the fog, the soldier at his heels. "Show thyself, wizard! Thy hour is come!"

"Wait up!" yelled Astuti, because having come this far there wasn't even a choice anymore. A shape ducked near them waving a burp gun.

"Halt!" it cried. "Over here! Here!"

Astuti rolled aside and shot wildly as the German missed him too and then the fog closed again. He was instantly alone, groping for his companion . . . he moved toward a general, rosy luminescence that he hoped might be the sunrise. He'd worked out that this was a prison camp and had vague ideas about just surrendering and waiting for the army to catch up, except everybody was shooting all the time . . . a pair of helmet-headed shapes passed . . . the sirens still moaned . . . something hit him, stars flashed as he rebounded to his knees, then realized he'd run into the side of what had to be a barracks.

He got up and moved, parallel to it, toward the glow and dense shouting and outcry. Screams and shots too.

His Majesty must be among'm from what I hear, he thought.

He peered in a slit window. Saw just dark.

"Hey," he called in, cautiously, "any Americans in there?" Nothing. He moved on past the end of the building . . .

Rosenberg stood with arms lifted in a great V over the packed victims, the wild mists prowling past the Orientals with their thin torches, waiting, appearing, fading, as the leader cried out:

"O lord of blood! O lord of blood! O lord of blood! Strike down those named in my inmost heart! Strike . . ."

There was commotion behind him. His eyes were rolled up, lips peeled back from gapped teeth. He heard nothing, not even when the sirens went off and some of the SS were instantly running back into the blotted-out prison yard.

Burly Sergeant Höss, jaw set in grim outrage, could stand no more: he snatched the nearest Oriental by the collar and ripped his torch from his hands.

"Enough is enough, you yellow swine!" he snarled.

Which seemed a signal because the remaining four

glanced at one another after staring out of the ritual long enough to take in the developing chaos, just as a hoarse, muffled shout sounded out in the mist followed by a long burp-gun burst (aimed at Astuti, in fact):

"The Americans! The Americans are here! . . . They're here! . . ."

And, even as Rosenberg raged and waved his arms, leaping to grapple with Höss, the Tibetan gentlemen, as one, ducked away into the fuming mist. Their torches were visible for a few steps until they tossed them away. The troops all scattered, either running for their lives or to fight. Except for Höss, because Rosenberg had him by the neck, clutching it in a spasm of fury.

"You filthy dog!" he howled, foaming with hate. "You're destroying everything! . . . everything! . . ." Clinging as the powerful soldier smashed at his head with his free hand, then with the torchbutt too as the little man bit him in the neck. People were now crawling and leaping out of the pit, helping one another, heading into the vaporous obscurity. While the party philosopher, teeth stained with the agonized sergeant's blood, screamed:

"The Jews! The Jews are getting away!"

And then the desperate and terrified guard pushed himself arm's length back, ripping the frenzied grip from his neck, his blows ineffectual against the maddened man. Then he smashed him with the flaming wooden torch, which snapped in two and dropped Rosenberg to his knees (Höss was already running, side by side with the few dozen victims who'd already gotten clear) as the flaming half arced up, end over end, and dropped into the gas-soaked mound of struggling flesh and blood. The flames instantly whoosh-boomed, shook air and ground: scorched reek, crackling hiss, screams, frenzy . . .

What no longer knew it was Kurt Fragtkopft was twisted upside down deep in the press of flesh, in the choking air and stink. He was talking constantly, clawing and wriggling deeper, seeing her just ahead, walking on a silver-green lawn past water-cool, twilight trees by a low garden wall, and he kept calling her name, Minna, Minna . . . just a moment more and he'd touch her . . . had to . . . just a moment more . . . and then the name was gone too and there was just the need . . . and the next water-soft landscape melted like a dewdrop and there was pain and pain beyond pain, ripping teeth, nails, and burning . . . burning . . . and he howled with the great howling and was tilted up by the immense struggle while demons wailed and human voices shattered into glassy screams and broken prayers and wordless outrage. His flesh hissed, body flailed, spasmed through the more fragile ones, all climbing, leaping, flopping, rolling, and then he was on top, wading, staggering over the convulsive, dying heap. In the fire and fog, roasting beings writhed from the edges of the pit, fell back, searing in hideous smoke and flaming screams. His uniform roared; hair crackled in his ears as his blasted limbs clawed to the top of the pile again and then sank him knee-deep, falling, hopping, treading on heads, faces, shoulders, backs. He was empty now of all but suffering and the blind body, fleeing through the roar of his own combustion among the other animate torches . . .

"My God," cried the SS lieutenant to a guard, "what the devil's happening?"

They were groping with leveled guns, peering into the flap and swirling all around.

As if produced in a magic trick by jerking a curtain aside, an SS man reeled past them, clutching his belly where what at first seemed tangled ropes hung and trailed under his feet, his eyes shocked wild.

"My God," the officer said as the man fell and the soldier stooped beside him.

"He's been ripped open, sir," he said, "like a gutted pig."

A bubbling scream and they whirled. Strained to see into the wet, blinding opacity.

"A . . . demon," croaked the man lying in his spilled entrails. ". . . there's a demon . . ."

"What's he saying?" the officer demanded.

"It's no bayonet wound," the other said, "—he's almost cut in half."

The floodlights were vague, grayish-shifting translucence. The two of them now moved slowly, almost back to back.

"Where did this damned fog come from so fast?" the officer wondered, pointlessly. "First those party maniacs and the damned Chinamen . . . in uniform, to boot . . ."

"Maybe," said the soldier, "they're a new type of Aryan."

"What pig-doings!" He strained to listen over the endless, painful siren dinning. "Did you see the commandant anywhere?"

"No, sir. I was busy with the prisoners."

"This is insane . . ." He spun left where shots sputtered in the deceptive blankness.

"You can't kill them with gasoline like that," the soldier was saying. "How stupid can you get?"

"The great Rosenberg . . . His book made no sense to me . . ." Groped at the fog. "I've never seen muck like this . . ."

"The barracks must be this way, sir."

"Do you have a compass on your backside, eh, Hoffman? I have no idea where anything is . . ."

"It's the British commandos."

"Take heart. They can't see us either."

"What a way to get rid of prisoners," muttered the soldier. "As if we don't know our own business here . . . I think—"

Shadowy movement ahead, and they crouched, guns ready. The siren brayed in metal pain. Hoffman was suddenly tottering and the officer wondered, abstractly, how he'd managed to duck his head so far down between his shoulders though his senses and gripped stomach already knew it was gone, even before the rest of him pitched backward and was lost in the glistening wall . . .

LXII
(LATE WINTER 1944)

Renga sat close to the fire which guttered and billowed as the snow wind rattled and shook the circle of wagons. The gypsies were huddled around the big kettle. Some children fought with snowballs under the dense pine trees. Horses were bedded down nearby. The flames were gradually changing from color to light as the day ended.

The chief sat beside him on the same log, sipping his terrifically spiced soup. His dark hair and mustache were flecked with metallic gray. Guerna, the chief, liked him. They were keeping out of the way, he'd said, while the outsiders killed themselves off. Renga had wheezed and coughed in a wagon for a week, mildly feverish. Most of his strength was back now.

He was staring into the fire as Guerna said, in Italian:

"It's not too wise, my friend, to go north. Wait for them to stop fighting."

"No sense."

"Eh?" The older man watched him with grayish eyes from the dark hook of his face.

"I have to find my wife."

"Didn't you say she was dead?"

"I cannot be sure." Rubbed his cold-reddened face. Why was he going to Germany? He knew he'd have to face it soon. As if something were whispering in his ear while he slept, *go back, go back* . . . because he'd jerk awake soaked in chill sweat, almost hearing it . . . except there would be only the sounds of the camp: coughs, an infant crying, the rush of wind or clitter of snowfall outside the tent.

"Ah, did Mayaska . . ." The chief squinted one eye at the lean-faced professor. Mayaska, his wife, raised her seamed, taciturn face and said nothing, her hands working a long needle through a furred vest, across the fire.

"Yes," Renga said, "she looked at my hand."

"You think Gypsies are fakers?" The chief sucked his yellowed, gapped teeth. "Eh?"

Renga shook his head.

"Some have the gift," he said, "some do not."

"That's good," agreed the big man. "That's the truth. What did she tell you?"

"She seemed surprised by something," Renga said, shrugging.

"That's right. She was. That's maybe why you got to stay here. Ain't you worried?"

"I've got nothing to worry about."

"You got your skin."

Renga stared at the fire, the flames flailing and

breaking off around the pot with each hollow suck and heave of the wind.

"My skin?" Renga repeated.

"Life is all a man has," the Gypsy said. Scratched himself under his woolens.

"No," said Renga, "it's all a man doesn't have."

The big man grunted. His wife was watching them across the fire, her face set like stone. Renga grinned at her.

"I am going to be killed soon," he said to her, "that's what you saw."

"You suffer, my friend," said the chief. "Drink the sweetness, digest the bitter. That's all we have in this world. And in the other worlds too." Slurped at a steaming bowl of soup. "The death and the dreaming. Take each one and then let each one go." Slurped.

"That's what you saw," Renga said into the leathery, rippled female face where the dark eyes showed nothing at all. She didn't speak. "I don't mind being killed so much," he said on, "but I think it's going to be much worse than that."

Eunice had never looked back at Dorian when the soldiers dragged her out of the car. They'd chopped him to pieces when he raised his gun. Now she knew he'd been lucky, after months of cells, camps, pain, and outrage . . . She wished, more than once, they'd have shot her, because life clung to life even in the bleak hell she'd finally arrived at, after being packed in a boxcar with hundreds of others for a nearly endless season in stink and filth until they were hearded out somewhere that was like everywhere else in a gray, seething downpour behind barbed wire among the others who also were shaved bald and shivered in the muck: the world was reduced to sufferers and the others, nothing else . . .

She made no effort to remember. Sometimes there were images or thoughts from the past, but they had no force. She was wept out. She had slogged through the days and night, always hungry, always hurting, until even shock had become ordinary and all the faces were the same: the captors with their remote, frightened cruelty; the captives showing almost nothing but gray weariness . . .

She was shipped, reshipped, and people died in their sleep, were shot, or they vanished, and everyone knew what happened and said almost nothing because words were too brittle and broke . . .

And then the night she sensed was the end, driven into the foggy yard, naked this time (which always meant death), only asking herself why it had to be so dragged out . . . because she now believed the camps covered the earth, that beyond the wire there was more wire in a universal, bleak darkness with only guards and the guarded . . .

She stared into the bitter vision that shaped itself in the vapors, not really looking at the middle-aged SS officer who seemed to be talking up ahead with one of the victims. A woman victim. She didn't listen but the voices brought something back . . . a flicker of something . . .

And the man was yelling and the woman's wasted profile stood out against the fog-blurred floodlights: a ghost, she thought, or hallucination or . . . but the distinctions were absurd because the woman was moving, running, fading into the mists as the SS man grabbed at her, missed, and Eunice suddenly felt a rush of strength pour through her tentative limbs and she staggered along into the officer's wake (she never even looked at him because he was a captor), forcing herself through the thickening crowd near the pit, crying out in a murmur, a ghost voice in the misty phantom world as she chased a long-lost image into the open mouth of hell before she fell and rolled and was tangled among the other wraiths, still mouthing:

"Minna . . . Minna . . . Minna . . ."

LXIII
(1945)
At the Death Camp

Thank thee O Lord, prayed the duke, *for concealing me from my enemies . . .* Because he moved with total certainty, feeling, as he'd been guided so far, he'd not be neglected at the end of his mission through this magical world. He believed that when he finally struck down the sorcerous lord, the spell would shatter and leave him free back in his own home country—with quite a tale to tell.

A black form appeared, wildly waving what he didn't know was a burp gun, chewing the air with a long burst that veered wild as, *snic snic,* the broadsword snapped into the man who fell, bone shatters poking from massive rents, screaming, into the siren wail in terrible shudders.

"Thy spells avail thee little, dark ones," the knight exulted.

Went on into the wet, blank chill vapors toward a new commotion and the edgeless rosy glow Astuti had taken for dawn but which he knew had to be hellfire that rose to embellish and sustain the dark master's throne. *"I come!"* he called over the wail and shouting and gushing flame-roar. *"I come!"*

Then, for a blink-space, Renga was back, staring wildly around, believing himself blinded, and then was gone back into the green-glowing underworld, where he was nude, forcing himself to climb the stone steps that circled the outside of the tower.

His feet were past pain now. He knew if he stopped walking they'd stiffen and cripple him. The blood was clotting.

He had climbed well ahead of the queen and the boy now.

* * *

Far above, near the surface, just having entered the fortress itself, General Rog and his Skull warriors regained their accustomed arrogance. Rog led them up a tilted corridor into the great battle hall where Relti (and the kings before him) had given speeches to the army leaders.

"Our task," the massive (for his race) general was saying to his intense, sharp-featured captain, "is to see to things up here. We will make ready for our master's return."

"Yes, my lord," the soldier agreed, squinting around the huge, vaulted hall draped with a thousand legionary banners, "but what if—"

He broke off because there was movement, a tinkling shuffling sound, among the thin pillars that made a forest of the floor. They all padded over, quick, silent, alert. Ran into about two dozen men, boys, girls, and women, all wearing loose, coarse, dark green robes, barefoot, a silver flicker at each ankle.

"You, slaves," Rog commanded, "halt!"

Most stopped reflexively, some didn't, and they milled and tripped themselves into an indecisive herd. The chains that should have linked the ankle bands were hanging loose and clinked on the pavement.

A young man and long-haired girl started to run for the shadows. Without a word (because it was understood no one ran), two soldiers whipped away a dagger each that hit so hard the couple was knocked flat. The male took it in the side of the head and died at once; the girl, hit in the neck, wilted but made noises for a while.

The rest of the slaves huddled together now.

"You were dressed for sacrifice," the captain observed. "How did you escape?"

A defiant, frightened middle-aged man with pale eyes proving him an outlander answered:

"We were freed."

"Hah," said Rog. "By what authority?"

"Where have you been, Lord General?" a thin woman said dully. "The city has fallen. Relti is no more. The children of the light—"

"Blaspheming bitch," the captain snarled. "Silence!"

"What's this?" wondered Rog. "What's this?"

"Lies," said the captain. "The city can never fall to those weak—"

"Hush," commanded the general. Frowned. Licked his lips. "It is no doubt true. We will have to come to terms with the new rulers."

"But, Lord General," protested the captain, "the master will return in a rage—"

Rog sweated and tapped the hilt of his undrawn dagger. The two warriors were retrieving their daggers from the bodies. Rog shook his head. The slaves or ex-slaves just watched them now.

"It is madness," he said. "He is lost. He will never be back. Our world is ended. Greatness is undone. I would weep but we do not weep. We will, instead, live and seek vengeance. Yes. We will bide our time and, in the end, strike in vengeance."

By the time Ner reached the flat roof of the tower, Relti was standing partly under the curve of the huge semitransparent emerald egg where the tremendous, dark, shadowy, ancient dreamer was stretched out in hibernative slumber.

Ner staggered and swayed on his agonized feet, chipped sword dragging his right arm down to his side. In the murky illumination (mainly from the surface of the imprisoning jewel substance), he tried to take in the scene through a wind that was not air, an unfelt wind that blew the mass of coiling and uncoiling snakelike single-horned heads that seemed to be growing from Relti's back, the heads that seemed to shudder, joyous, in the presense of the winged giant.

Ner, grimaced, shocked, seeing his brother's massive head dragged down by the weight of solid metal that filled the skull like melted wax in a socket. He had to hold his nerves at the sight of the stone heart in the ripped-out chest, throbbing in dull, coal-like fire. Had to accept the outsized metal hand that was reaching back in a fist to crack the crystal shell that had been (he knew from secret studies) formed by the impact of the defeated, fallen lord on the depths of the (then) still-smoldering world . . .

Relti half-turned, recognizing his brother, smiling, bobbing the weight of skull so that he appeared to be pondering his feet. The snake-heads seemed to hiss and glare, each horn glinting with menace.

Ner squinted to block out as much of the strangeness

as possible. Raised the sword. Moved forward. There would be no discussion, no reasoning with the thing his brother had become. He expected to die. Hoped, vaguely, leaning as if against the unnatural gale that swirled there, that they would both die. That would be enough. That would be a blessing . . .

LXIV
At the Bunker

I cannot grasp how the British and Americans can fail to see the Red menace . . . Stalin will chew up Europe, the British empire will fall to pieces . . . This war has drained them dry . . .

Hitler limped down the corridor and turned into the strategy room where the last generals stood around the map under the hooded light that splashed downward and cut their bodies off between belt and heart.

He stood blinking, not bothering to put on his glasses. What was there left to focus on? He faced silhouettes and glare. Kept his aberrant left arm close to his side where it jerked rhythmlessly. *How can they be so stupid?* he went on asking himself. His lips moved occasionally.

"My Führer," someone (he didn't bother to identify as Field Marshal Jodl) said. Others murmured greetings. He didn't respond. The Allies were madmen! *Must every savior be destroyed by blind malice?* . . . Stood still in the doorway, not focusing.

"Führer, I—" Keitel began, grave, doomed.

"I gave everything," Hitler rasped at the glare and shadows, at the silence flooding around them and the distant shell thuds. Gritted his teeth, with vacant fury. "You were all too weak." Hunched unevenly to the map table. "I kept myself from corruption . . . I have all . . . but the German people were not fit for this destiny . . ." Stared down without focus at the outlines of a shrunken dream, slashed and punctured with grease-pencil arrows, strangled by numbers and X's, crushed to a few broken tracings and lost abstractions, as the light swayed and dimmed and came back. After a long, flickering silence, he spoke again: "Well, is there nothing to report?" As if, Keitel thought, this were not the present. "What about Wenck's army? Hm?"

"No word, my Führer."

Hitler made a grimace that no one there knew was a smile. Then a sound no one took for laughing.

"What a surprise," he said. Then silence; echoing, ringing booms and failing light. "I dismiss you," he finally said. Shuffled from the room. Paused at the door. His voice was suddenly strong again: "Save yourselves, if you can. What we have begun is *not* finished. Don't imagine otherwise. My death is not the end!"

He went away down the gray-green corridor. He'd left the door standing open, so Keitel watched him stooping along in spasms until the jamb cut him from view.

"What now?" someone asked.

"What's the difference?" another answered.

"I forgot to congratulate him on his marriage," said a third officer.

"Oh, shut up," said lanky General Jodl. "He did his best."

"Best what?" interjected the first.

"We better have dignity," Keitel advised, still staring into the empty stone tunnel. "That's what we're going to get to keep."

Was that all? he was wondering, just a final parasenile outburst and a last limp to oblivion? Was that all there was?

"Dismissed," he whispered. There was no way to wake up, nowhere to run to . . . suddenly nothing, an empty world, no way to just take off his uniform and go home and sleep . . . no home to go to, anyway . . . "We're dismissed."

Himmler stood indecisively under a line of pine trees. His faint mustache was shaved away. He wore a black eyepatch. He wondered if it made him look like a pirate . . . Actually, one man had noticed that his features were so bland that simply removing his glasses was an excellent disguise . . . The rain sheeted steadily down over the flat, open countryside, sinking the world into pale gray mist.

Puddles in the road frothed mud and bubbles. In the distance shellfire rumbled like unbroken thunder.

The black Mercedes was dead. The young, pale, blond driver straightened up in despair from the open hood. His hair was plastered flat along his bare head.

Two officers in civilian clothes, Stein and Müller, stood beside Himmler who was staring acoss the empty fields.

"We'll have to walk," Stein said.

"How far?" the Reichsführer asked tensely, biting his lower lip.

Stein shurgged. He was short, wide-shouldered.

"Hard to say," he commented. "Once we're through the American lines we'll have to obtain another car and drive to the coast."

"Yes, I see." Himmler didn't look right or left. His glasses were misted over as he stared into the focusless world.

"We'll have to get out of these uniforms," Müller pointed out, already starting to strip down. Himmler was vaguely thinking that in civilian clothes he might not be taken seriously by the Allies, if captured. He had a misty idea of talking man to man with Eisenhower. Tried to decide whether he would simply click his heels and salute, or bow—perhaps both. Yes . . . "I take full responsibility for my men, Herr General," he would say . . .

He sighed and nodded. Stein was rummaging in a duffel bag, pulling out mismatched clothing.

"Shit," he said, "who collected these rags, anyway?"

"What did you expect?" wondered tall, ridge-faced Müller. "We were one step ahead of Ivan."

Himmler kept his hands motionless at his sides. The rain beaded on his cap and rippled down his dead-white cheeks. His blank glasses were an eyeless stare.

"Shit," said Stein as the young driver came up to them, looking nervous and disgusted, wiping his greasy hands on his black pants. "There's nothing here to fit the Reichsführer." They were tossing and snatching up garments like women at a sale. Stein peered at the blond young man.

"It's no good, sir," the fellow said. "The bearings are finished."

"Spare me details," Stein said. He held up a dress and bonnet. "This will serve."

"Serve what?" Müller wondered, rubbing his long chin.

But Stein was already holding the flower-print up to his leader with a cocked, appraising eye.

"It's you, Herr Reichsführer," he said, grinning.

"But," protested the young blood, "you cannot expect—"

"The Reichsführer's safety is of far more consequence than superficial dignity," Stein snapped. Grinned. Winked at Müller, peered into the blank gray glasses that framed the dripping, colorless, expressionless features. "Correct, sir?" And Himmler just nodded, once. Hands stayed pale and still at his sides. "Let me help you, sir." Stein was already working at the uniform buttons.

"Sir," asked the young man, "we were betrayed at every turn, weren't we?"

The coat and cap were gone. Stein set the round-rimmed bonnet on the close-cropped head, then freed the belt and dropped the trousers and knelt to free the soft, gleaming black boots.

"Yes," Himmler murmured. *Something went wrong*, he kept thinking, *something went wrong*, until it became words and Stein almost smiled.

"An astute analysis," he commented, getting the second boot off while Müller helped the leader keep his balance.

"Be quiet, can't you?" Müller wondered.

Himmler's droopy shorts and bony knees were now covered by the floppy dress that Stein buttoned up the back, wet, chilled fingers struggling.

The grayness stirred slightly, billowed into partial shapes for a moment. Himmler, as they fitted on the heeled pumps, said:

"There's still a last hope."

"Yes, sir?" wondered the young noncom, eyes sleeplessly bright.

"Sure," said Stein, "—that the Reds and the Yankees will get bored and go home."

"Watch what you say," Müller snapped. "We're still SS men and Heinrich Himmler is still Reichsführer."

"Except there's no more Reich left."

They were all dressed in baggy, mismatched outfits now: Stein wore a red checked shirt and short pants;

Müller, a dark suit; and the young man, an overcoat that hit his heels. Stein took off his leader's glasses. Then the eyepatch.

They started glopping along the muddy, trafficless road lined with broken, burnt-out, twisted junk iron and steel. Here and there a tank still smoldered . . . a shattered truck . . . the bones of a farmhouse . . . snapped telephones lines and trees . . . hundreds of craters in the soaked, steaming earth. And the smell of damp death.

Himmler wasn't really listening. He followed, with nudges and a hand now and then when he wandered toward the ditch or half-lost a shoe in the muck. He followed shapes without dimension or detail in his blurred vision's gray flatness. Movements vaguer than shadows on the blank sheet of the world . . .

But safely within his brain there was sharp focus: he saw the pit, the pyre flames ascending, heard the clear, superhuman cries gathering potency, spearing up like flame. As the great, avenging form took shape from fire, death, and wind, eyes like supernatural searchlights, in chill fury stretching his steel hands, leaping into the sky from the magical pit where the sacrificial victims had their souls sucked into invisible blazing (while the bodies crackled to ashes) . . . soaring, riding to storm and descending in ineffable terror: pictured Stalin, sitting at his desk, looking up as the pitiless, magnificent being tore out his mind with one clawed hand . . . then on to the others one by one, all the wormlike betrayers of glory . . . finally, alighting before his resigned, loyal, and lonely disciple, poor Heinrich being led in gray blindness like ruined Oedipus, through the shattered wasteland, staggering through the muck . . . embracing him . . . embracing him . . .

He smiled, a hint. He was unaware, as he watched these inner wonders, that they'd just entered a smashed village. He paid no attention to the sudden whine and grind of oncoming tanks. He didn't focus on Stein and Müller yelling at one another or see beyond the gray shifting. The pale blond young soldier was already running past the first crumpled house into the boggy fields. The tanks came in single file down the center of the street.

He smiled because the ineffable figure was already here, the giant hands in clubfists, smashing the enemy's

brittle weapons, tearing, flinging, crushing, trampling
. . . trampling . . . trampling . . .

Paid no attention as they dragged him to the side of
the road to let the screaming steel monsters slosh massively
past. Paid no attention because he was watching Stalin
scream and burst to bloody pulp, spattering the papered
walls with his squashed self in the clawed grip . . . then
Churchill, fleeing fatly down the Parliament steps, meeting
the terrible fist, left smashed and runny on the stone . . .

In the raving of the tank treads he heard the doom of
the world and shouted, suddenly:

"Victory! Victory! It walks among us! It stalks the
earth!" They were each on a side, locking his arms, walking
him past the slogging, weary, incurious Americans while his
reedy, high, penetrating voice raged: "The power of the
Jews is at an end! The power of the—"

Stein was shaking him.

"Be still, goddammit! Be still!"

His heart sank next, aware through the grayness of the
brown uniforms under a half-broken archway, just out of
the drizzle.

"—at an end! The Aryan spirit is freed forever!"

"Shut your damned mouth!" Stein raged, shaking him
in violent despair, then shoving him so that he staggered in
the baggy dress, lost a shoe, bonnet tilting over his
eyes . . .

LXV
(1944–45)

There was always snow and walking. Hills, valleys, frozen
rivers . . . walking . . . sleeping in broken buildings
. . . hayricks . . . munching sparingly the dried food the
Gypsies had wrapped in sacking . . . long, long days of
blank white expanses and stinging snow . . . he sensed, as
he gradually fasted into leathery leanness, this was prepar-

ing him, toughening, tightening . . . because he went for long, white stretches now without a single thought stirring, as if the chill silence was entering into him.

He ducked aside when he saw human movement; the frozen dead he crunched past as a matter of course: the heads, hands, reaching from the drifts; endlessly ripped, battered, and piecemeal human litter in the wake of the great armies he followed through the vastly effacing snow.

He seemed, more and more, to sleep without dreams, waking in iron mornings, crossing gray, chill afternoons into hollow, faintly luminescent evenings. His brain simply held images of each day and night and he numbered none of them. He hadn't actually forgotten his purpose, he simply didn't have to remember it. He strangely felt that the cold had somehow replaced his blood and flesh and left him relentless, indestructible . . .

At some point he found himself crossing and following a wildly twisting road through dense pine and rock country, country he almost recalled (as if from another lifetime) because he'd fought there in 1916 when the German and French armies hammered hopelessly at one another in the crisscross Ardennes forests. He was walking through the outskirts and grinding down of what had already been named the Battle of the Bulge. He worked his way through the American lines, and somewhere behind the actual, sputtering combats he lost momentum like a spent sprinter and lay in a drafty deserted barn . . . lay for uncounted time as bright and dim and dark showed at the interstices of board and sagged door . . . and then rain . . . warmer air . . . new clean smells . . . and he was out of food and it was spring . . .

Went out into morning brightness and started across the new green and yellow-blue spring-scatters, pausing to watch a farmer jerk his plough behind a weaving mule, then noticing the fine, light dust on the horizon and registered the roaring of trucks and tanks moving steadily north, and in the strange thawing of his body and spirit he understood what he'd been blocking out for so long: that he hadn't come looking for his wife at all . . .

He was toughened to pure stone in his center. The future was lost behind a wall of flame and darkness and the past was frozen away forever. He wasn't afraid anymore.

He even let himself think from time to time, working his way, by moonlight, past sentries, tents, parked tanks and cannon, all the immense paraphernalia. Finally, before dawn, reaching the edge of a forest, mysteriously sensing the other army across the pale valley. Paused, letting himself think again, careful, almost sipping at it . . .

What do I do next?

Because the fear really was gone. And the pressure too. He was past going back. He'd stood in the garden and asked the night to open its edgeless door and so, he knew, it would. Sooner or later. He was relaxed because a man without a future relaxes.

A little later he walked out of the dark silence of the trees into Germany. He was starting to understand.

He can't escape me, he thought.

So he smiled as he walked, bearing the edgeless power with him, the power that could never strike a blow or be struck either . . . no future . . . no past . . . just unending, unresisting, infinitely supple movement . . .

LXVI
(1945)
At the Death Camp

The camp guards had panicked. The wind had shifted and the fog was now billowing full of oily, biting smoke from the blazing gasoline and charring, bubbling flesh. They reeled and crept and froze too, blinded, shooting in spasms into blankness.

Head throbbing from the blows, Rosenberg backed up along the flaming pit where there was a thin strip of footing—where the full horror erupted as the mass of hideously tormented bodies heaved and struggled, crawled and twisted, leaped, danced, and rolled. Rosenberg found himself suddenly surrounded. Backed, then scurried into solid mist, dodging the smoking, seared phantoms that flailed, hobbled past—and into him too—howling, and he howled himself, old man's body beating with blood and failing.

Skin boiled loose and flapping, what had been Commandant Kurt Fragtkopft jerked and twisted, babbling, tripping over distorted limbs, wobbling upright, walking on heads, fleeing past even shock or terror . . .

The lean knight was surrounded by screams, feeling the stinging pressure of half-seen flames as a many-headed black shape lunged at him with the fire-spitting magic sticks he'd seen Astuti use to chop men down. He slashed at them and the many heads became many men, and only one dissolved back into the choking opacity intact.

Stupid magic, he thought.

"Show thyself," he challenged in his German, blinking, squinting.

He stumbled into a naked woman on her hands and knees. She was bald, charred . . . than a sizzling man capered madly past, seemed to form and unform in blaze and smoke . . . others too . . . incredible . . .

And then there was Rudolph Renga again aghast as the blinding, stinking curtain drew away and he saw the glowing horror of the pit, heard the muffled cries from beneath the crisping tangle, the bubbling and boiling . . .

He lost all his breath at once. Some, who'd gotten free, still burning, reeled blindly back out of the fog wall that now lined the trench and toppled into the human embers again. Renga covered his eyes and was gone back to the top of the spire while the duke was shoving past the suffering shadows, sensing the enemy close-by . . . cut and shoved through the steaming chaos . . .

While Astuti wandered (he realized) in hopeless circles until, finally, blundering into the shorted-out barbed-wire fence. Then he stopped and sat down, gun across his knees, and waited. Stared at the wild flickers and shadows and hints.

"I hadda follow that screwball," he muttered.

One searchlight still futilely and faintly probed. The

unseen pyre crackled. Horrible sounds, cries, and shots all around.

"I'd fucking surrender if there was someone to fucking surrender to," he bitterly muttered.

(In the Bunker)

He didn't think about anything at all as he opened the steel door for Eva. He had no desire to speak. He concentrated on each painful, physical movement, like a machine that could suffer, grinding on to the end.

He followed her into the sitting room and didn't look back at the people in the corridor, the blank-eyed or weeping women, the semidrunk soldiers and functionaries. Shut the door as she sat down, kicked off her shoes, and tucked her smooth, plumpish feet under herself, like a young girl. She was just a blur to him. She started, and kept biting her lower lip. She didn't realize she was whispering to herself:

". . . so . . . so . . . hand in hand . . . hand in hand . . ."

His ruined sight dissolved the room into a greenish mist where the single lamp was a yellowish blot. He shuffled and stooped to his armchair and sat down, barely conscious of the action. The strange energy or presence was here. He sensed it, filling the featureless dead end.

He drifted away into the green. A witness without feeling now, to where the self that both was and was not him stood sidelong, half watching the naked, bloody, frightened warrior Ner approaching him across the parapet and half gazing into the satisfying, shifting images that flowed within the substance of the emerald egg, the dreams of the dreamer, scenes of its great fall, stricken near the sun, wobbling on ruined wings, dropping stunned into the reeling, smoking earth that opened in flame and fury to gather it into stone darkness where endless ages and the pressure of the world had sealed it until its struggles died fitfully into seamless sleep and unending memory that troubled all mankind's imperfect slumbers . . .

Witnessed without emotion as Relti, followed by the great, toadlike, bronze-looking creature (that had eaten off the top of his head), charged at his brother Ner, clawed metal hand upraised, eyes full of smoky fire, open chest

pulsing with stone power, swirling horned beast-heads
arching as if to strike, resisting the gusts of dark, unphysi-
cal wind.

Ner was trying to say something. Gave it up. Raised his
sword for one, last, hopeless stroke . . .

Hitler stared at the green steel wall across from his
chair. Watched the scenes play themselves out in the
moments while his hand adjusted the gun and he vaguely
prayed for a final miracle, the angel of the last moment, of
reprieve, of comfort, who would announce the miraculous
victory, not listening to Eva still whispering to herself like a
child . . .

"Kill him," he didn't know his lips were forming. "Oh,
kill him . . . kill him . . ."

LXVII
(1945)
Central Germany

The two British military policeman were uncertain. The
American noncom had just come into the shattered chapel
and seated himself on a massive gray building stone. He lit
a cigarette and blinked pale eyes under sandy brows in a
wide, freckled, elfin face. Stared at the three Germans, two
in bizarrely mismatched coats and suits, standing a little too
straight and tense to really be civilians. The young man
puffed along, shapeless clouds of smoke into the dim
chamber. The brass pipes of the organ facade tilted over
them. The rain dripped where the roof was broken apart
and bubbled at the glassless medieval window arches.

Above him was a giant, half-burned, water-soaked
tapestry that seemed to depict an archangel with flashing
sword smiting down horrors that spilled up from what
must have been the gaping pit to hell: malformed, demonic, massed, many-headed . . .

The American kept watching the pale woman whose

face haunted him and reminded him, he decided, of an anteater. She stood between the other two, lips moving continuously so that he imagined she might be saying silent prayers.

"Hullo, Yank," the British sergeant called over. "What do you make of this lot, then?" He was middle-aged, bald, uncomfortable-looking.

"Beats me," the American said, exhaling through his nose. Outside tanks and trucks wheezed and splashed past in an unending roar that dulled the whooshing rainfall. The woman's pale eyes were staring at him, he thought. He tilted his head appraisingly. The baggy dress covered most of the facts, he reflected. Most . . . The bloodless mouth was smiling at him. He had a sudden, sinking feeling she was flirting.

Except Himmler, without his glasses, really didn't see him. He was actually absorbed in studying the fuzzy shape where his misty vision had blended smoke and man together. The broken wall behind seemed the gateway to a vast, colorless void—otherwise a leaden, lowering sky.

Himmler felt he recognized the shape, gathering its bones from stirred cloudiness. He felt protected now. Confident. Smiled in not-quite-smug recognition. He was safe. They'd come for him. He sucked on the unbroken poison capsule he'd lodged between gum and cheek.

"Rub her face," the American suggested.

"Ah?" The sergeant glanced at his long-limbed comrade who was half-sitting on the cracked altar. The panels were illustrated, but fire had turned whatever scenes and figures there once had been into bubbled chaos and blank char. He idly toyed with a small, part-melted brass cross, tapping it meditatively on the wood. Shrugged at his bald countryman. One of the Germans was suddenly talking in English:

"Sirs," he was saying, "this is, I am certain, a painful mistake."

"Ah, then," said the bald sergeant, "you may be right there, me lad. You were a bit quiet up to now, hm?"

"Sort them bloody out," the long dour one suggested, pushing off from the altar, spinning the cross in his hand.

"We were, you see," the German, Stein, went on, "my sister home taking."

"Home taking, is it?" commented the sergeant, digging his pinky into his ear and popping it.

"Yes . . . We were from the Nazis running away."

"Ah. You been running hard from them right along, I don't wonder."

"Rub her cheek," the American repeated. "She was running so hard I bet she forgot to shave."

Himmler was squinting at the flickering gleam in the tall man's hand. It frightened him, for some reason. He looked for comfort back to the smoky figure who was moving, rising, seeming to form a pair of spectral wings. As he floated nearer, the helmetless young man's fire-blond hair showed like a soft halo and the eyes were like burning blue sky, the wings filling around him.

Himmler lunged spastically forward, losing the flowered bonnet, raising both hands in wild invocation and salute.

"O Lord of Glory!" he shrieked. "Know me! Know me!" Crashed to his knees. "I am Heinrich! I am King Heinrich!" The American stared down at him, cigarette pumping smoke past his handsome face.

"For God's sake!" yelled Stein, waving his too-long arms. "You insane coward!"

"Strike them down!" ordered Himmler, imploring the gold and blue vision looming above him with mysterious wings outspread. "Lord, I have prepared your coming! Defend me!" And then it was gone and the harsh gray illumination cleared his brain like an icy douche. He looked around in panic and despair, at the cold faces and terribly wrong uniforms. Shut his eyes and stayed on his knees, suddenly dulled and calm. It might have seemed, to someone just coming in, that a woman had been surprised in the ruined church at quiet prayer and contemplation.

There was no color in his mind. Felt nothing. Thought nothing. Didn't have to hear the British boots clacking over behind him or the midlands voice saying:

"Look at that bloody face. Look there, mate."

"Christ on a crutch," exclaimed the American in recognition too, "it's him, it's him."

But he wasn't listening, as if shut sight shut off sound too. Worked the smooth glass between his teeth. Left his mind gray. And without a wince of expression he bit down hard and didn't really feel his body lock: only the gray roaring filling all space and time, the roaring that wasn't just the passing tanks and droning bombers or in his ears or head either . . . the roar of dullness . . . yieldless, dreamless dullness.

(At the Pit's Edge)

Roaring fire beside him, the duke charged through the obscurity, passing the anguished stick figures that burned and glowed in the swirling depths, screaming and silent . . .

. . . for a few steps there was greenish darkness and a monstrously deformed humanlike creature smashing the sword from his grip with a huge, steely fist (the duke's consciousness fading like afterglow) and himself reeling back, throwing a punch at the head whose skull was steel, little bones snapping on impact, reeling back in blinding pain and despair, the great form of the sleeper looming behind in the crystalline gleaming egg like a fly in amber . . . a toad mouth full of teeth gaping at him, a nightmare of snakelike faces striking at his, hissing giggles of laughter from the thing he now recognized in both worlds: the bony, harsh, strained face, the set jaw, the Führer . . . then the claw-fingers smashed down across his collarbone and ripped the front of him irresistibly open. A spume of blood sprayed. The great voice was mocking him:

"I will replace your heart too. Your body will serve me forever, weakling bastard!"

. . . shock, flung violently back into the present, the duke was back in the blinding vapor. He moved along the pit's side like a wirewalker. The roasting shadows now moved only from volitionless shifting and swelling, gestured by combustion . . .

. . . Renga aware he was Renga and Ner too, torn and dying, wobbling back near the edge of the sheer tower as his transformed and terrible brother stood over him, the big metal hand bloodstained. The great voice that he'd

heard in person and on radio and from loudspeakers
crashing at him, hurting his head:

"I shall free the sleeper and the whole world will be
changed forever. My power will never end. Only gods will
survive to rule."

The scenes were flipping back and forth, accelerating
until the overlap was like eyeblinks so that he was all three
persons at once: Renga, Duke, and Ner the dying warrior.
So in his disaster and triumph he understood at last.
Understood how history and time could be squeezed into
one hand's grip.

Accelerating until the worlds melted together into one
vivid landscape of smoke-mist, flame, glowing stone, demons, and mortals . . . the scenes fused together as the
Duke and Renga and Ner fused too. It was one thing, one
gesture, one time, one space, a single hope and despair.
Chaos and terror rose from the smoldering pit, the tower
grew there, in that unspeakable prison, rose up sheer, the
egg gleamed, swarming with nightmares, glutting on pain
and madness. The dreams were smoke. Stifling . . .

And Hitler's face in front of him, gloating over him,
smoke and solid. The burning hand digging open his
breast again . . .

At the same moment, in the fog and smoke-stink of the
sacrificial pit, a flabby-faced little man stood waving his
arms as if he meant to fly. The composite warrior didn't
know Rosenberg, who was shouting, flabby cheeks popping
with fury under his glassy stare. Floated in the choking,
dimensionless haze, a scrawl of frenzy in a universe of
featureless violence. To the warrior's strange sight he was a
changing outline, puffing with dark terrors one moment,
shrunken to a pitiful, pale worm the next. The scenes had
fused so that the warrior stood at the edge of the
smoldering trench and simultaneously on top of the
pinnacle where Hitler's face glared out of the shapeless
confusion. He paid no attention to the flabby man's shouts.
The words were just noises:

"What is that idiotic getup?" Staring at the lean man in
the shreds of damp and battered armor, lumpy shoes, bare
calves, and a bit of tattered housecoat holding a wet-bright
sword. "What are you doing here?" Rosenberg backed
away along the lip of the hissing trench. "Lunatic, put down
that weapon! Don't you see who I am?" The siren still

screamed its pressure through the muffling gray that closed them in bleak intimacy.

The warrior was about to strike because the flabby man stood where the worlds churned together and the evil face was his too with the beast rising from his shoulders, Hitler's face forming and unforming from the depths of time and nightmare.

"Abomination!" he cried. Raising his sword to cut into the hated face he felt the great clawed fingers tearing through his chest as if it had reached through the insubstantial form of the flabby little Nazi. Because Ner was dying and so Renga and the Duke were dying. "Abomination, I know you!"

Rosenberg backed away in panic because it was now the moment to shout the sounds of power that he'd memorized at the feet of his master, Haushofer of the Thule Society. Time to shout the unwords from dream time that would crack the wall between the bright earth and black chaos and rain the bolts of darkness on their enemies. That was the purpose of the sacrifice: to unplug the pit and let the terror flap to the surface and smite and poison and dim and destroy . . .

He was breathless to shout the sounds. In ecstasy to let in the everlasting force of the night. Panicked that the moment might pass as he scuttled back into the choking fumes on the charnal pit's brink, locked in his mockery of prayer, and began the cry.

The first syllables broke, shrill, from his straining, swollen throat. The stinking smoke seemed to gather over him, brooding. The composite warrior perceived the force now rising from the agony in the pit. He made out the winged shape, the shadow of the sleeper vampirically thickened with suffering, rising to Rosenberg's piping shrieks.

The warrior understood the sounds. Saw the livid face of Relti-Hitler as he cracked the egg of hell on the tower-top at the same dream-time moment, ancient and present. The warrior watched the shadow rise on unfolding black wings above the wounded world, crying like a hunting hawk: *Victory! Victory! Victory!*

The warrior saw the pale golden light dying under the

pall of the world-wide wings. Stared at Rosenberg's puffy
face overlaid by Relti's and Hitler's smoky expressions and
cried out again:

"Abomination, I know you!"

He charged at the flabby man who, still screaming the
power sounds as if his very breath had taken his body over
and was pumping it empty, ducked away from the warrior's
downstroke, scurrying like an animal. The cut just touched
his mouth, leaving him with four bleeding lips.

The smoky fury billowed around him; the unhuman
sounds still poured out like frenzied oratory in a nightmare
with no meaning. Because the spell was broken. The
warrior knew that. The sounds didn't matter anymore
because the flabby body had run away. That body had been
the doorway for the power and it was too late as the
already-fading shadow struck a clawed spite blow at him.

He knew: Renga knew, the duke knew, Ner of Lemuria
knew—all one soul knew he'd won. He stood a moment,
sword at his side, listening (over all the other terrible
sounds) to the hideous bellowing voice of the mad, possessed Nazi Reichsleiter fading as he fled in terror through
the inpenetrable fumes, tripping over dead and dying,
careening off the barracks, doubled mouth spilling blood
under his hands . . .

The warrior knew and was satisfied. He'd stopped
them. He could rest at last. The shadow would melt in the
coming light. Nothing more mattered. Not revenge . . .
nothing. He could rest at last, in peace . . .

An instant later he saw the shadowy claws rip down.
And then, as if the smoke had thickened, a bony, blazing-
hot body crashed into him, veering along the pit-edge,
knocking his bent sword from his grip. Hard bones and
skull face; fleshless teeth seemed to chew at him. A
clacking, ripping voice (that he couldn't know was the last
babbling of Kurt Fragtkopft) scraped jumbled unwords
across his ears.

Fragtkopft's charring body twisted the warrior the half
step over the edge and suddenly there was the falling that
lay at the end of everything . . . and he knew he was Ner
and was lying on his back, torn open on the towertop, blood
welling away across the dark stone surface, while the Hitler-
faced, transformed tyrant leaned above him as if to suck
out his soul. The metal skull flashed the fitful greenish light

and the dark gales that raged around the stirring sleeper in the jewel-like egg . . . and knew he was Renga too and had just been dragged by a corpse into the charnel pit in 1945 . . .

(moments earlier)

Pain. White. Blinding. Rushing blankness. Pain riding his body. Burning in his bones. Roaring in his ears. Beyond conception. Pain and raw sound driving him somehow on, only the SS boots left, the rest of Kurt a hairless, crisping, bubbling torch, blind, without even the memory of himself, everything consumed . . . consumed . . . plunging out of the stinging vapors, trailing smoke, careening straight into the misty, half-armored shape he couldn't see or feel either, already dead as he struck and dragged the warrior into the seething embers . . .

Falling . . . embracing the searing remains, Renga came back, pressed under a gigantic shadow that spread its wings out of the bitter smoke, rising to fill the sky . . . He was Ner too on the towertop staring up at the chomping, writhing horned heads, the wizard's gloating grin as he told him he'd eat his heart now and clawed it from his torn chest with the metal hand, gloating because the sleeper was about to rise and call down the eternal night and fire . . . pressing the bloody heart to his mouth—except the nail on one of the unhuman, metal fingers had scraped loose the tiny splinter from the shattered cup of light that had been aching in Ner's breast for so long, and in that strange, greenish darkness it pulsed with sudden, sparkling, golden fire, exploding in sweet silence. The beast on Relti's back shuddered and snarled its necks like a spasmed squid. The tyrant jerked back, eyes blank, stunned. Ner lay there, the chip blazing heatless glory in the open wound that was his chest; deep in his body's blood it sang with light and the blood bent colors all around as if his heart were a prism. That speck was bright as the sun's core and shone through all his flesh as if it were glass and showed him with bones of light and a head formed of golden fire.

He felt himself (as his changed and tormented brother twisted away, covering his face from the razor bite of that tender radiance) rising from himself, floating upward out of the dense dimness, weightless as a feather in an updraught. Without looking he saw clearly how the light (that was rising with him as if he were the first sunrise in that pit's eternal gloom, filling the huge cave with soft fold shimmer) stung into the massive emerald egg and flickered on the darkness of the sleeper. The sleeper stirred and Ner knew (and Renga too across the ages that were no time at all) it would stay partly conscious for milennia, pinched by the compassion that would light him forever in faint afterglow—as if (Ner thought), his whole real purpose in seeking his brother had been to strike a light in hell . . .

Rising higher he saw the beast with many heads collapse and drop, writhing, from Relti. Saw the tyrant stumbling, blinded, around the smooth towertop, metal hand and human hand pressed to his face. Saw Relti's wife, the queen, halfway up the stairs that circled the outside of the tower, blinking in baffled wonder at the golden gleaming that flashed everywhere in that vast, barren place like sun reflections from a stream. Saw the boy, further down, staring straight up at where Ner rose in a ball of light, smiling, rapt . . . And the dwarf with big feet shivering, alone where he'd reached the peak that didn't matter anymore and then the place tilted, turned, spun away, and there was no place and no movement and only gold and rainbow spatter without dimension and without end and there was silence that was music and emptiness more solid than the earth . . .

And for the final time Renga was Renga, staring up from the pyre, pain just distant unrelenting pressure now, his lungs solid with smoke and heat while his heart strained to lift the crushing world from his chest . . . failed . . . saw the billows of smoke open in a gust so that the sun was in his face, melting the sooty darkness—and (had he been still alive in the world) he would have smiled in recognition—and then he rose or fell or drifted some other way. He couldn't tell. He only knew he moved past heat, past weight, past pain . . . past past . . .

LXVIII
In the Bunker

Eva was still whispering but he didn't listen. Thoughts rose and fell, went past, and didn't matter anymore. He felt his heartbeats so distinctly that he marveled, from an inner distance, how much time each one actually took to gather, pulse, and fade . . . And she was whispering.

He held a glass cyanide capsule in one hand, the pistol in the other. The strangeness was close, waiting. She spoke clearly this time and he answered without having to hear her words:

"Bite down hard," he told her, not looking at anything. She said something else.

"No," he replied, "it won't hurt." He saw the process, step by step: the crushed, ampule glass in the mouth that didn't matter, then the jaws would lock in death's reflex. Then pull the trigger so there'd be no mistake about it.

And something more.

"All right," he said dully, and levered himself to his feet again. Leaned down to dryly kiss her. Stood there this time, the gun at his side, waiting. Her face swam in his sight, a little clearer now. He noted the tension in the wide, unfocused stare. Didn't react. Waited. Felt the cold.

Saw her eyes try to hold his, then stray, as she jammed her jaws shut with a wince as if tasting sour food and not oblivion. Felt the pistol buck in his hand: his hearing, erratic since the bomb last year, went into ringing silence . . .

Didn't look at her to check his aim. She was just sitting there on the couch without details for him. He'd seen her nap in that position. He was remembering the last miracle when the HQ had flown to pieces around him in a vast impact of silence, lifting him, floating him, whispering immortal things in the hush of time, and his mind listened

457

now, straining for a hint as his arm mechanically raised the gun to his head, feeling his heart speed hopelessly against his iron concentration, spitting the cyanide cap out with contempt, watching his brain make pictures from the past: something now like a reflection in a pool, intense as abstract tears, his mother in fluffy white standing in the enclosed backyard lit by honey-mellow bands of morning sunlight, seeming so tall, and he was trying to tell her something . . . trying . . . then gone . . . and he jerked the gun and squeezed, clenched it like a fist, felt the silent pressure and saw only flaming green and then recognized the vast hollowness pouring into him, through him, like a flood through an open doorway, spilling through the door of his death as if a dike had burst and his whole self had been the plug as Adolf Hitler melted like ice in a warm river rush . . . Saw only flaming green even as the shot echo died and the door opened, the first SS man biting his lip, standing still, framed there, hands suddenly clenching, white-knuckled, feeling a pale chill and wanting, for an instant, to run away, refusing to actually look at the heap of old clothes that seemed to have been flung over the cushioned chair beside the dozing woman—except the old clothes showed an awkward arm and a head whose ears and hair ran blood . . .

(Outside the Bunker)

The flames were thinning at the bottom of the shell crater where the two bodies lay side by side, gradually charring and flaking to pieces. The young SS soldier, glazed and vague, could now see the white edge of teeth and jawbone where the blackened cheek had split. Hitler. The woman's body hissed in its fats and seemed to melt away faster.

A second soldier came up, walking unevenly over the rubble brick as if he had a limp. He spilled fresh petrol from a big can and ducked back as the fire billowed up in his face. The smoke curled up and shredded into the iron-gray sky.

"It takes so much to cook a body," he said, sweating. Beyond the chancellery garden, beyond the broken walls and walks, small arms crackled constantly and there were flat, harsh shellbursts.

The other soldier just half-stared, glazed, sleepless, remote. Not even thinking about how the Führer was flaring up, smoking away to blackened, stubborn bone . . . stared as the gray sky dimmed and reflected distant burning.

"I'm getting out of here now," the other said. "Why get caught by the damned Russians?" Blinked at the first whose eyes were masked by the black helmet. Wiped his face nervously. "What do you say?"

The dazed-looking one shrugged.

"Not much," he murmured. Hitler's arm had just sloughed off, popping sparks like a burning log.

"What good's *he* going to do us now?" the other one asked, blinking under his uniform cap that was sweaty though it wasn't warm. "Everybody's got to save his ass." He stood there, strangely still despite his words, as if the last embers of the dream held them in inexplicable thrall. "I tell you, I'm getting out . . ."

The shooting was very close now. They could hear the tanks clearly. Shouts . . . cries . . .

"And go where, anyway?" wondered the seated soldier, staring.

"What's the difference?" He stood perfectly still, voice strident, almost furious. "I'm getting the hell away . . ."

The darkness rose, subtly, tidal, around them until their faces were just reddish sketches on the night . . .

LXIX
At the Death Camp

Astuti shifted his buttocks on the damp earth and stared into the vaguely lit billows of blankness, the Garand rifle across his knees. He wondered what he was actually waiting for. He'd lost the madman, that was clear. Here he was, inside some kind of German stronghold . . . the sirens still ripped at the air and he could hear the enemy shouting here and there and sometimes shooting.

Maybe, he considered, he was as safe here as anywhere else. The smoke and fog was perfect cover.

That guy, he said to himself, *was from the fucking moon . . .*

And then a shadow crossed the muted fire-glow, stirred the vapors. He got ready . . . An SS man. He aimed. *A fucking Jap!* he thought as he locked his finger and slammed a full clip into the short, tilt-eyed figure that was running straight at him, leaping out of the amorphous curtain, then, stopping in shudders, reeling back, without even a grunt, into the swirling blankness . . . in shudders . . .

Astuti was on his feet, reloading.

"Fucking Japs," he muttered. "What a fucking outrage."

He crouched forward and studied the sprawled, starfished form. The gaped mouth seemed to rigidly bite air. The arms had locked, with fists clenched. Astuti shook his head in amazement.

I come over here and I kill a fucking Jap . . . what next? Them Nazis, he thought. *What nuts you got in this world . . . speaking of which maybe I better go look up the world's champ himself . . .*

So he began poking his careful way into the vapor curtain. The sirens had finally ceased. And the yells and screams too. A few shots stuttered in the distance, scattered, fading. He couldn't know that the remaining guards, thinking the enemy was there in force, had retreated. The prisoners who could flee, had fled.

The fog seemed to be shredding a little. He went on, gun first, passing a burned body, still faintly smoking . . . then others. Opened then firmly shut his mouth as he stepped over and around the convulsed human ruins.

Stopped by a mother charred forever to her child. The mist was thinning from gray to light sky-blue overhead so he knew it must be morning.

What the hell is going on here?

At the rim of the trench he shut his eyes for a while. When he opened them there were long, slicing sunbeams here and there. The brightness struck sudden tears from his tired stare.

The charnal pit smoldered. The mists melted and the uncompromisingly factual sun laid bare what the dark could never have dreamt. And then he heard a sound down there, saw movement.

"Oh," he whispered to the small bodies, old bodies, bent, charred, boiled in themselves. "Oh . . ." Where an arm reached, a head turned. His eyes were flooding his face.

All that remained of Rudolph Renga was sight because the eyes were open. The first, sprayed sunrise beams poured into the center of what was left after all the images of a lifetime had melted away. Sinking through his liquefaction there was only the point of sun filling everything, a golden cry. Nothing left but seeing . . .

Astuti standing at the lip of the pit was just another shape lost in the ever-changing tints of blue that sparked the gold . . . hints of pure green that were no longer treetops . . . ripples of singing light . . . and then what had been Renga rose with a bird that lifted above the acrid smoke and wheeled in final lucidity . . . soared until there was only a strange roaring of brightness without end or edge . . .

Astuti lit a kinked cigarette and left it in his mouth-corner as he sucked it steadily, the ash growing, smoke pumping past his dark, expressionless face. His eyes were like still, dark water.

The fog was gone. The sun pressed its spring heat into the steaming earth. He glanced just once, all around, at the terrible place: the shattered tower . . . bodies . . . the single, now-fumeless smokestack.

He let out his breath and shrugged.

Mamma Mia, the things you gotta see . . .

Then noticed the empty shoes at the pit edge. Squatted down because he'd recognized them: Renga's, the only civilian shoes for miles. When they first had met he'd been blown out of his clothes and now, finally, he'd been knocked out of his shoes to die.

The innersoles seemed to be wadded and curling up. He was curious because there was a face there. He tugged free what turned out to be photos. Unfolded them. The face was a grayish outline; a room upside down, turned rightside up in his thick but delicate card-player's fingers, became ghostly horrors, vague but incredible outrages, stained, smeared, and cracking . . . he leafed through images of nightmare after nightmare, worse than what was around him because this place was hell but these were scenes of villages where flowers still had been growing and children had lately played . . . old men with white beards . . . infants . . . other things, other things that stained the sweet April sunlight . . .

His teeth stayed unconsciously clenched as he carefully refolded, wrapped, and tucked the pictures away in his pack. He shut his eyes for a moment and had an irrational fear that he'd always see those things, the young mothers, the flowers on the hillside where they were dying . . . and the things his mind was too stunned to even formulate . . .

"That poor fucker," he whispered without knowing it, "no wonder he was nuts." *Now he sticks me with it* . . ."Maybe that's the *reward* . . ." *He said I'd get a reward* . . . Almost smiled. Started walking away, not looking around. "Some reward . . ." *I gotta do something here* . . . *I gotta do something here or I'll fucking snap* . . . His guts stayed clenched into a knot.

LXX
(1946)
At Nuremberg

Rosenberg's hands kept wiping over the knees of his baggy prison pants. He never seemed to take his eyes from the featureless wall across from his cot. He kept his lump-scarred lips (that didn't quite fit together where he'd been slashed) pressed tight. The guard had noted this, but not on his clipboard. Neither did he note that, ultimately, he felt sorry for all of them because life was sweet and the men in this row were going to have it twisted out of their bodies shortly. A few last murders after the millions of the war. It was always murder, he realized, no matter what you said about it. As if the war wanted just a little bite more after gorging for so long, he sort of thought, then blinked the strange idea away, set his thick, narrow shoulders, took a slow breath, and checked off the blanks on his time sheet.

Rosenberg didn't look up at him framed there in the barred door. Above him the slit window leaked gray daylight.

Come to think of it, the guard had never seen him sleep. He always seemed to be sitting, facing the wall. Maybe he was counting minutes . . .

The military policeman shrugged and went on to the next cell where Göring stood with his face to the barred opening that overlooked the gray landscape, the dark turrets and gables and towers of Nuremberg.

Göring turned, watched, then smiled. He was pale, hollow-eyed, thinner than he'd been in twenty-five years.

"Good day," he said, in English.

"Hi," said the MP, who then frowned as a question crossed his mind. He was getting to be a little imaginative for his work. Up to now he'd taken these men for granted—the way he accepted deserters, rapists, killers, black marketeers, during all past years of his service. But this duty was a problem. He kept feeling the questions stirring in himself. "Hey," he said, leaning his round, too-red face close to the cool bars.

Göring blinked at him.

"Hm?" he murmured.

"Why?" the guard asked. "How come?"

"What for what?" Göring cocked his head as if his hearing were to blame.

"You know what I'm talking about."

"Ah," rumbled the massive man whose gray clothes flopped loosely over the paunch. "I see."

"Yeah?" The reddened face was smileless, somehow furious. Perhaps because he had to ask at all. The question was swelling in him like a vapor of doubt. This man had helped rule half the world for a while and now he was a bug in a box. He was going to die. The guard was feeling things about that. "Can't you tell me something?" he pressed, strangely vague.

Göring seemed to understand because he shook his head gravely.

"No," he replied, turning back to the window where the lost dream of outside waited.

"Damn you," muttered the guard, close to the bars, furious. "You know what I'm talking about."

Göring didn't turn around this time. Said nothing.

LXXI
(1980)
Spandau Prison

The old man paced along the gray-brick yard under the sky like beaten tin streaked whitish by billowing autumn winds. Draughts whipped and circled around the high walls. Leaves from the skeletal trees and the withered garden scraped and fluttered over the chill stones, caught and licked at his somber pants legs as he shuffled his shapeless shoes along, still limping from his parachuting injury when he'd bailed out over England forty years ago . . . He kept his hands locked behind his stooped back like an old professor.

The prison was virtually deserted. He was the last prisoner. There were not even any guards in sight. Where was he going to escape? And what would it matter?

Rudolph Hess turned his collar up carefully to keep the dismal gusts from his wiry, pallid neck. He really didn't look at anything anymore. Sometimes his lips moved, silently . . .

He knitted his long forehead in a frown. There was suddenly something he wanted to ask. What was it? . . . Speer would know . . . Yes . . . He'd have to ask Speer . . .

No, no, he remembered, *he's gone now . . . they're all gone now . . .*

He considered trying to get a message to the Führer

again but there was never any response. Obviously he'd forgotten him. His most loyal subject . . .

He didn't pay attention to the two men standing near the barred archway. They were just blurs in the general gray. He stopped at a stone bench facing the garden where dried rose vines swayed and flickered in the wind.

He was tired so quickly now. Shook his head and his lips silently said something pettish about it. The two men had come closer. One was blond, under thirty; the other, a middle-aged guard.

"You wanted to see relics," he said to the younger man. Hess didn't look up. "This fellow wants to talk to you, Hess. What do you think of that?" The guard was dark with a beaked nose and grayed dark hair. His padded hips and buttocks caused a floaty movement when he walked. He winked at the blond. "You can see how things are with the Nazis here," he told him.

"Yes," said the young American. He took in the old man's preoccupied, oddly unfocused gaze. He spoke to him: "Hello. I'd like very much to ask you some things."

"He's a teacher," prodded the guard, amused and scornful. "Professor Hess. A brain-worker like you and me."

The American couldn't tell if there was any real malice in the statement. Possibly not, he concluded. How could you hate this particular, pitiful shadow at the edge of oblivion?

"Want to ask me about why I flew the plane?" Hess suddenly spoke, voice whispery, creaky like unused gears. He blinked at nothing and sucked his teeth, rocking slightly on the stone seat.

"Ah," put in the guard, "he's talking today. His face struck the young fellow as waxy, even the loose-brushed mustache unnaturally stiff. "You're in luck, Professor."

"No," the teacher responded to Hess, "not about that."

The old man sucked his teeth. His voice was slightly cranky.

"That's what they all want to hear about. Well, too bad . . ."

The teacher rubbed his strong-boned hands together as he bowed over the fragile old man. The leaves scuttered around their feet.

"I'm writing about Hitler," he said. "I have certain

ideas about the effect his childhood had on his ultimate development. I have a number of ideas."

The waxy-looking guard was almost mirthful, saying: "What a surprise, Professor. Eh, Hess?"

"Have you seen him," Hess asked, fluttering one pale, time-changed hand faintly. "Have you seen him?" Anxious, eyes tracking around.

"Seen?"

The guard sniffed a little as if he was getting a cold. "Sure," he said. "The chief."

"But . . ." The teacher had a strange moment of doubt and something, perhaps, deeper. "He's dead."

The guard's dark, waxy face was twisted to him. His wiry hair didn't stir as the wind gusted and gushed a fine dust across the garden.

"That's what you know," he told him, frozen mirth seeming frosted into his eyes. "Hess knows otherwise, eh, don't you?"

The young man thrust his hand into his tweed pockets. Glanced around the cold bare grounds. The tin sky seemed to press down on the walls as the day went darker.

"How can he stay here year after year like this?" he asked, more or less rhetorically. "And not be insane?"

The wind contorted around them in a rising whirl of dust and shredded debris.

"He's not alone, Professor," said the guard. Then to Hess: "In America you can have such young professors, eh?"

The old man's hands were again motionless in his faded lap. His eyes kept wincing into the wind.

"You keep him company?" asked the young man.

"Not much."

Hess suddenly was peering, trying to focus, tilting his head around.

"Are you a Jew?" he demanded, plucking toward the professor's arm, falling short of his sleeve by several inches.

The pale blond head turned down to him. He was tense and suddenly cold.

"Do such things still matter to you?" he asked. "I cannot believe it."

Hess sank back, rocking slightly, resting on the weathered, splintery slats. The gray was a glow on his dead cheeks.

"They won," he whispered, "didn't they?" Shut his eyes.

"Why did you say he's not alone?" the young man asked the guard whose flesh seemed somehow inhuman to him now as the chilly twilight began to blur outlines. The barren garden was already a dark, mysterious pool. The walls and buildings were sinking into depthless suspension. He was upset. Wanted to get the conversation on a useful track, if possible. Tapped his notebook against his leg.

"Ask him," the man replied. In the failing light his mouth couldn't be seen moving.

Hess's face was pale vagueness. He was semi-sprawled on the bench now.

"What?" the American asked.

"Hitler comes here and visits him," the guard said. His features were edgeless, blotted together.

"Look," said the teacher, determined to get somewhere, "is there much hope of getting anything out of him?"

"Getting what?"

"About Hitler."

"Go to his cell and listen. He talks to him at night."

"So he's hopelessly mad."

"Is he, Herr Professor?"

The American was frustrated. It had cost a lot of trouble and favors to get permission for this. He was sure he had a key to Hitler's driving obsessions and wanted to coax confirmations out of his oldest surviving friend. The nearest thing to a friend perhaps he'd ever had.

"You said he hallucinates," he pointed out to the guard. "What would you call him, if not mad?"

"I don't call him, Herr Professor. Whom do you talk to at night?"

"What?" Then turned back to the dissolving outline on the bench. "Herr Hess," he tried, "did Hitler ever discuss his mother and father with you?" Waited. "Herr Hess?"

The old man didn't feel his body now and the voice came across a vast, dim, rushing distance that filled his ears with vagueness.

"Mother and Father . . ." he echoed in a whisper, in the gray of memory: long, long ago sat a wrinkled woman and a man with a drooping mustache in the cluttered, gaslit living room of his childhood.

"Hitler, Herr Hess," the academic pressed, "—do you recall anything he might have said about their relationship? Did his mother, perhaps, reject his father's sexual advances? Hm?"

"Mother and Father," repeated Hess. The rushing roar was drowning out the voices altogether. His breathing deepened, rattled . . .

"Excellent question, Professor," said the sardonic guard. "Probably Hitler talked about little else."

"There's a point to be made here. The key may lie in childhood. I've studied this for years."

They were all blending and fading. Sight could no longer tell where one seemed to end and another begin. And out of his hollow, dark, almost shape the guard replied:

"I think Hess is answering you."

The old man was gurgling down into a choking snore that shook him back awake with its force. He sputtered and said:

"What? What's that?"

"I used to think Hitler was dead too, Professor," said the guard. "For a long time."

The wind rattled and scraped the unseen leaves around the vacant yard.

"What are you talking about? The evidence—"

"Not in that sense. Not the way you think. Not the dead body."

"Eh?" The young man strained to see the other's face but got nothing but hints and fugitive gleaming.

"I think Hitler is here."

"What?"

"I've spent twenty years with Nazis. We're all alike, in the end. Just people. Haunted people. And Hitler's in us. Everybody. Take it from me."

The American was invisibly shaking his head. Hess was struggling through another snore. The cool air whooshed around them.

"No," the teacher said, "that's just rhetoric, my friend. Hitler's mind was shaped in a unique way. He was outside the ordinary world. That's the mystery behind the insanity and the genocide, the—"

He broke off as Hess cried out, between sleep and waking, screamed, hoarse, fragile:

"Ahhh . . . I tried . . . tried to . . . help you . . .
help you . . ."

Then silence. The clashing leaves that moved like
scraping feet taking broken steps over the stones.

"Incorrect, Herr Professor," the guard said. Seemed to
touch himself, his head. "Inside everybody. Nothing so
special."

Hess was weeping, the sound coming from somewhere
in the vagueness of bench and body, while the wind
prowled. And he was still talking, almost asleep, almost
awake. His voice fluttered, whispered, appealed, exhorted
. . . then wailed in an undertone . . . rose in hope . . .
suffered in murmurs . . .

The young teacher listened, bending over the blotted,
melted shape, the hint of a face, hands . . . He frowned,
with just his forehead.

"I can't make anything out," he complained, concentrating on the rush of whispery babble flowing almost
sourcelessly, running through emotion, intimations, with,
now, seemingly no more words than the wind itself. The
leaves and the voice rasped fragile implications that swelled, climaxed, and died all the while the American struggled
to filter out something he could use, asking his questions,
now and then, into the ceaseless sound that kept lapsing
into just breathing or blowing, erratic and soft . . . hollow . . .

"Don't you know whom he's talking to?" the guard said
with near scorn. Paused. "I think you do, Professor. I think
you know whom he's talking to."

LXXII
(1945)
At the Death Camp

Astuti picked his way across the camp trying not to look too
closely at anything. There was a lull in the distant firing.
Behind him the dark smolder from the pit stained the sky.

He'd seen a few of them and didn't want to deal with it:
those terrible burns . . . Shook his head.

I could fucking lose my mind, he reflected. *That's about it.
The nickel's worth I got left . . .*

The sun wasn't showing yet as the dawn went lighter.
He kept his head down and just picked his steps. When he
heard the voice he assumed it was just in his head.

There's nobody alive because nobody's moaning . . . He'd
been in enough battles to know that. Except there was a
woman talking. Just talking. So he stopped, near one of the
long, low barracks. Then went to the tiny window, leaned
up, and pushed his head a little way inside. The stink was
like hitting a wall, he more or less thought.

Holy shit . . .

He couldn't make out any words. Cocked his ear.
Decided (or assumed) it was German.

"Sorry, lady," he informed her, "I don't speak no
Dootch." Squinted into the rank dimness. Saw no one yet,
just bare planks with light working vaguely through them
. . . "Hey? You hear me? *Capisch?*" She'd stopped speaking. He waited. As his eyes adjusted he thought he saw
someone huddled in the near corner. "Hey?" he called.

And then the woman's voice, (he realized) probably not
talking to him, weak but fierce too, berating the empty,
foul, low room with words that were just sounds: except he
understood the anger there was too deep to ever merely
flare into heat and die . . . "Hey, lady?" he tried. "*Chè fa?*"

470

A silence this time. Something moved, seemed to shape itself from the blots and shadows.

"Italian," she said, in that language.

"Me? I'm Italian-American." Closed one squinted eye. "What about you?" Now he saw a sketch of bare limbs, over-bright eyes in the naked hollow of her face. She seemed to be floating there. "Eh?"

"Am I Italian?" she seemed to wonder, like a child. She came closer and one of the probing flickers of light creased across her bald head. The hollowness was a shock. "I think I was, once . . ." All these people, he thought with other words, had been worn and melted into suffering's ultimate uniformity. "Maybe I'm a Jew, though . . . not certain . . ."

He didn't hear that because he was looking for the door which he found around the side. He went in and groped to where she was. Found her hand. Tried not to be surprised by how it felt. Tried not to breathe too deeply either.

"Come on," he said in English, "let's get outta here."

"I am confused," she said.

"At least you're alive. That's something."

She came along without resistance. He felt if he pulled too hard her bones might come apart. He wasn't crying. He was surprised he wasn't crying.

"I'm sorry . . . I couldn't . . . I wanted to die by myself . . . I couldn't die outside . . . I tried to find her but she ran away . . . But I don't know if it was she . . ."

"Don't look around, you understand?" He supported her butterfly-fragile body with an arm across her back. "Keep your eyes shut." As he led her, his own steps were so careful he minced.

"My God," she said, "I saw her . . ."

"You're alive, okay? *Jesù . . . Jesù . . .*"

He floated her across the sun-bright, steamy compound toward where the fallen tower had flattened the wire. They crossed a water-filled rut that spattered the golden light like jewels.

"Where are you going? There's nowhere to go . . ."

"Don't remember, lady," he said, in English. "Don't worry about it."

She don't weigh nothing, he was thinking. Maybe he was crying now. Wasn't sure.

"The camps are everywhere . . . I've seen them. . . there's nowhere to hide . . ."

"Yeah," he muttered, stooped and lifted her when they reached the wire that lay sprung and knotted under his heavy boots. "You take it easy, all right?" *Madònna*, he thought, *Madònna* . . .

He suddenly went faster, almost fleeing with her out into the lull of green fields where the last vapors were burning away. Her naked, virtually sexless body lay loose and, he vaguely thought, seemed it would float if he set it on a firm curl of breeze.

". . . It's foolish to try . . ." she went quietly on. ". . . the devil never dies . . ."

"Sure . . . Take it easy, lady." Then, in Italian: "You will be fine." He felt his eyes streaming now, fatigue and tears blurring the abnormally quiet morning. No firing even in the distance that he could tell. He blinked but couldn't really clear his sight, and caught only bent, amplified, or dimmed versions of the first green on the trees, the new flowers, the mist-softened old hills.

". . . It was just a phantom I saw . . . That's why I couldn't catch her, you see . . ."

"You're outta that snakepit, you hear?" he told her, moving rapidly down into a little dell, not sure why he was fleeing, feeling (he noticed) a little like a kid running from ghosts . . . "You're outta that fucking snakepit . . . Excuse me," he amended. Then in the other language: "Excuse me, *signóra*."

Over the grass under the sun-stippled branches among a few bird-cries that fell like broken light.

She don't weigh nothing, he thought. Like carrying a ghost or a dream now up the wooded hillcrest, her voice floating near his shoulder as he broke into the terrific shock of direct sunlight on the reverse slope. His blurred sight drew no distinct forms on the bright gold and blinding blue. He bore the wisp of her away like an imagined princess from an imagined land. Half running still through the deserted lull that was almost the end of the war.

"You're safe," he told her, a little breathless. "Where's your home? Maybe I can help you get home." He tried to blink away the blurs and burning. Part of his vision had a clear view to the smoldering horizon while another part showed just splinters of light and stainless green.

"My home," she whispered. Her feather-light fingers plucked vaguely at his solid shoulders as he jogged along into the waking spring day. ". . . There are no homes . . . or contessas . . . all gone . . ."

He twisted to avoid a stream that was suddenly underfoot, except his tears bent it the wrong way and the blue sheen and shadow broke under him and then a shock of cold, drifted sidewise, then scrambled, holding her high, panting, and fell on the far bank. He lay there, soaked and sucking breath . . .

He cradled the naked fragility of her as if fearing she'd tear, break, or somehow simply fade away. The shock had cleared his eyes again. He stroked her as if by touch to keep her substantial. She had to live, to somehow be all right. He looked just at the water which shook the sky and his own image in sunblaze. His hands stroked as she shivered slightly. After all the others, he couldn't bear the idea of this one dying too. So he held her as if to keep the life in, and the substance, as if his tender hands gave her shape to keep.

"Possibly," she murmured on, "there was a lovely garden once . . . I don't really remember . . . Just ghosts now . . ."

The waterlight held him still as his breathing relaxed. The air was warm enough so being wet was no trouble. He watched the shadow of himself down there full of sun-shimmer, blue and deep green mysteries as the rich current changed . . . watched as his hands caressed the breath-thin life in his arms. In the distance there was some firing now, but he barely noticed, staring as the light and shade melted, bent, reshaped their images. He was amazed and calm.

"There were all nuts," he told her. Thought about the duke, the Nazis . . . everything. "Just you rest, lady. Just you rest . . . forget everything . . . there ain't nothing worth remembering, anyway."

ABOUT THE AUTHOR

From the beginning of his college days—Columbia University 1966–1969, where he studied English and Musical Composition—Richard Monaco has published and edited poetry; composed musical works which were performed and broadcast; and been commissioned to write screenplays by Universal, MGM, and Columbia Pictures. His novel, *Parsival or a Knight's Tale*, published in 1977, was a main selection of the Quality Paperback Book Club, was nominated for the Pulitzer Prize—and was a bestseller. Since then, he has had over half a dozen books published, including *The Final Quest*, another Pulitzer Prize nominee, *Runes*, *Broken Stone*, *Blood and Dreams*, *Journey to the Flame*, and *Unto the Beast*. He is currently at work on a novel for Bantam Spectra entitled *Shadowgold*.